# Apollo

## -by-
## Thomas A Farmer

ISBN-13: 978-0-9987679-9-4

ISBN-10: 0-9987679-9-9

*For everyone that's stuck by me over the years
as I've worked to become decent at this writing stuff*

# Chapter 1

Warm rain beat down out of the ash-gray sky. Fat droplets splattered on the aircar's windshield as it sped through the late evening sky toward the fringes of so-called civilization. Lightning crackled overhead and thunder shook the entire car like a toy in a child's bathtub.

From the outside, the car came across as old and well-used, something whose sole purpose was daily errands. It had been maintained well enough to be respectable, but had never been the sort of status symbol that drew attention. The gunmetal gray body was almost invisible against the dark sky—noticeable only by the faint glow of the thruster at its rear.

The insides of the car were another matter. The engine had been heavily upgraded with expensive custom parts that easily cost ten times the original value of the vehicle. They enabled it to pull an acceleration that would have turned a lesser aircar to scrap, and to maneuver at those speeds without risk of the driver blacking out.

Incidentally, the inertia dampeners and lateral stabilizers worked in time with the precisely maintained engine to produce a ride that was also comfortable for long distances. Years before, the outside would have matched the inside, but these days the man who owned the deceptive vehicle wanted anything but to be conspicuous. Performance was a utility, and while he enjoyed the luxury that came with it, the less memorable it was to others, the better.

Reality fell more in line with its appearance than its upgraded systems. Its owner made regular trips from his house in the foothills of the Visegrad mountains to the markets outside Londonsberg where he bought immediate necessities such as food. He often conducted his own business during those trips, engaging in work that those inside the City would find distasteful at best.

He always made his trips to the market as late in the day as possible. When the sun was out, even the outer parts of the sprawling marketplace were packed with people. The market expanded away from the gray monolith of Londonsberg, never coming closer than a few dozen kilometers distance from those imposing gray walls.

As the sun set, and the patrols from Londonsberg grew less frequent, the crowds thinned. The marketplace itself shrank, condensing from a sprawl to a tightly-packed knot of shops and vendors. Those who stayed after the market officially closed for the day referred to it as the Night Market. Others simply referred to it by its more literal name: the Black Market. Operating out in the open, in the shadow of a City that could not bring itself to care, they kept more interesting items in reserve to sell once the normal merchandise ran out.

His official City Issue ID card matched the one with Visegrad's stamp on it. Despite that, "Leo Barcelona" was only the most recent in a string of dozens of alternate copies of the same forged document he kept on hand. His real name, the one known by the few at the market fortunate enough to gain a few minutes of his personal time, was Apollo. Most simply recognized him on sight, never asking for his name—it was safer that way.

Apollo was not exactly fond of crowds, but his discomfort was of secondary importance. The Night Market was populated by people who, for their own reasons, either did not or could not do business inside the Limits.

As he neared the Night Market, Apollo scanned the parking area for other cars. Attendance was down, with only a few others braving the storm. Most were long-distance aircars like his, but not all. An expensive model, likely belonging to someone from inside the Limits, stood out off to the side. People like that came to the "Far Market," as they called it, because they believed the food to be better than the processed sludge they ate on a daily basis. The fact that that assumption was correct did little to curb his annoyance at the prospect of having to put up with some rich city-dweller walking around the market like he owned everything in sight.

Worse, he thought, that rich city-dweller was probably well connected. Well connected people knew other well connected people, and the chain might just be long enough for news of Apollo's presence to make it to the wrong ears. He debated turning around and making the trip another day, but he had appointments to keep. He would just have to be sure he avoided anyone who looked rich enough to buy their way through the Limits after dark.

A dark, blocky shape lurked beside the city-dweller's sportscar. Another hundred meters and it resolved itself into the side of a bulky freight truck. No deliveries ever came this late. Most of the merchants brought in their own food and goods anyway. Many of them set up shop as far away from authority and regulation as possible precisely because they trusted no one but themselves with their food.

It was not a perfect setup. Two years before, some would-be terrorist—or, if the conspiracy chain was to be believed, a government agent—set up a small shop selling fruit that had "accidentally" been exposed to a particularly virulent, and untraceable, cytotoxin. A dozen people died before the others put the pieces together and disposed of anything bought from that shop. The seller was long gone by that point, but six months later, a group of would-be customers tracked him down, brought him back, and executed him in the middle of the market.

Each one of them had been fined a year's profit for causing a scene, but no one had tried anything that heinous since.

For his part, Apollo was happy to have supplied the gun that did the job. Despite that, he kept his head down when matters of violence erupted in or around the Market. It was not that he had a reputation to maintain, but that he had a reputation to evade.

Apollo glanced down again at the boxy shape in the parking lot. A few people in the market used trucks that size, but they all parked near their shops. That left only two options—a delivery or a pickup.

He had already ruled out the possibility of a delivery. If it was a pickup, it had to be someone buying stock for a restaurant back in the City. Perhaps the owner of the fancy sportscar and the owner of the truck were partners. That happened often and, while it meant good business, it was a pain in the ass for the usual customers at the Market.

He cursed and dropped his speed. A younger Apollo would have rushed in, burning his engines as hard as he could over the last few kilometers to come skidding into the parking lot. He circled the lot once, ostensibly looking for a good spot to set down, but in reality his final pass allowed him a moment to do a last check before setting down. Most who came to the market made similar maneuvers, even if nothing ever happened to require them.

The delivery truck's presence continued to prick at the back of Apollo's neck, however. It sat there, unusual, but not threatening enough to chase away the feeling of having made the trip, done the same things, a thousand times.

He deliberately sat down near the truck. If its presence was going to cause a problem, Apollo supposed it was better that he be close by. He killed the engine and sat there for a moment, thinking about nothing until the feeling of suspicion faded into the background with everything else.

Apollo opened the car door and stepped out into the rain. He turned and causally closed it behind him, locking it with a palm-print scanner camouflaged next to a fake key hole. Deactivated, the scanner looked just like another part of the aircar's paintjob. The key ring on his belt was for show—none of the keys would unlock the car even though several of them seemed to fit.

He turned and leaned against the side of the car. He would have to head to the market, toward its makeshift buildings and awnings, eventually. For the moment, he simply stood and let the rain drum on his skull. Apollo pushed the idea out of his head that the truck's driver, almost certainly the rich city-dweller he was worried about, would buy up everything he came to purchase. He knew his clients well and he knew his regular merchants well, too. They would keep a stock in reserve for him, and he had no need to rush.

Besides, he thought with a strange sense of contentment, the rain almost made him feel human.

From his parking spot, the advertisement on the truck was clearly visible despite the pouring rain and gathering dark. It showed a steak, or a good simulation of one, with a bed of rice and vegetables sitting on a sizzling skillet. The slogan was written in Euronord, the primary language of the area especially among the rich and affluent looking to expand their social circle.

"Gunnar Michael's Steakhouse," Apollo read silently. "Serving real meat and veggies since 2990!"

He cursed again. Even out here, real meat was scarce. If this rich city chef had bought it all before Apollo could take any home, he would be less than pleased. Another deep breath and he reminded himself, for the second time now, that he could trust the people in the Market to look out for their regular customers.

It took control, but he leaned against his aircar for a few moments longer, allowing the rain to soften his mood. He craned his neck upward toward the blank sky, watching the rain come down in shimmering streaks. After a few moments, he looked down at the ground again and blinked the rain out of his eyes. He watched the raindrops splash in the puddles near his feet as warm water ran down the back of his shirt, slowly soaking him to the bone.

Nature had no agenda; it wanted nothing from him. Everything was so much simpler when it rained.

"Oy, you there!" someone called from across the parking lot. Apollo turned, brushing a lock of damp black hair away from his face. The caller was a tall man, pale, dressed in more expensive clothes than most people who frequented the market. In one hand was a large umbrella, while the other held the lead for an anti-gravity sled. The a-grav sled had its own covering, but that shroud did little to conceal the pile of goods underneath. "It's a bit wet to just be standing around, innit?"

Apollo noted that he seemed to be heading for the large truck, but stayed silent. After a few moments, it became clear the man wanted a response from him specifically. Apollo waved.

"Don't worry," the man called again, gesturing with the lead to the a-grav sled. "I didn't buy it all up."

Apollo looked from him, to the sled, to the truck, and back. The other man must have followed his gaze, because he added, "name's Gunnar. Gunnar Junior, if'n you want to get technical. Dad runs the business, see."

Gunnar also held out his hand for Apollo to shake, but Apollo made no move to do so. He did not want to go out of his way to be rude, however, so in a gruff voice replied, "Leo."

The man seemed to pause for a split second, perhaps trying to search his memory for a tidbit that would tell him whether or not "Leo" was an important customer of his. That passed quickly and the salesman's grin returned.

"Have you ever had real meat, Leo?" Gunnar paused again, just long enough for Apollo to open his mouth to answer before continuing his spiel. "Of course you have, that's why you're here, right? Well, let me tell you, our restaurant serves the best naturally grown food for ten thousand klicks. You come to Londonsberg much?"

Apollo eyed the man for a moment, suddenly suspicious. He was either too eager to make friends or to make a sale. Neither sat well with his intended target at that moment, but a quick visual survey of the man's clothes and posture told Apollo that Gunnar Junior was exactly who and what he claimed to be. Apollo shook his head once. "Never."

"Well," was the reply. Gunnar actually seemed genuinely surprised by the news. "Come inside the Limits sometime and sit down at one of our tables. I promise you the cost of the meal that you won't regret it."

Apollo stayed silent, but shifted his gaze toward the advertisement on the side of the truck. Rather than force conversation with a man obviously trying for a sale, he pretended to be interested in the image of the steak. A moment passed and Gunnar awkwardly towed his sled around the truck, saying, "well, I've got to get this loaded and get back inside before curfew. Nice talking to you."

Apollo nodded in his direction, carefully masking his knowledge that curfew, legally, was some time ago. He waited until he heard the back door to the truck open before pushing away from his own car and walking toward the market. After several minutes, he heard the truck's cargo door shut, then the driver's door open and shut again. He never heard it lift off; it probably had sound deadeners for operating inside the City.

He was unsure which annoyed him more, Gunnar Junior's assurance that his sales pitch would be enough to get Apollo to set one foot inside that damned City or the fact that he never once offered Apollo the use of his umbrella. Not that he would have taken it, he thought with a smirk, but the gesture, or lack of a gesture, showed where exactly he fell in the cityman's priorities.

He smiled into the darkness for a moment, then shook his head with amusement. No, he thought, Gunnar Junior and his steakhouse were no threat. Just a naïve city-dweller trying to edge out his competition.

Despite the rain, the Night Market showed no signs of closing down. More people were present than he expected, easily two or three per aircar in the parking lot. As the lights from the City went dark, the market carried on lit only by lanterns and flashlights. Most of the legitimate businesses closed up shop after sunset. About half of the ones who did, however, immediately opened other stores. A few continued their daytime business well into night, but they were a profitable minority.

At night, no one inside the City cared what happened to the people outside the Limits. Most were too busy securing their own apartments and houses against the dangers of city life to even spare a thought for the rain-drenched markets operating beyond their borders.

On the whole, if he had to suffer through crowds of people, Apollo was glad those crowds were full of the sort of people who visited after nightfall. Most of them were quite happy to mind their own business provided no one else tried to mind their business for them.

Apollo checked his pocket watch. The hands indicated 1948—twelve minutes until what the government of Londonsberg called "night." This early, things still looked like they did during the day. The transformation, though dramatic, was gradual. Here a man sold fresh fish—guaranteed to be toxin free—and there a team of jewelers flattered anyone close enough to hear their pitch, hoping to make a customer.

As much as the crowds hated being caught in one of the summer's frequent storms, the merchants loved it. Their eyes lit up with the prospect of a captive audience, people who would buy more than they intended when their choices lay between buying a trinket where they stood, and sprinting to the next awning and the next sales pitch.

Apollo was one of the few people braving the general walkways, which meant that even with the heavier crowd, he had plenty of space. He thrust his hands into his pockets, sauntering through the rain. Conversation on either side was a blur of noise lost in the sound of his shoes on the gravel underfoot.

Several vendors called to him as he passed. None called him by name. He ignored them, and they quickly turned their attention back to the people clustered under their roofs. One lost customer, even him, would be quickly forgotten when so many others with money clustered around.

As Apollo neared his destination, some of the more daring shopkeepers were already changing out their signs and adding to their displays. Next to his path, "Jamie's Quality Fruit" became "Jamie's Fine Rum" with a quickly unfurled banner. The woman behind the stall's counter bent down as Apollo walked past and the jingling sound of keys opening a lock box cut through the chatter around her stand for a moment. As her stall passed out of his vision, he could see her handing out bottles straight from the crate and stuffing money into her shirt. He suspected most of her rum would be sold before she set it out on display.

At the far end of the main thoroughfare sat the best butcher shop for days in any direction. Four walls and a roof set it apart from the other shops, placing it in a small minority of businesses who found continued success before and after sundown. No name cluttered the outside wall, only the place's logo: a stylized leg of lamb with a square-bladed cleaver buried in the top. Most of the stands sold out or went belly up before they could even afford a stall like Jamie's Fine Rum. Even fewer ever made enough money to support any kind of building, and even then most elected to spend it on more merchandise.

The entryway to the butcher shop was a heavy leather flap, probably made of real cowhide given the quality of the meat inside. The walls alone spoke volumes about the success of its owner, but the chill emanating from the inside, kept carefully cool to ensure the meat never spoiled, reinforced the image.

Apollo pushed the leather curtain aside and stepped through. The butcher tossed a pleased, if distracted, greeting over his shoulder as he worked on a machine leaning against the back wall.

Apollo returned it with something slightly less than the contempt with which he had regarded the merchants outside. He shivered at the chill inside the shop, refrigeration temperatures and soaked skin and clothes combined to make even him noticeably uncomfortable. He ignored the chill; it would be gone soon enough.

The butcher turned around, aiming a smile like a spotlight in Apollo's direction. He was a burly man with tattoos covering both of his arms. A handwritten name tag pinned to a bloody apron proclaimed the incredibly well-to-do butcher's name as "Sal." Sal dried his hands with a white hand towel as the leather door flap dropped solidly into place behind his customer.

Apollo was pleased to note that, while the selection had been decimated by customers, likely including Gunnar Junior, Sal was far from being sold out for the day.

"Good day, Mister A," Sal rhymed as he pulled on a pair of clear plastic gloves. He grinned. He spoke with an Imperial Manhattan accent. It would have immediately marked him as "not from around here" if not for the consistent quality of his merchandise.

Apollo hated the nickname, and intensely disliked Sal's overly-cheery tendency to rhyme, but he would never shop anywhere else. A lot of the so-called "natural food" sellers would cut their meat with artificially grown crap from a lab. The better ones could usually pass it off when dealing with most customers, but Apollo could tell the difference. Vat meat oozed clear protoplasm when sliced, but real meat bled real blood. Not only was Sal always well stocked, but he had never tried to slip vat-meat into anyone's order. If he was out of stock, he was out of stock—at least for everyone except Apollo.

"Just the usual, Sal." He put little emphasis into his order, suspecting that Sal already had the four kilos of meat cut and packaged for pickup. Apollo leaned sideways against the display cooler that made up most of the front counter.

Sal nodded and turned to the cooler behind him, where the better cuts of meat were kept. He took out several chicken breasts, a kilo and a half of pork loin, and several cuts of beef. He packaged the chicken and the pork without much fuss, setting them on the counter one by one. The beef, he cut into a dozen different pieces, packaging each one separately.

Sal slid everything into a bag and tied it shut, watching Apollo more than what he was doing. "You know, Mister A, for someone who pays f'r real beef, you ain't too picky."

"No," Apollo replied, detached. "I suppose not."

"Mind if I as—"

"I do," Apollo retorted quickly, but with little venom.

Sal shrugged and seemed to take it in stride. Sal always tried to engage him in conversation. It had never worked. "Total comes to a hunnet an' twenty Cees." He slid the package across the counter. "Keep the bag, it's watertight an' insulated. Call it a gift f'r y'regular patronage."

Apollo nodded his thanks and passed across the money. He paid, like most who visited Far Market, and everyone who patronized the Night Market, with actual physical cash. The antique paper and coinage was probably worth more in electronic credits than its printed value, meaning that any exchange done at the market was more expensive than any comparable transaction inside the City. But cash, unlike e-creds, was untraceable.

Taking the packaged meat and tossing the bag over his shoulder, Apollo turned for the door. He waved with his free hand. "Keep up the good work, Sal."

"Come back later if'n you got questions," Sal called. "An' say 'ello t' Jamie on y'r way out, yeah?"

Apollo paused with his hand on the door flap. "Later" would be well into the Night Market, long after the less dedicated merchants packed up. He looked over his shoulder, but Sal had already turned away and was busying himself with the keys to the cash box.

Apollo nodded and made a mental note to check the lining of the bag when he got home. He never missed a shopping trip, and Sal never missed a payment.

Back outside the butcher shop, the storm had somehow intensified. He shivered, annoyed that the pleasant rain from before had vanished only to be replaced with the skull-hammering torrent of a brewing thunderstorm. Before, the rain had been heavy, but the drops slow-falling and pleasant. Now, the air had a tingle in it and the wind was slowly getting faster. If it started to storm, the Market might close early after all. Apollo wanted to be long gone before that happened.

The crowds were smaller, but the growing intensity of the storm forced more of them under the awnings of the few merchants Apollo needed to visit. Most knew better than to try and engage the reticent man in conversation, and the few that tried were met with an icy stare. He bought a week's worth of vegetables and other food from a stall that promised "Real Dirt-Grown Edibles!" and dropped them into the sack with the meat.

Apollo's second-to-last stop was at a booth run by one of the many illegal distilleries operating in the Night Market. From them, he purchased two large bottles of a brown-gold liquor that promised to be Scotch. His bag was full, so he carried the bottles in his free hand as he made his way to his final stop.

Jamie's stall was still packed with people clamoring for the last few bottles of her rum. They parted reluctantly as she cleared her throat and pointed out who, exactly, was standing behind them.

Jamie eyed his bottles of Scotch and grinned. "Supporting the competition, I see."

Apollo almost smiled. Sal's boisterous humor might have grated on him, but Jamie's was much drier. He shrugged. "I can't help it if you keep making that clear stuff."

She laughed, reaching down under the counter and retrieving a small brown bottle. The label was thick, too thick to be a simple logo. She handed it across the counter as Apollo quirked a surprised eyebrow.

"For keeping me company last month."

Apollo nodded, took the bottle, and slipped it into his jacket pocket. As he stepped away, the crowd immediately shifted from slack-jawed awe, and a little bit of nervous fear, right back to clamoring buzz. He wondered how much new business that comment of hers would bring.

His errands finished, he walked a straight path back to the parking lot where he had left his car. The trunk of the aircar opened a moment after he touched the hidden palm reader next to the fake key lock. He secured his groceries, shut the trunk, and returned to the driver's door.

Absently, he noticed the fancy sportscar, the one he assumed belonged to some partner of Gunnar Junior's, was still parked there. Wracking his brain, he failed to remember seeing anyone dressed like they would have been driving such a car. He looked it over for a few moments as he passed by. Something was definitely out of place about it, but he could not put his finger on exactly what that was.

Before he could finish that chain of thoughts, a odd flash of color against the dull gray of his own car caught his eye.

"What the?" he muttered, noticing a rain-soaked piece of plastic stuck against the side window. It was an advertisement for Gunnar's Steakhouse. Disgusted, annoyed, and yet strangely approving of the man's persistence, he crumpled the thin plastic and dropped it into a nearby puddle before unlocking the door with his palm.

Apollo settled into the driver's seat, relaxing for a few moments. He had been fine until the storm got worse and forced him into the massed crush of humanity.

Devil, but he hated crowds. They made his hands itch.

He shook his head to clear the unpleasant thoughts forming there and tapped the power switch for the aircar's engine. It hummed to life and rose into the air, stopping at the standard ten meters above ground. Apollo hit the Ceiling Override key and manually took the aircar to a hundred and fifty meters, high enough that he could travel at top speed without worrying about other vehicles.

His house sat five hundred kilometers away, and much of the two hour trip would pass with the aircar on autopilot. Apollo keyed in a command to alert him when the car got within a klick of his house, or if anything disastrous happened, and closed his eyes.

***

The truck sailed smoothly through the open gates at the edge of the City. Technically, Legal Night started a few minutes before, and no one was allowed to come in or go out until the following morning. The small camp of people waiting to re-enter the City looked up at the truck with jealousy. Most of them recognized the brightly-colored advertisement of the side of the big vehicle, but none of them had ever eaten at the steakhouse it advertised. People with that kind of money had the money to get them past the guards at the Limits after dark.

Even in Londonsberg, money could not smooth over every problem. A high-profile restaurant like Gunnar's Steakhouse would not be allowed in and out of the Limits terribly often. The bribes to get through the gates, like all bribes, had a way of getting larger each time they were needed. But to do the job he had been hired to do required staying out past Legal Night, and he was just glad he had the clout—and the money—to get safely back inside the City again.

Gunnar Junior, privately, hoped he would not be needed again. He disliked the Limits; the place was gray, sterile, and generally everything that his father's festive restaurant was not. The guards there had no sense of humor, either. None of them ever responded to his attempts to charm his way past with food or other services, preferring instead to be bought off the old-fashioned way.

He hated cash and was glad to be rid of it. The irony of it was that he needed cash to get back in after dark, but the only place to come by the stuff without risking one's metaphorical head on the pike of a minor crime boss's mansion was the Far Market. There, people with the right connections could convert e-creds into cash with only minor markup. It was, he decided, a crude system but it seemed to work well enough.

Either way, as the Limits closed up behind his truck, he hoped he never would have to deal with that bunch of people again. The Far Market was noisy, crowded, and generally unpleasant. The people were worse. Here in the City, people knew who he was and they respected him for the service his family did for Londonsberg.

Gunnar Junior shook his head to clear it. Passing through the walls that ringed the City, the rain overhead had temporarily abated. That was another thing he disliked about going outside. He wanted music in his ears, not the incessant hammering of Mother Nature doing her business on his head.

Out of the tunnels and back into open air again—and back into the rain, he thought with a curse—he put his truck on autopilot and undid his seatbelt. Flight paths inside the City were strictly controlled and while it was technically illegal to leave the driver's seat during flight, he had no concerns about being caught. No one would pull a Gunnar's Steakhouse truck down.

He stretched and went to the back of the truck. He brought in less meat and vegetables than he would have liked, especially considering how much he paid for the stuff. Still, he could tell by smell that what he bought was a thousand times better than the artificial food they "grew" inside the City itself.

Normally other people, actual employees, did the run to the Far Market and they never did it with a full-sized truck. A briefcase full of real steak or pork would last his father's restaurant months and bring in enough money from their customers to pay his salary for a year.

His usual driver had been ecstatic about having the night off, and even more pleased with the bonus Gunnar Junior had given him. He cited the man's hard work, which was true, and now that he had seen the Far Market firsthand, Gunnar Junior supposed he deserved that bonus after all. Perhaps he would speak to his father about raising their drivers' pay rates when he returned. They could spare a few percent on their margins.

Especially, he added with a mental smile, after the payment he received that morning. Another payment, three times the size, would be on its way very soon. He brought up his bank account on the computer in the back of the truck, and his smile broadened. The most recent deposit, from an account registered to an 'Abel Baker,' which was one of the less creative fake names he had seen, had a rather pleasing number of zeros after the first few digits.

Satisfied, he keyed in a call number on the computer and waited. It took almost a full ten seconds before the call connected, and Gunnar Junior wondered how many layers of encryption it tunneled through.

Finally, it rang. It did that twice before the recipient on the other end of the line picked up. The screen lit up with what should have been a face, or at least a person from the shoulders up. Instead, a shapeless black outline greeted him. It looked like the privacy avatars people put up when they wanted to avoid telemarketers, but this one was buried beneath enough ICE to stop a military inquisition. This one also talked, though it spoke with a voice so distorted that he would never be able to identify the speaker in person.

"I'm done out there," Gunnar Junior reported.

"Good," the icon replied. It never moved. "Did you make contact?"

Gunnar Junior nodded, though he had no idea if the person on the other end of the call saw it or not. "Yeah. I tried to put a tracker on him, but he tossed it."

"Doesn't matter."

"It... doesn't?" Gunnar Junior asked, surprised.

"No." The single word reply was terse, and Gunnar Junior thought that was everything when it spoke again. "All I needed to know was whether or not he was there."

Gunnar Junior blinked in continued surprise. The job had been to make contact and track the man, not just to look at him and walk away. But if "Able Baker" wanted to pay him for that, then he was even happier.

"He was there," he confirmed. "I saw him land and talked to him for a minute."

"You spoke to him?"

Gunnar Junior recoiled slightly. Somewhere in the electronic noise filtering the other person's words was the edge of a threat. He wanted no part in that business. Watching, he could do, and it had been easy enough to fab a tracker that doubled as a flier for the restaurant, but he wanted nothing to do with any violence.

He did want to get paid, though. He spoke quickly. "Just for a minute or so, right after he landed."

"That was not part of the deal."

"I didn't give anything away, I swear. I just gave him the same sales pitch I give everyone."

"That was not part of the deal," the voice echoed. Gunnar Junior wondered if it was recorded or if the distortion just made the voice come out the exact same both times.

"I apologize, but..."

"Apology accepted."

He blinked in surprise again. This whole job was weird, he thought to himself, but this guy who hired him was even weirder. Distortion or no, he knew that last statement had been genuine. Not for the first time, he wondered what the hell was going on.

"I suppose speaking to him was a good idea," the voice said after a moment's pause. "Did you confirm his identity?"

Gunnar Junior nodded. "He said his name was Leo, but he matched the pic you sent me, plus a few years."

"Good."

"He didn't seem dangerous."

The line buzzed. "I assure you, he is the most dangerous man you have ever met. It's good that you were able to stay safe during your encounter."

"He never threatened me though."

"He wouldn't," the voice said. "He doesn't threaten people. If he wanted you dead, you would simply *be* dead. He is dangerous."

Well, Gunnar Junior thought, that put a damper on his mood. Aloud, he asked, "will, ah, will there be anything else?"

The line fell silent for a long moment. Gunnar Junior's heart thundered. He suddenly had the urge to look out the window of the truck, but was afraid he would see a targeting laser or the trail of a missile engine. He resisted that urge, whoever Able Baker really was, he had been unfailingly polite during their brief business relationship and Gunnar Junior had no reason to suspect that he would be killed now.

He was too important to die, anyway.

Finally, the line clicked once and the call ended. A text message replaced it.

"Good day to you, Gunnar Junior. Thank you for your hard work. You have helped me more than I think you realize. Attached to this message you will find the sum we agreed upon this morning. Spend it in good health. A."

He checked his account, finding another immense deposit from Mister "Able Baker." Truthfully, he could retire on the money he had made that day alone, but he was far too young to do so without becoming a pariah. He had to put in his due diligence to the City first, then he could retire. In the meantime, though, the social mores of Londonsberg had nothing bad to say about what he could spend his hard-earned money on so long as he continued to contribute properly.

# Chapter 2

Apollo trudged into his house. The pirated fingerprint reader on the front door failed to unlock properly again, drawing out a string of curses. Buying a new one would have been easier, but no matter how much over the theoretical fair market price he offered, no one in the Night Market had been able to acquire a replacement. The ancient key lock worked well enough, but it did nothing to deactivate the actual security of the house. In fact, the failed attempt at reading his print sent the system into high-security mode, which gave him roughly seven seconds to deactivate it before it triggered the explosives hidden in the walls.

Technology around Londonsberg had a horrid failure rate, especially if it came out of the City first. Some days, like the days when his door locks refused to cooperate, he entertained the idea of leaving. Novarus and Kingsmark, to say nothing of the nationstates raging against one another to the south, had superior technology to anything Londonsberg could produce. On paper, any of them should have been able to attack and conquer overnight.

Londonsberg had two advantages, however. The first, and most obvious was that the City possessed not one, but two functioning spacecraft. That alone set it above most of the other small states. The President-Duke never said it outright, but the threat that he might destroy one or both ships was a known quantity. No one wanted to invade and take that risk.

The real advantage was NoTech. Inside the Limits, Londonsberg was all but invincible. No military in the world could compete with a security system that could selectively disable all technology in its radius. Even the passive effects caused long term damage, hence the stream of half-functioning tech flowing through the Night Market.

Apollo visited those other places, but various things kept drawing him back to the outskirts of the one place on Earth he hated more than any other. Each trip brought a different reason, a different justification.

For instance, he left Novarus for personal reasons. The fact that he left at the head of a nationwide manhunt with orders for his execution was, while not the chief reason, among the top five reasons he decided not to stay. Kingsmark he left for similar reasons, though he had been more afraid that such a thing might happen, rather than leaving the country because it had already happened.

He never sold his house, and each time he left somewhere, he returned here.

Those places were too populous for him anyway, he rationalized. He actually rather enjoyed living where he did, with no one around for hundreds of kilometers. His house sat at the base of a small range of hills. Far to the south were real mountains, and he had considered living there, but the draw of Londonsberg was far too strong. Where he was, within driving distance of the Market, Londonsberg continued to beckon. Here, the call was dull, desire tempered by the regular sight of its ugly walls and hideous lights. Here, he could live with it—and himself.

His house was fairly small, but he lived alone. Just inside the door and separated by the only walls in the main part of the house was the kitchen to the right. Originally, it had only a small nook for a person to eat breakfast, but he used that space for every meal. To the left of the front door was the area intended to be the "dining room," which which he used as a workshop.

A couch and wallscreen took up the back corner of the room. The fourth corner of the open area led to the bathroom and bedroom. The walls were bare of decorations, though a few tall bookcases broke up the plain expanse of space here and there. The kitchen had decorative railings atop the half-wall between it and the front door, but those had been there when Apollo bought the place.

He shut the door behind him with his foot and made his way to the kitchen. The perishable food went into either the refrigerator or the freezer, depending on how quickly he planned to eat it. Other things, like the alcohol, he left out on the counter or put into cabinets. The packages from Sal and Jamie he took directly to the work table.

The first order of business was to check out the bottle Jamie had given him. He opened the top, expecting the nostril-burning scent of one-fifty-one rum. Instead, a pleasantly spiced, woody aroma greeted him. Apollo took a swig directly from the bottle savoring both the spreading warmth and the taste of the spices.

Smiling at the unexpected surprise, he peeled the label from the front of the bottle. Free of the glue holding it to the glass, the envelope behind the label expanded slightly. He opened it, finding eight hundred credits worth of cash.

He set the bottle on the table and started to drop the label beside it. The cheaper bottles came with printed labels, but Jamie sketched the art for this one herself. It looked like something she drew directly on the label material. Not one for keepsakes, he nonetheless picked it up and examined it.

Apollo's eyebrows rose in surprise as pieces of the art stood out. No one thing told the whole story, but the picture was dynamic, active, not the passive pinup that traditionally went on rum labels. The figure was backed by a bolt of lightning that bore a curious likeness to a scar running down his cheek. That drew his eye to an old-fashioned sand-filled hourglass that held very little sand in the top half.

"Might have been wrong," he muttered. "She's not careful; she's good."

Apollo set the label next to the cash. Its message that he needed to hurry the pace of his work came through loud and clear. Without knowing why, nor really caring enough to ask, he mentally moved her piece up in his timetable. The payment had been double her usual monthly installment, which was incentive enough for him. Going out of her way to give him a bottle of rum he would like and then hiding a message as she did were the proverbial icing on the cake.

Money was good, but he respected competence. He planned to keep the label this time.

Leaving the ostensibly empty bag from Sal alone for a moment, Apollo took off his jacket, and hung it from a peg by the door. Without it concealing them, his hands brushed across the pistol and knife at his belt. He made no move to take that off. He had not drawn either weapon in years, aside from cleaning them or practicing in his expansive back yard, but the weight on his hips was a comfort.

Returning to the table, Apollo picked up Sal's bag and rummaged around inside. He found no hidden pockets, suspicious bulges, or anything that would have told a normal person to look further. Like the message hidden in the label of Jamie's rum, a normal person would have gone right on by without ever noticing something was amiss.

Sal never failed to impress him. Apollo checked the stitching on the bottom again, looking for something that would indicate a pocket hidden in the bag's insulation. He found nothing, and withdrew his hand with a puzzled frown.

Surely, he thought, Sal had not forgotten. Sal never forgot, and so Apollo continued examining the bag. Apollo wondered how long the game would continue before he found the hidden pocket. Much longer, and Sal would have to be congratulated.

As it happened, several minutes passed by before he came upon the telltale triplestich where Sal modified the bag. This time the pocket was on the outside, which explained why he found nothing inside the butcher's sack. With his knife, Apollo carefully picked at the thread—it was a nice bag, after all, and he did not want to simply tear into it—until it unraveled and he could open the pocket.

Inside was a stack of cash, banded together with a plastic strip. Apollo drug his finger along one corner, treating the stack of money like a flipbook. The inspection was cursory, more out of habit than anything. He trusted Sal to have the right amount of money ready. But the pocket was large and he set the stack down and thrust his hand inside again to see what else might be hidden. There, he found a second stack of cash, nearly three times the size of the first one. Puzzled, he thumbed through it quickly, verifying that it was indeed a huge sum of money.

"What the devil..." he muttered.

He reached into the pocket one last time and found a single sheet of paper. To his surprise, the sheet was not plastic, not even the ultra-durable plaspaper that books and such were printed on. It was, in fact, real tree-pulp paper. At a market average of ten credits a sheet, the delicate material was hardly the sort of thing normal people wrote notes on.

He unfolded it.

"Apollo," it read. Sal's handwriting was at odds with his personality. The script on the page was neat, almost flowery. Rather than the blocks and lines of printed Euronord, the words on the page were filled with little hatch marks, loops, and dramatically elongated accents. Where a butcher learned to write like that, Apollo had no idea, but he read it anyway.

"A man named Gunnar Michael Jr. came by the shop a few minutes ago. Ordinarily, I would have not mentioned this to you, because cityfolk seem to be a sore spot. They are often a sore spot for me as well, not least of which because he was the sort who acted like I owed him a favor just because he was in my shop.

"But I'm getting distracted. He came in and demanded market price for everything I had in stock. 'It's late!' he said, 'I'm doing you a favor!' I knew his type. I quoted him a price triple what I would have charged you, Apollo, and then sold him everything except what I held in reserve for you and a few others who often come after dark.

"To my surprise, he paid my price without complaint, loaded his sled, and left. I kept what I needed of his money and thought you would like the rest. I still took in twice the profit I normally would have.

"The reason I wanted you to have his money, Apollo, is that this man made me nervous. I believe he would have made you nervous as well, had you met him."

Apollo snorted. That was not quite an understatement, but close enough. Gunnar Junior had not made him nervous, exactly, but the man's pushy attitude had set him on edge.

He was near the bottom of the letter, and continued reading.

"All the time he was in my shop, you see, this man asked about you. He seemed to know who you were, Apollo, and not just by name. I did my best not to reveal anything. He did not seem like a prospective customer for your business.

"I ushered him out of my shop as quickly as I could, glad to be rid of him once he was done loading his purchases. I am concerned that something bad is afoot, and that Gunnar Junior represents someone who wants you found, most likely someone in Londonsberg.

"So I thought it fitting that you have your share of his money. If people are after you, Apollo, the extra money should be of use to you.

"Incinerate this letter after you read it. I regret wasting good paper, but fire will cleanse any evidence of this conversation ever happening.

"Salvatore."

"So that's his real name," Apollo muttered.

The signature was broad, expansive, the signage of a man accustomed to using a pen to seal documents rather than his thumb. Apollo realized he had gravely misjudged his butcher. More went on behind Sal's broad forehead than he ever seemed to let show. The letter was nothing like the way he spoke, either, which was curious. If Sal wanted the letter destroyed, then the odds of Apollo having a conversation with the Salvatore who wrote the letter, rather than Sal the Butcher, were slim.

He shrugged and folded the letter up neatly. Crumpling it would have felt wrong, somehow disingenuous to the amount of work Sal put into hand writing the note. Apollo agreed with him; he hated to waste a perfectly good piece of paper, but if Sal was right and people were actually looking for him, then the fewer breadcrumbs left the better.

The access door for his underground incinerator was located just outside his bedroom. He took the letter and dropped it down the metal chute. The incinerator stayed burning most of the time, and he usually only turned it "on" when he had accumulated a large amount of trash. The low flames at the bottom of the pit would turn the letter to ash in minutes, erasing the evidence.

He stopped with his hand on the latch for the chute.

"What was it he said?" Apollo asked himself. "Fire cleanses? Where the hell have I heard that before..."

He stood there a minute, thinking. Nothing came to him, nothing concrete anyway. The feeling that he had heard that expression somewhere, not just in passing but from a source that would have been using it symbolically, never left. Fire was a common enough symbol that it could have been from anywhere.

He shook his head, banishing the thought. It was not his business, he decided. Sal had helped him out, and he would return the favor somehow. At the least, he would make sure the request in the letter was fulfilled. His tone, written, had been insistent, and Apollo felt no need to argue. He hit the activation button on the incinerator, increasing the temperature to over ten thousand degrees. In seconds, nothing would be left of the letter but a pile of oxidized carbon.

Apollo took a deep breath. The idea that people might be after him—might be hunting him at that very moment—filled him with unease. If the restaurateur was in on it, odds were good that whoever was after him lived in Londonsberg. That narrowed the list of possible subjects down considerably, but without more information, he was unwilling to restrict it that much. Just because travel was heavily regulated by the President-Duke did not mean that communication was as well.

Hell, he thought with a bitter inward twist, it was probably someone from Novarus out for his blood. The devil knew not nearly enough of *them* came chasing after him in recent years.

No, he thought. What bothered him was not being hunted. It had been a few years, true, but it still felt like a normal part of his life, something simply to be accepted and moved past.

The part that made him seriously uneasy was how that knowledge made him feel. Sal's message had not made him afraid, although it did spur a desire to double check his security systems. Fear was the normal reaction to being hunted, but what he felt was far different.

Apollo felt eager. Part of him was excited about the prospect that armed men might come kicking in his door any minute. It had been too long, he thought, since something like that had actually gotten his blood going. He did not particularly care for that revelation, wanting instead to go back to the gray fog of his daily life.

His emotions cared nothing for what his mind wanted. Whoever was chasing him, he wanted them to find him. Apollo wanted to fight, to feel the breaking of bones under his hands again.

And that was precisely why it could never happen. He forced his fingers to relax from where they had tightened into white-knuckled fists. Sal's note was right, he needed to take extra precautions for the next few weeks or months. Those precautions, however, had to place him as far away from any conflict as possible.

Apollo sighed. He had to know who was after him. Otherwise, he would jump at every shadow until it drove him to violence. If he knew who was after him, he knew who and where to avoid until the trail went cold.

He strode across the small house and picked up his tablet from its resting place on the arm of the couch. He tapped in a command.

"Speak to Sal about Gunnar Junior," he dictated. "Investigate possible connections inside Londonsberg. Stay low-profile. Do not interrupt the usual schedule."

Satisfied, he told the tablet to save the note and set it back down. He stared at the wallscreen for a moment, wondering if watching something to take his mind off of Sal's note would be a good idea.

After a minute's deliberation, he decided it was. His brain was too unfocused to get any real work done anyway. A little distraction would do him some good.

Apollo dropped lightly onto the couch and turned the screen on. It showed what looked like a Londonsberg Citycast, probably from earlier that day. The sun was out, high overhead. He did not remember leaving it on the news, and definitely not the Londonsberg news. The things the Citycast had to say rarely put him in a good mood.

He changed the channel. The next channel, and the one after that, all showed the same scene. A flicker of amusement stopped him and he imagined how utterly pissed Visegrad was going to be when it learned that Duke Charlie hijacked their telecom channels.

Hell, he thought, whatever this was had probably been broadcast to the DPR as well, and Dresden-Pilsen liked having their systems overridden even less than Visegrad, if such a thing was possible. Actually broadcasting into Kingsmark or Rhineland was probably out of the question, but Apollo knew Duke Charlie was going to try anyway. He had no real fight with Visegrad or the DPR, but the maps sold in Londonsberg, Rhineland, and Kingsmark told three very different stories about the territory to the west and north of Charlie's City.

Curiosity won out and Apollo settled in to watch. If something big had shaken up Londonsberg from inside, maybe that might explain why someone had decided now was a good time to dig up the past and come after him. Ultimately, he had nothing better to do right then—work could wait.

The screen showed Londinium Square. The central plaza for the City was wide and open, creating a sense of space and freedom for the citizens and providing a perfect field of fire for the snipers and guards that Apollo knew were on the tops of at least two dozen of the surrounding buildings.

Gleaming, modern structures flanked the plaza on all sides. When the President-Duke built Londonsberg, he destroyed or buried anything from the civilization that inhabited the area before the Succession Wars. The only things he kept were those he could use. Remnants of those past lives could be seen etched into pieces of the buildings here and there. On one building, he preserved a corner. Opposite that, a doorway from two thousand years ago still stood tall. Everything that survived had been selected and carefully preserved by the President-Duke's Office of History and Solidarity.

The most prominent piece of history was a section of wall on an otherwise typical storefront in the northeast corner. The Office of History and Solidarity had declared those few stones to be a historical landmark, even though most of the Euronord speakers that would see it would have no idea what a "Berliner Mauer" was.

According to the official literature, the piece of wall served as a reminder of a dark time a thousand years before. The city that came before Londonsberg had been divided by a great wall—something that Duke Charlie assured the population would never happen again. The wall had divided the people, setting brother against brother, but Londonsberg stood for all of its citizens—strong, standing together, united under the President-Duke.

Apollo had no idea if the official story was true. Privately, he suspected it was just a hunk of stone that the OHS dug up and chiseled some words into. The official story made too little sense for his mind. No intelligent ruler would build a wall across his own city. Only an idiot or a warmonger would do something so obviously misguided. Still, the people ate up the story with relish, no matter how illogical.

Restaurants, hotels, theaters, and shops all advertised their businesses as being the best in the City with brightly lit displays and demonstrations. Ordinarily, the square was packed with people milling around between the buildings. The people were still there, still milling about, but their movements had been restricted. Guards kept the mob of people away from the exact center of the plaza, where a large object stood shrouded in white plascloth.

It, and the small stage in front of it, was the gathered crowd's center of attention. A droning buzz of voices filling the air. According to the crawl across the bottom of the screen, a special unveiling had been planned precisely at noon. It went on to say that most of the unmoving crowd had been there for hours.

Apollo shuddered. The thought of that many people packed into one place made his hands itch. He felt an uncomfortable urge to look over his shoulder, despite knowing that nothing would be there but the wall.

He contemplated turning the screen off, pouring a drink, a getting to work on the backlog of orders he had let pile up over the last two days. His eye caught the time of the broadcast in the lower right corner of the screen, 11:58:17, and his curiosity got the better of him. Whatever was about to happen—correction, whatever had happened earlier at noon that day—was about two minutes from starting. He could wait that long, he decided.

Apollo tried to imagine the possibilities, but the list turned out to be fairly short. Whatever waited under that cloth stood tall and narrow—either a statue or a monument. The Duke did not need much of a reason to erect a monument, at least not to himself. Following that line of thought, he realized that Charlie never actually built anything to celebrate his trip to the Solar L4 space station when Apollo was young and still considered himself a Londonsberger.

At exactly noon, a short siren sounded to alert the people crowding the stage that the ceremony was about to start and to move out of the designated walkways. A squad of armed Marines reinforced the siren, moving aside those present who were not fast enough on their own. Though they were forceful, the troops were not overly violent with anyone in the crowd as they made their way through the mass of people, bringing order to their chaos. Their presence, armored and carrying enough weaponry to fight a war or put down a riot, kept the crowd in line. No one looked ready to fight, but Apollo knew, and twitched with the memory, how quickly such a large crowd could turn from passive observers to bloodthirsty rioters.

The squad then marched onto the stage and came to attention. They stood with ramrod straightness, shoulders drawn back and chests out. The only thing out of plumb was their eyes. Each guard scanned a different section of the crowd, watching for trouble. Outwardly, they seemed impassive, more like statues than people.

"They could give the Army of Novarus a run for their money when it comes to intimidation," Apollo mused. With a laugh, he added, "of course, I haven't had the Londonsberg police after me in years. I suspect the Novarussians train theirs better. Devil knows City flyovers can't spot a damn thing they don't already know is there."

Apollo caught sight of a few flashes of light from the rooftops as another group of Marines parted the crowd on the opposite side of the stage. The flashes, likely from rifle scopes trained on them, seemed to go unnoticed by the crowd. In truth, Apollo himself only suspected their presence. Those flashes he saw might just as easily have been glints from windows or antenna lights refracting through the dust in the air as the camera moved. Apollo felt in his gut, though, that those snipers were there. They were scanning the crowd even then, watching for unusual movement, hidden weapons, or anything the President-Duke's security would consider a threat.

Apollo wondered how much they would have cared if the crowd knew about the snipers watching their every move. The official story, even if someone had to be killed, would be that the snipers, like the armed guards, were all there for their protection and safety. The crowd understood such things.

Moments later, another squad of troops made its way toward the stage from behind the statue. Unlike the first, this second squad, totaling sixteen Marines in all, flanked a man in a very expensive suit. As the camera zoomed in on him, Apollo's practiced eye picked up the hidden weapons and armor under the jacket. Such details were lost on the crowd, who never came within speaking distance.

Everyone in that crowd could have identified the man in the suit from a hundred yards away, so coming that close was never an option. The most recognizable and powerful man in Londonsberg—as far as anyone in the crowd knew, anyway—was not someone easy to misidentify.

The troops flanking the President-Duke all held their weapons at a precise forty-five degree angle, pointed up and to the right. As the second group filed in between the members of the first group, they brought their weapons up as well. In unison, the entire detail shifted their rifles to their left sides, pointing them straight up. A loud bang echoed across the square as they dropped the butts of their rifles to the stage. Their hands slid down the weapons as one, lifting and spinning them in one smooth movement. When they finished the display, the weapons returned to rest, cradled in the guards' arms at a perfect forty-five degree angle.

With one final unified motion, the sixteen Marines turned on their heels to face the podium as the suited man stepped up to it. They all saluted sharply, then turned back to face the crowd.

One of the Marines, apparently wearing a microphone tied to the speakers hidden around the square, barked, "I am proud to have the honor of presenting Duke Charlie Maxwell, President of the Free City of Londonsberg and the surrounding lands!"

The Marine who had spoken turned on his heels and saluted the Duke, who returned the salute, before turning back to the crowd. He and the other Marines surveyed the upturned faces; anyone seen not returning the president's salute would find themselves visited by one of the Black Ties in the following days.

"People of Londonsberg!" The President-Duke spoke into a microphone on his podium. He had a had a friendly voice like a favored uncle reading a story. That voice rang out over the crowd in deep, resonant tones that turned his few words into a captivating speech. "Both those lucky enough to be here today to see this historic event in person and those watching at home or at work right now, I bid you good day."

He continued after giving the crowd a moment to cheer. "The Burning War ended one hundred and twenty-one years ago," another pause for effect and applause, "but mankind learned nothing. The Wars of Succession raged less than fifty years later, ending only with the founding of this beautiful City.

"This City was build on one principle: that the future of mankind should be a peaceful one."

Apollo grimaced. Peace was easy when the ones in power killed their opposition.

"Never again will a centuries-long conflict tear families and lives apart. Londonsberg stands against any who would use violence and force of arms to subjugate their fellow human beings. We are here today to celebrate one of the ways in which, day by day, our collective dream is being realized!"

Duke Charlie placed both of his hands on the podium and leaned forward slightly. He grinned with enthusiasm. "We are here today to honor the greatest hero Londonsberg has ever known, Alexander The Captain, Commander of the Special Guard!"

He pushed away from the podium and clapped with slow, even strikes. When he was convinced that enough of the crowd was clapping as well, he stepped to one side and turned. He held out one hand to indicate to the man standing out of sight on the ground to come on to the stage.

The crowd gasped as one unit. They had all heard of the man named Alexander. His story, or the official version of it, was the stuff of legend around the City. Despite his status, however, the crowd was shocked to see the President-Duke sharing visual space with anyone other than a coterie of armed guardsmen.

Alexander strode confidently onto the stage. No one in Londonsberg knew his full name, or if Alexander was even his real first name. "The Captain" was simply a title, not an actual rank, which meant he was not "Captain Alexander" in any military status. Even "commander" was not his rank, but a position. The Special Guard existed outside any proper military or police forces in the City, if it existed at all.

Despite the secrecy, he held a very important place for the people of Londonsberg. He was their hero, or so Duke Charlie's propaganda had propped him up to be. No one knew exactly what he had done, only that he had saved the Free City of Londonsberg several times from threats "too terrible to describe."

A handsome man with sandy blond hair and gray-blue eyes straight out of a thousand stories, he smiled with the self-assurance that told everyone watching that he deserved to be standing on that stage. He wore a white suit in contrast to the Duke's dark attire. A well-worn pistol holster hung prominently on one hip. Alexander was the only one present, other than the Marines, visibly armed.

Apollo seethed. Unlike the people of Londonsberg, he knew Alexander. He knew him very well, in fact. He also knew that Alexander and Duke Charlie had a more intertwined history than the official record showed. Apollo cared nothing for the official story, but seeing Alexander on the screen made his blood boil.

He wanted to turn the screen off. He needed to turn the screen off. Every nerve, every thought in Apollo's suddenly syrupy brain screamed at him to turn the damnable screen off and pretend that he never saw the man staring out at him with eyes the color of a gun-barrel.

He could no more obey those urges than he could have spat fire.

Apollo sat dumbfounded as the President-Duke turned back to the podium and opened his mouth. "I don't think I need to remind you how much Alexander has done for our City." He reminded them anyway. "He has kept us safe against enemies from the outside and enemies from the inside. He drove the Nightmare away! He has protected you, each and every one of you! And now it's time to give him something back."

Duke Charlie turned to the nearest of the Marines. "Major. The ropes?"

The Marine nodded, then gestured to the others in the squad. As before, they all moved in perfect unison, turning on their heels and marching off the sides of the stage and around to the cloth-covered thing behind it.

Turning to Alexander again, the President-Duke continued, "it's not much, but you'll accept it in the spirit it's given, I hope?"

Apollo gaped. The scene unfolding in front of his eyes was not, could not be real. It had to be some elaborate prank or hallucination. Maybe the people after him were taunting him. If they knew enough about his past to taunt him with this, his mysterious hunters likely would have already found him. Since that had not happened, he had no other choice but to accept that the blasphemy unfurling before his eyes was really happening.

"Pull!" the Marine Major shouted and the squad tugged on the ropes attached to the cloth. It fluttered to the ground at the base of a giant statue. The crowd made ooing and aahing noises as appropriate. Apollo waffled somewhere between gagging with revulsion and wanting so badly to scream that nothing came out of his rage-tight throat.

The pedestal alone, made of some glossy black rock, rose over three meters tall. Atop the pedestal was a towering statue of Alexander, identified by a four large brass plaques, one on each side of the pedestal. The statue itself stood seven meters tall, bringing the entire monument up to an intimidating ten meters. The whole thing was made of bronze so dark it might as well have been black. One hand rested jauntily on the hip and the other held a pistol upright. The unbelievable thing's face gazed out and over the crowd like an imperious god.

Alexander turned to the statue, regarding it with a satisfied smile. Taking the podium a moment later at Charlie's offer, he began, "thank you, President-Duke Maxwell. This is an honor. This," he indicated the statue with one hand, "is much more than I expected, but no more than what I deserve. In fact..."

Apollo blotted out the rest of his comment as he sprang from the couch. He went to his work table. He had things to do, but the damnable broadcast was still going on. Alexander's voice grated in his ears, threatening to turn his brain into red haze.

"Where's the control?" he snapped, snarling at the universe itself. He was in front of the screen again. Alexander was still talking, but none of the words made it to Apollo's ears. Between his own cursing and the roaring of blood in his veins, nothing of the outside world came through.

"Where's the damned control?" he yelled, then finally laid his hand on it. He almost threw it at the screen, but that would have done no good. Hammering the power button turned the screen off, then back on, then off, then on again before finally turning it off for good. He threw the control away.

He needed a drink.

Apollo stumbled into the kitchen while the opening words of Alexander's speech echoed through his brain. He wrenched open the bottle of Scotch he bought earlier and threw the lid in the general direction of the wallscreen. It bounced somewhere out of sight and was immediately forgotten.

He upended the bottle, drinking directly from the heavy two-liter container for a moment. Three hearty gulps threatened to overpower his senses and he stopped. He wavered on his feet, more from the rush of blood and the sudden sharp pain of the alcohol burn than from any effect of the drink itself. He was moving much too fast for it to affect him yet.

Apollo grabbed a shot glass from the cabinet and violently slammed it on the counter. He poured a shot, drank it, poured another, drank that one, and repeated the ritual three more times before giving up and taking a real glass out of the cabinet.

Meanwhile, Alexander still hung in front of his eyes. He saw his face in the blank black rectangle of the wallscreen. Even with it turned off, Apollo swore he could hear the speech continuing.

"Shut up. Shut up. *Shut. UP!*"

Words of empty thanks washed over him, words he imagined Alexander was saying. Even without the video to watch, his brain knew the kinds of things Alexander would say. Apollo downed his drink in an effort to make Alexander's voice go away.

He cursed and poured another drink.

"Leave me alone!" he shouted, stumbling out of the kitchen. He held the bottle tight in one hand and the glass in the other.

Some dim part of his brain told him that what he was doing was a terrible idea. Ten minutes before, he had been worried about security, concerned for the future of his isolation and his own job prospects. Before being exposed to the Citycast, he had been ready to work, to continue with his life.

He glared at the blank screen. All that had changed when he saw that *thing* on the screen. The statue that now stood in Londinium Square represented every single thing wrong with the world so far as it concerned Apollo. Duke Charlie's words burned, but they were a dull ache compared to the fury kindled at the sound of Alexander's voice.

Apollo dropped heavily onto the couch. Some of the Scotch might have sloshed onto his lap in the process; he had no idea. Everything had acquired a thick layer of insulating fuzz. He thudded the bottle heavily on the small table beside the couch and drank.

His hands itched. Every muscle burned with desire to move, to rage. As he finished yet another glass—a glass that once again held liquor though he had no memory of refilling it—he fought to control those urges.

What happened with Alexander was in the past, he told himself. Nothing could change what had happened. The Alexander of then may be the Alexander of now, but the Apollo of so long ago was not the man currently trying to drink the past away in his isolated house. The Apollo of then was long gone, long dead as far as the current Apollo cared.

In his last conscious thought, refilling yet another glass that he had no memory of emptying, Apollo wondered if everything that he tried to bury would come back to him like this.

# Chapter 3

Apollo woke half an hour after noon. His head pounded with the pain of a hangover not yet slept off. He had passed out on the couch, still in the clothes he had been wearing the night before. One of the two-liter bottles of Scotch he bought at the Night Market sat on the table at the end of the couch. A significant portion of the liquid inside was missing, and a little still sat in the bottom of a small glass beside it.

He sat up, rolling his shoulders to work out the cramps that sleeping on the couch had brought on. He rubbed his head. He needed coffee, but first he needed a glass of water to try and calm the red-hot spike digging its way through the side of his head.

Apollo remembered coming home the night before, unpacking his purchases, and sitting down. He remembered the letter, mostly the feeling of appreciation at the craftsmanship. He remembered its contents, and burning it, but that was it. The next thing to come across his brain was waking up on his couch with a murderous pain in his head and a liter of Scotch missing from its bottle.

Carefully, he pushed himself to a standing position, gritting his teeth against the hangover pain with every movement. Something was humming at the edge of his hearing, but the pain in his head superseded any stimulus other than the searing light streaming through the window.

Forgetting for a moment his desire for water, he stumbled to the window and drew the curtain roughly across it. The heavy blackout fabric, made somewhere outside the Limits and thus untraceable, instantly cut the light level to something more manageable.

With the lessened light, the pain in his head subsided to a more tolerable level and allowed Apollo to open his eyes the rest of the way. He rubbed his head again and headed for his small kitchen. There, he poured himself a glass of water. He drank the first glass in one go without checking it for grit, but if any contaminates made it through his filters, he was too thirsty to notice. He breathed heavily as pain, icy now from the shock of the water, flared in his head, then filled another glass.

The water came from a tank buried underground and fed by rainwater sent through several filters. Apollo trusted the area's groundwater even less than he trusted the piped water from Londonsberg. The water still had a chemical tang from the filters he used, but that was better than drinking a glass full of dirt and plasmetals.

The Scotch did its job as advertised. The label read "New No. 7 – The Mind Eraser" and it had done exactly that. After he passed out, even his dreams were nothing but blackness.

He struggled to remember exactly what sent him into the drunken spiral the night before. Putting up with that restaurant grunt's overly-familiar attitude certainly put him into a sour mood, but that was normal. Nothing he called to mind seemed responsible for the string of memories that he had thought to be long buried.

He wondered if Sal's letter had something to do with it. The warning that he was being researched—no, he thought, being hunted—certainly put him on edge. Something had triggered memories he thought had been left deep underground, and he could not shake the feeling that he was forgetting something.

Something sparked each and every one of those memories to come clawing back to the surface. Surrounded by people, the thrill of the Night Market's illegal activities filling the air with adrenaline-laden sweat, always put him on edge. Now, Apollo had been reminded of things he preferred to forget.

Those memories mixed with the ones from the night before. The rain on his face and clothes, so much like blood, had not helped matters in the slightest.

Now, he reminded himself, someone was hunting him. He still needed to know who, and preferably why, but that could wait. He had to get his emotions back under control before he even thought about interacting with other human beings again. Losing control in a place like the Night Market would be unacceptable.

Apollo finished the second glass of water and set it on the counter. He hit the "BREW" switch on the coffee pot to get it started before opening the refrigerator with every intent to make a large, greasy breakfast to take care of his hangover.

The refrigerator was closer to the main room than the rest of the kitchenette. As Apollo rummaged around inside it, the noise of the TV forced its way through the thick fog of his brain. He had no memory of turning it on the night before. He almost never turned it on, especially not when he was drinking and preferred to be alone.

He leaned around the corner, expecting to see some mindless entertainment channel that, in his drunken stupor, he had decided would be a good thing to watch. Instead, the first thing he saw was the official seal of Duke Charlie superimposed in the lower-right corner. A gleaming, gaudy statue dominated the screen. Its face was turned toward the sky. At its feet, a man in a white suit addressed the crowd.

"Wait a minute..." he muttered, shuffling across the small room to the couch where he had slept. In one hand, he still had a pair of eggs from the kitchen, but they were quickly forgotten as the realization dawned on him that this was the same program he had been watching before passing out the night before.

Despite remembering watching something, he had no real memory of what it was in the first place. He knew the man speaking on the stage. The President-Duke stood next to him, along with a retinue of guards, but the man at the podium bore a face etched into Apollo's nightmares.

Apollo grabbed the remote and turned the volume up. As the realization of who exactly was on his screen set in, he found himself unable to do anything but watch.

"...and it is precisely that sort of evil that I have dedicated my life to destroying. No more will the people of Londonsberg have to fear the robbers, the murderers, the rapists. No more will the selfish plague you. All that I have done, I have done for everyone!"

It all came rushing back to him. The memory of Duke Charlie's speech and the unveiling of the statue assaulted his mind with pain that could only partly be blamed on the hangover. He remembered pouring the first drink the night before as the President-Duke spoke. Like now, he had been unable to to turn the screen off as the words washed over him.

"You son of a bitch!" Apollo swore, unthinkingly flinging the two raw eggs in his hand at the TV. They splattered across the small screen, obscuring Alexander's image as the camera zoomed in on his face. He jabbed the volume down button, holding it until the screen was completely silent.

He tried to hit the power button, but could not make his thumb move to it. He flung the remote at the wall, where it bounced off with a loud crack, and stormed back into the kitchenette.

"A statue? A goddamned statue?" he snapped, screaming at the empty air. "You don't deserve a fucking statue! You deserve my knife in your throat, is what you deserve!"

He gripped the edge of the table until his knuckles turned white. He shouted loud. His voice broke, but still the rage poured out. "I swear to God, I'm going to fucking kill you one of these..."

Apollo stopped mid-sentence, closed his eyes, and took a deep breath. His fingers relaxed on the edge of the table. "No." He took another long breath. "No. That's the past, and the past is past. It's over, got it, Apollo?"

He stood there, breathing in and out slowly, fists clenching and unclenching with every breath. Breathe in, he told himself, breathe out. He closed his eyes, willing himself to a place of calm.

His eyes flared open. "The past is not past!" he snapped, slamming a fist into the tabletop hard enough to rattle loose articles around the room.

He inhaled deeply again, forcefully placing his hands at his sides, and then repeated the deep breathing exercise.

"Let it go, Apollo," he told himself. "Leave it be. This is not you anymore."

He stood still for several minutes more, breathing in and out, before turning back to the counter to resume making breakfast. His head pounded from his outburst, but at least the coffee was done.

Apollo mindlessly went through the motions of making breakfast. It only took a few minutes, and when he turned to set the dishes down on his single-person table Alexander was still speaking on the muted TV. Apollo closed his eyes for a moment, then reopened them, forcing himself to set the plate and mug down on the table gently and without breaking them.

He turned to the wallscreen, still covered in dripping raw egg, and glared. He shook his head, telling himself once again to just ignore it. With a tense sigh, he turned his eyes away from the screen and trudged to the bathroom, returning with a large towel which he draped over the front of the screen.

Muted and covered, he could put the memories out of mind for a little longer.

Satisfied, he returned to his kitchen table, which was little more than a desk facing a small window, and sat down to eat. The effects of the hangover were turning his stomach, making what would have been a pleasant meal into a nauseous ordeal. He head should have cleared as he ate, but the fuzzy feeling persisted.

His tablet sat on the opposite side of the table. He remembered making a note on it the night before and then leaving it in the kitchen when he poured his first drink.

He picked it up and checked the calendar. With a bitter sigh, he tapped his way through the previous day's to-do list. The final item was labeled "one more day" in block text. He tapped it complete as well, then ran through a quick calculation in his head, glancing over his shoulder at the towel-covered wallscreen as though expecting it to have come uncovered somehow.

He could still see Alexander's face, despite the towel. Despite completely covering the screen, his mind still saw that smug, self-assured smirk. He felt Alexander's eyes burning through the heavy cloth, searching for him.

"Searching for," he whispered, "Son of a bitch, no. There's no way."

Apollo closed his eyes and could still feel the blood.

"Six years, two hundred and seventy-five days," he muttered, turning off the tablet's screen with a flick. "Two more months and it would have been seven years."

* * *

Apollo left the wallscreen covered for the next several days. He refused to go near it even to clean up the mess he made after seeing Alexander on the Citycast. Every time he glanced at the fabric-draped spot on the wall, his brain rewound to the moment Alexander's statue had been unveiled. Apollo had no idea what he had been thinking, why he thought watching that damnable program—twice, no less— was a good idea, but he had. Now the memory was seared into his brain like a brand.

His work had slowed down before the Citycast, which was bad because he had a deadline coming up. He had multiple deadlines coming up, in fact, and none of them were completely finished. Every weapon he worked on reminded him, in some way, of Alexander or Duke Charlie. Even connections that made no logical sense kept cropping up in his mind.

Things like, "what if the President-Duke owned one like this?" and, "had Alexander ever picked one of these up in his 'missions?'" kept barging into his thoughts, causing him to make small mistakes that ordinarily he never would have made.

He barely slept at night, especially the next night after his hangover. Apollo swore the hangover persisted well into the second day, and blamed the insomnia on it. When he barely slept the third day, he realized his mind was still troubled.

Apollo barely went outside at all, forgoing his usual daily walk around the countryside because the open sky made him uneasy. Not only was Alexander's Citycast on his mind, but Sal's note was as well. He still had no idea where to start with it, and the scrambled feeling that Alexander's speech left in his brain only made matters worse. The meager knowledge it gave him was just enough to make him jumpy and nervous at the idea of being outside for too long.

However, after a week spent looking at the same series of walls from waking to sleeping, spending most of the day in silence, even Apollo was starting go to stir crazy. The idea of being caught was starting to seem appealing again. Not, as it had before, because of any promise of violence, but because it would mean an end to the infernal waiting and tension that had been plaguing his every waking moment.

If only he could kill something, he thought for what must have been the hundredth time in three days, that would ease so many of his tensions. But he rejected that possibility, shunned the very idea until keeping himself under control was once again second nature. Even if he could have gone outside without being spotted by a flyover—the fact that that never happened before continued to elude his rambling brain—even hunting would produce a more visceral reaction than he wanted to deal with.

Instead, Apollo had kept busy working on various knives and guns he had been commissioned to repair or customize over the last couple of months. He had a reputation of having a long turnaround time on his work, but his work was also widely recognized to be some of the best weaponsmithing outside the Limits. His long turnaround time was not because he worked slowly, rather that he worked sporadically.

Apollo could do his work—well paying work at that—very quickly when he found himself with a large backlog, but rarely did. Working on weapons was one of the few things he allowed to transfer over from his previous life into his new one. The feel of a knife handle or the grip of a gun in his hand still sent an addictive euphoria through his veins, and so he tried to limit the time he allowed himself to work to avoid going down that path again. He had become very good at it, and with tight control over his emotions and his schedule, he could continue that work.

Weaponsmithing was lucrative, especially outside the Limits where it was also technically illegal. Because of it, Apollo never came up short on money no matter what expenses he incurred. People always needed weapons, and his were the best. He was doing these people a service, and not even charging them the exorbitant rates he could have if he truly wanted to. If he worked through his entire backlog, it would mean a momentary boon in money, not that he needed it with the gift from Sal, but he had to be careful about his reputation. He did not want people to think that this pace was normal—Apollo enjoyed handling the weapons too much to allow that.

Despite that, his paranoia remained in overdrive. By the third day after the Citycast, he even kept his curtains closed and avoided his windows. That only made the problem worse, because without a view outside, his feelings of cabin fever intensified dramatically. He needed to tend his garden, but as nervous as the open sky now made him, it would have to go un-weeded for a while longer.

Voluntary exile inside did have one advantage, though. He fell into work with a passion and speed he had not allowed himself in years. Before the week was out, he had worked through months of backlogged projects and commissions that otherwise would have taken him another few months to complete at his usual pace. With the jobs he finished, he could avoid working on another piece for more than a year if he could keep the boredom away for that long.

But he was still going stir crazy staring at the same walls all day, every day.

Finally, eight days after Alexander's speech had been broadcast across the area, he returned to the wallscreen and reached for the towel covering it. He paused with his hand in midair for a moment before it shot out like a snake and threw the towel aside. The screen beneath was black; it had turned itself off automatically at some point. The yellowish residue of dried egg still coated the screen from that day, and he scraped at it with a putty knife until it came clean.

The towel had absorbed some of the egg, and he threw it into the laundry. Though Apollo still could not get the image of Alexander and his appalling statue out of his mind, the sting was starting to fade without the towel in his vision.

He looked at the blank screen and laughed, wondering if the stupid towel had been the actual source of his anxiety. With it blocking the screen, he had been constantly reminded that he was ignoring something. Now that it was gone, he was already thinking of the wallscreen as just a wallscreen again. The imagery of Alexander's speech was fading from his mind, gone like the unpleasant memory it ought to have been days before.

It continued to eat at him. The elected royalty of Londonsberg called Alexander their hero, but they had no idea what sort of person he was, what he would do in the name of "the people's safety." Alexander hunted people, made them disappear, and—an electric shock went through Apollo's brain as the thought again registered—he had been after Apollo before.

"No," he forcefully told himself. He shook his head, willing that thought away. "Alexander wouldn't come after me, not after all this time. But... No. Just, no. If he wanted me dead, he would have done it a long time ago." Apollo laughed. The sound was amused, bitter, frightened, and angry all at the same time.

Seeing his face again just put him on edge, and that was that, Apollo told himself as he tidied up the mess he had made over the past week. The people of Londonsberg needed something new to fix their attention on, and so the President-Duke gave it to them. Publicity stunts were not his concern.

"Hell," Apollo said with a rueful shake of his head. "They don't even know why they're praising him, only that their Duke told them to."

That thought, unfortunately, sent his mind back down the dark paths he had been fighting to stay away from. Apollo shook his head again, more violently this time. He had to get the image out of his head somehow. He turned, eyeing the bottle of Mind Eraser on the side table with interest. If another week passed by without his notice, it would not have been a bad thing, but he had deadlines to keep and he was not going to screw over his schedule just because his brain was in a bad place.

One more night would not hurt. Perhaps this time, when he awoke again, the thoughts would be gone for good. He could sink into the bottle today and continue his work tomorrow and the next day. That still left several more days to get everything settled on the business end of things before he made his next trip to the Night Market.

Anything, he thought, to be rid of the urges making his hands itch.

He had crossed the room, picked up the bottle, and taken the stopper out of the neck when someone knocked on his door.

"What the?" he asked himself. No one ever visited, which was exactly how he liked it. He visited the Night Market every other week for food, supplies, and to do business. None of his clients, not even Sal, actually knew where their weapons were being taken when they handed them over to Apollo. He lived five hundred klicks away from Londonsberg's Limits because he did not want any visitors—ever.

His house was by no means actually hidden, but who in their right mind would randomly stop at a lone dwelling so far from any of the big cities?

The knock at the door came again, and Apollo gritted his teeth. As he crossed the room, he instinctively grabbed the nearest of his commissioned pistols and stuffed the hand-engraved, silver weapon into the back of his pants, hiding it with his shirt. It was the last piece he worked on, and was still loaded from where he had been testing the custom slide.

Something felt different that morning, and he never buckled on his usual belt of weapons after waking up. Despite the previous few days, he felt different. In truth, the feeling was worse, and perhaps he had been afraid of what would happen if he had a gun on hand and he started drinking again. That had been then, and now he felt the need for a weapon because there should not have been someone at his door.

He stopped in place. One hand reached for the pistol with the intent to set it back down on the table. He hold himself that it was not needed, that he would just tell whoever was at the door to go away and that would be that. He had no desire to fight a random passer-by, and the quicker they could be on their way, the better.

The would-be visitor knocked again and Apollo took his hand off the pistol and lowered his shirt back over the checkered wood grip. Surely whoever was trying to get his attention would leave him alone after having the barrel of a gun shoved in their face. He would scare them away, have the drink he was about to pour, and try to make himself relax.

Apollo flung the door open, revealing a startled, mousy man. A few dozen meters behind him was parked a small truck with no logo on the side. Apollo was not terribly tall, but he seemed to tower over the man, who had shrunk considerably in the few seconds since the door opened.

"What?" Apollo snapped, leaning on the door frame with one hand. His other hand seemed to be casually thrust into the back pocket of his pants, but rested only a few centimeters away from his hidden pistol.

"H-hello, s-sir," the mousy man stuttered. "M-my name is Jason Connor and my p-partner and I sell..."

"Go the hell away," Apollo growled, shifting his weight off of the door frame so that he could shut it.

"Sir, p-please," Jason said quickly, trying desperately to get his pitch in before the door shut in his face. "It's v-very important that you see what we ha-have for sale."

Apollo took his hand off of the door and reached for the pistol in his waistband. With a fluid motion, he drew it and held it at waist level. "Important why? I visit the Far Market every other week. I have everything I need right now. Leave me alone."

"Sir, m-m-my p-partner was very insistent that we stop here."

"Here? In the middle of nowhere?" Apollo found himself laughing despite his anger. He moved out here to get away from people, so it was ironic that the one thing to follow him was the most annoying by-product of civilization: the door-to-door salesman.

Jason nodded. "Yes, sir."

"Was he more insistent that this?" Apollo demanded, raising his pistol slightly.

Slowly Jason nodded again. "He was. He... he threatened to fire me, sir, if I didn't stop the truck here."

"Interesting," Apollo drawled. If these two idiots were from Londonsberg, where employment was guaranteed to all citizens not guilty of a crime, then the threat of being fired was a strong one. An employer would frequently trump up charges against an employee before firing them, thus ensuring as "convicts" they would never work again.

Against his better judgment, Apollo felt curiosity getting the better of him. Something was missing from the little man's spiel, and Apollo wanted to find out what. "Alright, fine, what are you selling?" Apollo asked, replacing the pistol in his waistband.

"Most of it's in the truck. If you'll follow?"

After a moment's hesitation, Apollo did just that, following the small man to where the small truck had been parked. Apollo kept a careful eye out. He was still not completely over Alexander's broadcast, and the suspicion that this was a setup gnawed at the back of his mind.

Apollo also wondered if these men were in on the scheme Sal's letter warned him about. He decided to ask. Iron control kept his voice casual. "You guys ever been to Gunnar's Steakhouse?"

Jason looked up, surprised. Apollo thought he caught a flash of worry across his face, but it vanished in half a second, replaced by mousy fear. "Once. Boss took us all there as a reward," he said. After an almost imperceptible moment of hesitation, he quickly added, "I never met the man myself."

"What about his son? I heard Junior does a lot of the meet-and-greet."

A laugh whose nervous shake came from sheer terror—terror that Apollo again noticed was not directed at him—answered him. "Not that I remember."

Apollo nodded, filing all of that away like pieces of a puzzle. He stood well back from the truck as Jason unlocked the back.

Apollo's knees were bent, his hands ready to go up to defend himself or draw his gun in case his paranoia paid off and armed men lurked in place of freight. Something still felt wrong with the way things were happening. Jason's movements were tense, jumpy. Too much anxiety radiated from a source that was not Apollo for Apollo to feel entirely comfortable.

The cargo door of the truck rose, rolling smoothly into a hidden compartment in the vehicle's roof. Inside sat a perfectly normal arrangement of crates and boxes. It appeared to be packed tightly all the way to the front, leaving no room for attackers. The interior was also well lit, letting Apollo see all the way to the plain metal wall.

It was highly anticlimactic.

Apollo looked over the interior of the truck, asking himself why his fighting instincts had kicked into high gear the moment the door slid into position. The cloudy haze in his mind kept him from identifying the possible threat.

Jason started rattling off the various things they had for sale. None of it seemed very interesting, especially to a frequent customer of the Night Market. Apollo suspected that most of what the man had to sell had been grown in a vat somewhere. He had no liquor, no weapons, and food that was only food in the nutritional sense.

Apollo quickly tuned him out, relaxing his hearing to pick up any strange movement or unexpected sounds. His finely-tuned danger sense kept telling him that someone was hiding somewhere. He had no idea who, or what, it might be. He saw no sign of anyone other than the mousy Jason Connor the entire time.

The feeling never left the back of Apollo's neck. Somewhere, just out of sight, someone was waiting for his back to turn just far enough. Apollo shifted in place, relaxing his muscles so that he could spring in any direction he needed to. He turned his back to everything but the inside of the truck, hoping to spring the trap.

He heard a single footstep.

"How are you finding our stocks?" asked a new voice behind the two of them. He spoke with an Eslavic accent.

Logically, part of Apollo's brain realized that the only other person around should have been Jason's supervisor. He had been in enough similar situations that he should have seen, or at least heard the man coming. The fact that he had not spoke volumes about his intent. People trying to make a sale did not sneak up on their customers like that, especially not with a pistol drawn and ready.

Apollo spun on his heels, already reaching for the pistol tucked into his belt.

"So it is you. Just like I thought," the second of the two salesmen said. Apollo's hand was halfway to his own pistol when the man spoke again. "Ah, don't touch that. I'll be the one with the gun this time."

Apollo gritted his teeth, extremely unhappy. Whoever this man was, he had waited until Apollo's head was turned just enough to one side to sneak around the edge of the truck, using the ever-present distraction of Jason's prattle like a rehearsed skit.

"Who are you?" Apollo asked, forcing calm. Inwardly, his mind raced with one thought: how did he find me?

The man gestured with the barrel of his pistol. "Hands on your head first."

Apollo narrowed his eyes, growling deep in his throat, but did as ordered. The man's grip on the gun was firm, but not tense. He clearly was familiar with the weapon and Apollo, as every instinct screamed that he had fallen into his trap, was at a clear disadvantage. The disparity in power did not make him any happier the longer it drug on.

"Don't I get an introduction? It isn't polite to kill someone without giving them your name first," Apollo growled with a mixture of sarcasm and promised violence.

"You don't remember me, Apollo? I'm hurt." His tone indicated that he was anything but that.

"No, I don't. I want the both of you to go your merry way. You're intruding on my life, and I don't exactly appreciate it. Leave here and leave me alone, understand?"

The man snapped back at him. "Not happening, Apollo."

"And how do you know my name?" Apollo demanded, knowing that he had taken every possible step to erase the record of his life. Every banking record, every credit number, even driver's license and ID codes had been erased in every corner of the network. He had been a ghost for seven years. If even a shred of his life remained buried, forces from Londonsberg—men far worse than the President-Duke's Black Ties—would have paid him a visit long ago.

"It's not a name I would forget easily," the man growled.

"I'm going to ask you again." Apollo spoke with his temper under forceful control. Despite that, and despite the man's threat, his hand inched for his gun. "Who are you?"

"Let me jog your memory. Eslav, the city-state of Novarus, nine years ago."

Apollo's eyes went wide. The list of things he could have been referring to was short and nothing on it was pleasant. More important, the memory of Novarus was one of the things he had spent the last week trying to avoid. There were explicit connections between his feelings for Alexander and his feelings about Novarus.

"Get the hell out of here," Apollo growled. Venom laced his words. He wanted the man in front of him dead, burned, forgotten by the world. How he could dare bring up a thing like that here at Apollo's own house was lost on him. That was the past, Apollo thought, and the past was dead and buried.

Apollo became dimly aware of a shift in his own balance—knees subtly softened and hips tilted outward. The difference was so small he doubted either of the men noticed, and if they did, they would have no idea what it meant.

In his mind, however, Apollo willed everything to relax.

"Uh, Edward, boss, I think we should do what he says," Jason, hiding inside the truck, supplied. Jason was either a flawless actor or he truly had no idea what his boss had planned for this particular "out of the way stop." Either way, Apollo did not like feeling that he had been played for a fool.

They had to leave. He could not kill the men who had invaded his home and his privacy. There were things he could not excuse, but he could not kill them. It was precisely because he wanted to cross that line so badly that he could not let himself do so.

"Leave my house."

"Not until I get what I came for," Edward growled.

Apollo realized his tone bordered on pleading and accepted it. "Leave. Please."

Edward laughed and spat in the dirt at Apollo's feet. "You think you can just play nice and get me to walk away, after what you did?"

Apollo tensed every muscle in his body as Edward took a step forward. Perhaps Edward mistook his tension for a final readiness to fight because a smile crept across his features. Instead, every fiber of Apollo's being was pulled taught in order to restrain his desire to launch himself forward and break this man's neck.

Edward obviously came for a fight, but if he persisted, there would be no fight, only a slaughter. Again, Apollo willed his muscles to relax. When he spoke it was very quiet, very controlled. "Listen, Edward, the man who did that is dead, understand?"

"Dead? 'The Butcher of Novarus' is dead? I find that hard to believe."

Hearing that name, a name he had thought long gone, stirred something deep inside Apollo's spirit. His facade cracked and the world went sideways.

Faster than the other man could react, Apollo drew his gun, dropped to one knee, and shot. Edward's reflexive shot sailed over Apollo's head while Apollo's own bullet smashed the gun out of Edward's hand. In the blink of an eye, Apollo crossed the two meters between them, and took Edward by the collar.

He shouted at him. "My name is Apollo, you understand me?"

Apollo lifted Edward into the air and shook him like a side of beef before dropping him roughly onto the ground. Memories, emotions, and instincts that he never wanted to feel again flooded into his mind as adrenaline supercharged his pulse.

"Boss?" Jason called.

Edward stood, facing Apollo again. Apollo remained impassive, hoping he would take his underling's pleading at face value and leave. "Quiet," he snapped. "We're doing this."

"Boss you didn't come here to sell to him did you?"

"No, I didn't. Now shut up."

That was real fear in Jason's voice, Apollo realized. He really had no idea what he was getting himself into when Edward landed the truck here. Apollo almost felt sorry for the poor bastard.

Almost.

"After nine years, you're going to get what you deserve, you bastard!" Edward growled through gritted teeth. Even though his gun was gone, he still stood ready to fight. One hand was clenched into a tight fist and the other, streaming blood where Apollo's bullet tore through it, was doing its best to match.

Apollo glared, tightening his grip on his gun with every finger except the trigger until his knuckles turned white. He wanted to pull the trigger. The weapon's sights rested lightly over the sweet spot right between Edward's eyes where the heavy round from Apollo's gun would blow the back of his head apart.

Apollo wanted nothing more than to pull the trigger, to empty the gun's entire magazine into his lifeless body and then bludgeon his lackey for the crime of being in the wrong place at the wrong time.

But he would do no such thing. His hand tightened to the point that the checkered grip dug into the skin of his palm painfully. It took every ounce of effort and self control that Apollo could muster to not allow himself to caress the cold metal of the trigger.

Quietly, Apollo said, "please." There was a tremble in his voice as he continued. "Leave me alone."

"Nine years!" Edward roared. "Nine years ago you took everything from me! Now I'm going to take it all back!"

Edward lunged toward Apollo, hands outstretched like a champion grappler.

In an instant, Apollo's rage melted away. Replacing it was the cold, unfeeling void that had been his only companion for so many years. In slow motion he watched Edward spring into the air, watched the muscles in Edward's arms tense to try and grab him around the neck.

For those long moments, the world narrowed to nothing but the two of them. Everything else but the violence was a blur, an unimportant crashing of waves at the back of his consciousness. The fight was crystal, clear and beautiful. With a terrifying clarity of action, Apollo ever-so-gently pulled back on the trigger of his gun with the light touch of a lover.

The gun spat fire and thunder.

Edward's body spun away, spraying blood, as the world jumped back into focus. He turned, saw Jason trying to run with knees that threatened to collapse out of terror, and calmly put a bullet in the man's back.

Apollo stood still, breath coming in short gasps for several long moments as his heart continued to race near the bursting point. His fingers loosened on the grip of his pistol. It fell unheeded to the ground. Moments later, he sank to his knees next to the forgotten weapon as Edward's blood soaked the grass.

With his face in his hands, Apollo quietly wept.

# Chapter 4

Apollo did not know how he had gotten back to his house. His first memory after collapsing next to Edward's body was waking up in his bed. He had showered and put on clean clothes at some point during the interim, but he had no idea how long he was unaware of what went on around him.

Low light streamed in through the windows in his bedroom. Those windows faced west, which put the time as early evening. That meant it may have only been a few hours since that hideous moment, or an entire day could have passed. He had no idea what day it was.

He panicked. If too much time had passed, flyovers from Londonsberg would surely have spotted the two bodies laying sprawled out and bloody in his yard. They often brought police, or Black Ties if the situation warranted, suspiciously quickly, even here in Visegrad. Apollo had seen it happen before. More to the point, the fliers were armed themselves, and a fresh murder scene would likely bring swift and immediate retaliation from the Londonsberg armed forces.

Apollo forced his thoughts, and his pulse, to slow. One deep breath, then two, and he sat up in bed. He rubbed at his temples. His head hurt with more than the hangover-like pounding of dehydration. His fists came away dry from his head—he was not bleeding, which was good.

He passed the bathroom, and an odd sight caught his eye. Whatever chain of logic had gone through his head while blacked out, he had dressed in some of his old clothes. He recognized them, specifically, as things he had not worn in years. They were little different on the surface than the simple pants and button-down shirts he normally wore, but he could tell they were old. They felt old. He could spot the tells here and there, especially with the memories painfully fresh in his mind once again. Sweat stained the collar of the white shirt he wore along with splotches of other stains that never came out completely. The pants, plain black cargo slacks with extra pockets on the thighs, had a long scar running down the front of one leg where they had been ripped open by the spike on top of a fence and sewn back together.

He had no idea where the clothes he was wearing before had been left, nor did he have any idea why or how, out of everything in his closet, his unconscious mind selected this outfit. In truth, he thought he disposed of this particular shirt and pants a long time ago. Why they remained in his closet was a mystery, but he had not seen either article of clothing since leaving Novarus so long before.

He hung his head in the only mirror in the house. Black hair made unruly by sweat and sleep hung limp in front of his face. His blue-gray eyes were rimmed in red, with black around that. Despite all that, a light shone there. That light seemed to be drawn into the wicked scar crawling its way down his right cheek, illuminating the jagged white line from within.

A tight smile, one that never touched his eyes, sat unwanted on his lips. He had not seen the man in the mirror in years. The man staring back at him from the polished glass was, if possible, the only person on Earth that Apollo hated more than Alexander.

Disgusted, he stripped quickly out of the old clothes. Regardless of the reasons they were still around, he must have simply forgotten about them as time passed. The irony of it was that if he could have forgotten where the stains came from in the first place then their presence would not have been a problem.

Perhaps that had been his plan, he thought. Whatever the case, he wanted the damned things gone now. Buttons flew from the shirt as he quite literally ripped it off of it torso in his rush to disrobe. The pants were sturdier, but he removed them with no less fervor.

Apollo carried the bundle of bloodstained fabric to the incinerator and shoved the entire outfit into the chute. He slammed the activation key with his fist and waited until he could feel the warmth radiating from the door before turning away.

"Good riddance." He turned away from the incinerator and took a deep breath. "No more reminders. No more past. Let it all fade."

He returned to his closet to look for any other clothes he might have missed. He ransacked the racks and drawers, but never found anything older than seven years, and so he locked the incinerator and left it to burn. It would continue to burn at solar temperatures until whatever objects its sensors detected had been reduced to component molecules.

In the living room, the gun he had killed the two men with had been placed back on the work table where it had been before they arrived. It looked as though it never moved, and Apollo had the sudden flash of thought that he might have dreamed the whole thing. He picked it up, and the gray smear of burned powder around the muzzle betrayed any possibility that it might have been a dream.

He felt the weight of the gun, judging it less like the weapon that just killed two men and more like a piece for sale. It felt heavier than he thought it had the day before. Idly, he wondered if the client would like, or mind, the extra weight that the silver designs added. He pushed the thought aside—he could worry about it later.

Apollo checked the magazine. It had been reloaded and a round left in the chamber. He stared at it for a long time without ever actually thinking any thoughts before locking the safety and setting the gun back down.

Not for the first time since waking up, he wondered what exactly had happened to him. Killing was nothing new in his experience. Even being taken by surprise was relatively old hat after the things he lived through—things the past week had brought back to the front of his mind.

"And yet," he muttered, "I blacked out. What the fuck."

Apollo went to the door and opened it cautiously. The truck sat where it had been before, still open, but the bodies were gone. He looked around, checking to see if they had been carried off by animals or picked up by anyone. Some of the cargo in the truck had been disturbed, but that had probably happened when Jason tried to run.

Outside, he found no signs of any presence other than his and the two dead men, which meant that no one came looking for them while Apollo slept. He had to have disposed of them somehow. The furnace was an option, but there was no blood on his floor. He crouched down in the grass where Edward's body had fallen. The damp dirt still smelled of the iron tang of blood.

The scent of blood called more of his memories back to the surface. He remembered roughly shoving things around inside the truck until he found a crate of fabric. He had wrapped the two bodies in several layers of uncut jacket wool before throwing them into the incinerator.

He shook his head, clearing the fog. A second look in the truck revealed his memory was right. A box near the back had been torn open, revealing a few bolts of the heavy fabric still inside.

He wondered what to do with the truck. It was full of food and supplies, even though the food was likely vat grown and the gear substandard. As far as Apollo was concerned, it was free as of Edward's death. He searched, but found no useful identification, log books, or anything that would have pointed him at a place to return it. He had no idea where it came from, or even if the men flying it had been the legal owners at all.

Apollo laughed, realizing that his plan to return a stolen crime scene, a crime scene now rife with his DNA and fingerprints, to its rightful owner was probably one of the stupider ideas he ever had. His brain was still foggy, like he was coming out of the pit of a drunken stupor even though he was sure the effects of his last drink had been long since slept off. His movements were sharp, but every thought felt like it had to be vetted two or three times before his brain registered.

He thought about trying to sell the food. It was likely crap, and the odds were decent that he could pass it off as coming from someone paying their bill with food. Apollo did not make his living on "decent" odds, however, and quickly abandoned that plan.

Rewiring the truck's guidance computer took the better part of the afternoon. Whoever decided to send a half-trained mercenary, or whatever Edward actually was, after him seemed to have spent more time worrying about vehicle security than anything else. Still, the task was not hard, just time consuming. Part of him was surprised by the calm with which he set to his task after his mind finally began to clear.

With his memory of the events after the brief fight coming back, Apollo wondered how he managed to lose control so badly before. He thought he had been in control the entire time during Edward's failed assassination attempt. The man attacked him, he remembered, but then Apollo simply reacted. He could recall no thoughts on his part, only a frigid certainty and mechanical precision in his movements as his body acted on instinct a thousand times faster than his conscious mind could have directed.

It was like remembering a dream, he realized. The memory of disposing of the bodies was even hazier. Those moments felt like trying to remember something he had done while drunk. His brain held on to snatches of movement, color, and feeling, but nothing that he could pin down in any meaningful way.

That had been then, and "then" was the past. It had happened, and though Apollo hated himself for losing control, he could no more blame himself for what happened than he could blame the weather for storming on his last trip to the market. The past was over and done with. In the present, he had an empty truck to dispose of.

He looked the truck over one last time, checking to make sure nothing that could identify him had been left inside the vehicle. Satisfied, he set the truck's autopilot to fly north at maximum altitude until it ran out of fuel and then crash into whatever was most likely to destroy it, probably the ocean.

He thought for a moment about loading it with explosives to make sure the wreckage was destroyed, but that would create more suspicion than a "simple" crash.

As the truck lifted, Apollo spotted something small in the grass, gleaming with reflected light from the truck's lift engine. He bent to examine the object, and found Edward's gun. A bullet was lodged in the underside, splitting part of the frame and shattering the finger guard. He suspected his shot had also destroyed, or at least damaged, the inside as well. It would make a decent project to tinker with in his spare time—certainly, he had repaired worse damage in his career.

He stuffed the weapon in a pocket, surprised again at the detachment he felt. The previous owner of the wrecked gun on his pocket had used it only a few hours before to try and kill him. Now, here he was pondering how best to fix the thing up and sell it.

The truck continued its rumbling rise until it looked small enough to be a toy, then the rumbles turned into a full-fledged roar as the vehicle's thrusters kicked on and it slowly accelerated its bulk toward the northern horizon. Apollo stood idly, hands thrust in his pockets, and watched until it disappeared out of sight.

He felt empty inside as he went back into his house. As the door shut, that feeling coalesced into fury. He was angry at himself, angry with Edward and Jason for wasting their lives like they did. He raged, pacing the living room and seething before hitting on a realization that gave him a focus for his anger. It was stupid, what they did.

He came here specifically to kill me, Apollo thought. He wondered if Edward was truly who he claimed to be, or if he had simply been a hired scapegoat. If it was the latter, then his death might actually cause Apollo some problems. "Edward" was certainly not a normal name for a Novarus man, anyway.

And Apollo had begged him not to fight. He remembered pleading, not for his own life but for Edward's life. He attacked anyway, and Apollo wondered what that said about him. He was either desperate, or had been paid a lot of money to throw his life away on a fool's errand.

Both answers, Apollo thought, were stupid. He paced, finally coming to rest in front of the wallscreen. For a moment, he thought he saw Alexander's face peering back at him from the black surface.

"No," he growled. He raised a finger and pointed accusingly at the blank screen. His mind's eye saw the scene from the week before. "This is your fault, Alexander! You hear me?" His voice was a shrill shout now. "Your fault! You piece of shit! None of this ever would have happened this way if not for you! It's your fucking fault!"

He took a deep breath, once gain forcing his heart to slow to a normal rate. Quietly, he added, "somehow," to the end of his tirade. He knew it was pointless, even stupid to blame Alexander. He had not been there.

"Although," Apollo muttered. "If that dumb bastard had been hired, and Alexander did it..." He laughed and shook his head. "No, Alexander's a piece of work, piece of shit, actually, but he wouldn't pay a man just to kill himself on my gun.

"Would he?"

Apollo shook his head again and stepped away from the screen. Something felt wrong, but Alexander was not at the core of it. Seeing his face on the screen the week before had been a fluke, a freak accident of fate.

It would not happen again, he swore.

His tablet was where he left it on the breakfast table. He picked it up, checking the date again. The numbers had yet to change, which was a slight relief. If he had only passed out for a few hours, admittedly a few hours after blacking out and burning two bodies, then perhaps things were not as bad as they looked. He could still keep his schedule.

Perhaps with another month, maybe another year if he was unlucky, he could put it behind him and go on like he had been doing. On his tablet's calendar, he made a brief entry for the day, writing out, "Slipped. Today marks a new Day 0."

He tapped the screen's power button and stared as his face in the reflection. The unmistakable resemblance was there. His cheekbones were the same shape and while his jawline was squarer, their chins bore more than a passing resemblance as well. Set in the middle of it all, though, were the same eyes.

Despite that, Apollo reminded himself that he was clearly his own person; the similarities were there, but they were only skin-deep.

He slammed the tablet down on the table on frustration. He had gone for years without thinking about Alexander except in the most abstract of terms, and it had been years since the memories of that time surfaced. Now, with just a few seconds of a broadcast, things were going bad quickly.

Apollo looked at the still open bottle of whiskey where he left it hours before. Once again, he told himself that that was what he needed—a drink. He would down as much of the burning amber liquid as he could before losing consciousness, and he would do it again and again and again until his memories were buried once more.

Less than an hour later, Apollo was deep into his third glass. His mind had long since gone past merely being "fuzzy." Now, a gray and woolly pall had descended over his thoughts and actions. The memories were gone for the time being, as was his ability to construct abstract thoughts about anything other than what was directly in front of his face.

Somewhere, kilometers away from his head, he heard a banging. It came a second time after what seemed like hours, even though the volume of liquor in his glass had not decreased—or had it been refilled? The sound seemed to be moving through thick grease, reverberating through the murky water in front of his eyes with curious slowness. The third series of bangs, coming after a long draw on his glass, tripped a switch in Apollo's brain that suddenly brought the real world crashing into normal speed and focus.

Someone was knocking at his door. His drunken mind first thought it might have been Edward or Jason. With effort, he forced himself to remember that they were dead; he had killed them and they had bled on his grass. They were real, but they were dead, and the person at his door was real and not dead.

A stab of actual fear shot through his gut as he realized that it might be an associate of theirs, come to see why they never checked in after their stop. But their stop was a ruse, he slowly reminded himself, mouthing the words as he thought them. They had tried to kill him and so they deserved to die.

The knock at the door came again and Apollo came to his feet. Every single movement between the couch and the door took effort. He could not simply tell his body, "walk to the door." Instead, the thoughts came as very specific, very small orders: "Move my left foot. Move my right foot," for more than a dozen slow shuffling paces.

Looking out the window told him that the sun was setting, but his exterior lights were turned off. Whoever was at his door had better have a good reason for rousing him off the couch, not that he could do much in his drunken state other than possibly fall on them and knock them over.

Another stupid decision, a surprisingly cogent voice in the back of his head chided. Here he was again, too drunk to fight. If violence was coming for him again—and why, he wondered, could he not take an evening to just rest?—in his current state of intoxication, he knew he would not walk away from the encounter with all of his blood where it was supposed to be.

He cursed again, alternating between his own stupid decisions and the plethora of furniture and other objects that had somehow been left in his path.

So long as he kept his mind on exactly what he was doing, he could function well enough to move and speak. Anything he tried to do was slow, but he had been falling down drunk enough times in his thirty-three years that he knew how to work around the instability and cognitive issues.

I can move, he thought silently, slowly. "But can I fight? We'll see, I'm sure."

At last, he reached the door. Whoever was on the other side must have heard him coming, bumping into things and cursing the entire way, because the knocking had stopped. At the door, Apollo stared at the handle as though trying to remember how to make it work before lifting his hand, dropping it on the handle, and twisting it downwards.

Apollo's door opened inwards, and he had to take an unexpected shuffle step to one side to avoid smacking himself in the face with the edge. His other hand had been raised to throat level, ready to put on a show of defending himself should he have to use force. Fighting drunk was not exactly his favorite activity but, much like walking and talking drunk, he had been forced to do it enough times that he could expect to cope well enough to survive.

It rained outside, and the weather had turned cold in the hours since the sun set. The drops that fell from the blackening sky did so on a freezing wind. Apollo, warmed by the liquor, stood in the doorway for a few seconds and enjoyed the feeling of the frigid air as he tried to make his eyes focus on the figure standing under a black umbrella a meter away. They made no threatening moves.

The sound of rain served to calm his nerves, as well. The steady, dull roar of nature's most persistent weapon ate away at his tension in seconds.

"Apollo?" the figure asked. The voice belonged to a woman but the darkness was making the alcoholic haze over his eyes worse, preventing him from being able to make out any of her facial features. Her voice was a warm contralto that purred in his ear, somehow easing every one of his tensions. He thought he saw diamonds glittering on her neck and wondered who in the hell would visit him with such expensive luxuries out in the open.

"Who... who're you?" he slurred. With one hand he held himself shakily upright against the doorframe, but the other was raised in his best approximation of a boxer's guard. The defensive stance was reflexive, but the alcohol, her obvious lack of threatening intent, and her voice worming its way into his brain, sapped his will to fight.

"Can I come in first?" Her voice carried tones of authority now.

He extended his fist slightly, wavering, pointing with his index finger. "You know who I am. And you," he stopped as his train of thought derailed into the murk of his fuzzy mind.

She waited patiently, red lips quirked in a smirk. "Yes?"

"You," he continued, "want to come into my house?"

"I do," she replied.

"I don't." He wavered. Something was wrong. "Don't want nothing to do with you."

She spoke after a moment's silence. "My name is Catherine."

"Don't care," Apollo retorted, but the wheels were turning in his mind. "Go back home."

"Apollo."

Before she could finish her sentence, Apollo slurred, "damn it, how d'you know my name?"

"I have an important message for you, and a job if you'll take it," Catherine said. Apollo narrowed his eyes slightly, trying to figure out if she was avoiding his question or answering it. If she was bothered by the rain, she gave no hints in that regard.

Apollo stared at her for several more moments before pushing away from the door frame and stumbling backward back into his house. Superficially, he had not changed his mannerisms since opening the door, but the sense that something was not normal had returned and the resulting adrenaline rush allowed him to focus his thoughts. Even if his body would not respond exactly as he wanted it to, he knew he was in control again.

Control, he thought, was good.

Crossing the room, he now veered into things deliberately, or told himself he did so. The lurch in his step from before was done on purpose now, as were the exaggerated hand movements.

"This's my fuckin' house," he slurred, gesturing toward the dwelling with an expansive sweep of his arm. Only half of the wool in his speech was from the alcohol. He was definitely drunk, but if he kept up the charade of being out-of-control drunk, it might just come in handy if things turned into a fight. "Welcome."

Catherine stepped demurely across the threshold, turning to close and shake her umbrella dry outside the door before setting it against the outside wall. She stepped out of the way of the door, closed it, and seemed to be about to say something when Apollo grabbed her by the shoulders and pulled her face close to his.

Something in her movements set off his sense of danger more than her presence alone had. They were too calm, too controlled. If she truly knew who he was, then she was being entirely too calm about stepping into his house where he could, and did, have no end of traps or hidden weapons. The danger did not bother her; even his alcohol besotted brain realized that, and that meant that she herself was dangerous.

She had wavy black hair, not a strand out of place, and deep brown eyes. She was roughly his height as well, and he held her at almost eye level. Her features were soft, cheekbones high but not pronounced. Alcohol-scented breath assaulted her nostrils as Apollo searched, mad-eyed, for any familiarity or recognition in her facial features.

Something stirred at the edge of Apollo's memory. Feelings not of lust or power, but of frustration and anger. Something buried deep in his brain screamed that he knew who she was, but nothing, not even her name, made any real sense. He had no idea if he had forgotten or if alcohol was messing with his ability to think.

He rushed forward awkwardly, hands still gripped tightly on Catherine's shoulders, and slammed her into the closed door. He took one hand off of her shoulders and pressed the side of that forearm into her throat. Physically, his muscles were operating on memory alone and the movements were sloppy

Despite difficulty breathing, Catherine neither struggled nor even looked afraid in the slightest. She kept her eyes carefully leveled at Apollo, regarding him with the same intensity he had displayed moments before.

"Let me go, Apollo," she said gently, but firmly, and without fear or anger.

"Who are you?" he grated.

"I have a proposition for you if you'll listen."

"And if I don't?"

"Then you don't."

"If you know who I am," he drawled, feeling the fuzziness of the alcohol coming back, "then you should know how stupid it was for you to willingly come into my home alone."

"You're not going to kill me." Her voice retained the same firm-yet-gentle tone as she continued. "So let me down and we'll talk."

He growled at her. "I'll kill you just as easily as the rest."

"You won't."

Apollo stared into her eyes for several seconds, trying to find the fear he knew had to be there, just underneath the mask of false confidence. With each passing second, his heart beat faster as he realized that not only was she genuinely not scared of him, but her lack of fear was somehow terrifying him instead. Not only that, the feeling that he should know her continued to eat away at his own confidence.

"There's nothing you can do to me, Apollo. Once you understand that, then we can start talking."

"There are plenty of things I can do!" he snapped. "Killing you just happens to be quick and easy."

"This would be easier if you were sober, Apollo."

"Maybe," be admitted before thinking about his words, or the underlying lack of killing resolve they displayed. It would be easier if he was sober. Maybe he would hear what she had to say and then send her on her way, never to return. Maybe she was just a prospective client who sneaked past the Limits after legal night.

He considered that he might be overreacting. So far, this woman named Catherine had not made a single threatening move, but he was treating her like an assassin. She was overly confident, true, but that was hardly cause for his harsh treatment.

Apollo asked himself if he, subconsciously at least, was right and there was more to her than it seemed. His reactions could just as easily have been explained by the tension from the past week.

Searing pain interrupted his thoughts. It felt as though a white-hot knife had been plunged into his temple, somehow burning and twisting without actually killing him. Somewhere in the pain was the realization that Catherine had touched the skin of his arm.

He fell to his knees and then to the floor. Being stabbed hurt worse. Being shot hurt worse. Being beaten and left to die had hurt worse, but all of those pains had came with the threat that they might kill him. He felt no such threat with this pain, only a dim sense that whatever it was, it was something to be endured and not fought against.

As soon as he could move again, he would kill Catherine. She had done this to him, somehow. She had some device from the City for subduing people like him with minimal effort.

It must have been Alexander. He told them to come looking for Apollo. After years of solitude, the time to pay for his past had come. Alexander hired Gunnar Junior and Edward, and now Alexander had hired this woman.

And yet, he was neither being cuffed nor beaten.

He craned his head upward, growling and wincing with every millimeter of movement, and glared at Catherine. Her face was not gloating or triumphant as he expected, but seemed to show a trace of sadness. He had been right, those were diamonds around her neck. She also wore a silky black dress, cut low in every important way, that looked like she had just left a party thrown for the elite of Londonsberg.

In a flash, the pain was gone, replaced by a shuddering emptiness behind his temples. He sprang to his feet, all traces of intoxication gone and took a step toward where Catherine still stood.

Then he realized who she was and felt a strange pang of longing, regret, and the seething rage of years of bottled resentment.

"You." Apollo snarled with every ounce of hate he could muster. "You've come back to torment me again, haven't you?"

Catherine looked him dead in the eyes. She nodded once, but her mouth remained an implacable line of ruby lipstick.

"Get the hell out of my house," Apollo snapped. He was beyond mad, beyond furious even, to see the woman who called herself Catherine. The only reason he had not killed her where she stood, or so he told himself, was that she had spared his life when he had been too drunk to fight back against her moments before.

He also doubted that he could kill her, should it come to that. The problem was not willingness, but he had attempted violence against this woman before. Whoever, whatever, she was, she served a god more powerful than any technology.

"Let me tell you what I came to tell you and I will leave once you have made a decision on my offer," she replied coolly. Her accent was decidedly not Euronord, but her speech was perfect nonetheless, with the same lilting Scottanian accent he remembered from years before. In fact, it was better than perfect. She spoke with the mechanical precision of someone who learned a second language in school.

Apollo glared, fuming silently as he tried to figure out what to do. He could attack her and kill her, finally giving him the revenge he wanted years before. He could also attack her and lose, and the dead do not hold grudges. He could listen to whatever she had to say, get rid of her, and then try to put not only Alexander's presence on the Citycast but Catherine's return both out of his mind.

He had already tried once to kill her and failed, one of only two such failed attempts in his entire life. That left only one realistic option. But the more he thought about it, the less appealing it became. Catherine could have killed him when they fought the first time, but never did. Given the power she displayed when he tried to kill her so many years ago, she could have easily done him in the moment he opened the door.

Despite his better judgment, he wanted to know why.

Apollo smiled as the thought percolated through his still-recovering brain. Whatever brought her to his house was important. Only he could take care of it. That realization melted through his icy wrath like a torch. He would be getting the one thing more dear and more desired than revenge.

He would be getting vindication.

That, he thought, might just be better than any other reward she could have given him. Simply knowing that she needed him, that after so many years, he won the argument, was enough. If she was not going to leave him alone and let him bury the past where it belonged, then this was the only consolation prize he would accept.

Apollo silently turned and walked to the kitchen, bypassing a very tempting knife block on the way—he still felt uneasy around Catherine, and old habits died hard. Catherine watched him with a combination of amusement and genuine confusion given the rage he had been expressing moments before. From a small fingerprint-locked cabinet, he produced two crystal tumblers and a small bottle of Scotch worth over a hundred times what both bottles of Mind Eraser cost him.

Appearing to ignore Catherine completely as he crossed the room again, Apollo set the green glass bottle down at one end of his work table and turned the label so Catherine could read it. Among other things, it proclaimed, "Talantach – Anno 2770." Next to the bottle, he set one of the crystal glasses. He circled the table and, with a backward look at Catherine, roughly placed the second glass in front of her.

With a ceremonious gesture, he swept all of the tools and components of the gun he had been working on the day before to one side. The table was hardly what he would have called fancy, and the expensive liquor and glasses were a stark contrast to the disassembled pistol, but he worked with what he had.

He indicated the chair opposite the bottle. "Sit."

"I would rather stand."

"Sit," Apollo ordered.

Catherine watched him for a moment before her lips turned upward in a wry smile. She sat, folding her hands on the table and keeping her eyes on Apollo as he made his way to his seat and the bottle.

Apollo poured a finger of the Scotch into his glass, then reached for Catherine's glass to do the same. He stoppered the bottle and set it aside before sliding her glass back to her.

"You know I don't drink, Apollo." A hint of a demure smile crossed ruby-red lips.

He shrugged. "Don't care." His tone, almost jovial, was such a sharp change from mere minutes before that it seemed to take Catherine off guard.

Her discomfort amused him. He supposed that it was only fair, given the conflicting emotions she had been stirring in his brain ever since he opened the door. He folded his hands on the table in mimicry of the way Catherine sat.

He shifted in his seat, leaning forward slightly. He left his realization that she needed him unspoken but heavily implied. He knew the sudden shift in his outward confidence would be enough. "It's my house. That means we do things my way."

"As you wish," Catherine replied with a sweet smile that never quite touched her eyes. Rather than simple pleasantry, they held the icy dominance he knew from years past. However, now something new lurked in them: amusement that bordered on self-assured pleasure. She made no attempts to hide her feelings, perhaps because she knew how much Apollo would be struggling to understand them.

"Now." Apollo raised his glass with a businessman's smile. Light refracted in the crystal, creating a play of tiny rainbows across the intricately cut facets. He took a sip of the golden liquid inside, reveling in the complex flavors. He held it in his mouth for a moment, savoring it, before swallowing. The Scotch hit his stomach and blossomed with warmth that radiated through his body.

Yes, he decided, life did have its pleasures after all.

Taking her cue from him, Catherine raised her glass and took a small sip as well. She smiled, seemingly genuinely impressed by the drink. Apollo could tell little else for sure from her expression.

"You said you have a proposition for me?"

"I do." She kept her glass in her hand, holding it near her face and using the swirling liquid to gesture. "We need you to hunt someone down for us."

Apollo stared at her over the rim of his glass, too incredulous to finish the motion to bring it to his lips. He took a moment to think, and covered that moment with another sip of the exquisite Scotch. Catherine would not contact him for simple mercenary work. It was beneath him, not to mention that she still had one skilled killer who would come at her beck and call. It made no sense, unless she wanted him to track down one very specific person.

He smirked. "You want me to hunt him down for you, don't you?"

She smiled. Nothing about it was friendly. "You're perceptive."

"It was obvious," he admitted. "You want a man found, you hire a hunter or bribe a Black Tie. You want a powerful man found, you call your head attack dog. And if you want your dog killed..."

"We call you," she cut in.

"Exactly. You need me." Apollo laughed. After a slow pull on his drink, he added, "and that's exactly why I won't do it."

Catherine's eyes widened. She clearly had not expected that answer from Apollo, given their shared past. Given how Apollo had reacted before to not being offered a similar job, the thought that he could decline must never have occurred to her or her masters.

"You," she paused, "won't?"

"No."

"Why?"

Apollo swirled his drink once, then set the glass down on the table and very deliberately leaned forward with his hands on his knees. When he spoke, his tone was as even and hard as polished steel. "Why the *fuck* should I?"

"Because it's what you've wanted for years," she pleaded, still obviously trying to get her bearings.

Apollo picked up his glass and bowed his head to eye the Scotch inside. He swirled it a few times, ostensibly more interested in the patterns of light in the liquid than in Catherine.

With his head still down, his eyes shot upward. "Perhaps it is. And perhaps I don't care anymore. Perhaps I just want him out of my life, you out of my life, and that whole goddamned mess left far behind me."

"I know you, Apollo."

He raised his head, then followed that motion by sinking backward into his chair. "The fuck's that mean?"

"You still want this," she said, voice flat. "I know how the thought of a fight worth your time excites you."

"Not anymore," he grated.

She eyed him for a long, tense few seconds as Apollo took another sip from his drink. Catherine sighed. "We may," she slowly began, chewing on her bottom lip. She considered a moment, then finished her confession, "we may have made a mistake."

Apollo chuckled derisively. "I told you that years ago." He took a sip of his drink without taking his eyes off Catherine's face. "Why should I think things are any different now? Tell me that."

Catherine set her glass down and shifted nervously in her seat. Apollo reveled in her apparent discomfort. He wondered what precisely could make Catherine and her masters change their minds now. When every appeal, every threat, every wound inflicted, and every drop of blood spilled in years past had not.

Finally, she quietly admitted, "he doesn't listen to me anymore."

Apollo nearly choked on Scotch when she spoke, caught as he was between surprise and raucous laughter. The laughter won out, mixing sardonic glee with vindictive cackling. It went on for some time, long enough that Apollo needed a moment to catch his breath before going on with the conversation.

"He what, now?" Apollo asked with intense and quite genuine surprise. She could have told him that the sun would rise black from the western sky in the morning and it would have come as less of a shock.

"He won't listen to me," Catherine repeated. "All he cares about now is his fame and how he can use that to barter anything he wants, kill anyone he wants."

"And I'm supposed to feel sorry for you?" Apollo demanded, the fire in his voice back. Suddenly, the vindication was gone, replaced by anger at being their second choice again. She had not come because she recognized Apollo's inherent superiority, only because her previous choice had proved to be an inconvenience. He had moved on, or so he had told himself for years, and Catherine's problems were no longer a concern of his.

"Not necessarily, but..."

"No deal. He's your monster. You kill him. I don't want to see his face again. Ever."

"But..."

Apollo interrupted venomously. "I don't want to fight him. I don't want to fight anyone!"

Catherine sat still with her eyes downcast for several long moments, deep in thought. When she looked up again, she said, "you've made your decision."

"Damn right I have." He wondered if he sounded as bitter as he felt.

"Should you, ah, should you change your mind." Catherine slid a scrap of paper across the table to Apollo, who picked it up and read it. He eyed her over the top of the paper coldly. "My frequency and number," she added. "Call me if you decide to take me up on the offer."

Apollo pocketed the paper despite his misgivings. "No promises."

Catherine stood, finished her drink, and crossed wordlessly to the door. Umbrella in hand, she left Apollo to finish the rest of his glass in solitude as the rain beat down on his roof.

He did not feel like returning to the bottle of Mind Eraser. Especially after the Glenfiddich, it would seem like little more than turpentine and he did not feel like passing out on the couch again. He had a lot to think about, and he needed to keep a clear head.

He stared at his drink in silence for a long time before finishing it. For years, he had avoided the question of what he really wanted, and now it seemed like he was being forced to make that decision at last. Part of him called for blood and revenge, while part still wanted nothing to do with Catherine or any of her promises. A third part still clung to the fleeting vindication he felt when he realized she came to him with a reason.

Maybe he would call it an early night and things would be clearer in the morning.

# Chapter 5

The City of Londonsberg rewarded those who served it faithfully. Chief among those rewards, from an objective standpoint, was liberty to act without worrying about whether the President-Duke's Black Ties were going to arrive with unpleasant questions in the middle of the night. On a more personal level, Alexander, whom most simply knew as "The Captain," found that his favorite parts of being the Hero of Londonsberg ran to a more pleasurable nature.

With the Black Ties under orders to turn a blind eye to his activities, Alexander could come and go freely from the City. He rare did, but he would frequently contract other people to visit the outer areas for him. The irony of shopping outside the Limits, he quickly found out, was that while the food was of a far better caliber than he could get anywhere in the City—short of his favorite steakhouse, which itself bought food from the Far Market—the alcohol was terrible. That, he had to import from elsewhere.

He lifted his glass and swirled the liquid inside. Sunlight, itself an even rarer commodity in the City than the illegal liquor he drank, streamed in through his window and turned the contents of his glass into liquid gold.

Alexander repeated the small ritual, ignoring the world around him for a moment. He could hear the guards outside his door shuffling in place. They were not there to keep him contained as they would another high-profile individual. Nor was their job to protect him. Alexander suspected—no, he knew—that he could kill both of them without breaking a sweat. Instead, they were there for the second oldest reason in the world to surround an important person with armed thugs. They made him look important.

The few people who visited him in his personal quarters reacted appropriately. Few of them knew Alexander's true power—the opulence and legal authority he wielded were enough. The ones who knew the truth were either dead or part of the system doling out treasures to satisfy his every whim.

His current guest was not on the short list who knew who and what he was. Despite that, he seemed to be terrified to share the same room with Alexander. His reputation, it seemed, was doing most of his work for him.

He eyed the Black Tie over his glass. "You're sure?"

The Black Tie nodded. Alexander was no stranger to reading people's body language, and the thoughts going through this man's brain were clear. His stiff formality betrayed his frustration at their power imbalance. Alexander detected resentment, but that was fine. He did not resent Alexander's accomplishments or even his fame. What this Black Tie resented was that he was not the center of the conversation.

Alexander nodded absently, following his own train of thought while the Black Tie sat, waiting on him to continue the conversation. The Black Tie took a long sip of his drink, obviously savoring the decadent reward Alexander bestowed upon him. True, he resented not being the one in Alexander's position but he had proven to be as smart as he was greedy and that was something Alexander could work with.

They both knew that by taking Alexander's "rewards," the Black Tie had bound himself to Alexander's service. He could never tell anyone about the work he did for The Captain, nor what sort of payment he received. Alexander might be above the law, but he was not.

"Explain," Alexander ordered.

"It was like you suspected, sir," the Black Tie said. His manners continued to be stiffly formal. He watched Alexander take another drink, emulated the act, and continued with perhaps two percent less starch. "For the past three months, the man named Apollo has been visiting the Far Market every other week, remaining long after nightfall, doing business in what the locals call the Night Market."

"Did you make contact?"

The Black Tie nodded.

"Let me see."

He nodded again, then slowly reached inside his jacket and produced a pistol. From the outside, it seemed to be a perfectly normal firearm. He held it out, holding it by the barrel so that Alexander could grasp the handle.

Alexander took the proffered weapon and looked it over. Superficially, the report was accurate. It looked exactly like a weapon made in the City, in this case for a Black Tie's personal arsenal, but with a few subtle differences. The grip was different, slightly, and the sights had been altered to increase their visibility. He racked it, found the slide moved more smoothly than any mass-produced Black Tie weapon would have.

He had one test left to conduct. Alexander turned in his seat and pointed the pistol at the door. He squeezed the trigger. The rapport echoed around the room, bringing his guards bursting into the room in half a second.

"Sir!" one shouted.

"Are you alright?" the other asked on reflex. He noted the pistol in Alexander's hand, now pointed at the first guard to enter, and closed his mouth.

"Is the NoTech still active in the tower?" Alexander asked.

The guard, already sweating as he stared at the gun in Alexander's hand, bobbed his head in a nervous nod. "It may have malfunctioned."

"It didn't," Alexander countered. He slipped the pistol into his pocket. "But your report will say that it did."

"Understood."

"And have the door fixed."

"Yes, sir."

The guards left the room as quickly as they had entered. Once they were gone, the Black Tie turned back to face Alexander. "We have proof that he's making illegal weapons, sir, should we go after him?"

Alexander shook his head. "No. If we send someone to his house, he would just kill them. I'm prepared to risk a lot to bring Apollo in, but not if it means sending people to their deaths for no reason."

"Sir..." The Black Tie paused, trying to figure out the right words to use. A moment later, he settled on honesty. "I respectfully disagree."

Alexander cocked en eyebrow. "Do you now?"

"Yes, sir," he replied. He spoke quickly, nervously. "All of my men are ready to lay down their lives in the service of the City if need be."

"I don't doubt that, but sending them against a man like Apollo would not be 'dangerous.' It would be suicidal."

"Sir?"

"He's easily as capable as I am, and he's completely ruthless. He would kill your men just because he could, and I don't see any benefit to arranging things so that happens."

"I understand."

His answer was just a little too slow, a little too reserved, and Alexander knew he was lying. He could not blame the man for doubting him. No one was that strong, that skilled. No one, that was, except for the two of them.

There were legends about Apollo, and about Alexander, but most just dismissed them as stories to impress, or terrify, the population. Ultimately, Alexander did not care whether the Black Tie believed him or not. He was second in authority only to the President-Duke himself. If Alexander told him to keep his men at home, then at home they would stay.

"You've done enough." Alexander's smile was warm, charismatic, but something deadly flickered in his eyes.

"Thank you, sir."

"I mean it," Alexander said. "I have a schedule now, and if there's anything I know about Apollo it's that even after all these years, he never misses an appointment."

"That's been my observation as well, sir," the Black Tie agreed.

Alexander smiled again. "Excellent. You've helped me more than you can know. By the end of the week, I suspect the City will be free of the last great danger to plague it."

"Thank you, sir."

Alexander raised his empty glass in salute. "You are free to go."

The Black Tie stood and regarded his own glass which still held a significant amount of contraband liquor. Alexander gave a tiny nod, and the Black Tie downed the remainder of his drink in one swallow, then left the room.

To his retreating back, Alexander called, "you'll find the agreed-upon numbers when next you check your balance."

The Black Tie said nothing. He was already out of the room, though not out of earshot. Publicly, no one knew he was there. If anyone happened to wander into the corridor, they could not see him acknowledging Alexander's comment in any way.

Alexander finished his own drink in silence, thinking. He appreciated the man's spirit and his willingness to do the proverbial "dirty work." This one, perhaps, would survive their tenure together. His predecessors had all met with terribly unfortunate accidents, but this was one Black Tie that Alexander thought might merit some extra care.

He nursed his drink in blessed silence. That was another perk of his position. At street level, the noise never ceased until Legal Night. His was the top suite in one of Duke Charlie's towers, and the noise of the street was all but gone at his level. After nightfall, even that little bit of noise would cease as the Black Ties took to the streets. They would not touch him, but he did like his sleep, and never ventured out after dark if he could avoid it.

Such unheard-of quiet also meant that Alexander could hear anyone approaching, theoretically. His guards outside never reacted, never let anyone in, but he heard the sound of a pair of feet striding across his carpet nonetheless.

He jumped, spilling his drink onto the floor, and drawing his own pistol. Like Apollo's guns, it would still work despite the NoTech in the area., though for a different reason. Alexander's weapons were exempt, not immune. In a moment, the sights of his gun were level with the intruder's forehead.

He froze. Catherine stood demurely in his doorway. The door itself was still shut and his guards outside, meaning that in her own frustrating way, she had simply appeared in his room without passing by his security watchdogs first. Her hair was done up in a simple braid with wisps here and there that had escaped. She wore a simple pair of slacks and a Manhattan-style button-down shirt whose casualness matched her lack of jewelry or makeup.

When Alexander realized who his visitor was, he bit back the curse on the tip of his tongue and holstered his pistol. His brown-red pants and gray shirt, the same as what any one of a thousand other relatively important people would have worn on his day off, suddenly felt inadequate.

He knelt. "My lady Catherine."

She folded her arms across her chest. "Stand up, Alexander. You know you don't need to kneel."

Alexander rose. "Of course. What brings you here?"

"You know why I'm here, Alexander."

He recoiled at her sharp-edged tone. "My lady, I would do anything you commanded me to. You know that. But you cannot ask me to give up all of this," he swept the apartment with his hand, "simply because your superiors feel it's a distraction. I can promise you, it's not!"

Catherine closed her eyes and shook her head sadly. "You know that's not the root problem, Alexander."

"Then tell me what you need me to do," he pleaded.

"Giving this up is only the first step. You've let yourself get too wrapped up in the things of this City."

"I made this City the safe place it is today! I deserve this!"

"We have more work for you." Her voice was flat with tones of authority.

"And I will do as you ask." His voice hovered on the edge of pleading. "Just give me time to finish my work for the Duke."

Catherine shook her head and pursed her lips into a tight line. "You will stay here, if not in this room then you will at least remain inside the city, until I return."

"My lady," he protested, "I can't. I have work..."

"We will not have this conversation again, Alexander. This is your last opportunity. We have found another."

Alexander's world snapped into crystal focus. She had made that threat before, but something in her posture and voice now told him that she was telling the truth. He did not have to ask who the "other" was; he knew in the very pits of his heart that Catherine's superiors would only ever consider one other person on the face of the Earth.

Alexander could not let that happen.

"Give me time to think," he said at last, though his mind was already doing exactly that.

She eyed him and not for the first time, Alexander felt her gaze penetrating down past his facade and into his very soul. He wondered what she saw there. Finally, she nodded, apparently satisfied.

Alexander closed his eyes and let out the breath he had not realized he had been holding. "Thank you, my la—" The words stopped in his throat when he opened his eyes and realized that she left his room as silently and suddenly as she arrived.

Alexander knew what he had to do, and he only hoped there was still time.

***

Half a megameter away, Apollo was enjoying the one thing that had been denied him for a week after Alexander's Citycast: sleeping in. Things had not been clearer the morning after Catherine's visit. In fact, things had only grown so progressively more unclear that Apollo felt forced by necessity to pretend the entire encounter had never happened. He still felt a swell of vindication knowing that she had asked for his help in person, but he never regretted sending her away.

Instead, he once again buried himself in his work. Unlike the previous week, when he had been avoiding dealing with seeing Alexander's face again, he felt strangely at peace. After years of fighting against the past, he felt like he had finally shut the door on a part of his life that he never wanted to deal with again. Catherine was gone. Alexander was probably whoring it up somewhere in the City, likely on the people's credit and under the guise of working for the common good of Londonsberg.

His regular trip to the market was scheduled for that night, when he would offload many of the weapons he had been working on for the past two weeks. Ordinarily, he felt a bit of nervousness prepping for the trip. The trouble he could find himself in for selling weapons to civilians outside the Limits was far worse than a visit by the Duke's enforcers. He was always careful, and never sold to anyone who would get word back to the Black Ties that his business was illegal arms manufacturing.

Far Market had no real organizing force, and the Night Market had even less of one. At best, it represented organized anarchy where each person was responsible for his or her own work and nothing more. Unlike the other vendors who operated out of specific plots either rented or borrowed, Apollo conducted his business from a suitcase. Every once in a while a new merchant would raise a fuss, but Apollo could usually cut a deal with the offended party, usually involving a discount on a custom pistol and a veiled threat to use it if they neglected to pay.

Apollo shook his head as he loaded two large suitcases with weapons. One case held most of his finished commissioned work. Some of them had agreed to meet him that night specifically, but most were regular customers—or other vendors— and would be there whether they contacted him or not.

The other case held a variety of other weapons that he planned to sell to new customers, mostly modified standard stock. Here and there a few pieces original to his workshop sat amid the mediocrity. Apollo was always interested to see who picked those up—they often became regulars.

Apollo finished loading his aircar half an hour before Legal Night. He planned to arrive at the Night Market an hour and a half after nightfall. That gave the market plenty of time to thin out, leaving only the serious buyers and expensive merchandise. He also had a stop to make at Sal's, where several choice cuts waited for him.

Apollo made the trip in his usual time, still buoyed by that strange elation. Once again, the thought that he had finally moved on came to the front of his mind. It made him happy, which was something he had long since ever given up hope of feeling again. Perhaps tonight he might even stay and socialize for a few minutes.

This time, he hoped, things would stay calm, letting Apollo concentrate on actually living for once.

His thoughts continued along the same lines, hopeful if reserved, as he neared the parking area for the Night Market. From the air, the number of people milling around far exceeded the stock he brought.

Good, he thought. That meant that the ones who were lucky or rich enough to get his weapons before they were gone would show the others and would increase overall interest. It would also draw more customers to the Night Market, which meant more customers for the other merchants as well.

Apollo laughed quietly to himself as he exited the aircar. "So this is what teamwork feels like."

From the trunk, Apollo withdrew the two suitcases. He made little effort to announce his presence once he hit the market proper. Word of mouth and sight of the suitcases did that well enough, and he was quickly followed by a sizable crowd.

Apollo kept the crowd in his peripheral vision, pretending not to notice them at all, until he felt that a suitable number of people had gathered. At last, he stopped and turned to the crowd, saying simply, "can I help you?"

If his voice held less than the usual amount of contempt, no one in the crowd seemed to notice and they all shrank back for a moment, before a well-dressed man in the front row spoke up. In a thick Marrakeshi accent, he asked, "we were wondering if you were here to sell tonight."

Apollo grinned. "As a matter of fact." He dropped the suitcase of spoken-for weapons on the ground and set the second one on top. He opened it and allowed a few moments for the greedy eyes of perspective customers to take in the suitcase full of pistols, broken-down rifles, and weapon parts before he stepped in front of it.

He turned to the crowd for a moment, surveying their eager faces with blank disdain. Perhaps he had been wrong about his mood. The press of people and faces still sickened him and set his nerves on edge as it always had. Perhaps there was no moving on.

He shook his head, disguising his derision of the crowd as simple showmanship. They, of course, bought it completely and assumed that the rumors about Apollo and his temper were all true.

From the case, he drew out a simple pistol. The black metal reflected the lanterns of the Night Market dully as he swept the barrel along the crowd—creating a disturbance even among those who were use to dealing with him—then held it above his head.

"I am," he said, finally finishing the sentence.

The pistol in his hand was the cheapest of all his stock. Best to save the more expensive weapons for the ones who held out deliberately for them after the cheap pieces were gone. "This is a custom-tuned Wescott Model Six Service Pistol. The trigger pull has been smoothed and softened. It has an upgraded security lock on the targeting suite and custom physical sights in case that fails. It will hit reliably at ranges fifty percent longer than a Black Tie's standard sidearm." Apollo rattled off the rest of the gun's features with a tone that sounded more like he was giving orders than a sales pitch.

"One thousand credits," he added, bringing his hand down and holding the gun closer to belt level. Someone quickly met that offer, then was shouted down by other, steadily higher, offers. In the end, the simple gun sold for two-point-two thousand credits to someone who would probably take it home, leave it unloaded, and bring it out at social events to show his friends how tough he was.

Over the next hour, Apollo slowly sold off the contents of the suitcase. He sold an antique pistol, complete with documentation dating it to at least 2466, to a man who Apollo was reasonably certain was a Londonsberg weapon collector with a taste for illegal wares. He had sold more than one gun to him in the past, though by mutual unspoken consent, they acted like they had never seen one another before. The final piece was an extremely ornate weapon, black with an action and grip etched with gold. It had had every internal upgrade Apollo could squeeze into the frame, and had taken him hundreds of hours to finish. It sold for twenty-five thousand credits to the man from Marrakesh who handled it with more familiarity than most.

Most of his official clients, the ones who had directly commissioned his work, typically met him in predetermined locations throughout the Night Market. As the night wore on, he found them one by one and traded their weapons for exorbitant amounts of cash. Per hour worked, he charged them rates that were much more fair than what the anonymous mass of people paid for their stock weapons

That continued until he had one left.

Apollo pushed aside the leather curtain of Sal's butcher shop. Sal's eyes immediately fell on Apollo's suitcases and he grinned with excitement. Sal set his knives down on the counter and pushed aside a large chunk of beef so red that Apollo had to do a double take to make sure it was not still bleeding.

"Finally got'er finished, Mister A?" Sal asked with a smile.

Apollo nodded, feeling the ghost of a return smile touch his lips. He was still trying to figure out what exactly was going on with his moods. As the night had gone on and he fell into the comfortable routine of buying and selling his work, the good spirits he felt on the drive to the market returned.

"You look happy," Sal observed. "Must've come out looking nice."

"You know, Sal? I suppose I am."

"Good," Sal said. "You're a good'n, Mister A. Hate to see you angry all the time."

If only you knew how wrong you are, Sal, Apollo thought with a frown. I know exactly what I am. He forced the half smile back to his features. "Thanks. I assume you want to take a look at it?"

"You got it. Just lemme wash m'hands."

Apollo set the suitcases down on the ground and took the last of the weapons out of its case: a silver pistol with checkered wood grips. The metal had been extensively engraved with ornate scroll work that caught the ambient light in a thousand different directions.

It was also the gun that killed Edward and Jason, though he had not quite finished working on it at that point.

Sal's eyes widened at the sight as Apollo stepped up to the counter to pass it over.

"It's loaded," Apollo warned. "I tested it before bringing it to you."

Sal nodded absently, already going through the motions of checking the magazine, chamber, and safety. Apollo silently wondered where Sal had learned to handle a weapon, considering he seemed more familiar with the pistol in his hands than the majority of the people outside, especially those who bought his more ornate guns.

"And the verdict?" Apollo prompted.

"More than I ever expected." For a moment, Sal's accent was gone and Apollo wondered again where exactly Sal was from.

"Old gun like that's got to have history," Apollo mused.

Sal nodded. "My pa fought in the wars," he drawled, then, "Granddad, too." The accent was still absent. The man speaking now, Apollo realized, was the man who had written him the letter. With a sad grin, he added. "Fought against the Londonsberg Army, in fact. Explains why my family and I weren't exactly welcome within the Limits, hey?"

Apollo nodded. The Second Succession War, commonly referred to as the Validian War, ended thirty-six years ago. Londonsberg as a political entity existed at that point, in fact they won the war, defeating the Validian army after thirteen years of fighting. With the war over, President-Duke Charlie erected the walls around the Limits, creating the world into which Apollo had been born.

Sal slipped the gun behind his butcher's apron. "This was his gun, see, and pa always wanted to get it engraved and done up fancy like this, but after our side lost the war, well. To say we fell on hard times would be an understatement. He taught me how to use one and how to clean and respect one."

Apollo listened with surprising interest to Sal's story. He knew he had a reason for elevating Sal above the rank and file merchants and general filth that did little else beyond occupying space and taking up resources. To hear that the man's family had fought against the doddering totalitarianism that Londonsberg represented almost made Apollo like him.

Perhaps humanity was still worth a shit, he thought, and wondered what Sal would think of Apollo's own reasons for hating Londonsberg.

"Well," Sal said, breaking Apollo out of his reverie. "I suppose everyone here has their reasons and their own story to tell."

"Yes," Apollo agreed. He was in no mood to go over such unpleasant and anger-laced events right then. "I would say everyone does."

Sal persisted. Even without saying anything, he clearly expected that it was now Apollo's turn to share something. The look on his face and posture said enough.

Apollo grimaced, hoping it did not show on his face. "Let's just say that I was born in the City and leave it at that."

Sal nodded, clearly deciding not to press the issue. He still seemed pleased that his years-long quest to get Apollo to open up a little had paid off even a little bit. "Well, anyway," he said. His accent returned a moment later. "I owes ya, what? Twenafive kay?"

"Twenty," Apollo countered, and immediately wondered where the came from. "Consider the other five a gift for the story."

Apollo spent a few more minutes talking to Salvatore, rather than Sal, as the butcher packaged his bi-weekly purchases. When he turned to go, Sal, in his faux-Imperial Manhattan accent, said, "y'done good, Apollo, thanks. Y'done real good. Ma Pa would'a been proud."

Despite himself, Apollo smiled. "You're welcome, Sal. See you in two weeks."

Apollo hurried through the rest of his errands, walking fast enough to appear busy, but slow enough that he could keep his ears open to see who was talking about his weapons. From the general buzz, he expected to be approached by more than one person on his next visit to the market. Business would be good for a while. He felt several pairs of eyes watching him as he made his way through the crowd, all familiar-feeling, none threatening.

At his aircar, the sky began to sprinkle rain. Apollo looked up, watching the silver streaks falling for a moment. The moment passed and he pressed his palm against the hidden reader and opened the trunk, depositing the two empty suitcases and his groceries in the back of the car. He was thinking about taking some time off from working, when a voice from behind him spoke.

"You know, it's illegal to sell weapons to civilians, especially outside the Limits."

A chill surged down Apollo's spine and he shot straight up, slamming the trunk lid in the process. It was not the authoritarian tone to the voice, nor the implied threat of imprisonment or worse under Londonsberg's laws that made Apollo take notice. Rather, what set every nerve he had on edge was the fact that he recognized the voice itself.

It would seem his past had caught up with him, after all. Alexander stood two meters behind him. He wore the white suit he had on the day his statue had been dedicated—Apollo wondered if he ever wore anything else. In his hand, held casually at waist level and pointed at Apollo's spine, was the gun he carried every day since they last met.

Apollo turned his head, putting on a face that was a mixture of mirth and spite. "You wouldn't shoot a man in the back would you?"

Alexander smiled and Apollo saw the muscles tighten in his hand at roughly the same instant that two other things happened. First, his reflexes which had been placed on a hair trigger since he heard Alexander's voice moments before threw him to one side and into the dirt. Second, Alexander's gun went off with a sharp crack. The bullet missed Apollo's shoulder by a few centimeters and the round slammed into the armored side of his aircar.

Alexander tisked. With scorn he said, "Armor plates? I knew you'd planned for this, Apollo. That just makes this all the more deserved. You knew this was coming, and now I'm here to deliver!"

Apollo sprang to his feet, drawing his own gun from its holster as he did so. He came up in a two-handed stance, firing as soon as his instinct told him he was level. He should have hit Alexander—he never missed a shot, even without aiming, from so close—but Alexander was not there. He judged the speed at which Apollo would stand, and dove out of the way at the exact second to make Apollo's shot miss.

Alexander fired from the ground. The first shot went wide, and Apollo ducked behind his aircar before Alexander could aim and fire a second shot. He was never quite as good a shot as Apollo.

"Stop this, Alexander," Apollo called as Alexander got to his feet. "You don't have to do this."

"Oh but I do, Apollo." He sounded much closer than he should have. He laughed. "I do."

"No you don't," Apollo argued. "Listen to me. Things are... Shit!"

Apollo's sentence was cut short by Alexander vaulting onto the roof of his aircar with his pistol pointed at his head. He dove out of the way as the bullet slammed into the tightly-packed dirt of the parking lot, sending up a shower of dry earth.

Apollo used the momentary cloud of dust to dart behind the next aircar in the lot. "Damn it, listen to me. Things have changed. The past is the past!" That phrase had become his daily mantra over the years. Somehow, he doubted that Alexander would buy the argument.

"I know what you are, Apollo. I know what you've done," Alexander chanted, mocking, as he slid off of the roof of Apollo's aircar.

"And I know *what* you are!" Apollo spat back.

"Then you know this fight is already over, Apollo. Give up. Give up, Apollo, and die."

"I've changed! The past is the past," he repeated, hoping the second time would get through. He had fought Alexander before, and nearly won, but after meeting with Catherine, he wanted no part in anything to do with his past.

Apollo sprang out from behind the second car, firing several shots at where Alexander should have been. Once again, he was gone. Not just to one side or on the ground, but completely gone. Apollo stood with his gun at the ready, scanning the parked cars and trucks for any sign of Alexander's presence.

Behind him a piece of gravel squeaked. Apollo spun and fired twice. Both shots missed, making Apollo wonder what was going on. Yes, he was agitated, but the adrenaline in his veins usually made him more accurate, not less.

Was he actually afraid of fighting Alexander and of unearthing that part of his past?

He shook his head to clear it as Alexander lunged at him. Apollo pivoted on one foot, grabbed Alexander, and hurled him over his shoulder and to the ground. Standing over him, he aimed the gun at Alexander's chest. Instead of pulling the trigger, he gave his assailant one last chance. "Leave, Alexander. Go away and leave me alone. The past is the past."

Alexander was up in a flash, sweeping Apollo's legs out from under him with the same motion he used to get his own under himself. Apollo hit the ground hard, knocking the wind out of his lungs. He dove forward, under another shot from Alexander's gun, and tackled him in the knees.

Apollo stood, aiming his pistol now at Alexander's head. "I've changed, Alexander. I can't make up for the past, but I can move on, and I have. I don't want to kill you."

Alexander laughed as he came slowly to his feet. He moved like he was mocking Apollo's unwillingness to shoot. His laugh was the same hollow sound a headsman might make after cracking a joke at the expense of a condemned man.

"Don't want to kill me?" Alexander laughed his hollow laugh again. To Apollo, it felt like something was missing inside of him, or that something cold and inhuman had taken its place. "Well, it seems you're as bad at lying as you ever were. We don't change, Apollo. People like you and me, we are who we are." His lack of expression chilled Apollo's blood. His eyes were wide with fervor as he added, "nothing stays buried forever; the tide of time washes away all the filth."

Apollo grit his teeth. He had spent years telling himself that his past was behind him. He repeated that fact daily, marking the slow passage of time as each day put him further and further away from people like Alexander. If he would have just turned and left, Apollo would have done the same, but now it seemed like he had no choice.

Maybe Alexander was right. Maybe the past would always come back for him. If that was true, he needed to ensure that everything he left behind him stayed dead and buried where it belonged. No one else was strong or skilled enough to deal with this problem. Even if he did walk away, leaving Alexander near the Night Market seemed like a recipe for blood.

Apollo would have to kill him.

Alexander, who had been slowly walking toward Apollo, suddenly broke into a run. He was faster than Apollo had ever seen him move, and was on him in a second. Apollo managed to squeeze one shot off, but, despite the line of red that appeared on Alexander's side, it seemed to have no effect.

The barrel of Alexander's pistol came whistling toward Apollo's temple. He managed to jerk his head out of the way and grabbed Alexander's wrist with one hand. His pistol was in the other hand, and he struck the outside of Alexander's arm with the butt of the weapon, loosening Alexander's grip.

With both of Apollo's hands busy, he was unable to block the punch that struck him in the side. The blow sent a sharp jolt of pain through his body and sent him flying at least three meters through the air. Apollo skidded to a stop on the hard ground, gasping for air and sure that several of his ribs were broken. He was dimly aware that he had dropped his gun at some point before hitting the ground.

Alexander calmly walked towards him, waiting until Apollo got to his hands and knees before dashing forward again and slamming his foot into the mercifully unbroken side of Apollo's ribcage. The hit sent Apollo flying again, and he landed on his back, again trying to force air into his lungs.

"Apollo the Destroyer," Alexander chanted mockingly as he approached the spot where Apollo fell the second time. His voice dripped with disdain. "I thought, given the stories people tell about you, that you would be a better fighter than you were all those years ago. Instead, it seems you've grown weak and soft. And I thought this would be a challenge. I should have come after you years ago."

Slowly coming to his feet, Apollo grated, "don't ever call me that again. I've changed. Things are different now. Listen, damn it!"

"No." Alexander again spoke with that cold, flat inflection. "You die here, Butcher of Novarus. You die, Nightmare of Londonsberg."

Apollo growled and lunged forward, hitting Alexander with an uppercut to the jaw. Alexander was strong, but Apollo had always been stronger, so when his fist seemed to do nothing, it took a split second before Apollo realized it.

In that split second, Alexander slid forward and kneed Apollo in the gut. Fighting back the pain, the nausea, and the stars in front of his eyes, Apollo retorted with another uppercut to Alexander's jaw using every ounce of strength he could muster. He followed it up with several more blows from his fists around Alexander's face and neck, before ending with a kick to his sternum that should have been hard enough to shatter a wooden door. The familiar wet crunch of breaking bone, one that he should have been able to feel all the way up his leg, was missing.

The last hit did knock Alexander off his feet, at least. Apollo whipped his head around, searching around for either of the two guns. He found his less than two meters away and made a dash for it. Before he could reach it, Alexander was on him again with a chop to the side of his head that sent Apollo sprawling on the ground. His gun was just out of reach.

Apollo jumped to his feet, throwing another punch to Alexander's face. It should have hit him in the nose, breaking it and caving in the front of his skull, but his target was not where it should have been. Alexander had moved to the side, melting out of the way like fog, and grabbed Apollo's arm. He pivoted slightly, capturing Apollo's elbow in an arm bar. Rather than throw him as Apollo expected him to do, Alexander pivoted again and landed a solid blow to the outside of Apollo's elbow, breaking it inward with a sickening tearing sound.

Apollo crumpled, too stunned to scream.

Alexander lifted him roughly off the ground, turning Apollo so they were face to face. "Listen, damn it," Apollo sputtered. "The past is..."

"What defines us," Alexander finished. His eyes were wide, almost like he was happy to have finally caught and probably killed Apollo. Alexander cocked one fist back. Apollo tried to block, but Alexander's other hand brushed his arms aside like twigs before hitting him square in the face with the force of a crashing freighter.

The blow snapped Apollo's head back and he fell limp to the ground. As the world faded around him, he was dimly aware of a thud and jolt of intense pain as Alexander kicked him in the ribs again. Somewhere in the blackness, a white-hot lance of agony shot through his body, but that was the last thing he knew.

# Chapter 6

Apollo awoke to a blinding light. Everything hurt, inside and out. His ribs ached, his nose was swollen and impossible to breathe through, and one arm seemed to be completely immobile. Every breath burned like fire as he forced air into his torn and shredded lungs.

His mind raced. He had lost. He demanded, of himself, of Alexander, of any deity listening, to know how that had happened. Alexander had never been that strong or fast before. He had never been able to beat Apollo in an arm wrestling contest, let alone an all-out fight of life or death.

That single question burned in Apollo's mind. He no longer cared about who Alexander had become, or even who he had been years before. Now, all he wanted to know was what Alexander was now. He was something more than human, Apollo was sure of that much.

His mind ached with a mental pain that burrowed deeper than any of the physical agonies wracking his body. He needed revenge. He did not simply want revenge or yearn for it. Rather, he needed revenge like an addict would need another fix. Every pain-soaked inch of his body and mind called for revenge to be paid in kind. He would tear Alexander limb from limb, cutting and smashing, and burning his body while he was still alive. He would break him and destroy everything he was before finally launching his body into the sun so that no scrap of the man who was Alexander would ever touch Earth again.

Apollo reveled in the thoughts. The fantasy pushed the pain to a back corner of his mind as he imagined his hands awash in blood once more, but this time it would be Alexander's blood that would stain his skin and clothes. One last death, he thought with relish, yes that would be a delightful end to all things.

After so many years, Apollo could end on a high note. All he had to do was find Alexander again and then the hunted would become the hunter, the way it should have been from the beginning.

As his mind raced, his eyes adapted to the light around him. He was in his bed at home. The last thing he remembered was falling to the ground outside the Night

Market. He had been beaten, broken, and left to die. He seemed to remember Alexander shooting him. He felt his chest, digging beneath thick bandages he did not remember applying, and found a thumb-sized hole in the middle of his chest on the right side.

He pressed against the hole and a fresh wave of pain and nausea threatened to reduce him to a gibbering wreck. The wounds were real, so the fight had been real. Now, he was home, and he struggled to remember what happened after darkness took him outside the Night Market.

There was nothing there. No memory came to the surface to explain how he survived or made it back to his house. He remembered fighting, falling, and pain. Then darkness more complete than any sleep, and now he was here.

He shook his head, which summoned up even more agony. That did a fine job of banishing his thoughts of the night before—at least, he hoped it had only been one night ago—and focusing him again on the present.

Apollo rubbed his head, brushing aside flakes of dried blood. He had seen enough head wounds to know that even minor ones bled a lot, but the lack of dirt and other debris surprised him. One of the few things he clearly remembered was tumbling on the ground more than once. He looked down finally, realizing that his clothes bore none of the rips, tears, and cuts he knew had to be there. Someone had washed his body and dressed him in clean clothes after bringing him home.

"Shit," he muttered. "I'm dead, aren't I?"

Wafting in from the living room, he swore he could smell coffee. He never programmed the coffee maker himself. He supposed being dead might not be that bad if it came with free baths and coffee, but the burning pain coming from every part of his body attested to the fact that nothing, even Valhalla, was perfect. It seemed like a gross miscarriage of justice to kill him and still expect him to deal with his injuries.

If he was dead, then he would never get to exact revenge. His heart chilled with hatred at that thought and he wondered if he could find his way back to Earth like a demon out of the old myths. Then, he would kill Alexander and throw his soul down to hell where he belonged. An eternity sitting on the precipice of hell and mocking Alexander while he burned seemed to Apollo to be sweeter than honey.

He slid to the edge of the bed, then off and promptly fell into the floor in a tangled mess of limbs and pain. One arm was braced with a splint and he dimly remembered it being violently broken. That arm would not support any weight, and his broken ribs resisted any effort to use his core muscles to support himself. He was unsure whether his legs were whole or if they were just slightly less broken than his upper body, their pain drowned out by the pain in his torso.

Without testing himself, he would learn nothing. With what seemed to be the only working muscles in his body, Apollo grabbed the nearest bedpost with one hand and pulled himself to his feet. His legs seemed to be able to support him—if only barely—but the lacerated muscles around his ribs were still too weak to do their job without intense pain.

He had a rifle above his bed, an antique from the previous millennium that had been one of his first restoration projects. He shuffled along the edge of the bed until he could reach it with his good arm and took it down off of its display mount. With one hand on the barrel and the metal-shod stock against the floor, it made a decent enough crutch for his purposes. Using it, he was able to limp into the bathroom, toward the only mirror in the entire house.

To say he looked terrible would have been a gross understatement. Blue-black bruises interlaced with brownish-red gashes covered his exposed skin. The hair on one side of his head had been plastered flat to his skull with blood, despite the appearance of having been bathed relatively recently. It seemed an odd thing to notice right then, but the blood drew his eyes to his scalp where sandy blond threatened to make a reappearance.

Apollo avoided his eyes. The black rings around them were nothing new. He had been hit in the face before, though usually those fights ended with him winning. Apollo knew what he would see in his own eyes if he looked at them. He knew what was there because he could feel it stirring deep in his soul, and he could do nothing about it. He knew with every fiber of memory that he would hate the man he saw in the mirror, and so he made the choice not to look at that man at all.

Apollo knew *he* had returned.

His breathing rattled in and out of lungs too bruised and damaged to function quietly. Above that noise, he heard movement in the other end of the house, and his mind immediately jumped into overdrive. His first thought was to wonder if he could muster the strength to use the rifle as a club. He then wondered if he could kill anyone in whatever afterlife he found himself in. Even if he could, Apollo then asked himself if there would be any point to it.

The part of his brain that still clung to thoughts of the real world tried to convince itself that whoever was in his house must be the person who saved him from the market's parking lot. He had no idea how long he had been asleep, but whoever it was had plenty of time to kill him already. They had not, which served to simultaneously calm his nerves and put an entirely different set of nerves on edge.

He kept a tight grip on his rifle-turned-crutch just in case.

Apollo hobbled into the living room. For a moment, he was so focused on the pain radiating from every part of his body that he only registered two things. First, another human being was in his house and, second, that human being was not trying to kill him. When his mind resolved the identity of the human shape, however, his knees threatened to give out and send him plummeting to the floor.

Catherine sat at his table, watching him. Her hands were folded in front of her, between her body and what appeared to be a small cup of coffee. She wore the a similar low-cut silk dress to the one she had worn at their last meeting, only this one was a deep blue, accented by a necklace of blood-red gemstones that drew his eye to her breasts. She nodded approvingly at the rifle he was using to support himself.

"Hello, Apollo."

Her voice had a hint of warmth, but was reserved in a way that clearly communicated she was holding something back. Given the way their previous conversation went, Apollo suspected she was waiting to see how civil he was going to be. His mind flashed back to his thought from moments before: if she wanted to kill him, she could have done it already.

He decided civility, or attempting it, was the best route and took a deep breath. Another, and it turned out that civility lasted exactly seven seconds. "That settles it. I'm dead and this is hell."

Catherine smiled, amused. "Then who am I?"

Apollo glared. "You're the archdevil herself, who else?"

Catherine smiled again, a much more genuine gesture than Apollo remembered her ever using. He failed to place the emotion behind it, only that it was not quite amusement. Under his watchful eye, she went to the kitchen, retrieved a second cup of coffee and brought it to the work table.

"Sit," she offered.

The way in which she seemed to dominate the room, *his* room, bothered him more than anything else. "Go to hell."

"According to you, we already are. Now, come, sit. Your coffee's going to get cold." She turned her familiar demure, amused smile on him before speaking again. "Besides, isn't this how things are done at your house? We share a drink before we talk?"

Apollo growled, annoyed that she was using his logic against him, but the coffee did smell inviting. Gingerly, he set himself down at the table, leaning the rifle against his chair so that it would be close at hand when he needed to stand up.

Catherine cradled her mug in her hands, smiling overtop. "First, you're not dead."

Apollo laughed. The pain brought on by the laughter only made him laugh more. Every ache told him that he had to be dead. No one could survive being thrown around by whatever Alexander had become. But if he was actually still alive, then that meant he would have another chance to get revenge. If he was still alive, then he could still make Alexander pay with blood for everything he had done.

"How?" Apollo finally demanded. Having lost to Alexander, he felt that his grip on reality was tenuous at best. Perhaps he was right after all, and he was dead, and part of his punishment was to have this damned inane conversation with the last person he wanted to see for all of his godforsaken eternal afterlife.

"I watched him attack you," Catherine admitted.

"You were there?" he snarled. "And you didn't call him off?"

"I couldn't," she admitted, looking away from Apollo's bruised face. To his surprise, she actually seemed ashamed. He thought for a moment that his injuries were somehow bothering her, but blood had never been a problem of hers. A moment before she opened her mouth again, he realized the problem was her relationship with Alexander, or current lack of one.

Before he could pounce on that sudden, crystalline thought, she continued. "I already told you, he won't listen to me anymore. I ordered, and even threatened, but he went on his way."

Apollo felt an unexpected pang of guilt, a sensation he was long unused to experiencing. Alexander had mentioned his selling weapons at the Night Market. Apollo tried to convince himself that he cared very little for the people there. Yet, the thought of the carnage Alexander could have caused after leaving him a crumpled heap in the parking lot sent a shudder up his spine. If he considered anyone his friends, the scant few people he talked with at the Market were them, whether he admitted that truth to himself or not.

He felt his energy ebb, and the next question came out quietly, almost an echo of Catherine's ashamed tone. "And the Market?"

She averted her eyes for a moment and Apollo felt another pang of guilt. "He left them alone," she replied after a moment. "After he shot you, he got in his aircar and left the area."

Apollo nodded, strangely relieved. However, as soon as that relief hit, it was gone. His emotions surged again and he pointed an accusatory finger across the table. "If you, with all of the power you command on behalf of your masters, couldn't stop him, then why the hell did you think I could?"

She did not answer, leaving him alone with his thoughts for the moment. Apollo wondered if the whole thing had been a trap. She could have visited him, watched him, and then told Alexander his habits and schedule only to have her attack dog jump on him exactly when she wanted him to.

But if he was still alive, and Catherine had saved him, then perhaps her offer was more serious than he thought. Especially given how strong Alexander had become, Apollo reasoned that he still had something that Catherine and her masters needed which no one else could give them.

Dead or not, the feeling of vindication flushed his broken body with energy and new life. He would heal, he would plan, and then he would wring every last drop of blood from Alexander's body scream by scream. The first two would be easy, especially if Alexander thought that he was dead in the dirt outside the Night Market. If he knew where Apollo lived, he surely would have attacked him at home long before. Catherine found him easily enough, but Alexander had never showed his face.

With a deep breath, he forced himself to be calm. The desire to see Alexander bleeding in a ditch somewhere never left, but his conscious brain finally hammered into his unconscious brain that blood-lust would not help him. Alexander would die, but he would die cleanly.

Finally, his calm restored, he asked, "what is he?"

"As you said, he is our monster." Catherine's eyes were on her coffee, avoiding Apollo's penetrating stare. Fortunately, his desire for answers at the moment outweighed his desire for blood, so he was willing to talk as long as it served that goal.

"Look." Apollo shifted painfully in his seat. He took a long drink of the hot coffee, a moment which he used to gauge Catherine's intentions. She seemed pensive, almost afraid that he would refuse again.

Good, he thought, let her continue thinking that for a few moments longer. He had to give her time to remind herself why she needed him. Even more important than her wishes, Apollo added, were those of her masters. The Immaculata needed him and Catherine was just an agent of their will.

"Look," he repeated, setting the coffee mug back on the table. "You know what? You were right before. I want Alexander dead. More than that, I want him to suffer for what he did *and* what he took from me. So tell me what you want from me and as long as your plan ends like mine, with his head severed from his neck, then we have ourselves a deal."

"Our plan goes far beyond killing Alexander."

"How far?" Apollo asked, narrowing his eyes with suspicion.

"Far enough that you would get what you wanted from the beginning."

"You've already promised me Alexander's head. What else do you think you can give me that I want more than that?"

"Don't forget the original offer that was made to you both. The one we gave to Alexander and not to you."

Apollo growled involuntarily from somewhere deep in his throat. The wet rattle of blood in his lungs made what should have been a brief flash of anger into an animalistic gurgle.

"You would..." he started to say before losing himself in thought again.

Before the fight, he had neither spoken to nor even seen Alexander in person since that day. Apollo had even avoided the broadcasts of his exploits and speeches until the day when the President-Duke decided that Alexander getting a statue was something everyone for a thousand klicks needed to see. Catherine had agreed with his statement that Alexander was their monster, but he had meant it only figuratively.

He asked himself if she could she have meant it literally. Had her masters made him into something more than human?

He voiced his thoughts aloud, took another long sip of his coffee as he watched Catherine shift uncomfortably in her seat again, then punctuated his deductions with, "if I do this for you, then I become their Champion? I take his place, the place that I should have had from the beginning?"

Catherine nodded. "It won't be easy. You will have to pass three tests, Apollo. Alexander passed each of them, and with the final test he became stronger than we had expected."

"You're afraid you won't be able to control me."

"That is a concern, yes," she admitted.

He narrowed his eyes. "Remember. I wanted this from the beginning. Give me his blood and I will do whatever other tasks your masters see fit to give me."

"Given what has happened with Alexander, if we feel you are displaying," she paused, looking away from him and back to her coffee again, "rogue tendencies before you pass the final test, then we will find another and have you killed in much the same way."

"I get it." He gave her a dismissive wave with his good hand. "I'm a tool for your masters, just like you." He grinned like an animal, showing his teeth. "I know what sort of tasks they're going to give me, just like I knew why you showed up at my door a few weeks ago."

"What assurances do we have that you won't do the same thing?"

Apollo laughed with a wet rattle. "Alexander, quote, 'went rogue' end quote, because he got hungry not for power, which you seem to have given him plenty of, but for fame. I saw that bastard on TV, soaking in the glory of the crowd and the praise of anyone with authority."

Apollo leaned back in his chair and a self-satisfied, smug expression crossed his face. "Me? I don't give two shits about most of the people in Londonsberg, or anywhere else for that matter. Send me to Moskgorod, or Brisbane for all I care. I want this for me and me alone."

"You will still have to follow our orders," Catherine reminded him.

Apollo nodded. "I know."

"There's nothing else?"

Apollo held up a single finger. "You've already promised me an end to Alexander's life. Good. I want you to promise that your masters aren't going to," he coughed up blood, nearly spat it on his carpet, and then thought better of it. He took a moment to collect his thoughts—again. "Promise me my freedom when I'm not working for your masters."

Catherine quirked an eyebrow. "Meaning?"

"Meaning I have work to do," he retorted, "a garden to tend."

"Unless we need you, we will not disturb your life." Something dark crossed her features and she added, "and we hope it will be a very long life indeed, Apollo."

He leaned across the table, choking down the furious pain that erupted in his ribs at the movement. He smiled a smile that was part pleasure and part animal fury. "I'm in."

Catherine stood. Her demeanor changed, becoming more businesslike. "In order to fully carry out our orders, you will need power, which we will give you as you pass each of the tests. But to have that power, you must understand what it is that you will be inflicting under our guidance."

Apollo eyed her, but remained seated. He took another drink of coffee, watching her come around the table over the cup's rim.

"Pain, fear, and death are to be your weapons, Apollo. And you must understand them if you are to use them." A moment passed and she ordered, "stand."

Apollo looked up, wondering if this was part of the first test. He had known pain enough in his life that he would have thought the first test was already passed. He chuckled, asking, "getting my ass kicked by your ex-dog wasn't pain enough?"

"No." Catherine shook her head, then repeated her order. "Stand!"

Apollo did as ordered, shakily using his one good arm and the gun crutch to come to a standing position. Catherine moved the chair aside and beckoned Apollo to the center of the room. He followed, wondering what exactly she was going to do. Even after taking her offer, he still did not entirely trust her. The memory of their first meeting, buried under what should have been the weight of years, was still raw in his mind after having been dredged up again and again recently.

Catherine lightly placed a hand on Apollo's swollen cheek. Her skin was soft and warm, her touch light. He almost found himself enjoying the feeling of her skin touching his when the pain hit.

The injuries suffered against Alexander were nothing but a dim candle compared to the roaring inferno of agony that consumed his every nerve. It ate away at his sentience until all he was was pain. He was no longer Apollo, but a soul of pure tortured agony, twisting for all eternity as a white-hot blaze beyond mortal comprehension.

Apollo screamed until it felt like the air had been burned from his lungs, and again was no more.

***

He awoke after what seemed an eternity, shouting and clawing his way out of the white void of agony. He found himself on the floor of his living room. Catherine stood less than a meter away with her hands clasped lightly in front of her body. She held her head bowed slightly, watching Apollo with curious interest.

He pushed himself up to a sitting position and came smoothly to his feet. He was about to threaten Catherine, to demand that she tell him what she had done that had caused him so much pain. He had even raised his hand to point a menacing finger in her direction when he realized the hand he was waving around had been securely wrapped in a cast moments before.

"What...?" he asked, examining his body. The catastrophic damage to his elbow had been repaired, his ribs were whole again, and even his nose had healed itself.

He saw no bruising anywhere. If he had not clearly remembered the fight and its humiliating aftermath, he would have sworn that it had been an alcohol dream while passed out on the floor of his house one afternoon.

Catherine's presence reminded him that his memories were real. Whatever his logical side told him about his injuries, he knew that one moment he had been nearly crippled and the next he was whole again. The cast, split open on the floor, and the bandages wrapped around his torso reminded him too well of reality.

He saw two downsides. The first, and the only one of them that was a true problem as far as his current mindset saw, was that he was ravenously hungry. The second, though his brain was in no position to complain about it just then, was the euphoria surging through his mind and body. He knew, in some deep corner of his brain, that such feelings could be problematic, especially since this one was making it hard for him to focus. He found himself unable to care about any possible downsides just then.

Catherine took a step back and looked Apollo up and down with a warm detachment that reminded him more of the way in which a scientist would regard a favorite research animal than a new colleague. Despite that, the sudden shift in her bearing shocked him.

She smiled. "You passed the first test."

A fresh wave of euphoria washed over him as he flexed and moved his restored muscles. Giddy, he asked, "what was that?" He intended it to be a demand, but he felt his face, driven by the ecstasy in those same muscles, twisting into a smile.

He forced his brain, with considerable difficulty, to focus. For a moment, he thought he could ignore the fresh energy in his limbs in favor of determining what other advantages the crippling pain brought. The ability to spring back from any hurt would serve him well enough against a normal attacker, but against a superhuman like Alexander, it would do little other than give him the chance to be pummeled longer.

His mind suddenly flashed back to when he and Alexander had first parted ways so long ago. They competed fiercely, but Apollo came out of every challenge victorious. Stronger, faster, and smarter than Alexander, Apollo won by being ruthless. The very first contest had been a foot race, one which Apollo won not by being faster, but by crippling Alexander's legs.

And Catherine, acting on the behalf of a higher being that called itself—or possibly themselves, even Apollo was hazy on that point—the Immaculata, had chosen Alexander to be the one to carry out their plans, despite Apollo's superiority. Overcome with jealousy, Apollo had gone to Alexander that night and beaten him bloody.

Had that been his first test, Apollo asked himself. Had Alexander passed the test of pain after Apollo left?

"You're a third of the way there." Catherine's announcement brought him back to the present. "From now on, almost any injury you sustain with heal in a matter of seconds. Even severe wounds will heal quickly if given proper rest."

"So I'm immortal, is that it?" Apollo asked, folding his arms across his chest. "Better question. Is Alexander immortal as well?"

A tense silence hung for a moment, broken by a sudden giggle from Apollo. For a moment, he had no idea what the strange sound was. So rarely in recent years had he actually laughed, and even then never in a way that could be described as a "giggle," that at first he did not recognize it at all. The sound had come unbidden; something in the universe itself had simply struck him as funny right then. He found himself unable to hate that slip of control, and the absurdity of it all elicited another intoxicated laugh.

"No," Catherine replied, keeping a carefully straight face. "To both questions, the answer is no. You both will be hard to kill, but not impossible. Were you to be shot with a small round, your body would heal fully in under thirty seconds, but a sufficiently large caliber bullet to the skull would likely still mean death. That's why Alexander left the Night Market alone, even he couldn't stand up to that many armed people in an open arena."

"And the downside?" Apollo asked, growing skeptical. The giddy feeling was receding, leaving him more able to focus. Nothing that good came without a price, he thought. "More than this damned hunger, I mean."

Catherine smirked. "The pain you felt was your injuries all rapidly healing at once. Your threshold for small injuries, cuts and scrapes, is higher now. In fact, you'll probably not notice minor injuries at all."

"So," he said, thoughtful. "I'll feel all of the pain, all at once, but it will be over in seconds?"

She nodded. "In effect, yes. It is nothing you are not ready to handle. Lesser men would have been killed by the test alone."

Apollo grinned. His pulse quickened. Her praise inflated his spirits, even though a part of him knew that she deliberately calculated for that exact result. She was right and he knew it, so it mattered little if she was only complimenting him to make him more pliable to the plans of her masters.

"It's not the pain I'm worried about." He was already formulating ways he could use a near-perfect regeneration ability to his advantage. In time, he suspected, he might even grow to enjoy the experience—pain telling him that he was alive, rather than warning him of his impending death. If Catherine was right, then he would never feel the pain of anything that would kill him, and so every ache and every wound would be a reminder that he was stronger and better than whoever he was fighting.

"What do you need me to do?" he asked, feeling at peace with his new arrangement with Catherine and her masters. They made a mistake, he told himself for what must have been the thousandth time in his life. Now, they were rectifying it, and all was right with the world once more.

"Find Alexander." Catherine's voice had taken on an icy, threatening edge. "Find him and kill him. Are you sure you can do that?"

Apollo laughed, already picturing the confrontation and Alexander's shocked expression as death finally catches him. He would do as they asked, and then finally he would have peace.

"Oh, yes. I'm sure I can do that."

\*\*\*

Catherine left later that evening. They had, much to his surprise, enjoyed the afternoon together. Now that he no longer wanted to kill her, Apollo found her to be a rather pleasant person. To his amusement, it rained again; it seemed to do that every time she visited him.

Apollo stretched out on the couch shortly after her departure and had not moved in hours. In her absence, Apollo was left wondering once again about the timing of her visit.

Rationally, he suspected that Alexander's attack and her visit both stemmed from the same cause. He had gotten power hungry; that much was certain. Apollo had seen the joy on his face as Alexander soaked up the crowd's praise. Alexander always was too eager to please others. He had even had the gall to apologize to Catherine for losing to Apollo in her masters' contests.

Years of unending praise had taken their toll on his mind and pushed him away from the Immaculata and their plans. That was the only logical conclusion Apollo could reach. By contrast, Apollo cared only for the opinions of a select few. He would not be swayed by the praise of faceless masses.

However, doubt still ate at him. The timing seemed too perfect to be coincidence. Shortly after turning down the offer, he had been brutally attacked, and Catherine had been right there to pick up the pieces. No matter how pleased he was at this new arrangement, he could not shake the suspicion that her line of, "Alexander won't listen," might not have been entirely accurate.

Apollo suspected that Alexander still listened to her, or at least could be swayed one way or the other, even if he consciously ignored her orders. If that was the case, then his lot was not so much to kill Alexander for straying from their path, but to replace him as a better executor of their wishes.

He shook his head. Even if he were right, he found that he actually cared very little. So what if he was being set up, he told himself. He would play along because their plan was his plan. He stood to win either way. If Alexander really had gone rogue, then he did their work and got his revenge at the same time. If it was all a test, and Alexander still worked for them, then he would pass their test once more, kill Alexander, and get his revenge anyway.

Most important, he would do all of that and still remain "Apollo." He was, and would continue to be, his own person. That had been part of Catherine's original pitch when they were younger, and why he knew Alexander had not simply "gone mad," but had always been on the tipping point of madness.

Apollo wondered if Alexander even knew who he was the way Apollo knew himself. He suspected not. He suspected that Alexander thought of himself as having the moral high ground in all things—whereas Apollo knew, as every look in the mirror reminded him, that spot would never be his.

Apollo shifted on the couch, looking at the small house in a way he had not done in some time. Years before, he hid guns and knives behind panels on the walls or false bottoms on the tables and counters. He designed everything so that no matter where he was, he would always have a weapon within arms reach. As the years went by, he made himself forget about many of them, locking each one away along with a piece of his past until everything was a blur.

Now, the time came to bring it all back into focus. Apollo surged to his feet and went for a very specific gun hidden beside the front door. Unlike the others, this one was not just a gun he owned, or even a gun he liked, it was *his gun*. He carried it for years, even before parting ways with Alexander, and it never failed once.

He opened the simple spring switch with a tap. It swung open, revealing the black pistol exactly as it looked the last time he laid eyes on it. Its holster and belt were there, as well as two dozen loaded magazines and enough boxes of ammunition to load a hundred more. He gingerly took the belt and holster off of its peg, feeling the leather beneath his hands, and buckled it around his waist as though no time had passed between its last use and the present.

Unlike the others, he never forgot this one. It had not been fired in years, but Apollo kept it clean nonetheless. Even so, his first task was disassembling and meticulously checking each part. The design dated to before the Burning War, with fully mechanical parts and no taclink whatsoever. Dirt and damage barely affected it, and NoTech did not even slow it down.

Satisfied, he slipped the weapon into its holster. Mentally, he was instantly transported back in time to the last use of that gun. He still remembered it as clearly as if it had just happened. For the first time in years, he was not actively trying to suppress the memories, and so was free to remember every life taken by his hand, and how he had felt with each one.

He remembered feeling alive, exhilarated with the rush of power. It never was about punishment or justice, sex or violence. No, it had always been about power. None of them had anything he wanted or needed, they were just the means to an end, the drug to fuel his next rush.

Until the last one. He had killed several Black Ties in a dark alley, but someone had seen. He heard the scuffle of fleeing footsteps and fired into the darkness. The bullet hit home, splattering the blood of the eavesdropper across the bland cinderblocks of the nearby buildings.

He had gone to check on the body, to make sure that no one would live to tell the story of what they had seen, and found it to be a small boy. He had been no more than ten, probably homeless and with no one who would listen to his insane story about a man in black leaving a trail of bodies in his wake.

On that day, Apollo realized he was out of control. He returned to his house far away from the City, vowing never to pass the Limits again unless he had a damn good reason. For years, he kept that promise, but now it seemed like he would have to break it at last. Catherine's arrival, her interruption of his life, forced him to reevaluate certain things, his self-imposed exile among them. Killing Alexander turned out to be worth far more to him than staying on one side of the Limits set up by the Londonsberg government.

He was not turning over a new leaf, as it were, but he was not altogether turning back time either. He was moving forward, he realized, accepting the past for what it was. He would use the past as the tool it was meant to be, and with it he would shape the future to be exactly the way he wanted it to be, Alexander be damned.

With a sense of purpose he had not felt in years, Apollo slid a dozen magazines into their respective places on his gun belt. A knife, his knife in much the same way the gun was his gun, hung from one side of the belt as well as several tools secreted in its small pockets.

Behind a panel in the back of his closet was his old jacket, as well. In normal light, the loose, black garment looked like suiting wool or some similar artificial fiber. When it moved, it produced a moire effect that blurred his movements and helped blend into the shadows. Numerous pockets held more weapons or tools, including a pair of gloves and mask should he need to conceal his identity further.

As with the weapons, he examined the jacket to make sure nothing had worn out with its years of disuse. It seemed to be in as good a condition as it had been before, not that he was surprised. Durability was one of the reasons, aside from the advanced fabric itself, that the jacket had cost him close to fifty thousand credits. Mirage fabric, as it was called, was rather high on Londonsberg's list of materials prohibited for civilian ownership.

He pulled it on, comforted by its familiar weight. The gun belt could actually be buckled over the jacket, but he left it underneath for the time being. Sneaking into Londonsberg was going to be hard enough, and carrying a pistol openly like that would only make it harder.

The time for intimidation and threats would come, he assured himself, trying to assuage his baser instincts. For now, he had to make do with stealth.

And if you lose it again? A voice in the back of his skull demanded. The voice was not his, but was not strictly a hallucination either, or so he told himself. It was the construct of his deeds and the consequences thereof. He had silenced it for years, but perhaps now it would be good to embrace it like he had embraced everything else about his past. It might be the only real link to his sanity he would have inside the Limits of Londonsberg.

Back in the living room, Apollo's eyes fell on the bottle and a half of Mind Eraser still sitting out. He grimaced at them, crossing the room to pick up and examine the bottles. The cheap hooch did not deserve the title of "liquor" any more than coal deserved to be called a diamond.

He grinned—time to test out his gun.

Apollo went out into the night. The area in which he lived, legally part of Visegrad, was home to very few people. Light pollution that would have plagued a city like Novarus was absent and a thousand million crystal stars glittered overhead. Insects buzzed in the massive oak nearby, one of the few to come out of the wars intact. Otherwise, silence hung like a curtain; even the wind was still.

He set the full bottle down next to his feet and hoisted the half-full one by its neck, drawing his pistol in his other hand. With a grunt that sounded loud against the stillness, he flung the unbalanced bottle into the air, where it quickly disappeared. He raised the gun and fired a quiet round into the darkness, then picked up and threw the other bottle. He fired at it as well. Inspecting the yard with a flashlight would have told him that both shots hit their targets, but Apollo did not need light to tell him that.

He would keep the expensive liquor, he decided. The Mind Eraser had been a crutch, but the Glenfiddich, along with the rest of his collection, were vices and a distinct line separated the two.

In the wake of his moment of destruction, a breeze blew the mingled scents of gunpowder and blooms from his garden back at him. He nodded, feeling for a moment like he and the wind were holding a conversation about the destroyed liquor bottles.

With that out of the way, he went back inside to plan. Brute force would not work, at least not yet. He had to out-think Alexander to to kill him. Apollo smiled. Out-thinking Alexander had never been hard.

Doing his job properly would require more than his old ways. Alexander was still stronger than him, and would probably be able to shrug off all but the most accurate gunfire. Apollo needed a plan, but first he needed information.

He checked the time, finding it barely past Legal Night. He had plenty of time to get to the Night Market and question the merchants and patrons. Surely some of them had seen something that night, or maybe even knew something about Alexander's whereabouts.

Apollo had not broken his regular pattern in three years. If Alexander had laid another trap for him, just in case he survived, the odds were in his favor that the trap would not be laid tonight.

# Chapter 7

Apollo made it to the Night Market after most of the merchants had run out of stock, packed up, and left. A few aircars remained, including the same particularly fancy one that had been parked there the day he met Gunnar Junior and received Sal's hand-written warning. That brought out a mild sense of suspicion, but he dismissed it.

In the market itself, the crowd around the outer stalls had grown sparse. Closer to Sal's shop, the crowds started to return to their usual density as the more profitable shops continued to operate.

Conversational noise came and went in bursts. On the surface, none of it was terribly incriminating. Even here in the market people spoke in coded phrases when buying or selling certain things. No one shopping paid him more than a cursory glance. Without his suitcases of weapons, he suspected most did not even recognize him.

In truth, Apollo preferred these smaller crowds. He was not fond of dealing with people one-on-one, but it was preferential to being surrounded by faces he had no connection to. If his primary reason for visiting had not been food, Apollo knew he would likely come at this hour more often, but most of that sold out hours ago.

When he had stock to sell, the larger crowds were a benefit. Customers often outbid one another in their rush to spend, resulting in a tidy spike of profit. That was their only benefit as far as Apollo was concerned.

The smaller crowds held another, practical, advantage. He could go directly to Sal's shop without having to snake his way through people milling about. Now, they were all glued to the various booths, not bothering him, and he could simply walk around. With nothing to distract or slow his progress, the walk felt much shorter than usual.

As he went, Apollo reflected on one more benefit of the clientele he passed. They had expensive and esoteric interests that often put them in touch with interesting people, the sort who were likely to hear and see things. While most were taciturn, or even aggressively isolationist, the ones who did talk picked their would-be friends carefully.

Apollo spotted a few faces in the crowd he recognized and nodded a quiet greeting as he passed. None of them signaled that they had anything important to tell him, and he continued on his way without stopping.

Three-quarters of the way to Sal's, Apollo felt the hair on his neck rise. Someone was watching him. He could not have pointed out who, even in that small crowd, but he knew the uneasy feeling of having intent eyes on him all too well. He looked for out of place faces, but saw none. He failed to recognize several around him, but no one stuck out like an agent of the City would have. He shrugged mentally and continued on, though his brain refused to leave high alert.

He still had on the Mirage jacket, but he wore it open with the mask and gloves stuffed into his pockets. Despite the feeling of being watched, he had no real need to hide among the Night Market's patrons. Stealthing around the market with his face obscured would do no good, and probably raise more suspicion than anything. Mirage fabric was not active opti-cam, all it did was obscure his silhouette and make it easier to hide in darkness. The Night Market was well lit and offered few places to hide, turning the Mirage jacket into a fashion statement rather than combat gear.

If Alexander, or someone in his employ, were waiting to ambush him again—Apollo shuddered at the thought, but then wondered how his new regenerative power would stack up against whatever Alexander was—then hiding was no good anyway. If it came to that, he would fight Alexander head-on, and kill him this time.

Apollo pushed aside the leather curtain that served as Sal's door and stepped inside. The blast of chilled air was a refreshing shock on his face as Sal looked up from his work. Apollo, though he would never admit to being bothered by the cold of the butcher's shop, once again marveled at Sal's ability to stay in the near-freezing temperatures for hours at a time in short sleeves.

"You's early, Mister A." Sal greeted him with a good natured grin and fake Imperial Manhattan accent. "Wha's a'matta? You trow a party and run outta meat a few days early like?"

Apollo shook his head. "No, I'm still pretty well stocked. Probably won't be at home to eat it this week either. I came here to talk."

"Wha's there to talk about?" Sal asked, laying his hands on the counter and leaning his large frame against it. With another deep belly laugh laugh, he added, "You ain't been too keen on talk before, yeah? I'm a butcher, not y'r therapist."

Apollo felt himself grin at Sal's demeanor. He had to admit, now that he was starting to make peace with himself, he found that other people were not nearly so deplorable and dismissable as he had treated them. He amended that idea: some people, anyway. Sal was among those he found himself unable to hate, but that list was still a very short one.

He shook his head again, pushing the front of his jacket aside to reveal the holstered gun. "No." He wagged a finger between himself and Sal. He was unable to resist a grin as he added, "you and I need to talk, Salvatore."

Immediately, Sal turned serious. When he spoke again his accent was gone. "Just give me a second here and let me lock up." If he had not heard his real voice before, Apollo would not have believed those words came from the same heavily accented would-be foreigner.

Sal circled the counter, producing a set of electronic keys from a pocket on the back of his apron. He slid a part of the small building's wall over the leather door. It fit into place with a resonant click. Sal tapped the e-key against the lock and the bolt slid home with another click of metal on metal.

Sal turned, crossing his arms across his chest. His forehead creased into a frown, putting an odd set to his eyes that Apollo found familiar. Something about Sal's sudden shift in bearing reminded Apollo of news broadcasts from when he was very young. His large size and tattoos made Sal impressive enough, but with a little effort he could be very intimidating. "Now, what's this that we need to talk about?"

"I've found myself a temporary new job," Apollo said, clasping his hands behind his back. He could easily kill Sal if problems arose, he knew, but he did almost like the man. More precisely, Apollo did not really hate him the way he hated everyone else, and he wanted to try and avoid killing him if possible. Additionally, Apollo felt that he might be able to rely on Sal for more than information.

"Go on." Sal punctuated it with an encouraging hand gesture.

Apollo had no desire to brag about the personal failures that led him to the point where he was at, and even the good parts would take more time that he wanted to spend in the cold shop."To make an extremely long story short, I've been contracted to hunt and kill someone very important inside Londonsberg."

"Well!" The belly laugh that followed was the same one he had when maintaining his false accent. "You've got my attention already. I'm guessing you didn't come for weapons; it'd be like me going to one of those dogs outside for beef. So how can Ol' Sal help you, Apollo?"

"I need information," Apollo stated. "Sightings, whereabouts if you have them or know where I can get them."

Sal cocked an eyebrow. "What makes you think I can help with that?"

"I found a letter tucked away in a bag a few weeks ago," Apollo returned. If Sal was confident enough with the door locked and sealed to drop his facade, Apollo felt like he could mention the erstwhile secret letter, too.

Sal grinned. "Wondered if that made it into your hands."

"I'm very observant," Apollo said, dryly.

"I'm sure I can help." Sal smiled conspiratorially. "News travels fast out here, especially news the President-Duke doesn't want people inside the Limits to hear.

Who are you after? Tell me it's Duke Charlie himself and I'll sell my shop and come with you."

That stopped Apollo for a moment. He knew Sal's father and grandfather both fought in the Succession Wars, but what other history did he have with Duke Charlie's City? "No, not him. Not unless he gets in my way."

The grin returned. "Well, maybe he should get in your way, hey?"

Apollo returned the grin. Internally, his blood started to heat up as thoughts of raiding the stronghold of the President-Duke himself stirred more of Apollo's lust for violence. He knew he would have to keep careful rein on it and temper it with judgment, but complete suppression was no longer in his best interests. The grin turned feral. "I suspect he will, to tell the truth. I'm after Alexander, the Captain."

Sal took an involuntary step back. His face betrayed shock and even a little bit of fear as he processed the information. "Yes," he said after a moment. His voice was lower, more inward-facing, than it had been before. "Yes, I suspect the Duke will get in your way if you go after his attack dog. Who in the deepest hell hired you for a suicide mission like that?"

He shook his head. "Can't tell you."

He probably could tell most of the story, possibly even mention the Immaculata, but all that would do was paint him as a madman working on the orders of an invisible god. Given the true nature of his "employer," keeping some of the information secret made sure his story was believable.

Sal only hesitated a moment. "I saw him not too long ago. Come to think of it, I've seen him twice lately. Once a month or so ago, and again right after you came through the other day to bring me my pa's gun. You don't think he was looking for you, do you?"

Apollo nodded, his face grim. He contemplated showing Sal the bullet scar, but decided against it. Bullet wounds did not heal that fast, and a fully+

-healed scar would invite more questions than it would answer. Instead, he said, "oh, I know he was. Bastard found me outside of town and tried to kill me."

"Was this before or after you took the job to kill him?" Sal asked, waving one hand around like he was moving physical pieces together in front of him.

"A few days before."

"You think it was related to your being hired?"

Apollo started to answer truthfully, that a woman named Catherine had hired him and that she represented Alexander's former masters. Once again, telling the whole truth would do him little good. "Let's just say that Alexander's newly-ex employers aren't happy with him."

"Why do I get the feeling you're not talking about the Duke's men?" Sal asked with clear reservation. He would fight the Duke, but Apollo suspected that Sal's focus would quickly turn to ambivalence if he could not keep Alexander connected to the rulers of Londonsberg.

"Because I'm not. Alexander's working for Duke Charlie now, wholesale. The people he's supposed to be working for, well, they're not happy that he's not working for them anymore. So they hired me to kill him."

Sal eyed him for a moment. "Apollo," he began, "I've heard rumors about things that happened out east. You're not mixed up with the Novarussians again are you?"

Coming from anyone else, the mention of his past in Novarus might have been enough to trigger a reaction of pure rage from Apollo, but the concern in Sal's voice stifled the flare of anger before it formed.

"Not them," Apollo replied.

Sal nodded as a bit of tension left his shoulders. "Tell you what. I'll pass on anything I hear about him to you, no charge. You might find your meat's gone up in price about ten percent, but we'll have to chalk that up to unexpected operating expenses. Those insulated bags are a touch pricey, you know."

Apollo nodded. Sal's plan was sound. Apollo always paid in physical cash, and a little extra cost would go unnoticed by anyone other than Sal and himself. The money would be labeled, unsuspicious. "Deal. Don't talk to anyone else around here unless they come to you first."

"He's that dangerous?"

"More," Apollo growled. He could not reveal much of Alexander's nature, or at least what he suspected of it given what he learned from his fight and from Catherine, but if Sal was going to help, he needed something. Apollo settled for another half truth. "He's been enhanced. Leave it at that."

"Is there anything else I need to know?" Sal asked, moving to the door with his key in hand.

Apollo eyed him for a moment. "Keep your gun close by," he said quietly. A lucky shot from anyone could still kill Alexander, but after the frighteningly fast way he moved when fighting, Apollo had his doubts that anyone would be able to get a shot off, lucky or not, should it come to that.

As Sal unlocked the door and slid the panel aside, Apollo reminded himself that the ultimate fight was going to be between himself and Alexander. No one else, no one normal anyway, would stand a chance. That was just fine by Apollo's reasoning, because he knew with every thing that made him who he was, that he was better than Alexander.

"Pleasure doin' business wit'ya," Sal called loudly, once again using his fake accent as Apollo pushed aside the leather curtain and exited the shop.

The crowds remained outside the shop. A few had gathered close by, watching the door with interest. To Apollo's knowledge, it was never shut before the shop closed for the night. That would start rumor enough, but seeing Apollo enter and leave would add to those rumors.

Four of the market's other patrons continued to watch him as he exited Sal's shop. They already showed more observational capacity, and confidence, than the majority of the crowd. He considered approaching them and conscripting them as information gatherers, or killing them. At the very least, they could be cannon fodder in case Alexander showed his head again, giving Apollo a few extra seconds to get in a possible killing shot.

He decided against bringing them in on his plan after a few seconds. He cared nothing for their well being, and truthfully doubted their usefulness in general. Killing them would solve nothing, and might even ruin his arrangement with Sal if the butcher thought Apollo would randomly slaughter potential customers just because they might start an unpleasant rumor. No, something else had caught his eye, someone else to be more exact.

A dozen meters away, standing innocuously beside Jamie's rum stall was a woman. She was lightly built, her hair a perfect generic brown to match her lightly tanned skin. Both would pass unnoticed in any crowd anywhere. She stood at precisely the right angle with her head tilted so that she could see Sal's shop in her peripheral vision without actually looking at it. She wore glasses as well, unusual ornaments rarely seen outside of the Limits unless they provided useful information beyond vision correction.

Whoever she was, she was good, Apollo noted. He had no idea whether she was friend or foe, or even anything more than another interested patron who happened to be good at observing things unnoticed, but he knew instantly that she was the one who had been watching him on his way in.

Apollo's pulse raced as his instincts defaulted to hostility unless proven otherwise. If she was an enemy, perhaps a spy in the City's employ or even working directly for Alexander, then Apollo would have to kill her quickly before she could report back to whoever pulled her strings. If not, then she might prove to be useful for his purposes, and so he memorized her face so that he could find her later on, and made a note to keep her within eyesight and intercept her before she left the market.

It seemed the woman had a similar plan, because as Apollo maneuvered around the market to address a few other people that he had spoken to off and on over the years, she moved as well, always keeping him with sight. That helped narrow down the options in Apollo's head. She was actively tracking him, which meant her attention on Sal's shop had not been accidental. Whether or not she was working for Alexander or the City, or if she could be pressed into Apollo's employ, he was still not sure. The crowd milled around chaotically, and he saw the same faces again and again at various stalls, hers among them. She made no move to approach him, but Apollo suspected a normal person without his experience or instincts would have never noticed.

Some of them were people he had not exchanged any more than the basic pleasantries with, but by virtue of having approached them at all, Apollo already held them in slightly less contempt than most other people. None of them were willing to help, however. Once they caught the scent of danger, all had other places to be. Money tempted some, but even they backed out, terrified, after hearing who Apollo was hunting.

Jamie the rum seller agreed to help, which came as the barest of surprises. Unlike Sal, she had no personal grievance against the government of Londonsberg—at least none he knew of. He appreciated her, which was a rare thing for Apollo to admit, and was glad in a way that she was the one who agreed to help.

They carried on their conversation in snippets as customers moved around, never saying more than a few words within anyone's hearing. "And you promise you're not going to screw me?" she asked.

Apollo smirked at her choice of words. Any other day of his life, he would have taken her comment and ran with it, promising to do exactly that. Today, however, Apollo was preoccupied with Alexander and, for the first time in a long time, did not hate the fact that Alexander was foremost in his mind.

He nodded once. "Yes." Then, smiling, he followed up that simple answer with, "and trust me. I do not break promises, especially to other bootleggers."

She returned the smirk. Apollo wondered again what motivation she had to risk her well being by helping him and decided to ask about it. After all, it would be more than foolish to trust her with something without exploring her motivations.

In response to his question, she replied with a sarcastic flick of her eyes and, "Apollo, I distill and sell liquor outside the Limits. I'm already in violation of enough Londonsberg laws to see me a lifetime in prison, so what's more one?"

Apollo shook his head firmly. He tried to make it seem like his concern was directed toward her personal safety, when in fact it was mere concern over the possibility that she might take his money and run after seeing the magnitude of the threat Alexander posed. "There's more than Londonsberg law going on here," he said with carefully measured seriousness.

She smiled conspiratorially, reminding Apollo of the hidden messages passed to him in the artwork on her liquor bottle labels. He knew she was up to something, and found himself willing to be a part of it as long as her help proved useful.

"I sell alcohol. You," she waved a friendly hand in Apollo's direction, "are the one chasing the Duke's man. All I'll be doing is having a friendly conversation with you every now and then."

Apollo nodded in satisfaction. "Conversations that you'll be well compensated for, of course."

Jamie continued to grin. "One k-credit for a friendly chat?"

Apollo shook his head. "No, I think I'll just be buying a bottle of that *very* expensive spiced rum every so often."

She nodded understanding. Like his arrangement with Sal, this meant no unlabeled stacks of cash lying around. "I could do worse."

Probably not, Apollo thought silently. It would be difficult to do much worse, or more dangerous to her health and well-being, than entering into a partnership with Apollo. Inwardly, he shrugged, betraying none of his thoughts on his face. Sal was strong, and more importantly well-armed, and so Apollo had little doubt that he would at least be able to wound Alexander should it come to that. Jamie, on the other hand, would probably go down faster than he could blink against Alexander's inhuman speed.

Still, if she could be useful, then he would let her do her part. A few thousand credits, easily replaced by even a small pistol repair job, was a meager price to pay for information. And if she got caught in the crossfire, he thought with detached certainty, then someone else would take her place.

Apollo felt a sudden something he could not quite describe. It stung almost like guilt, but for something that might happen in the future. She knew what she was doing, or claimed she did, and Apollo had no connection to her other than an appreciation for her distilling abilities. He asked himself why he suddenly felt uneasy at the thought of her getting caught in the crossfire.

She was innocent, relatively speaking, of his fight with Alexander, he realized, and it would be unfair to her to treat her trust as something expendable.

Apollo wondered where the sudden pang of conscience came from, and told himself that it was simple business sense. If he let his contact get killed, the next one would not be so eager to help out.

He looked down and noticed that she was holding out her hand to shake. He frowned, but went ahead and shook her hand after seeing the insistent look on her face. He needed Jamie to believe that he appreciated her help as more than mere utility, at least for the time being.

Leaving the immediate area around Jamie's stall, Apollo noticed that the woman who had been watching him before was still keeping an eye on him. At the moment, she was at the far end of the market, pretending to examine a vase being sold by a new pottery merchant. But as before, she was standing at the exact angle that let her keep an eye on Apollo without seeming to do so. He was starting to seriously wonder what she was up to, and as time passed and he ran out of legitimate business to do at the market, he realized he needed to confront her and find out where her loyalties lay If she was an enemy, he could not afford to let her walk away having seen him doing business with Sal and Jamie.

Apollo made his way around the market, moving more or less randomly around the various stalls and booths. Every time he moved, he kept an eye on the woman watching him, slowly working his way towards her. Surely, she had to know what he was doing given the way he was moving. In his mind, his path was carefully planned to seem as unplanned as possible. Yet, if this woman was as good at observation as she seemed to be, she probably already knew what he was doing.

Eventually, he ended up in front of a fruit seller a few meters away from the vegetable cart she was perusing. After a few minutes, she spared him a look over her shoulder that betrayed no surprise at seeing him so close, and turned for the parking area.

Apollo intercepted her in the darkness between the market and the parking lot at a spot where his Mirage coat would make him all but invisible. With the gloves on as well, his hands were hidden in the gloom. If things went past simple discussion, he wanted to be prepared to strike quickly and be done with the problem before it spiraled out of his control.

Moments before he was about to step into her path, she stopped and turned her head slightly from side to side as though surveying the area and looking for him.

Wait a moment, Apollo thought, where were the two bags of groceries she had been carrying?

"Come out," she called, zeroing in on Apollo's location in the darkness with unexpected accuracy. When he stayed still, gambling on it being nothing more than paranoia telling her that someone was waiting for her, she called out again.

Apollo stepped out from behind the car. His hand rested lightly on the handle of his gun, but for the moment he kept it in its holster. He smirked. "It's not polite to stare."

"Nor is it polite to stalk a lady through the darkness," she replied. Her voice had an aristocratic flair, Apollo noted. It was real as well, or at least as convincingly faked as Sal's had been. That accent did not come from from Londonsberg with its fake nobility pretending to have sophistication to give their vapid lives meaning. No, he realized, she was from somewhere to the north—Kingsmark, at the very least.

"Only returning the favor, lady." Apollo placed a mocking emphasis on the word "lady."

She raised one eyebrow, but said nothing.

Apollo narrowed his eyes, trying to wait out her silence. A minute passed, during which he quickly grew increasingly frustrated and impatient. "Care to tell me how you knew I was out here?"

She tapped the temple-piece of her glasses with a demure smile. "The Mirage fabric was a nice touch, something we haven't seen since the Validian War, but it doesn't mask the heat coming off of your body."

Apollo's grip tightened on his gun and he started to slip it from its holster.

"I wouldn't," the woman warned.

Apollo ignored the implied threat, drawing the gun the rest of the way. Before he could level it, a clod of dirt at his feet exploded with a sharp crack. He had seen no weapon before she used it, but the muzzle flash came from her hand. Then he saw it, matte black nestled against black gloves, a tiny derringer.

"I said," she repeated calmly, "I wouldn't."

Apollo scowled, but lowered his gun to his side. He kept it in his hand, muzzle pointed at the ground. With his new healing ability, he could easily take a bullet and still kill her, but he needed to know what was going on first. "Alright, you've got me. Care to tell me what you were doing?"

"Sal's a friend of mine," she said. "I know he doesn't lock his doors unless there's something more important than beef sales going on in his shop. And I know who you are. More importantly, I know who you were, so I want to know what you and he were talking about."

"You're from Kingsmark, right?" he asked, ignoring her initial line of questioning.

"Your ear is good. If you want to be precise, I was born in Svalbard and moved to Kingsmark as a girl."

"What's a Marksman doing this far south?" he demanded.

"As I said, I'm a personal friend of Sal. We share certain interests."

There had been rumors that Duke Charlie was threatening to expand northward. He was boxed in by Rhineland on the west and Centrope to the south. Eslav and Visegrad, the latter being where Apollo's house technically resided, were to the east and would be much better targets should the President-Duke grow more arrogant than he already was.

Attacking Kingsmark to the north would be stupid, Apollo thought, but then again, Duke Charlie was certainly a stupid man. On the other hand, Kingsmark possessed a functioning spacecraft, one of the few worldwide that could get past low orbit. It would be entirely in-character for the President-Duke to attack them solely to improve his monopoly.

"So." Apollo slowly moved his gun back to its holster. "The rumors are true."

"Perhaps," she said. "Perhaps not. Rumors are never anything more than that until they become fact. There are certain elements who would prefer those rumors to never become facts, you understand."

Apollo nodded. "I don't want any part of Kingsmark's war with Duke Charlie."

"We wouldn't expect you to, but I need to know what you and Sal were talking about."

Apollo grinned, laughing quietly. On second thought, another war—and the resulting death of thousands—would be the perfect distraction for Duke Charlie's forces. If they were preoccupied fighting against Kingsmark, or defending against Kingsmark once the Duke's arrogance brought the wrath of the Marksmen down on Londonsberg, then Apollo could do his job with little to no interference.

Yet, he thought with an inward scowl, Apollo did not want thousands to die. Aloud, he said, "I'm hunting someone. Alexander, the Captain."

She kept her face carefully impassive. Despite her control, her voiced wavered with what seemed like excitement as she replied, "then it seems we may wish to discuss some things with one another, after all. Allow me to introduce myself properly."

She pocketed the derringer and held out a gloved hand. Apollo felt himself slightly more willing to take her hand, the hand of someone with strength and power versus the hand of a mercenary liquor seller. They shook once before she introduced herself formally. "Captain Vivian Jensen, Kingsmark Royal Services."

Apollo grinned, feeling a surge of interest in this woman's assistance. It never hurt to have friends in high places as well as low. "Apollo." He grinned. "But you knew that. Now, what's the KRS's interest here?

"Alexander killed our ambassadors about a month ago. We believe he was acting under orders from the Duke at the time."

Apollo laughed. "Well, well." Yes, he thought, this might just be an alliance worth pursuing in depth. If the KRS wanted Alexander dead, then his prospective pool of resources just increased a hundredfold.

First, he had to check on her story. "Follow me for a moment." He turned and walked back toward the market, never looking to see if she came or not.

Evidently, she followed, because when Apollo stopped in front of Sal's shop, she came up behind him a second later. He turned and regarded her with detached interest. Part of him almost wanted to believe her story outright, so useful would her help be. However, he still had his doubts, and those doubts had kept him alive more than once over the years. Someone had once quoted the old saying, "trust but verify," to him, to which he had replied, "verify only, execute anything that doesn't check out."

Apollo held the leather curtain aside and gestured with his head for Vivian to enter the shop. His free hand rested again on the grip of his pistol, ready for anything even inside the butcher shop. Over the year he had been a customer, Sal never lied to him, and that was as close to trust as Apollo would get.

"Vivi!" Sal called in his fake accent as she stepped inside the shop. "How's..."

Apollo's entrance interrupted the rest of Sal's greeting. For several tense moments, no one spoke. Apollo's hand stayed on his gun and Sal's inched for his as well with what seemed like instinctive movement. Sal's face looked concerned, worried there might be trouble, or worse.

"Vivi?" Sal asked, cocking an eyebrow. For the moment, the accent was still present.

"I told him what's going on."

Sal's relaxation was visible as his shoulders drooped slightly and his hand swept away from his hidden gun with practiced casualness. Apollo spared a grin at the possible irony of being shot with the gun that he customized, and took his hand off of his own weapon. The tension in the room lowered dramatically.

Sal addressed Apollo with his real accent. "I hope this doesn't change the circumstances of our agreement."

"No. In fact, it puts my mind at ease," Apollo replied with a thoughtful air. In truth, he was rapidly running through possibilities in his head and only paying partial attention to the conversation. Had Sal not dropped his accent, he would have turned on Vivian right there, but the butcher's maintained a fake accent for a reason, and he would not have trusted an agent of the City with the knowledge of his true country of origin. "No," he repeated, "I don't think so. I only wanted to make sure her story was true."

Sal smiled, relief written across his face. "Good, good. I didn't intend to deceive you, Apollo." He spoke quickly, still with a hint of nervousness in his voice, but it seemed to be nothing more than someone in a hurry to lay out facts. "In fact, I hadn't seen Vivi in over a year. Didn't even know she was here until today."

"I wasn't here until today," she supplied.

To Sal's credit, Apollo believed him. He wondered, privately, just how connected this KRS agent actually was and how widespread the anti-Londonsberg sentiment was outside the citystate's borders. Admittedly, isolating himself for years had not done much for his knowledge of current events. If war, or even rebellion, was coming, he did not want to be in the middle of it. One gun amid thousands was not his place.

Apollo turned and reached for the curtain, saying, "all right, thanks, Sal."

Vivian met him moments later outside the shop. Her face showed a combination of anger and amusement that Apollo could not help but be entertained by. "Satisfied?" she demanded.

Apollo nodded. She had passed his test, and he believed that her story was—at least mostly—true. He still had his reservations, and he doubted that she told him the entire story, but he was satisfied that the parts she covered were not lies. He trusted facts and observations, not people; never people. And if she was lying to him, then he would have to plan for that contingency as well.

He regarded Vivian for a moment, wondering how useful her talents and knowledge would be. She was at least interested in Alexander's death to simplify things for Kingsmark. He had intended to go straight from the market to the City, sneaking or fighting his way through the Limits in the dead of night, but another evening to revise his plans would not hurt.

After looking her up and down twice, once to estimate her tactical usefulness and a second time to appreciate the woman herself, he pointed over his shoulder with his thumb. "My aircar is parked this way."

Vivian cocked an eyebrow. "I brought my own."

"You want my help," Apollo said, "you ride in my car. Otherwise, you'll never find my house."

She seemed to consider that for a moment before offering a small shrug. With an equally small, if dismissive, wave of her hand, she said, "Sal can watch it for me."

"Good," he said "Now, if you want to help me take Alexander down, come with me. We have plans to make."

# Chapter 8

For the second time that night, Apollo realized something changed after Catherine's last visit. When Vivian agreed to accompany him to his house, Apollo found himself forming plans to use her resources to kill Alexander. The thought that a reasonably attractive woman would willingly accompany him alone five hundred klicks away from civilization and, presumably, her KRS support chain only crossed his mind once. At least, it only crossed his mind in relation to her attractiveness once. Even then, his only acknowledgment of the thought was a recognition of his lack of recognition.

They spoke some, and his mind was alive with ideas and plans. He told himself that his ambivalence about her presence was due to his focus on finding and killing Alexander, but the truth was that he simply felt no need to dominate their relationship. He was aware of a physical attraction, but he had more important things to do than act on it.

Not only that, the little voice he refused to acknowledge told him, but she was a human being with her own reasons for being where she was. It would not be right for him to take unwanted advantage of that.

With an inward laugh, he reflected on the fact that the concepts of "fairness" and "right" had entered his mind twice that night. It had been a long time since he gave any thought to those ideals. The world was what it was: unfair.

Yet Vivian's presence reminded him that killing Alexander was more than simple revenge. He was finally working for the Immaculata—making revenge merely the garnish on a succulent serving of vindication. Out of the three billion people living on Earth, he and he alone had been elevated above the masses to carry out the will of the gods.

With force, he reminded himself that the Immaculata were not gods, only beings more advanced than humanity. Alexander lost sight of that fact, turning respect into reverence and gratitude into sycophancy. At least, Apollo thought, until he decided he was more important than they were.

He laughed quietly at those thoughts, reminding himself once again that his rise to power as their "servant" was because it fit in with his plans, not because he wanted to be their sycophant. If they crossed him, he thought, even gods could bleed.

Vivian turned in inquisitive eyebrow in his direction, and he shook his head. He knew he was mad on some level. Why else, he thought grimly, was it so easy for his control to slip and for him to become the monster he never wanted to be again?

Vivian did not need to know that particular bit of information.

She never once tried to engage Apollo in chit-chat during the two hour trip to his house. They talked about Londonsberg—touching on some things, courtesy of the KRS, that even Apollo did not know—and Kingsmark itself. He learned that the KRS had been tracking him for years, but until very recently had considered him too unreliable to pursue relations with. Vivian's superiors had, she said, held a meeting some time back that changed that opinion.

"I'm not even supposed to know that it existed," she explained, "but if I never found out about it, what sort of 'elite' agent would I be?"

Apollo grinned, then laughed. She had a point. "I imagine your superiors would grow tired of finding their secrets are no longer secret."

She shrugged. "Perhaps. But I've made my loyalties clear over the years. Anything I uncover is for my use and mine alone. It's good to know what I'm getting into when they send me on a suicide mission."

Apollo quirked an eyebrow. "Then you know what we're up against?"

An inscrutably look passed over her features, gone in a moment. "I know what the KRS knows."

"Which is?"

"I'm to take out Duke Charlie," she replied. "They told me not to engage the man named Alexander if at all possible. 'Capabilities unknown,' his file says."

"Then be glad I'm along." Apollo's facial expression hovered in a gray area somewhere between a predatory grin and fulminating anger.

"They don't have much on you, either," she confessed. "But the KRS knows that you and Alexander have fought before and that you're one of the few to walk away from it."

Apollo grinned. "Capabilities unknown."

She eyed him for a moment. Apollo felt like she was sizing him up, trying to figure out if that last quip had been about him, Alexander, or possibly something else entirely. He let her wonder. She would find out soon enough.

In the following half hour of silence as his car crossed the last bit of distance to his house, Apollo's mind mulled over the problem ahead of him. Given that Vivian was a member of the KRS, she would have considerable assets to bring to the hunt. If Apollo could tap into them, and if he could win her over to his side completely, then he could requisition anything she could. His mind reeled with the possibilities and the advanced tech he could acquire.

He ruled out the majority of it for the hunt. Apollo preferred to use his antique low-tech guns, the ones without hackable components, especially if he was going inside Londonsberg where NoTech was everywhere.

He would have to be careful not to overdo it, though. Asking for advanced weaponry right at the start would raise too many red flags. He was going to have to draw the hunt out as much as possible, invent reasons to have more and more things delivered to him and then bide his time as much as possible so that he could reverse engineer it. A feeling that might have equated to joy in anyone else welled up inside him thinking about the engineering challenges he would face trying to steal official KRS gear. So excited was he about tackling the internal workings of new technology, that the idea that he could quickly become richer than he ever imagined by reverse engineering and then selling KRS gear was a distant thought in his head.

Having Vivian along would, at the very least, provide an additional set of eyes and guns, and possibly a human shield against Alexander's augmented strength. At most, she could get in the lucky shot to wound or even kill Alexander. That thought bothered him for a moment, but he pushed it aside. So long as he got to watch Alexander die, Apollo cared very little who actually pulled the final trigger.

That left the problem of force. Should Vivian agree to get her hands dirty, and he expected her to do just that, that would be all the active help Apollo would take. Too many people would get in one another's way, possibly alerting Duke Charlie's private police force that someone had infiltrated the City. He shuddered to think of the chaos that a full invasion would cause.

That was the worst case scenario—Kingsmark invading before Alexander could be killed, letting him escape during the fighting. He brushed that aside. If Vivian and the KRS had even an inkling of what Alexander could do, they would stay far away until he was confirmed dead.

Apollo grinned, finally putting the pieces together. He had wondered for years why no one ever invaded. Londonsberg was small and antagonistic and sat on a plot of land that would prove useful to anyone who conquered it. Duke Charlie had no friends among the countries around him, but the President-Duke had never been attacked, or even openly threatened.

Of course Alexander was his trump card, he realized. With a pet superman on retainer, Duke Charlie could do, almost literally, whatever he wanted.

One thing was settled, then. Kingsmark must not invade until his own mission was done. No matter what Apollo had to do to stall their invasion, they had to stay away from Alexander. At least until his plans were finished. The Marksmen and their feud with Duke Charlie would wait on his whim. And if he played his cards right, they would wait on his whim all while thinking it was their plan all along.

That left the issue of Vivian. She could get in his way, and that would be a problem. Even if she never did, she would not have the enhanced abilities that Alexander had. By the time they fought, Apollo would have them as well. Whether she lived or died at the end of the day was little concern of his—was it? Demanded the still-ignored voice in his head—but he needed her full involvement right up until the time when she walked away or got killed if he was going to get the most out of this would-be partnership.

So he would have to keep her alive as long as possible, Apollo decided. She was not necessary for his plan, but she was not exactly expendable either. To make sure he got what he needed from her, both her skills and her resources, she would have to be fully invested in the hunt—in *his* hunt.

More importantly, she had to trust him. Whether or not she trusted him as a human being was immaterial. In fact, he wondered if it might just be easier to have her distrust his "base" nature while simultaneously trusting his professional nature. Finally, he decided that, no, that would not work. For her to be fully invested, she would have to trust Apollo as a person, not just Apollo as a businessman. He pondered various ways to acquire that trust, to prove to her that for all of his faults that he was a man of his word.

Either way, he needed her, and he knew it. Apollo supposed Vivian knew it too, which would make negotiations difficult. He had to know he could trust her, as well.

He trusted that her story had been true, at least the parts of it she told him, but he still did not trust the woman in the car with him, not exactly. He spent the rest of the ride back to his house mulling over that thought. It was a strange, foreign concept to him: trusting another human being to be anything more than a customer or an enemy.

As the car landed outside his house, he was forced to admit the truth to himself. He had no idea how to trust another human being, and he wondered again at the transformation that was happening in his thoughts.

He had to figure it out quickly, though, because he did not want to put off his holy mission any longer than he had to.

*\*\*\**

Alexander paced the length of his luxurious apartment. The curtains had been thrown open, letting in the resource that put his apartment out of the reach of all but the richest citizens: unobstructed sunlight. Even as he passed through the warm beam, and again on his return trip across the room, he failed to take notice of the window. A thousand thoughts raced through his brain, each vying for control of his attention.

His contact with the Black Ties, the one he met with in private rather than the "official" liaison officer assigned to him by the President-Duke, had left only minutes before. As far as official channels were concerned, his inquiries did not exist. He knew others knew about them, at least other Black Ties and possibly even Duke Charlie himself, but because these meetings did not officially exist, no one but his lone contact ever spoke to him about them.

Alexander wracked his brain, trying to figure out the game Apollo was playing. The information he had was scattered around his mind like pieces of broken crystal. He examined each in detail.

First, Apollo survived. Truthfully, that did not come as a surprise. Even without the Immaculata-granted power that Alexander enjoyed, Apollo was damnably hard to kill. He knew, after all, because he had tried before. Still, he had not suspected that Apollo would be back on his feet so quickly. The fingers he kept in the Night Market told him Apollo showed no sign of scarring, or even injury.

"Did he go all the way to Novarus for medical care?" Alexander wondered aloud. He laughed. "No, they'd kill him on sight, even the doctors. Centrope, then. That's possible, I suppose, but still not likely."

He filed that piece of information away. Perhaps it would fit somewhere else.

The second thing on his mind was that Apollo had broken his pattern. As far as Alexander knew, and he had known Apollo for a very long time, he had never broken with an established pattern. That was the only thing that allowed Alexander to survive their first true fight. Apollo became predictable in his attacks, allowing his outmatched opponent to, if not win the fight, at least survive it. If Apollo was acting unpredictably, then Alexander's attack had shaken him up more than he expected.

"I never expected to kill him," he told the open window, finally acknowledging the setting sun. "No. That's a lie. I did expect to kill him. So how the hell is he still alive?"

He shook his head angrily. That did nothing but bring his thoughts back to where they had been minutes before. It proved to be no more useful the second time around. Regardless, if Apollo was acting outside of his patterns, perhaps Alexander needed to start searching on his own. He knew Apollo lived within driving distance of the market, possibly even of Londonsberg itself, but that left a huge area to cover.

He would go to the President-Duke, he decided. Duke Charlie would, if Alexander phrased his request right, be more than willing to allocate a few extra patrol craft to the task. All he had to do was to stress how dangerous Apollo really was. Duke Charlie would tell him to take care of it himself, and then Alexander would emphasize the need to find him quickly before he, "became a danger to the City of Londonsberg in general and the Office of the President-Duke in particular."

Alexander grinned. That piece of the puzzle still lay unfitted to anything else, but now he had a solution that would allow him to ignore the entire puzzle if it panned out.

The third problem, and the one that was causing Alexander the most mental consternation, was that Apollo allegedly left the market in the company of a woman. His contact said she spoke with a Kingsmark accent, which spelled trouble.

Well, he thought, it spelled trouble for Londonsberg, at any rate. He carefully did not give actual voice to those thoughts. Though he was held in the highest esteem by Duke Charlie, voicing such seditious sentiments out loud could easily lead to his request for more surveillance being denied. Even Alexander had to play the game, and he was very good at it.

His thoughts returned to the woman. She had gone with him willingly. She was not a captive, not a hostage. That part, he did not understand. Unless something had changed drastically in the years between their last meeting and the fight outside the market, Apollo never worked with anyone. He could barely tolerate other human beings.

"There's something there," Alexander said. He mentally imagined trying to fit two puzzle pieces together, only to find that their edges did not quite line up. "So what am I missing?"

His frustrations were only compounded by Catherine. They had not spoken in a week and the lack of contact put Alexander on edge. Typically messages went one way or the other at least once every few days. He would report to her for her masters and she, in turn, would relay orders to him.

The last few months had seen fewer orders coming in, however, as he had been busy with "things to do" for the President-Duke. Most of those things had fallen into one of the three classic categories of "wine," "women," or, "song," but that was hardly his concern.

He stopped in his tracks. No way would she would go to Apollo—hell itself would freeze over, spill out into the mortal world, and then freeze over again before that happened.

"But she said..." He stopped. "No. No! There is no way. But what if..." he trailed off, then resumed a moment later. "Was she actually serious? Did they... No. They wouldn't. They couldn't. They can't! Can they? I'm their hero, goddamnit!"

He took a deep breath. It calmed his nerves, but that did nothing to still the righteous fervor in his veins.

Those thoughts would not leave him alone. Wide-eyed, and with more conviction that he knew he should have been expressing around the Black Ties' ubiquitous bugs, he said, "if she was telling the truth, then I need to know that. I have to find her. I have to! No. I have to find *them*."

A grin spread across his face as he contemplated his next move. Apollo could wait. He had gods to confront.

***

Morning sun streamed into the room through the small gap between Apollo's bedroom curtains. It gave the room a pleasant atmosphere that he had, to his knowledge, never appreciated. Perhaps, part of his brain told him, because he would never be able to again. His house saw plenty of sun, but the streets of Londonsberg were mired in dust and hidden by skyscrapers. He had always taken that particular luxury for granted, and, like anything else one takes for granted, now that he was on the verge of possibly losing it for good, he found he actually liked it.

As it was, Apollo rarely closed the curtains to avoid diminishing the view through the windows. The ones in his bedroom were placed so that he could have a full view of his garden outside without having to move very much. From a more pragmatic standpoint, the curtains got in the way of his ability to see anyone coming across the flat plain outside. Especially since his encounter with the man from Novarus, he preferred clear sightlines over visual privacy. Anyone close enough to violate that privacy would be dealt with one way or another, putting the possibility of someone catching a glimpse of Apollo in his underwear among the least of his concerns.

However, it had been requested of him the night before to close them. At the time, he had not wanted to argue. He rolled onto his side and Vivian's arm slipped across his chest, reminding him exactly why he had not wanted to argue the status of the curtains. Her arm absently passed over a dozen obvious scars, and an uncountable number of lighter ones, as she readjusted. Each and every scar cost the one who wounded him dearly—usually with their life—with only one exception. The scars from his fight against Alexander had yet to be repaid.

She stirred after a moment, then rolled onto her back and slowly opened her eyes. Apollo watched her for a moment, appreciating what he saw. Her naked body was covered in scars as well, though significantly fewer in number and depth than Apollo's.

The sex the night before had been rushed, frantic, and rough. Apollo wanted her to feel swept up in the moment, and to feel like he was as well. Nothing that he did gave any indication of how carefully he planned every word and movement. That was not to say, however, that he had not been swept up in things. He knew she had had her way with him almost as easily as the reverse had happened.

"Tell me," he said. "Why you?"

"Do you start every morning off like this?"

He smirked. "Usually, coffee comes first, then work," he replied. The smirk faded as quickly as it had appeared. "Usually."

"Why me?" Vivian asked aloud, echoing Apollo's question. "Because I'm the best at what I do."

"And what would that be?"

"I hunt and kill dangerous people."

Apollo smirked again, this time with genuine amusement. "All sanctioned by the Kingsmark government, of course."

Vivian returned the smirk with a conspiratorial gleam in her eye. "Of course."

Apollo held her eyes for several seconds. Something more than a simple field agent lurked behind them. A cunning intelligence was at work inside her head. He had known from the start that her presence on the night he came to get information on Alexander was not a coincidence. Now, he suspected that her mission from Kingsmark might have involved him from the beginning. With a wry smirk, one that he let mysteriously show on his face, he realized that she thought she was playing him just like he was playing her.

Well, Apollo thought, he would just have to be better than she was. He needed what she could give him almost as much as she needed his skills—if not more, the voice he was quickly identifying as a conscience reminded him.

He decided to start with honesty. He wanted her to think he knew what was going on. That would throw her off balance, perhaps even get her to reveal more than she intended to. Then her game would change, and Apollo would be able to watch it from the beginning and carefully craft every event so that things would go exactly the way he wanted.

He sat up, leaning back against the cool wood of the headboard. "No." With a gesture that encompassed the bed, the room, and the two of them with a single sweep of his hand, he asked. "I mean why this?"

Vivian sat up as well. Apollo noted that she slid a few centimeters further away from him as she moved. He reminded himself that the end goal before they left his house was to gain her trust. If he moved too quickly, asked too many questions, demanded too much, then she would push away and his door would close.

If that happened, he would have to kill her. He wanted to avoid that outcome, especially considering how her untimely death would make his final plan more difficult. He could kill Alexander without Kingsmark's help, that had been his plan all along, but he was not, quite, so self-aggrandizing as to turn down powerful help when it came his way.

And, nagged that newly-insistent voice, he did not want to kill her.

"I'm sure I don't know what you mean."

"You know who I am, right?" he asked, putting a little extra wide-eyed emphasis on his words.

She nodded. "Of course. You're Apollo. You've no last name on file. You work as an illegal weaponsmith whose undisguised hatred of Alexander, the man Londonsberg calls 'the Captain' has caught a few ears back home."

"If that's all you have on me..."

"Not so fast," she said with a cautioning rise in her voice. "We also have a full psychological profile on you, and..."

"Really?" he asked, again with exaggerated surprise. With forced theatrical arrogance that deliberately barely concealed a layer of violent bravado, he said, "well then you must know what kind of person I am."

"We do."

He shifted around putting both hands on the mattress between them and leaning heavily forward. "Then you must know that I use people like you. And when I'm done with you, I spit you out and walk away."

Vivian turned as well, mimicking Apollo's posture and placing their faces only centimeters apart. The intensity on her face was far more of a distraction than her bare breasts. "This time it's different." She had an edge in her voice to match Apollo's. "You need what we have."

"Do I?" Apollo asked, narrowing his eyes.

"You help me take down Alexander, and Kingsmark rolls in and rips power right out of Duke Charlie's hands. We destroy everything that was his, burn it all down and let fire cleanse him from the world." An inviting smile spread across her features. "Then we make you a hero, give you the statue in Londinium Square."

Apollo had to admit that the offer, and the implication, was tempting. He hated people, crowds and cities especially. But that level of recognition and widespread adoration—no, he thought, idolatry—was exactly what he deserved. Perhaps the statue could have his foot crushing Alexander's skull, immortalized for all time in the same bronze used for his atrocity of a monument.

He also knew not to let such things go to his head. It would put his entire plan in jeopardy. It was entirely possible—no, not just possible, but probable—that that line of thinking and that attitude were what ruined Alexander in the eyes of the Immaculata. Apollo knew Alexander had always been full of himself, and that would only be the logical outcome.

The other difference, the difference that Apollo knew finally forced the Immaculata to send Catherine to apologize, was that Apollo knew what he was. Alexander paraded through life as though he were the hero of his own story. He accepted any honors sent his way as nothing more than his due in life, and all the while he spent his days and nights thinking that he was a "good guy." Apollo could, finally, look in the mirror and understand what he saw there. He was a monster, he knew that, and that knowledge would be the only thing keeping him from plunging into the same abyss that had swallowed Alexander.

Now, if he could get his revenge and still manage to secure fame with Kingsmark, his day would be, as they said, made.

Apollo reminded himself that win-win situations existed, but he had to play it right. "What makes you think I want that?" he asked, leaning back slightly.

"We know you, Apollo. You want to feel important."

He wondered how much of what she was saying was going to be true and how much was the deliberate mislead. He would have to watch her closely, and not just physically. "Perhaps," he replied at length. Silently, he added, yes, but not by you and certainly not by Kingsmark. People like you, he thought, are only the icing on the top. Aloud, he added again, "perhaps. But if that's why you think I'm going after Alexander, then your intelligence is sub-par at best."

She looked shocked, but the reaction was controlled. The expression disappeared after a moment, replaced with calm serenity, but the flash of surprise had been genuine as far as he could tell. The jab had been unfair, he knew, because no one other than himself, Alexander, and Catherine knew about the Immaculata, but he needed to gauge her reaction.

"Then why..."

"Because I fucking hate him, that's why!" Apollo snapped. He allowed his abject fury to consume him for a moment, letting her see the fire in his eyes without any filters or pretense. He would not elaborate, at least not yet, but all she needed to know was that the sole driving force in everything he did was hate.

The reaction was immediate. She recoiled instinctively, but he could already see the gears of her mind turning, trying to figure out how to use it to her advantage. As long as she understood that he would stop at nothing to end Alexander's life once and for all, then she would never put that goal in danger because she needed him for Kingsmark's plan to succeed.

There, he saw it in her eyes. She had decided on a plan already. Most people could barely function before getting dressed and having coffee, but her shrewd mind had already locked onto the next step. He could see it written across her face. Whatever Kingsmark wanted her to do would be done. Even though it would come second to Apollo's vengeance, and he knew she knew that, it would be done.

Vivian settled back slightly, crossing her legs and tossing the sheet aside. She stretched, arching her back so far that her ribs stood out amid the muscle and scars. It had its desired effect, drawing Apollo's attention for a moment, letting her evaluate his reactions.

His eyes traveled up her hips, past her breasts, and finally to her face. The self-assured smile lazily plastered across her lips told him one very specific thing: she won.

He slid out of the bed, grabbing a gray robe from a nearby peg on the wall and throwing it across his shoulders. Idly, he kicked aside the pile of clothes in the floor, left over from the previous night's mad dash into the bed. Sensors in his room detected the moment he woke up—a change he made after Catherine's visit—and by the time he made it to the kitchenette, the coffee pot was full.

He took two mugs down from the cabinet, calmly pouring the same measure of the hot black liquid into each one. Vivian had thrown her shirt and underwear back on and waited at the table when he turned around. Without asking her preference, he set one of the mugs in front of her and took his to the couch.

After several invigorating sips of coffee, he spoke. He drew things out, musing aloud more than actually talking directly to Vivian. Or, he thought, that was how he wanted it to sound. "You know. I could kill you where you sit, kill Alexander, and then tell Kingsmark that you were tragically killed in the line of duty, and still get everything you promised me."

She raised a supremely confident eyebrow. "You could try. They didn't send me because I was a slouch, Apollo."

He laughed, amused by her bravado. He did have to admit that anyone willing to threaten him, even a veiled threat like that, would have to be supremely competent to be able to even utter the threat without soiling themselves. Perhaps she would not be a burden after all.

Apollo calmly set his half-full cup of coffee down on the end table next to the couch. He dove forward, tucking in tightly with his hands between his knees to grab the pistol stashed under the cushion. He came up out of his roll, pistol cocked and leveled, to see that Vivian was no longer under his sights.

She had tipped her chair onto his side, using the seat to block her movements for the half second it took to snap the throwing knife free from the underside. Part of his brain congratulated her on even knowing it was there. She crouched, braced with one knee on the floor and her knife hand curled beside her head. From this distance, the razor edge of the knife would be just as deadly as a bullet provided she had any aim with it. Given her form, Apollo was sure she could put it in his eye with ease.

"Are you threatening me," she purred, "or flirting with me?"

In the heartbeat that followed, he debated whether or not to let her see his trump card. It would only be fair, considering Alexander would have the same ability, and his reward from Kingsmark would be more lavish should she survive that encounter. And survival is bred from knowledge, he reminded himself.

The old adage held that knowledge was power, and power was something he would not give up without reason. Equipping her with the knowledge to plan against Alexander, however, gave him the knowledge that his back would be that much more competently protected.

He shifted his aim slightly, pointing the white sight marker mere centimeters past her head. The subsonic round was big and slow, designed to shred the insides of anyone he shot without making a hole in his wall. The gunshot echoed in the confined space, but not quite to the eardrum bursting level of a high-velocity round.

Her knife streaked through the air with a single rotation. Apollo watched it cross the short distance in slow motion. He felt that with enough effort, he could dodge or even catch the speeding blade but his body was lead in contrast to the lightning of his senses.

It struck hard, burying itself to the hilt in his throat. The pain was intense, already worse than any stabbing he had ever received. Vivian was damnable good with a knife; the wound felt more like a gunshot than a stab.

Through the intense pain, the part of Apollo's brain that clung to reality knew his Immaculata-granted healing was already kicking in. Euphoria already lurked at the edges of his psyche, threatening to drown out the fire in his throat.

Apollo used the agony to focus. The force of the knife's impact snapped his head back and the sudden shock to his system sent him backward against the front of the couch. He pushed himself upright with one hand, gripping the rapidly warming metal handle with the other.

He grunted, wanting to scream but refusing himself that show of weakness, and slowly pulled the knife out of the wound. It gushed hot red blood onto his robe, soaking it in a matter of seconds. With each heartbeat he expected to feel his world dimming, the pain lessening until subtle warmth replaced it, but instead the pain only got worse.

Every heartbeat brought new agonies for him to experience, new levels of pain that he never imagined the human body could produce. His nerves were fire, burning with fury stronger than his hatred for Alexander.

Apollo gritted his teeth against the searing, maddening agony. In the space of a few seconds, moments that stretched across time to the heat death of the universe and back a thousand times, the pain started to lessen. He lay there for a full minute, watching Vivian's shocked expression grow confused and still more shocked with each tick of the clock.

In a minute, the wound was healed up and the pain was rapidly being replaced by the same fuzzy-headed rush that enveloped him when Catherine first granted him the ability. His bones burned as his marrow fought to replenish lost blood.

Another ten seconds passed, and Apollo stood up. He was woozy, though from the effects of healing so rapidly rather than the pain. Blood still covered his neck, but the wound was nothing but a small pink stripe across the side of his windpipe.

The pain vanished, leaving him with a single overriding thought. He felt *good*. More than that, he was *invincible*. His brain reeled with the possibilities, wondering what he could survive and what would actually kill him. Fire and ice coursed through his veins together. He was strong, he was mighty; nothing that stood against him would survive the attempt.

His vision swam. His muscles moved properly, but his brain felt drunk.

"What in the gods' names are you?" Vivian asked, staring up at him. All pretense was gone from her expression. From her perspective, she had just watched herself kill a man only to have him bring himself back from the brink of death by nothing more than his own willpower.

"Isn't it obvious?" Apollo asked, gesturing to the blood-soaked robe. He stopped and laughed. The sound hung on the ragged edge of sanity, pulled from somewhere where only the strongest psychotropics went. "I'm Death!"

She shook her head, unfazed by his intoxicated theatrics. "No, there's got to be something. Some sort of augmentation, something our scientists don't know about."

Apollo laughed again, a mocking giggle. "It's definitely something your scientists don't know about. Better yet, it's not something you can replicate. Only two people on this burnt out husk of a planet can do what I just did."

Apollo could all but see the proverbial lightbulb above her head go off as she said, "and the other one is Alexander, isn't it?"

With a killer's grin, Apollo nodded. The euphoria was fading. It left him feeling normal. He did not burn for more, nor did it leave a hole like drugs would have. It was simply there, elevating him to heights untold, and then it faded.

"Precisely. And now you know why you need me much more than I need you." He left, "and Kingsmark will know my price just went through the roof," unsaid. Nevertheless, he felt sure she understood the implication.

He stood, gathered up his bloody robe, and made his way back toward the bedroom and the incinerator chute.

"So." She had not raised her voice, not even to make sure he heard on his way to the incinerator. From the sound of it, she might as well have been addressing him at his work table as though the previous few minutes never happened. "What do we do now?"

Apollo returned from the bedroom in a pair of black pants and a white undershirt. He gathered up the two coffee mugs and refilled them, placing both on the table at opposite ends before replying.

"Now," he announced, gesturing to the table, "we discuss how we're going to kill my brother."

The shock on her face was a close approximation of her expression at watching Apollo heal from a near-death wound. He suspected that, had she been holding her mug, it would have fallen from her hand and shattered to a great many pieces on the floor.

"Sit. We have much to discuss."

# Chapter 9

Vivian proved to be exceptionally competent at planning their mission. It got to the point that, over the previous three hours, Apollo had taken on the role of sounding board as she worked her way through the potential pitfalls the two of them might run into. During that time, Apollo drained the rest of the coffee, set out a hearty breakfast, and migrated to the couch. Vivian had attempted to join him, but a glare kept her at the table. Despite their intimate night, she still made him uncomfortable for reasons he had yet to fathom.

The previous night had been animal instincts. He had no desire to establish anything with more depth, he told himself. As it was, he had already built more of a bridge with Vivian than anyone alive truly deserved from him. No one else, no one alive anyway, knew where Apollo lived and what the inside of his house looked like. Whether or not he would be able to say that again in a few weeks remained to be seen. He had already extended her more trust than he had anyone else in a very long time. The sex had only been a part of it, a time when he let down his physical guard for a few hours, but the real exercise of trust was going to be mental.

He tried to tell himself that his feelings of unease stemmed from stress and the disruption of his normal schedules, but something more continued to bother him. He was starting to trust her, and he was aware of that fact.

Distrust would have been comfortable and easy. He was used to not trusting people. Trust, on the other hand, left him feeling uncomfortable.

Apollo crossed one foot over the opposite knee. "So."

"So?" she asked, still walking the line between seductress and assassin with her mannerisms. Despite the serious nature of their work, she never bothered with pants.

"You're not wearing your glasses," he observed.

She shrugged. "I don't need them to see. Outside of a NoTech zone, they provide me with useful information."

He raised an eyebrow. "Like?"

Another nonchalant shrug. "The sorts of things most people stuff into a combat visor. It might be less durable this way, but people get antsy if you scan them with active optics."

"If you're obvious about it."

She smiled. "Which I am not. No one gives a second thought to a woman with glasses in a crowd."

He nodded. "Smart. What other fancy equipment did Kingsmark provide you with?"

She shifted in her seat at the table, posture coming more upright and becoming more businesslike, at odds with the way she only buttoned a single spot on her shirt. "Weapons, mostly. Some gear for breaking past Londonsberg's Limits. As little as they could get away with, truthfully. A whole bunch of Kingsmark tech showing up in the middle of Londonsberg one day would be a little suspicious, wouldn't you think?"

Apollo smirked. So, their bases were covered, good. "Most likely. And your intel on the City itself?"

"Flyover maps, power grids, a few safehouses. Not much. Duke Charlie is a lot of things, but 'low-security' is not one of them. Judging by your jacket yesterday, you've probably got more gear here than meets the eye, too."

He nodded. She found the knife under the dining chair easily enough. He was sure she had spotted at least a few more hidden stashes, but he was not about to tell her. Anything else she found would be because of her own skill at her job. Unless he had to equip her himself—and if he did then it meant her story was a lie and she would probably be dead anyway—he expected that the vast majority of his weapons would remain hidden.

But, in the interest of efficiency, if nothing else, he replied, "I do, yes."

"That jacket was Validian, wasn't it?" she asked, again trying to draw him out.

He chuckled slightly. "It sure as hell didn't come from Londonsberg, I'll tell you that."

"Or Kingsmark."

"Nope." The silence drew on for several more minutes before Apollo asked, "they figured out how to use NoTech in Kingsmark?"

She shook her head, clearly frustrated with the answer she was about to give. "None of our scientists have been able to crack it."

Apollo raised an eyebrow. "It's just a suite of targeted hacking programs and EMP disruptors."

Vivian chuckled and Apollo felt a stab of annoyance of his own. As she answered, the initial annoyance faded. She was not going to hold things over him, which was good. "It's far more than that. There's a quantum element to it we can't emulate."

Apollo nodded. Knowing how it worked would be nice, but knowing how to beat it was better. "You bring anything to deal with it?"

She shrugged. "A few things. Nothing permanent," she admitted. "Anything powerful enough to disrupt the City's NoTech for more than a few seconds, or over more than a few meters, isn't going to fit in my pocket."

Apollo smirked, leaning forward. He just found the exact place in their plan that he was supposed to fill. Inwardly, he smirked even wider. His price had just gone up again.

"You have something you want to say?" she asked.

"Your intelligence really never figured out why I made such a, pardon the pun, killing at the Night Market?"

"We assumed it had to do with quality of your workmanship."

Apollo smiled. That much was true, he admitted to himself, but there was more to it. "That's not all. Every gun I build, like the one for our friend Salvatore, will work in a NoTech zone."

He adjusted his posture away from conspiratorial and back to pure business. "Like you said, he's not low-security. Duke Charlie's a paranoid bastard. There's NoTech all over the City. Most of the major streets are NoTech zones, along with just about every important government building, and the ones that aren't can quickly become NTZs."

"And your solution is what?" she asked, cross. "Old guns?"

Apollo stood and went to the bedroom. He returned a moment later carrying his personal pistol in one hand. With a light thunk, he set it on the table and slid it across to where Vivian sat. Wordlessly, he sat back on the chair opposite her, waiting to see what she would do. It was still loaded, making this as much a test of faith as one of observation and skill.

Vivian eyed the gun for a moment, then picked it up and looked it over. The first thing she did was drop the magazine and rack the slide, emptying it, and Apollo hid a nod of satisfaction. She examined the safety and touched the trigger with ease that spoke more about her experience than anything else had, finally setting it back on the table. She did not, Apollo noted, replace the magazine.

She pursed her lips in appreciation. "This *is* old."

Apollo shook his head. "Not as old as it looks," he admitted. "Some people pay extra for thousand-year-old styling is all."

"Twentieth-century tech won't overthrow Londonsberg."

He leaned forward, resting both elbows on his knees. The smirk on his face was triumphant. He pointed a single finger at it. "That gun will still shoot inside of a Londonsberg NTZ."

"Seems like a lot of expense to go to just to keep your customers alive."

Apollo laughed again. This time the sound was full of scorn, mostly directed at his customers. He could not care less about most of them as people, he told himself.

They existed as sources of money and excuses for him to do one of the few things he actually enjoyed. The fact that Vivian would think otherwise, even after only knowing him for a short time, amused him.

And yet, that feeling in the back of his brain that he was lying to himself persisted. It told him that she read him better than he could. He chose, once again, to ignore it and focus on the conversation at hand.

"That's my gun," he stated with an emphatic raise of his eyebrows.

"And the ones you sell...?"

He shrugged. "Made to the same standard. No wiring whatsoever. They're all mechanical and chemical. NoTech scrambles the electronics, disabling firing pins and detonators alike. The higher strength ones will disable communications as well, but we shouldn't have to deal with too many of those. You know what else NoTech doesn't stop?"

Vivian narrowed her eyes, making her annoyance at his posturing clear. "What?"

Apollo held up a small tube. "This."

"And that is?"

"Suppressor."

Vivian snorted. "Silencers are shut down just like everything else."

If Apollo felt like laughing just then, he would have. Instead, he simply allowed a little more of his gloating to touch his face. "This isn't an active silencer. It's a suppressor. Not as effective, but," he shrugged, "it works inside the Limits."

A little too quickly, Vivian asked, "how many more of these do you have?"

Apollo grinned. It seemed he would have to outfit her after all. In true Kingsmark fashion, the KRS had ignored the obvious solution in favor of the expensive, complicated one. Their oversight was his gain, and he found no fault with Vivian herself for her superiors' failings.

He plastered on the same salesman's grin he gave his customers. "Many." With an expansive, almost welcoming, gesture of his arms, he continued, "I'll even offer you a discount, since you're working for the KRS. Or," the grin widened, "trade. Gear you need, for gear I want."

Vivian tightened her jaw. Apollo wondered how vivid the sensation of her KRS superiors tightening her purse strings were from her perspective if the impression was strong enough for Apollo to feel it across the room. After a moment's thought, she said, "what do you need."

Apollo shrugged with feigned casualness, carefully noting that her statement had not been a question. He was about to tell a half-truth, he realized. Not an outright lie, because he could easily produce a laundry list of things he would like to get his hands on from Kingsmark's armory, but he knew he should save that request until the hooks were in a little deeper.

"Not sure. I'll get you a gun, and let you know when I figure it out."

"Guns," she corrected.

He quirked an eyebrow. "Guns?"

Vivian nodded. "Yes, guns. Plural."

Apollo grinned, imagining the weight of the cash in his hand already. "Done."

"Just remember how much they're actually worth and don't try to cheat Kingsmark."

Apollo's grin returned. "Trust me. I know exactly how much it's worth to you. I'll make sure it's fair."

She grimaced, but hid the reaction quickly. She had done her research, after all, and except when someone ran the price up too high in a bidding war, Apollo never overcharged for his weapons. A few more tense moments passed before her eyes lit up with something a little more violent than joy.

"Apollo." The pleased lilt in her voice bordered on a purr. "How much ammunition do you have on hand?"

"Enough to," he said. A moment later, a grin split his face as well. He was torn between being impressed that Vivian had come up with the idea and being annoyed that the idea had escaped him. He finished, "enough to outfit a small army."

"And you can promise me, in writing if that's what the KRS requires, that all of your weapons are manufactured to the same standard?"

He considered his options for a moment. He would not lie to an ordinary customer, but he might fudge things, especially numbers. The KRS, on the other hand, would find out quickly if he had done that. Finally, with a shrug, he admitted, "more or less. Some people want cheap crap, so I sell them cheap crap. Others..."

"But," Vivian interrupted. Apollo glared as she finished. "It's all the same mechanical gear right?"

He nodded slowly. He already knew where she was going with this. He had known moments after she had asked about his ammunition stores, in fact. He found himself so impressed with her lateral thought process that he forgot to be annoyed at his own oversight.

"Of course. Do you think I'd still be alive if I put the same military uplink hardware in my guns that the Duke uses? I can't have someone trying to link into some asshole's homemade tac net with my gear. The odds of the Duke's men coming out here are small, but if someone tried to set up something like that, the Black Ties would make a special trip out here to see me."

"Why, Apollo," Vivian teased, "you almost sound afraid."

He scoffed. The emotion he felt toward the Duke's elite enforcers was hardly fear, more like an uncomfortable knowledge that, while he could kill several of them, they would keep sending men to "retrieve" him. Eventually, even he would make a mistake, and the Black Ties would keep crawling over the hill of their own people's bodies until he made that mistake. Their skill, individually, did not concern him. Desperate men, however, made him profoundly uncomfortable.

Vivian was silent for a moment after Apollo gave voice to most of those thoughts, only keeping his feelings towards fanatics to himself. He watched the gears turn in her brain once again. Finally, she asked, "how many have you sold?"

"Over the years?" he asked, closing his eyes for a moment to multiply the numbers together. "Several hundred, at least. Less than a thousand, let me put it that way."

Before Vivian could say anything, Apollo continued, "I see where you're going with this. I never sold any of them more than a single box of ammo at a time. There might be a handful of people with a couple hundred rounds but..."

Again, she interrupted, saying, "Kingsmark is prepared to buy as much ammunition as you're willing to sell at one-point-two-five times market price."

Apollo raised an eyebrow, suddenly intrigued. She had tipped her hand more than she knew, too, jumping out with an offer that big. Apollo now knew exactly how much latitude she had been given for her mission. He suspected she could probably commandeer a battleship for the right reason. She had played earlier at having a tight leash on her money reserves, and had done so convincingly, but with her offer, he knew instantly who really wrote the paynotes for her mission.

Or, he thought, had she really tipped her hand too early? The way his mind immediately latched onto that thought made him second guess himself. He did not like to second guess himself, ever. Yet, the fact she had maneuvered him so easily into it drug a bit more appreciation from somewhere inside his brain.

He needed someone who could think like Captain Vivian Jensen of the Kingsmark Royal Service. He also needed her to know that. Apollo had to keep some of the strings in his hands, at least.

He learned forward on his elbows again, visibly and deliberately showing his interest in the openness of his face. "Kingsmark is welcome to anything I'm willing to part with."

"I'd recommend you then sell it at what appears to be a huge loss, telling everyone in the market to 'be ready.'"

"Well," Apollo leaned back against the couch and draped his arms over the back. When he spoke, his voice was smooth as silk. He suspected he knew where her previous statement had come from, but he wanted to be sure. "I expected Kingsmark would want to keep the civilians out of the fighting."

"*Kingsmark* would prefer that, yes, but *I* know many of the people living outside the Limits, like your butcher Sal, would jump at the chance to fire a few rounds at the Duke's men." She shifted in her chair slightly, lowering her eyebrows and turning her head in a motion Apollo immediately recognized as a deliberate, and effective, attempt to be seductive. After a moment, she teased, "unless you're concerned about their welfare, Apollo."

He scoffed again, reacting before he could suppress it. She again led him exactly to the point she wanted with the line about Kingsmark, then sunk her own claws into him just like he had been trying to do to her. No matter, he thought, let her use him all she wanted as long as he got what he wanted from their deal.

Momentarily, he wondered exactly how much she had been reading him as they had been talking. He had told her the truth, because she would know a lie, and because his truth was necessary to uncover her truth.

Apollo shook his head to clear his thoughts. She was getting under his skin, and he was not yet sure how he felt about that. On the one hand, he ought to kill her on general principle because she knew too much. Reliance on someone else was a weakness in the long run, no matter how much she may promise to watch his back. On the other hand, a strange part of his psyche was thrilled to have uncovered a woman with the same ruthless determination and cunning mind that he had. She was, he reflected, interesting.

He would deal with that later, though. For now, he had money to make.

"Deal. I'm keeping enough to keep my personal stock comfortably loaded and whatever we take into the City with us. Call it five thousand rounds. Everything else," he said with a sincere smile and an expansive gesture with both hands, "is Kingsmark's."

"Good." Vivian smiled. "I'll transfer the credits..."

"No, no," Apollo interrupted. "I only work in cash. That's how this works out here, no tracers."

Her smile quickly turned into a frown as Vivian furrowed her brows in thought. "There's no way I can get you that much cash inside of two weeks."

Apollo shrugged with deceptive nonchalance. "I'll write your superiors an invoice. Tell them I want it delivered in person by one of their agents."

"And how much do you have that you're going to sell?" she asked, taking out her tablet to write the amount down.

Apollo smirked again, but his voice was all business when he spoke. "Five hundred-thousand rounds. Market calls for anywhere from one to five credits per round, depending on caliber. It'll average out to three credits per round. You can search it all and audit it yourself if you like." The next thing out of his mouth was significantly more taught and threatening than he had been moments before, "but we don't have the time, do we?"

She narrowed her eyes. Apollo noted a small flare of anger, but most of her thought seemed bent on trying to determine whether or not Apollo was lying or not. "Deal," she said, echoing his statement, but tinting it with annoyance instead of greed.

Apollo suspected she would get chewed out by her handlers after the mission was over, but he also saw that she thought the expense was worth it. Maybe she thought the would-be militia could be helpful, or maybe she just wanted to maximize Londonsberg casualties, he had no idea. He smiled. "Excellent."

"Three-point-seven-five credits a round," Vivian announced. "That nets you one million, eight hundred and seventy-five thousand credits to be delivered as cash in person."

"Good," Apollo said coolly.

"One more thing," she said, blanking the screen. "If I die, you get nothing."

"Bitch!" Apollo shouted, rising from his chair. Regardless of how mad her presumptive action made him, the part of his mind that she intrigued appreciated the kind of guts it took to do something like that.

She smirked.

"You... you..." Apollo snapped, searching for the right words. Finally he sat back in his seat and smiled. That odd feeling of appreciation was back. "You're a fucking cutthroat. I think you and I will work together just fine when we get inside the City."

Vivian stood a moment later, crossing to Apollo and wrapping her arms loosely around his neck. "I agree." Apollo detected no trace of a plot—not that he had seen any of her other knife-twists coming.

He was still tense, though. Upset that she had, in effect, tried to cheat him. She had also forced his hand, ensuring that he would do whatever it took to protect her against Alexander when the time came. A normal human would not survive more than a few seconds in a fight against the sort of monster the Immaculata made him.

He also realized that she expected him to stab her in the back and this was her insurance against that happening. In her defense, he would have made the same assumptions.

Apollo chuckled. It would be difficult, but nothing he could not handle, especially as he passed more of the Immaculata's tests. After all three, he would once again be better than Alexander in every way.

He was his own monster, after all.

"Now," Vivian purred, "about my gun."

Apollo chuckled, turning and pushing her toward the bedroom. "I have another idea."

*** 

Salvatore Alfonso Maximilian the Second, known to everyone as "Sal" or sometimes "that butcher who works at Far Market," double and then triple checked the lock on his shop. It was secure as ever, but the current contents and occupancy gave him little incentive to take risks.

Everyone knew his shop was one of the few permanent buildings of the Far Market. No one, not even Vivian and her Kingsmark friends, knew that it was armored as well. The walls, ostensibly insulated metal to keep his shop at the proper frigid temperature, were just a touch too thick for that to the their only purpose. The double layers of insulation were usually separated by a pocket of air to further prevent heat loss, but instead of air his walls were filled with a reactive polymer gel.

Soft and pliable under normal conditions, it closely resembled the expensive insulation found inside Londonsberg freezers. Unlike regular insulation, the stuff in Sal's walls would temporarily solidify hard enough to stop bullets.

Originally, the armoring had been because of paranoia. Anyone who knew Sal as anything other than a simple butcher from Manhattan living on the outskirts of Londonsberg could cause personal trouble for him. Apollo knew, Vivian knew, but no one else did. Sal assumed that if word of his paternal lineage ever got around, the President-Duke's forces would find themselves tasked with bringing the son of a certain "Baron Maximus" to Duke Charlie on a one-way ticket.

On the other hand, if the last conversation Sal and Apollo had was any indication, he was already being given the invitation to visit Duke Charlie, only it was not the sort of invitation he had always been afraid of.

Sal nodded in satisfaction as he looked over the small crowd assembled inside his icy butcher shop. He liked the cold, dry air of the shop. Sal could take or leave the ubiquitous rain most days, although the warm Rhineland rain was not terrible by an objective measure, but he had always enjoyed the cold. As a child, he wanted to move to Eslav or Moskgorod. After the war, the lure of Londonsberg, and the promise of revenge one day, kept him firmly anchored.

The people assembled in front of him all shared those sentiments for one reason or another. Most had family or friends who disappeared not-very-mysteriously after being visited by the Black Ties. Others had been slighted by the City itself in one way or another. Businessman had been forced out of work, artists hounded for painting the wrong thing in the wrong place, and on and on the list went. The only motivation not present was money. Sal wanted to avoid dealing with people in it just for the money for as long as possible. It would eventually be necessary he knew, but the "command staff," as he was beginning to think of his assembled guests, needed to be people invested in the cause, not in profit.

Behind the crowd was a shipping palette with a large metal box resting on it. The lid to the box was open, revealing more handguns and rifles than even Sal thought Apollo possessed. They rested on boxes upon boxes of ammunition and cleaning equipment. He had been floored by Apollo's price, and tried to argue, but Apollo insisted.

"For all of that?" Sal had asked. "You're serious."

Apollo then nodded, saying, "I am."

"That's only a little more than what I paid you for my pistol."

"If the price is too high, I can come down."

Sal had stared at him in confusion, unable to articulate the words he needed to ask what was going on. He wondered if Apollo was simply liquidating his assets because he was leaving on a suicide mission to Londonsberg. When he could, Sal had given voice to that thought. Apollo had laughed.

"No," he said. "Don't worry. I'm coming back from that City one way or the other."

"Then what?"

Apollo hesitated then, the first time Sal had ever seen him unsure about saying exactly what was on his mind. Finally, he admitted the truth. "Let's just say the KRS is involved."

Sal almost interrupted, but kept his mouth shut as Apollo continued.

"Vivian wanted these distributed, Sal," Apollo told him. He explained the deal he and Vivian worked out, including the KRS's incentives. "Sell them as cheap as you can justify. Just get them, and the ammunition, into the hands of as many people as you possibly can."

"What's my deadline?" Sal had asked. As Apollo had given his explanation, understanding slowly dawned. He did not have to ask for what purpose Apollo, and by extension Kingsmark, wanted the weapons distributed. That puzzle was easy enough to solve.

"I don't know," Apollo then admitted. "But soon. I don't know if the KRS expected you lot to actually help or to be cannon fodder," Sal remembered grimacing and growling at that thought, "but I expect you to lead these people and storm Londonsberg right alongside the Marksmen."

"I'll be there."

To Sal's surprise, Apollo had offered his hand to shake. Sal had never seen, in all their years of knowing one another, Apollo be so friendly. Whatever darkness had always hovered over Apollo's soul was gone. Danger continued to hover over him—not that he needed any confirmation of danger other than the crate of weapons Apollo delivered—and a new darkness had joined it. Whatever gargoyle now crouched over Apollo's soul made him sharp and focused. Sal saw happiness, too—not that Apollo would have acknowledged it.

Apollo then bid him farewell, told him to wait for the signal, and left Sal alone with more weaponry than he had ever seen in one place. That had been four hours ago. Sal then spent the next three and half of the intervening hours collecting everyone he wanted to share the news with.

Jamie cleared her throat. Across her chest, with the strap resting distractingly between her breasts, was the compact carbine she paid Apollo a great deal of money for. It had been on the top of the crate of weapons with a handwritten tag. "Sal? You were saying?"

He nodded, coming back to the present. He looked Jamie over. Her parents had been killed, Sal knew, by the Black Ties in an "unfortunate aircar accident" after they were overheard expressing something less than complete satisfaction with the President-Duke at an affair of state. She fled, taking what she could of the family business to the Night Market with her, and had been selling to other unsatisfied ex-citizens for ten years.

"The origin of these guns does not leave this shop," he said. "Is that understood?"

"Why?" a man near the back of the group asked. He made jewelry, and had made the decision to leave Londonsberg on his own terms rather than duress or threat. The Black Ties had insisted on taking a share of his product as a tax, in addition to the steep taxes he already paid to the President-Duke, and rather than fight them he simply paid off the right people and had been secreted out of the City in the middle of the night.

"Because," Sal continued. He spoke with his natural accent, not the fake Imperial Manhattan accent everyone present knew him by. That alone had been a shock to his guests, but one quickly forgotten when they saw the crate of weapons. "If word gets back to the City that Apollo just dropped off a box of guns, what do you think their logical conclusion would be?"

"Point taken," the jewelry seller replied.

"Each of you is going to get your pick of weapons for yourself for free."

That statement caused a stir almost as sudden and surprised as the reveal of the guns themselves had. The murmured among themselves for a moment, their focus suddenly lost, when Sal's voice cut through the noise.

"Quiet!" he barked. Some part of his mind wondered where the voice of his father came from, but he continued. "We're going to hand out every one of these guns to you as well. Your job, to be done as soon as possible as with utmost security, is to sell every one of them at no more than half their standard value, then bring me back a quarter of whatever you make."

"What?" another voice asked. Sal recognized the voice, though not the face because the short woman was hidden behind a burly potter, of Far Market's premier fishmonger.

"You heard me," Sal growled. "This isn't about profit. This is about fighting. I want Londonsberg burned down as much as any of you do, probably even more. I will not let that goal be sidelined by people trying to make a quick credit scamming some poor, dumb bastard. Am I clear?"

"Crystal," Jamie the rum seller replied. Louder, she demanded of the crowd, "ain't he, boys and girls?"

The replies that came were hardly the unified shouts of even a half-trained militia, but enthusiasm was something none of them lacked.

"Count off!" Sal barked.

They did, totaling fourteen aside from himself.

"Go bring your cars around," he ordered, "and bring boxes to carry this stuff in."

"What are you going to be doing?"

"Jamie and I," he indicated her with a wave of his hand, "are going to divide that," he pointed to the large metal box behind them, "into fourteen equal parts."

"You won't be selling any of them yourself?" the jewelry maker asked.

Sal shook his head. "Apollo left me a few other things that are going to be taking up my time between now and then."

"And when is 'then?'" the man asked.

"'Then,'" Sal replied unlocking the double lock on his shop door, "is about ten minutes after I say it's time. That's all I've got, so that's all you get. Be quick about it. Go!"

The group scattered, heading to their various aircars and trucks to bring them closer to Sal's shop. The last flyover had been nearly six hours before, two hours before Legal Night, but no one wanted to take any more risks than they had to. It was no secret that people sold weapons at the Night Market, but seeing so many moving at once would surely tip off even the densest analyst.

"Well," Jamie said as the last of them filtered through the leather curtain that served at the building's door most of the time. "This is not how I expected to spend my evening."

"Nor I," Sal agreed. "But if Apollo has any chance at all..."

"Does he?" she interrupted.

Sal shrugged his broad shoulders. He shut and bolted the door, just to be safe. "I think so."

Jamie nodded. "Good. And you?"

"And me?" Sal asked.

"Yeah. And you. What do you think the odds of us succeeding are?"

"Apollo's going after Alexander," he said. "And the KRS is after Duke Charlie. I think our odds are pretty good."

"None of us are trained," she pointed out.

"Not completely true," he countered.

"You're the exception."

"I'd rather not be," he admitted, "but you're right. We've got a motivated group here, though, and if they enlist one person for every gun in that box," he pointed again to the large metal rectangle taking up most of an entire corner in his shop, "then we'll have quite the force on hand to help the Marksmen."

"Aren't you worried about them running wild?"

Sal shook his head. "I thought of that. When the Marksmen roll in, everyone with us is getting assigned to one of their platoons as auxiliary troops. We help the Marksmen with some extra firepower, and in turn they keep anyone with the urge to do something," he paused, "unfavorable in check."

"Sounds like you've thought this out already."

Sal shrugged. "Pa taught me a lot."

"Apparently."

"Anyway. We need to get that box sorted out before everyone else comes back."

"Did Apollo give you an inventory list?"

"He did not."

Jamie rolled her eyes. "Of course he didn't." She laughed. "Oh well. We'll just have to figure it out as we go."

A minutes of silence passed before Jamie spoke. "I heard a rumor th' other day."

Sal cocked an eyebrow. "Oh?"

"Yeah," she said. After a moment, Jamie went on. "About th' Duke."

Sal laughed quietly. "There's enough of them going around to write a book."

"Well..." She hesitated. Whatever she had to say was not something she wanted to give voice to. Sal urged her on with a wave of his hand and she finally added, "it's his name. I heard his name wasn't really Charlie Maxwell."

Sal froze. Slowly, very slowly, he straightened his spine. Standing tall, and with a voice that was dark and deep, he rumbled, "what did the rumor say his name was?"

Her eyes went wide, but her mouth remained shut.

"Jamie," he said, keeping careful control over his voice. An idle thought percolated through his mind and he wondered if this was how Apollo felt most days. Trying his best to sound friendly, he asked, "what'd the rumor say?"

"Maximilian," she said. "I heard his real name was Charles Maximilian."

Sal's heart thundered as his mind fell back in time, hearing his father tell the stories of how the Validian War started. He nodded once, feeling his fingers and hands start to tremble with adrenaline. "Don't tell anyone," he muttered.

"I'm sorry," Jamie replied.

"Nothing to be sorry for. Never apologize for sharing information or for asking for it. Never apologize for the truth."

"So it's...?"

He nodded again, repeating, "don't tell anyone."

Ten minutes later, just long enough for the two of them to start making piles, a knock came at the door. Sal drew his pistol and approached it. The metal was thick, nearly soundproof, which was why he installed a small two-way microphone in the door. The sound of someone knocking came more through it than it did through the door itself.

"Who's it?" he asked in his fake accent.

"It's Singh," the voice on the other side told him.

Sal relaxed slightly and reached for the door lock to let the jewelry maker inside, but stopped with his hand on the lock.

The Imperial Manhattan accent remained for a moment longer. "What sorta ting did I say to you on the way in?"

"You talked about how much you liked bluebirds."

Sal relaxed the rest of the way and slid his pistol back into his holster. Singh's answer had been true. If he had said anything else, Sal would have known he was not alone. If he mentioned red birds, then whoever was with him was affiliated with Londonsberg or the Black Ties. Neither had happened, and so Sal happily opened the big door again.

"Welcome back," he said in his real voice.

"Am I the first one here?" Singh asked.

"The first one back, anyway."

"Good," he said. "Let me help sort."

Sal grinned. "The more the merrier, as they say."

Singh grunted. "Not where I come from, they don't."

"Well," Sal countered, "we're going to be changing that very soon, aren't we?"

Singh nodded, conceding the point. "That we are, Baron Max. That we are."

Sal eyed him for a moment. That was his father's title, not his. He shrugged and went back to work.

# Chapter 10

In the dead of night, even the towering Limits of Londonsberg seemed serene. The blank gray walls surrounded everything that was Londonsberg proper "for its own protection." After the Validian War, Duke Charlie ordered everything outside the arbitrary boundary he then termed the Limits to be bulldozed for dozens of kilometers. Londonsberg had no suburbs as a result, only towers that arched into the sky like steel sentinels. Even long past Legal Night, the Duke's soldiers regularly patrolled the Limits. They ignored anything beyond; the President-Duke built the walls for a reason.

He would not admit it, at least not out loud, but Apollo knew he had no idea how to get past the guards. Fighting them was an option, but while he could take out several of them—possibly upwards of a dozen or more if they were stupid and came at him one at a time—even he could not get through with the entire Londonsberg security force after him.

Apollo never had to sneak *into* the city before. He had no desire to see the inside of that labyrinth of glass and steel ever again. Getting through the Limits turned out to be one of the few things Apollo was glad to turn over to Vivian.

Visiting Sal was the last thing they did before leaving his house behind. The visit had gone better than he expected. Sal took his offer as quickly as Apollo expected him to, and already seemed to be formulating a plan to use the weapons even before Apollo left. It may have been his imagination, but Apollo would have sworn that Sal actually seemed sad to see him leave.

Sal could not have been worried about him, he asked himself, could he?

Apollo ignored the implications of that thought. He had a business to run and a brother to kill. Vivian was pleasant to work with, doubly so given her competence at nearly every task they had so far undertaken together, but making friends was not on Apollo's to-do list. Nonetheless, he had given five hundred rounds to Sal for free. He declined to explain exactly why, only that he suspected Sal's gun would need extra ammunition. Apollo had no idea how Sal planned to divvy up the rest of the weapons, but he, at least, would have more than enough to defend himself against any aggression by Londonsberg.

They gave themselves three days. Vivian insisted that taking any more time would endanger the groundwork laid by other KRS agents. That gave Apollo plenty of time to check, clean, and pack enough weaponry to outfit an entire company. On her end of what became their workroom, Vivian worked on the KRS tech she brought with her. When Apollo ran out of weapons, he tailored his spare Mirage suit to fit Vivian.

The two of them spoke very little those days, though they did develop a rather companionable working relationship. After the day's work was finished, their nights turned out to be vocal enough to fill any silence left while the sun was in the sky.

He still resented her for her trick with KRS's contract for his ammunition, and he resented the fact that it had quickly become clear that she was doing her best to play him as a pawn in Kingsmark's schemes. Each time those thoughts threatened to burn in his mind, he reminded himself that he had been doing the same thing to her. Each of them had goals, and they both needed the other person to achieve those goals. By the third day, Apollo was even beginning to find her presence enjoyable.

Even if he still harbored some displeasure over the way she had carried out their contract negotiations, they were overridden by his appreciation of her skill. What was more, he had to trust her. He had to protect her until Alexander was dead. Otherwise, no paycheck would come from the Kingsmark Royal Service. Apollo knew that she understood that she could not kill him once the deal was done as well. His "miraculous" healing had seen to that in the short term, and he would make sure his performance in their mission together would impress upon the KRS that he was an asset worth retention.

That thought nagged at his mind, reminding him again that getting too caught up in Londonsberg corruption was what pulled Alexander from the Immaculata's service. The paycheck, and even the partnership, given by the KRS was nice enough, but he knew who held his real loyalties.

Vivian assured him that she had a plan to get inside. She had been generous with her weapons and gear, perhaps feeling that she owed it to Apollo for providing her with weapons that would work despite the City's NoTech. In addition to a few other useful gadgets, none of which bore any Kingsmark stamp anywhere, Apollo now found himself in the possession of a small bandolier of flash-bang grenades. He had to admit that he was curious as to their effect on Alexander's heightened system.

The trip to the City had been surprisingly uneventful. They took turns keeping watch for Londonsberg fliers as Apollo's aircar came in low, slow, and more often than not under manual control. They left his house right as the sun was setting, and if Apollo had driven the way he drove to the Night Market, they would have made it in a little less than five hours. As it was, with the aircar hugging the hills and valleys of the landscape at low speed, the trip had taken almost nine so far.

They landed several klicks outside the Limits, much closer than Far Market ever came and within sight of the towering walls. Apollo set the aircar down under a rocky overhang at the base of a steep valley, doing his best to wedge it as far out of sight as possible. A few extra scratches and dents would not harm it, he thought, shutting the engine off. He had parked so close to the wall—actually scraping the rock in the process—that he had to wait for Vivian to get out first and then crawl across and exit through her door.

After piling some brush around it, the aircar was virtually invisible against the natural backdrop of the rocks and shrubs. Its black market heat diffusers would have it cooled down in a few minutes, long before a patrol would be by, assuming any were flying that late—or, judging by the clock, that early—in the first place. Some nights they hovered right over the Limits, and others they came further out. Apollo only remembered one night when the fliers came as far as the Night Market, but nothing came of that visit. He assumed the watch commanders, each a differing level of corrupt, would push the fliers farther out depending on whether someone was paying them to keep the patrols close or to send them out past the Limits.

The climb out of the valley proved to be harder than either of them had expected. The rocks were loose, brittle river sediment left over from when Londonsberg diverted and drained its source for water. After another hour, they finally scrambled to the top. Apollo had been surprisingly helpful during the climb, offering Vivian several handholds and keeping her from falling when the rocks gave way. He had to make sure she trusted him, and he was keeping a running tally of every time he held her life in his hands, or trying to. The debt was quickly mounting, but every time he thought about it found he could never remember the number quite the same way twice.

"Thank the gods for long nights, hm?" Vivian said, craning her neck upward to stare at the stars.

"It'll be morning soon. We should go as far as we can before it starts to get light, then dig in for the night."

"I thought you didn't know anything about this area." Apollo expected to hear a tease in her voice, but none was present. She seemed honestly curious.

"I said I don't know anything about the outer defenses," he growled. "I snuck out of this damn City the last time I came through here, not in. That doesn't mean I don't know where we can hide for the day. There are still ruins here."

"Our intel says that Duke Charlie destroyed the previous city."

"Then your intel is wrong!" Apollo snapped.

She eyed him for a moment before replying. Her voice was kept carefully level. He was dangerous, she knew, but a brain lurked behind that temper of his. If she should stay in contact with it, and not with the angry reflexes he had built up over the years, she would do just fine.

"Apollo, there are things you have to understand about the way my job works. I am not an invasion force. I'm the reconnaissance, sent here to make sure we know where everything is, to open the gates when the army rolls up to them, and, perhaps most importantly, to find a way to deal with Alexander and the NoTech."

He took a deep breath, folded his hands behind his head, and looked up at the stars. He held that pose for a moment, taking several deep, calming breaths before he turned his attention back to Vivian. "I know that."

"And?"

Apollo gestured toward the uneven landscape. If he registered that Vivian was not-very-subtly asking for an apology, he ignored it. "When Charlie built his City, he destroyed everything that remained of the cities before it, but you have to remember how he thinks. He didn't touch the ruins outside the Limits aside from running a demotank over them and planting some grass to cover everything up."

"Then, it's still here?" Vivian asked with wonder. Apollo would not have pegged her as a history buff, but it seemed her interest was real enough. From what he had heard, Kingsmark did have a deeper interest in the past, studying and learning from it anyway, than places like Londonsberg. Unlike the City, the Marksmen actually valued history as an educational tool, not an arm of propaganda. If they were smart, the KRS would never let on that they would value the ruins that much. Likely as not, Duke Charlie would bomb the catacombs and destroy the ruins just to spite his enemies.

"That's what I said. Follow me. There's some sort of audience hall about a klick that way." He gestured in a vaguely northern direction, then turned and started walking without waiting for her to follow.

Halfway there, a predawn patrol passed by overhead. On the relatively open plain, Apollo and Vivian both saw it coming several kilometers off, and managed to find cover. Vivian curled herself tightly into a ball beneath a wild shrub, while Apollo trusted in his Mirage-fabric clothes to hide him in the darkness in the shadowed side of a hill. The flier circled once, then a second time and seemed for a heart-stopping moment that it had found them, but quickly sped away to continue its search pattern.

They waited until the patrol car was a dot on the horizon before moving.

"Come on," Apollo hissed. "That's why we're staying underground until nightfall."

"Is there any chance we can take the catacombs all the way into the City?" Vivian asked.

Apollo narrowed his eyes, not quite a glare not definitely an unfriendly gesture. "Don't be stupid," he growled. "When I told you that Duke Charlie demolished the ruins, I meant it. He sunk the foundations of the Limits fifty meters into the ground. Nothing inside Londonsberg connects with the outside world."

Vivian silently nodded, her face an impassive mask. For the moment, Apollo did not care enough to try and decipher what was going on in her mind. He had more important concerns, and finding a way into the catacombs below was chief among them. He kept moving in a more or less straight line, refusing to stop and search any one place for more than a few moments because of the threat of another flyover.

It took fifteen more minutes to find an entrance. The hole was small, barely bigger than Apollo's shoulders, but the tumbled and cracked stone covered with a thin layer of dirt told him that he was in the right place.

"In," he snapped, watching the sky as another patrol car appeared as a speck in the distant horizon.

"Are you su—"

"In!" he snapped more forcefully, punctuating it with a rough shove in the direction of the hole. Vivian managed to squeeze through the vines covering the cave entrance in a matter of seconds, cursing quietly as a thorny bramble caught and tore at her arm. Apollo watched the patrol in the sky as she struggled through the hole, then was right behind her.

The patrol car roared by overhead, barely ten meters high, as Apollo ripped his way through the last of the thorns. His scratches bled, but the marks themselves healed before he noticed them.

From down the tunnel, Apollo heard Vivian pushing aside some of the rubble. "What was this place? Can you read this?"

He crawled down the tunnel a short ways until it widened enough to stand. Vivian stood beside a pocket lantern that illuminated the cavern with ruddy light. Scattered around were pieces of the facade of a huge building. Letters were carved on the broken blocks. "It's the same alphabet as Euronord, but I can't tell you anything else. There's a hundred pieces and I have no idea what the original order was."

"Could you read it if it was in the original order?" Vivian's eyes were wide, almost excited. It seemed she shared her nation's love of history.

Apollo shrugged dismissively. "Probably."

A moment passed a Vivian turned her attention to the cave itself. "So, we're camping here until night?"

"We don't have many options. Kill the lantern, too. If the fliers spot the light, it's going to be bomb first, question later."

She took one last look at the ruins around them before reaching down to extinguish the dim light. The cave was instantly plunged into intense, velvety darkness. Outside, the moon and stars provided enough light to see, but none of that silver light made it underground.

"It's going to be dark even with the sun out. That hole's not big."

"I don't mind the dark," Apollo said. He had excellent night vision and would, probably, be able to use whatever meager light filtered in just fine. Sitting in darkness with nothing to do for hours made his hands itch, but he ignored the sensation and the urges that went with it.

One more day, he told himself, then the blood on his hands would finally belong to the one person who deserved to die above all others.

"I'll take first watch," Apollo added a few moments later. He suspected Vivian was just as awake as he was, but her mental state factored into his calculations in only a minor way. He could make himself sleep when his turn came, and he wanted to be as rested and energized as possible for the next phase of their plan in case things went wrong and they had to fight as soon as they crossed the Limits.

"We'll leave in twelve hours," Vivian said. "You're up for six, then I'm up for six and I get you up and then we go knock down the door."

Apollo grinned at the metaphor, finding once again that he did have a certain interested in the way her mind worked. Perhaps he hated Vivian a touch less than anyone else, or perhaps endorphins from picturing Alexander's dead and bloodless body at his feet were to blame. Either way his thoughts made him smile the sort of smile that a normal person would have found disturbing.

With nothing to do, his watch dragged on. Eventually, he realized the patrol flights passed by every thirty minutes and used that to calculate time. The day passed a little more quickly after figuring that out, but not by much.

After the tenth flyover—he had started counting after the second one—he woke Vivian. She had fallen asleep against a massive block of stone engraved with the word "DEUT." Her jacket was bundled behind her head, offering as much comfort as could be expected from napping in a cave held up by the broken pieces of some dead civilization's capital building.

The two of them traded places quietly. The only words that passed between them were Apollo conveying his discovery about the patrol timing and an admonishment to wake him up immediately if anything happened.

That said, he found a relatively flat spot, bundled his coat underneath his head, and stretched out. Forcing his mind to be calm, using the same mental exercises that had enabled him to sleep most nights for the past seven years, he quickly slipped into a light but recuperative sleep.

Some time later, his eyes snapped open as a rumble shuddered through the cave. The roof above him was collapsing, raining stone and dirt. In the pitch blackness, he could feel dust and pebbles on his face and smell the scent of disturbed earth. Vivian was somewhere between the cave mouth and where he was laying. He heard her footsteps, loud and echoing against the stones of their soon to be ruined hideout. She ran, shouting his name, but her voice was muffled by the rumble of stone grinding on stone. The noise quickly grew in intensity, building to a crescendo that first drowned out her footsteps, then voice, then everything but his own thunderous heartbeat.

A piece of the ancient building making up the roof above him broke loose. In the pitch darkness, he was not sure how he knew it was directly above him, but it was. Apollo curled and sprang to one side, but he was too slow. He got one leg out of the way, but the other was pulped beneath the enormous stone.

The pain flared up as his body tried to heal, but with the weight still crushing him, it was no use. The pain mounted until he blacked out with the cave collapsing around him.

***

Apollo awoke some time later, first becoming aware that he was, and apparently had been for some time, screaming obscenities at the top of his lungs. A heartbeat later, the pain from his crushed leg rushed back into his mind with a force like the cave-in that dropped the rock in the first place. He was dimly aware, at his edge of his senses, that Vivian was scrabbling at the crushing stone, trying vainly to free him.

He could feel his limb trying to heal itself. A dim part of his mind realized his healing ability was more or less indefinite so long as the injury was not fatal. Whenever they got the rock off his leg, he would simply have to put up with another short bout of agony as he healed for real and then they could be on their way. Unlike before, when the feeling had been a pleasurable high, the euphoria was now so intense that it rapidly became more unpleasant than the pain itself.

He took a deep breath, doing his best to push everything out of his mind. Years of meditation took over and the pain receded, becoming the crash of waves at the beach rather than a tidal onslaught of oceanic fury. The pleasure was harder to force away, but even it was eventually buried under the all-consuming directive of, "get me the hell out of here."

Calm, he got a look at the rock that lay partially atop his lower body. It rose above him in Vivian's lantern light like a gray monument to futility. It had to be ten meters tall, and maybe half that across. From size alone, unless it were somehow miraculously hollow, it would be heavier than even a team of people could move without serious equipment.

Apollo laughed at the futility. The twinned-agonies of crushing pain and dazzling pleasure seemed to recede further as he laughed madly. He was stuck, pinned under a chunk of stone twice the size of his aircar, with no way to move it. Perhaps, given a day or two, Vivian could dig out under it and free him, but nothing said that the stone would not simply settle as she dug or spontaneously topple one way or the other and reduce her to a smear of blood against the cave wall.

The pain burned worse than anything he had experienced, even recovering from his injuries against Alexander. He passed out during that particular event, or at least had mercifully blocked the memory from his own mind. This time, however, he was wide awake for the whole damn thing, and the only thing keeping him from literally writhing in pain was the boulder itself pinning him immobile against the stony ground. Yet the pain was constant, and like the sight of one's nose, he could push it into the background of his awareness after some effort.

"You're," he rasped, then coughed a brick's worth of dust out of his lungs, "you're not going to just blow the damn thing up?"

"Explosives are," Vivian panted, not stopping in her attempts to dig under the mammoth stone, "pinned under another rock." She stopped then, looked up, and tried to force a smile on her face. "I figure if I can free you, we can move that one together and blow our way out of here."

In her fatigue, Vivian had dropped all pretense of whatever character and ploy she had been playing at before. Apollo, even wracked with pain, could read her face clearly. He saw concern, genuine concern for his well-being and not just a concern for a potential asset in the coming conflict. He also saw determination; she was not going to give up on digging just because she had gotten tired and dirty. He had never met her in his life before their encounter at the Night Market, but something in her face told Apollo that her hatred for Duke Charlie was more than KRS business. She had joined the KRS in the first place for this very mission— something had happened to her in the past that pointed her entire life to this spot.

Who was she? Apollo asked himself. Focusing on her let him ignore the pain while his unconscious mind worked to figure out how he would avoid eternity trapped under ten tons of stone.

He studied her face more, fighting at the same time to keep the crashing waves of pain buried. Her features were plain, forgettable unless someone had a reason to remember them—her concern, whether he admitted to it or not, gave him that reason right then. Her eyes were small, set close together, and hard. Her cheekbones were, he thought, somehow recognizable.

It hit him.

"Shit," he grunted. "You're one of them, aren't you?"

Her head whipped around and her eyes narrowed. Suddenly the mask was back and she stopped her work to sit back on her haunches. "One of who?" she demanded coolly.

"Validian," Apollo said, then laughed. "That's why you're so damned hardcore about bringing Londonsberg down."

For a long moment she continued to glare, and Apollo wondered if she was considering leaving him in the cave to fend for himself. Then her features softened almost imperceptibly. The mask remained, but less overt anger seethed from behind it. "So what if I am?" she asked with forced calm, turning back to the small hole in the ground she had made with her hands.

"Nothing," he said, turning his head to look up at the darkened ceiling of the cave. He lay there for several long moments, thinking. The Validians had been conquered by Londonsberg eight years before Apollo and Alexander were born. Everything he could find on the Empire suggested than the war had been territorial, with no underlying causes. If he could call bullshit on a historical essay, he would have, because it was just short of impossible for a citystate like Londonsberg to spring up almost fully formed atop the Validians' grave because of "territory."

A man named Baron Maximus had ruled the Validian Empire in its twilight. Some of the older patrons of Far Market, and especially the Night Market, talked as though they knew him personally, which was entirely possible. Londonsberg had been built on the site of the old Validian capital at the same time as the President-Duke had the few remaining Validian cities, like Bram's Haven, razed.

He was not going to worried about it right then. Perhaps when they were cleaning Charlie's blood off their knives, he would get Vivian to tell her side of the story.

Apollo turned his head back to face her. The even tone in his voice came as a surprise, even to himself. "You realize I'm probably stuck in this damn cave, right?"

"I'll get you out eventually," she said with the same determination he witnessed before her mask went back up. "Besides." She smirked. "It's not like you can starve, right?"

Apollo blanched, at least the sudden chill in his face felt like it had gone pale, anyway. He asked himself what it would mean if she was right, and he could not starve. If, somehow, his ability to heal extended to starvation as well. It meant that he could very well be stuck where he was for a long, long time. Spending the rest of his life until he died of old age pinned under a rock was not something he wanted to consider. In fact, the very idea came as close to frightening him as anything in his entire life had done.

And if he never died of old age? His mind raced. What if the Immaculata's "gift" of healing meant he was effectively immortal as well?

The idea of spending not just one lifetime immobilized in a cave, but potentially eternity in isolated darkness dug up deep seated fears of death and the unknown that he thought to be long buried.

He would never eat or drink again, never work again. Potentially, the sun itself might not be cut off from his eyes forever, but how long would it be until someone uncovered him? Worse, he would never know the comforting warmth of a strong drink, and he could never again feel the rush of holding another's life in his hands and snuffing it out. He had lost all opportunity and freedom in a freak accident.

In effect, Apollo realized, he had been thrown into a waking hell for the rest of what could possibly be an agonizingly long life.

Suddenly, he was terrified. He felt his heart quicken and sweat break out on his face. He felt around for his knife, intending to amputate his own leg to prevent that nightmare from playing out. His fingers tingled with fear-adrenaline and they fumbled at the weapon's hilt once, twice, and then closed around it.

He tried to come to a sitting position, gritting his teeth against pain that seemed to double with every movement. No matter how hard he tried, the boulder had pinned him in such a way that he could not twist his body enough to reach it.

His panic increased, fighting with the pain for the foremost spot in his mind. Surely, he would go insane long before whatever black oblivion that awaited him finally claimed his bloody, damned soul.

His thoughts chased themselves around and around, becoming ever more desperate. Surely, Alexander would find him here just like he had found him at the market. That bastard would spot his aircar, even if it took months, and then search until he found the cave where whatever was left of Apollo waited for death.

Enraged, he screamed, "mother fucker!" and stabbed the knife into the ground at his side with all the strength he had left. It buried itself past the hilt and all the way to the edge of Apollo's hand in the hard dirt.

He twisted again, furiously scrabbling against the ground with his arms and pushing against the boulder with his good leg. By that point, Vivian had backed away, visibly unsure of how to proceed, but she was the least of his concerns at the moment. He cursed again and again and again once more as he pressed with all his strength against the massive rock.

Veins stood out on his neck and face from the effort, and the edges of his vision and even hearing started to go gray and then black as he poured every last ounce of strength he had against ten thousand pounds of ancient stone.

He was afraid for the first time in his life, afraid of what would happen if he could not get that damnable chunk of rock to move even a little bit. Eternity alone in the dark with nothing but his thoughts and his pain to keep him company fueled his terror and opened up a new well of strength he never realized he had.

Somehow, the pressure on his wounded leg lessened slightly. The change was almost unnoticeable amid the pain and effort and fear and hate. Then the pain in his crushed leg spiked to a whole new level of unbelievable intensity, and he realized that it was actually healing and not just struggling ineffectively against the rock.

He roared. Whether from effort or from an entirely new world of white-hot agony, he could not be sure. Effort, pain, fear, and hate all mixed with the euphoric rush of his healing and drowned out his conscious thoughts.

He felt his wounded leg move and forced his eyes open. A fifteen centimeter space—bigger right then than the whole universe—yawned underneath the monolith that had almost been his damnation sentence. From underneath, Vivian hauled a vaguely leg-shaped mass of blood and flesh out. Apollo barely registered the glazed, stupefied look on her face as she got his leg clear of the stone and he scrambled away with his arms.

It crashed down with a thunderous sound, but he was free. He breathed deeply, forcing his racing pulse to slow as he felt the sweat on his forehead chill against the underground air.

Suddenly, he remembered Catherine's cryptic warning. "Pain, fear, and death," she had told him. Pain had been suffering the agony of his first enhanced healing, and surely he had just passed the test of fear.

Apollo came to his feet, unsteady on his still healing leg, but he refused to let the pain and weakness stop him. He limped on the good leg and crossed the dim space to the rock that Vivian indicated earlier. It was much smaller than the one he had been beneath, only a meter and a half on a side. He squatted, grabbing either side of the stone as though it were a simple weight to be lifted. With a grunt, he stood, heaving the thousand pounds of stone to one side. Underneath, mostly crushed by the rock's weight, was the bulk of the gear not kept in their pockets.

"What was that?" Vivian demanded.

"This plan of yours still going to work?" Apollo asked, turning and keeping most of his weight on his good leg. The pain in the other had almost subsided, but the euphoric rush was making it hard to think.

"What the hell was that?" she demanded again.

"That," Apollo replied. "Was the second test. All you need to know is that my fight with Alexander just got a lot more interesting." His head swam, forcing him to pause for a moment before saying, "so, I'll ask again, is this plan going to work?"

She stared for a moment with the same combination of calculation and confusion she displayed when she first watched him heal. Then, with conviction, "yes. It will. The key components were in my jacket pockets when the cave collapsed. If we can get out of here, we can get inside the Limits before sunrise tomorrow."

"Good," Apollo said with a hungry grin.

He turned his attention to the rest of the cave in, and their crushed supplies. Digging through it with Vivian's help, Apollo was able to salvage a few more things. Out of all of it, he was most glad to see that their food, as much as meal bars counted as food, was still mostly whole. Whether or not they tasted like cardboard, they would assuage the hunger that crept up on him in the wake of the overwhelming pain and fear.

Surveying the damage, Vivian spat in the dust at her feet. She gestured bitterly to the parts of the cave-in blocking the entrance to their ruined hideout. "I said, 'if.'"

Apollo came up with meal bar, one intended to be two days worth of calories and nutrients, and took a bite out of one side. He chewed the sugar-covered bitter substance with disdain, glad to have food of some kind.

He pointed at the stone that had crushed his leg. Around a mouthful of processed nutrients, he slurred, "d'you see me move that f'n rock?" As the healing euphoria continued to wash over him, he let out a giddy laugh. "There's no 'if' right now. Right now, I can do anything! Alexander, Duke Charlie, hell, the entire Londonsberg Army had better sleep with one eye open tomorrow night, because I'm coming for them and hell's coming with me."

\*\*\*

After a short bout of digging prolonged by Vivian's cautious insistence that they had no idea what awaited them on the other side—Apollo had intended to simply punch the offending rocks out of the way—Apollo broke through the last of the collapsed stone covering the cave's mouth. As the euphoric high from healing wore off, he found himself agreeing with her caution. An armed Londonsberg air wing was one of the the things he could not fight on his own, probably.

Beyond the cave that had almost been their tomb, the sky remained black. They saw no sign of any patrol cars in the sky, a fact which took a metaphoric ton of weight from their shoulders. Upon further inspection, however, they found that the ground around the entrance had been torn up.

Vivian noticed it first. Apollo was busy gazing skyward, wondering how many more stars would disappear into Londonsberg's light pollution if the city kept them on at night.

"Apollo!" she hissed.

He spun, on edge from the wary tone in her voice. "What?"

She indicated the cave mouth. The stone around it had been blackened or blown away in an irregular pattern. As he approached, he realized that the grass underfoot was no longer grass but crunchy black carbon. Apollo ran a hand over the rocks. Except where they had been blown free, the rock was smooth to the touch.

"The hell did this?" he muttered.

"You've never seen damage like this?"

Apollo looked up sharply, meeting Vivian's eyes. He had not realized he spoke aloud, but now that the words were out, debating their existence was pointless. "No," he admitted. "I haven't."

She ran one hand over the smooth stone. Her fingers probed the spots where it had simply been destroyed, then felt along the glasslike surface again. She tapped on one of the rough spots with a finger. "This was just a weak spot in the stone. Probably something that could have been dislodged with a hammer." She touched one of the smooth spots again. "This, on the other hand, looks like someone hit it with a thermobaric bomb."

Apollo recoiled in surprise, then looked up at the sky again in a panic. "There's nothing up there."

He was not sure if he was trying to convince Vivian or himself.

Her eyes followed his. "I suspect whoever dropped it expected it to do the job."

Apollo growled. He had been upset enough at a natural cave-in. Controlling nature itself was something he never aspired to do. He never wanted that responsibility—too many ways nice days could turn into storms. No one could fight the planet itself. A human being with a fire control switch, on the other hand, was something Apollo could kill.

The unnamed pilot would be back to check on his handiwork, and Apollo had no idea when that would be. If the flyovers could detect them even underground, that left speed as their only remaining option. Apollo said as much out loud, then, "we have to move."

Vivian nodded. "Can you see any better at night?"

"Than what?"

"A normal human."

"I am a nor—no. I know what you're asking, and nothing special has happened to my eyes. All I had was that night vision scope."

"And it was..."

"...in the pack the rock flattened," he finished.

"Of course," she muttered. "Mine, too."

"We'll do it the old-fashioned way," then, Apollo said, dramatically widening his eyes.

Their cave had been a kilometer and a half from the Limits, a distance which they both covered as quickly as possible. The urge was to run at full speed for the Limits and minimize the time spent in open ground. No other caves offered shelter. Even trees and rocks, anything to break sightlines, were few.

By mutual consent, running was out of the question. Instead, they moved between the ever fewer patches of darkness, always looking ahead and behind at the same time, watching for movement from the returning air patrols and the walls both.

After an hour, they made it to the Limits. The great gray face of the City rose hundreds of meters above them, stretching for several klicks as it encircled Londonsberg like a fortress. Nothing happened atop the walls during their approach, and Vivian assured him that they were invisible to the City's passive sensors. The Mirage clothes seemed to be doing the job aided by personal heat sinks and other small KRS devices that survived the cave-in.

She claimed everything with enough sensitivity to detect them through the distortion of their stealth tech was turned inward. The ones that faced the rest of the world, the ones Apollo knew about and the reason they ditched the aircar in the first place, were larger, designed to detect power sources or large groups of invaders.

Apollo stood close enough to touch the monolithic walls, and the tallest of the towers rose even higher. From above, the city would have looked like a dish, with concentric rings of ever smaller towers that tapered to ground level at Londinium Square. At the edge of that flat area, the gleaming obelisk of Duke Charlie's own tower lorded over everything.

As cities went, Londonsberg occupied a rather small plot of land, but the sullen hive of towers had a population that a normal city would have fit into eight or nine times the land area. That was another thing Duke Charlie had insisted upon, "for the City's protection." None of the outer buildings had windows facing outward, either. The effect was stark—great sheets of metal and concrete abruptly rose from the ground, unbroken by doors or windows. Only the President-Duke's tower—likely where Alexander was to be found—could see out past the Limits to the world beyond.

Apollo hated the City. He hated everything about it and everything it represented to the world and to him personally. The City meant the past. The past meant pain, failure. The past meant Alexander as well. For the first time in his life, Apollo felt a pang of sympathy for the people living inside Londonsberg. No one deserved to be caged like that, even people who would mindlessly cheer at every word from the President-Duke's mouth. They would likely die when Kingsmark brought the walls down, assuming Vivian's mission was successful, but Apollo would be long gone by then. What did he care if the common rabble were trampled underfoot?

He watched Vivian work, calibrating the small bundle of electronics she claimed would get them inside the Limits without tripping any alarms. There had been no time for Apollo to learn to use them, so he was content to watch for incoming patrol cars as she worked. He assumed the patrols thought they were dead and would not be looking quite as hard, but that only meant it would be easier for him to spot their aircars. Whoever bombed their cave would sound an alarm as soon as they returned and found the rocks covering the entrance disturbed—assuming they looked that closely.

"Come on." She pocketed the latest of three devices. She pointed off to her left. "Ten meters this way is a door that will get us inside."

Apollo almost stopped to ask, but decided against it. That would give the patrols more time to circle back and spot them. Instead, he asked his question as he followed her. "A door, hidden, unnoticed and you just happen to have the key?"

"Remember when I said we had three days before we *had* to leave your house? This is why."

"If the KRS can do this, why don't you smuggle a whole legion of Marksmen in through it?"

Vivian did not roll her eyes, but the effect was the same. "Because two can sneak in much more easily than a thousand. Plus, well, you'll see."

The spot Vivian indicated seemed to be blank, but she pressed the device she carried against the cold concrete nonetheless. It hummed slightly, the sound an overworked computer might make, and a section of the wall half the side of a door shifted a millimeter.

"In," she hissed, pressing the door inward. It swung silently on hidden hinges. Apollo, bent nearly double, followed. The rough tunnel expanded as they crawled through the thick wall, eventually becoming human-sized at the end.

Vivian turned, pressing the trapezoidal door closed. It slid into place as silently as it opened. It neither clicked nor made any noise at all to signal whether or not the lock had been reengaged, and Vivian took out her device once more and pressed it against the inside. It hummed again, then a small, faint light inside the tangle of wires turned green. Sealed, it was just another section of the wall.

Apollo looked around them as Vivian pocketed the device. They stood in what might have been any one of a thousand identical storage rooms inside the physical structure of the Limits themselves. He was almost impressed, wondering how long it took the KRS to cut a hole in the Limits without anyone noticing.

With a finger over her lips, Vivian drew her pistol and gestured to the room's door with her head. Apollo moved to flank the door opposite her. Latched with a simple metal crash bar and no window, this door gave them a good estimation of how little security to expect.

Slowly, Vivian pressed the bar into the door. The click as the latch disengaged seemed loud as thunder against the silence of the previous half hour, but no alarms sounded.

The corridor beyond was dark, not even lit by emergency light. Typical, Apollo thought. As soon as Legal Night hit and everyone was required by law be at home, there was no need for emergency lighting. Any Black Ties out on "business" would have their own lights.

Vivian knew, or at least seemed to know, where she was going, so Apollo let her lead. He did not want to admit, even to himself, that the dark interior of the Limits reminded him a little too much of his projections of his future trapped under the cold earth for eternity. That memory messed with his ability to think, and he jumped at shadows and random noises. He kept those thoughts in his own head.

After several twists and turns, they came to another door. Apollo tried it with his free hand, but the handle was locked tight and would not wiggle. He strained slightly, and the door creaked. If he pushed a little harder, he knew he could tear it off of its hinges. He held back. Commotion like that would surely bring whatever guards were in the area. Part of his mind did not really care—let them come, he said, that way he could kill them all.

No, the more rational part of his mind argued. They needed to be stealthy as long as possible. That part of his mind won out at as Vivian attached her electronic lock-pick to the door. A few seconds later, much quicker than the exterior doors, the lock clicked and she removed it.

Be reasonable, Apollo, he admonished himself.

He waited until she removed the lock-pick device and tried the door again. This time the handle twisted smoothly in his hand. The door swung away with a quiet creak, revealing a deserted street, dark and ominous with its lack of people. As much as Apollo enjoyed his solitude, the sheer size of the buildings flanking the streets combined with the abject lack of human life made the entire vista seem more like the hell-scape of his imagination than a city.

But he remembered the City. Little had changed, now that he got to look at it. The buildings were—almost—exactly the same. Paint and patches, most applied too expertly to notice unless one knew they were there, held the buildings together like tape on a cheap vase.

He hated the City, but now he had a job to do.

# Chapter 11

Being in the City reminded Apollo why he left in the first place. At his home, hundreds of kilometers away from the oppressive atmosphere of Londonsberg, the nights were dark and quiet. Inside the Limits, however, that same quiet darkness carried an air of crushing weight. It was like something was missing and, rather than taking comfort in the cool stillness, it felt ominous. Apollo felt like there could have been, should have been, armed men lurking in the dark corners around him. Instead there was nothing: no wind, no light, no noise alleviated the sense of walking through a city built for the dead.

He shook the feeling off—too much time in his garden and under the open air. Now, he was back in his element. In the dark, helped by his Mirage jacket, he could move unseen. Yet without the gentle sigh of wind or the constant buzzing of insects, his carefully measured footsteps slammed the ground like thunder. His pulse thudded in his ears and every step he took was measured, carefully paced to move him exactly where he wanted. Still he knew something terrible was lurking just out of sight.

Of course, he thought, if he started feeling like he was at home, or even comfortable, that was when the terrible thing would stop being hypothetical.

The thing that was missing, he realized, was life itself. It was eerie, a bit disturbing, and a significant letdown. He had built the City up in his mind as some sort of hive and now he was here in person only to see the same landscape of absolute blankness he remembered. Without anyone to populate the City, he had come all this way for nothing. He could not question an empty city about his brother's whereabouts.

More distressingly, without people he had nothing upon which to take out his frustration. His fingers itched, longing to feel the kick of a gunshot, the subtle resistance of a knife in flesh. Perhaps, he thought, the empty streets might have been a good thing just then.

He knew he was on edge, and the strange second-guessing voice in his head told him that was good. If he started to feel too self-assured, and someone attacked, Apollo knew he might do something that would ruin their stealth. The voice warned him to avoid fighting. He knew it was right, and he was not sure how to feel about that.

Once the dawn came, he knew the press of the Duke's mockery of civilization would return, but for the time being the City slumbered in coma-like sleep. Vivian's plan would have them off of the streets long before the sun crept over the artificial concrete horizon. Now that he was listening to the quiet reminders in the back of his head, he agreed with her.

"How much time until dawn?" Vivian asked, quietly coming to his side.

Ever since the ordeal in the cave, he had been aware that her concerns extended to more than just their mission together. She had shown genuine concern for his well-being during the cave-in. On Apollo's side, the feeling was unusual, possibly even unpleasant. He wanted her to be invested in the mission, and he had convinced himself that he had to keep her interest in him as a person to do that, but now that it had happened, he was unsure how to proceed.

Whether her feelings were simple self-preservation or something stronger, he could not say. In a way, his own inability to understand what was going on in her head frustrated him more than being unsure how to handle it.

Either way, he had also become acutely aware—given the way in which he had acquired the second of his "enhanced" abilities—of precisely how fragile she and every other human being actually was. If Alexander was even half as strong as Apollo had become, he would have to keep her as far away from him as possible. He knew he had to keep her alive in order to get paid. More to the point, if she died and Kingsmark's invasion failed, the KRS might just decide he was their next target. The President-Duke's Black Ties might have been dangerous, but they were thugs with expensive weapon suites. The Kingsmark Royal Service, on the other hand, was actually dangerous.

Kingsmark could not have known about Alexander's power—even Apollo had not known until that night outside the market. They had unknowingly sent one of their top agents into unfathomable danger and certain death. If the entire KRS was as skilled as Vivian, they might have taken down either Duke Charlie or Alexander, but not both, and certainly not without massive losses. They needed him and he needed Vivian to stay alive long enough to direct the might of Kingsmark against Duke Charlie.

So why, he asked himself again, did the thought of her dying at Alexander's hands genuinely bother him?

He knew he held the cards until Alexander died, at the very least. What would happen after Alexander's death was still up in the air. Most likely, he would turn his back on the whole affair and never look back. He certainly had no intentions of signing on with the KRS, no matter how much they paid him.

Vivian herself, on the other hand, was a different matter. He suddenly had a vision of the two of them, years down the road, traveling not just the planet but all of settled space taking down the sort of bloated dictators that Duke Charlie could only dream of being. It was, he realized, not an unpleasant idea.

"Apollo?" Vivian asked moments later, drawing his attention away from his wandering thoughts.

"Hm?"

"How much time until dawn?"

He glanced down, realizing he had been caught woolgathering. He slipped a hand into an interior pocket in his jacket and withdrew a small silver watch. Of all the weapons and tools that survived the cave-in, he was most pleased that this archaic, spring-driven timepiece came through undamaged. He depressed the stud at the top and checked the ornate face. "Twenty minutes until sunrise. Not that you could tell, surrounded by Duke Charlie's prison walls like this. The sun probably won't be above the walls for close to two hours," he said, then, "there's a little more than an hour until Legal Dawn, though. We want to be long gone before then."

"The Duke's 'police' come out an hour before Legal Dawn, I know," Vivian replied. "The flyovers are bad enough. I don't particularly want to meet a team of Black Ties before the sun rises."

Apollo grinned, teeth flashing in the predawn gloom. "Not scared, are you?"

"Not of them, no," she retorted, insulted. Hastily, she added, "even without you here, a team of Charlie's thugs wouldn't do much more than put me off my breakfast. What I don't want to happen is for them to know we're here."

"Not until you show up unannounced at the Duke's tower and put a bullet in his brain, anyway," Apollo replied with a slight chuckle.

"What do you mean 'you?'" Vivian asked with a raised eyebrow.

"I mean you, not me." He spoke quickly, hoping to drown his earlier thoughts in a sea of uncaring revenge. He was partially successful. "I don't particularly care if he lives or dies, personally. He's just another body biding its time until something makes it stop functioning. I'd kill him as soon as anyone else in this concrete hell. But you," he turned a half-turn to face Vivian where she stood. Pointing a finger at her chest, he continued, "to you, killing him means something."

She smiled, but it quickly turned venomous. With the same strange mix of implied violence and joy he heard in his own voice, she gave a simple, "thank you."

Let the Validian get revenge for her people, he told himself, ignoring the implication that he was doing a personal favor for Vivian because he wanted to. He cared about the Validian Empire slightly more than he cared about Londonsberg only because they were gone before his birth and he had no reason to actively dislike them.

He turned a ghost of a smile in her direction. "I'm just here to get you in the door and kill the watchdog. A watchdog that, I might add, would crush you without a second thought. So you need to lay low until I tell you he's dead, understand?"

Vivian looked like she was about to object, but then her mouth closed. Apollo could see her replaying his healing and strength in her mind. Then she seemed to remember that Alexander was just as strong, and nodded once in agreement.

She promised she would be ready, then asked, "what's the signal?"

Apollo shook his head. "No idea. That depends on how long it takes me to track Alexander down and kill him." He smirked. "It'll be obvious."

"I'll keep an eye out."

He turned toward her again, facing her fully this time. "Now. I meant what I said about Alexander. You stay the hell away until it's time for your part of this, alright?"

She turned the same smirk on him that he showed moments before. "I didn't know you cared."

He narrowed his eyes, but the corners of his mouth turned up slightly anyway. "I don't," he lied, "but if you die, then I don't get paid. So you're going to stay nice and safe until it's time for you to ride in like the cavalry and open the doors for the rest of your people."

"Tomorrow."

"No."

"Yes, tomorrow," she repeated, more forcefully this time. "The Black Ties are going to be taking to the street in a few minutes. If we get caught, we'll have to wade through a pile of bodies to get where we're going. And I don't think you want that."

"Ordinarily, I'd start burning this place down first thing. Hell, I'd probably make that part of the plan. Kill enough people, blow up enough property, the watchdog comes out of hiding, and I kill him. Then you call in the KRS, sweep this damnable place off the map, and we go home."

She missed, or ignored, his choice of pronoun and asked, "so what's the problem?"

"This is going to take a while."

"I thought you had a plan."

Apollo make an expansive gesture at the City around them. "Again, unless you want me to go Dresden on this place, it's going to take a bit of work to even pick up his trail. Then," Apollo added, ticking off a point on his fingers, "we have to figure out how to lure him, just him, out without alerting the rest of the City, and," he trailed off as she interrupted him.

Vivian laughed and held up a hand. "I get it. That actually makes it easier on me, too. The longer you take, the more time I have to set up..." She paused, grinned. "...*surprises* for the Londonsberg military when the time comes."

"Anything worth doing is worth doing right," Apollo said, temporarily taking on a haughty, if mockingly haughty, air.

"To be honest, I'm surprised you're *not* chomping at the bit to burn the City down."

"I never said that," he retorted. Again, he felt the itch in his fingers. "I want to see this place on fire, cleanse it as 'your people' would say, but I'm not going to rush it. I'm a lot of shitty things, but hasty is not one of them."

"True enough." She nodded. "Anyway, we need to get off the street."

"You have a place in mind." It was not a question.

"Several, actually. Believe it or not, we didn't go into this blind. The KRS has been planning this for close to a decade."

"But you never heard about Alexander?" Apollo demanded, incredulous. If the mission had been planned quickly, in a matter of weeks or even months, he supposed the KRS could have been that ignorant.

"We'd heard about him, sure." She sounded defensive, and probably really was this time. "After all, Duke Charlie made damn sure every Euronord speaking country and state for ten thousand kilometers saw the broadcast where he unveiled that statue."

"I'm going to take some special pleasure in shooting that damnable thing full of holes," Apollo growled. "Small caliber holes, too. That way I can shoot it more times."

"Anyway," she continued not sparing more than a momentary grin at his bloodthirsty comment, "none of our intel said anything about him other than what was publicly available. He's a hero, according to official propaganda, but nothing suggested that he was anything more than a highly skilled soldier."

Apollo grimaced, thinking. "It's probably a safe bet that even the Duke doesn't know what Alexander really is. He probably just gives him a grocery list of people to kill and problems to solve, then sits back and eats peeled grapes while Alexander does his work."

"Sounds like the life you might want for yourself," Vivian needled.

Apollo glared sidelong at her for a moment. Alexander did have the blank check that Apollo always wanted, but he would not be able to stand working for someone like Duke Charlie. The Immaculata were far better masters, he thought, then added with surprising mental haste, no, the Immaculata were far better allies.

No one but Apollo was master over Apollo's life.

Still, the Immaculata's authority was not something he could disregard. That line of thinking was at the root of Alexander's betrayal. Apollo knew he was walking a thin line of logic, but the fact remained that the Immaculata were better than any mortal authority.

Yes, he reflected, that was a much better term because he was not doing their bidding like a dog, like Alexander had done until he went mad. Authority meant power, even power over him, but not absolute control. Apollo did what they asked because their wishes were aligned.

"Perhaps," he said at length. "But I don't fancy doing it for this City. My reasons are private." After a pause, he added layering disgust thick in his voice, "there's not enough green here."

Vivian was silent for several long moments, during which Apollo's tension slowly grew under her analyzing gaze. She tilted her head, more like she was analyzing a particularly stubborn piece of electronics than a human being. Once again, he felt like she was dissecting him, or at least his mind and motives, with her eyes. Being undressed by someone's eyes was somewhat less pleasant when the undressing went straight to his soul. Finally, she said, "you were born here, weren't you?"

"That's got nothing to do..."

"That's why you hate this place," she supplied.

He glared. She was troublingly perceptive, a trait that had already earned her his suspicion more than once. After holding her eyes for a second, he said with his voice somewhere between an angry growl and a suspicious probe, "I thought the KRS knew who I was."

"The KRS has files on you," she corrected. "What I said was that I knew who you are, and..."

Footsteps.

"Damn it!" Apollo hissed between clenched teeth. "We screwed around out here for too long."

"Follow me and don't make a damn sound," Vivian whispered, equally quiet.

To his credit, or so he told himself, he did as she ordered. He moved immediately, staying no more than three steps behind Vivian at any time. As they crept through the streets, her training in the KRS grew steadily more apparent. From Apollo's perspective, it was obvious that her training extended to more than fighting and using fancy gadgets. She made even less sound than he did and, despite looking right at her, more than once Vivian melded into a shadow so completely that Apollo almost lost sight of her.

She moved with catlike grace, and Apollo cursed the necessity that forced the loose-fitting Mirage jackets on them both. He suspected that underneath the advanced shadow camouflage, her skin and muscles were moving with the same taut grace he found so appealing their first night together.

Briefly, he wondered if seduction was part of the standard KRS training regimen for agents like her. She managed to keep herself in his thoughts, if not at the forefront then at least somewhere off to the side, for some time now.

"In," she ordered, unceremoniously ushering Apollo through a waist-high door in the side of a building.

A small cleaning drone, currently shut down, occupied the majority of the space. Chemicals and tools left enough space for a single very small person to hide. Neither Apollo nor Vivian were terribly small, which left little room for either of them to do much more than breathe after she shut the outer door.

"This is your idea of a good hiding place?" Apollo demanded in a quiet voice. The space was so cramped that he could not even enjoy having Vivian's body pressed against his. Bones, weapons, and tech all pressed into his flesh. He suspected things were no more comfortable on her side, either.

"This is as good as we get for the moment," Vivian hissed. With as much of a head movement as she could manage, she retorted, "do you want to get caught by them?"

Apollo growled. "You know what? I wish they would catch us. That way we can kill our way through Duke Charlie's little police force rather than sneaking around."

"I thought you were patient," she snapped.

"I'm trapped like a fucking rat. That's trying my patience just a bit."

"It's just for a few minutes. Just until the patrols pass. You'll get your chance, Apollo."

The footsteps passed by outside. Several minutes later, they returned. This time, they went slowly down the alley where Apollo and Vivian were hidden. Whoever was outside was not patrolling and the citizenry would not be out on the streets this early.

That only left one option.

Apollo swore as the door hissed open and brilliant artificial light spilled into the tiny space. He could see a pair of black-clad legs but nothing else.

"In the name of President-Duke Charlie Maxwell, I order whoever is in there to come out," the man attached to the pair of legs announced.

They froze until the Black Tie spoke again. "Six-Six-One-Seven requesting permission to deploy nerve agent three." A pause, then, "understood. Denied, yes. Understood. Agent two cleared? Understood."

Louder, he announced, "you have ten seconds to show yourself."

Apollo glared daggers at Vivian. Neither of them could move very quickly and he would have to wait until she was completely out before exiting himself. Watching her stiffly crawl from their makeshift hiding place, Apollo suddenly realized that the Black Tie outside had no idea two people had been in the tiny cubbyhole.

He could simply wait for the door to close again and abandon Vivian to whatever fate Duke Charlie's secret police reserved for agents of enemy governments. Seconds passed, during which the Black Tie questioned Vivian mercilessly, before Apollo made a decision. He refused to allow the Black Tie to endanger her—or endanger his paycheck, he told himself, ignoring the cold feeling in his gut when the thought of the Black Tie dragging her away shot through his brain.

Stealth be damned, he thought, this was something he could fix.

Apollo grabbed a small piece of sheet metal from the cleaning drone's stock and, using his knife, roughly sketched the word 'MOVE' on the piece of metal. Apollo shifted around, getting his knees and feet under him as much as he could in the close confines. Knife in one hand, he slid the metal with its etched warning out through the still open door with the other.

He heard footsteps outside, lighter than the Black Tie's had been on his approach, and he braced against what passed for the ceiling of the tiny space.

Apollo pushed, pressing upward and outward against the wall overhead. Whatever the source of energy that gave him his incredible strength was, it seemed to have no limit on use. The steel directly above him buckled and shattered and the wall exploded outward in a shower of bricks and wiring.

Blowing through the wall also propelled Apollo's shoulder into the Black Tie's torso. He sailed across the alley and into the opposite wall. He had felt little resistance, meaning he missed the man's ribs, but the blow to the stomach and subsequent impact against his spine stunned him well enough.

The Black Tie opened his mouth, whether to scream or to actually say something Apollo had no idea. Either way, the attempt was cut off as Apollo drove his knife point-first into the side of the secret policeman's neck and sliced his throat open.

The Black Tie fell to the pavement, twitching, but making no sound. Apollo stood over the corpse, staring into his eyes as the light slowly went out. It felt good.

"You idiot!" Vivian snapped. "Just what the hell were you thinking?"

Apollo eyed her without blinking. Every part of her was in perfect focus. Every action seemed to be slowed down. "I was thinking that you would be grateful that I saved your life."

"Saved my life?" she retorted. "I was about to kill him. But I was going to do it fucking quietly!"

Apollo pointed at her with the knife. Every word came out with careful measure and ultimate precision. Ice turned to fire as he spoke. "Black Tie communication gear works inside Londonsberg's NoTech zones. They know someone's here. You can bet the Ties have already sent backup! We didn't have time for your to play with your food!"

When she replied, it was clear every bit of control she had went to keep her from yelling. "They're going to call a fucking manhunt. I swear to all the gods, Apollo, if you've fucked this up..."

"Devil take," he snapped, then stopped. His knife was still in his hand, the textured handle biting into his palm hard enough that his regenerative ability was trying to kick in. He stared at it for a moment then dropped it to the ground with a feeling someone else would have called disgust.

He stood there, doing nothing but breathing for several moments as the crystal edges of reality dulled back to normalcy. "We don't have anything to worry about."

Vivian glared, but the moment he took to calm himself seemed to have helped her as well. "Apollo, if he's seen my face, so has his camera."

Apollo frowned, stepped over the rubble, and grabbed silk neckwear that gave the Black Ties their name. He almost used his enhanced strength to rip it off, decided against it, and undid the knot so that he could stuff the entire tie in his pocket.

"There. Video is stored locally. Now none of the witnesses can talk."

Truthfully, he cared more about the symbolism than the practicality just then.

Vivian continued to frown. "And the 'backup?' Just what the hell do you think it's going to do to our mission to have Black Ties searching for us?"

Apollo took another deep breath, held it, and then let it out. The urge to explode again was there, but with effort he forced it down. "People murder Black Ties more frequently than you'd think."

"And they always find the person responsible," Vivian snapped. "We've never seen the Black Ties fail at tracking someone down."

"The propaganda machine here is very good."

"Meaning?"

"If they don't find the actual person responsible, they find someone who they 'prove' is an 'enemy of the people' and make him disappear." Apollo pantomimed being hung from a noose. "Give them a few days and we'll be fine."

Before she could say anything, Apollo continued. "Next you're going to ask me how I know that. Well," he let out a dark, quiet laugh. "Let's just say I was a 'person of threat' long before I relocated to Visegrad."

Vivian's eyes went wide with surprise that slipped through her control. "The Nightmare."

Apollo nodded once, carefully concealing the urge to spit at the mention of hearing that name.

"And how are you going to explain this?" She gestured to the rubble from the smashed wall.

Apollo shrugged, then withdrew a small brick of gray clay from a sealed pouch in his jacket pocket. Wires and a small control box came out of another pocket, all of which he assembled with only slightly less ease than he was used to. He placed the explosive near the center of his destruction, set the timer for five minutes and stepped away.

"The chips all have Rhineland stamps on them," he explained, answering a question she had not asked.

Vivian made a noise that was part sigh and part growl. "Fine, just follow me and try not to do anything else stupid."

He took a breath, reminding himself that he had to be patient. Especially now, he thought with a grimace, wondering what idiocy drove him to cause such obvious destruction. They had a dead body on their hands and a crumbling building facade that marked the scene of their crime—both mere minutes after he had expounded on the need for patience.

The City was getting under his skin, making him jumpy. That was the problem, he decided. For the time being, he sank back into himself, letting her lead again.

***

The nearest of Vivian's safe houses was three blocks away. Hidden inside an electronics repair shop, or an electronics parts store that desperately wanted to be a repair shop, waited a hidden vault.

No one was in the shop, which Apollo found very fortunate. The two of them could not exactly sneak into a hidden room together without being caught. Vivian's face might not be plastered on wanted boards across Londonsberg or ingrained in the populace's mind, but that would not stop word of their passage from reaching sensitive ears. Especially, he reminded himself for the tenth time in as many minutes, now that he had left the first dead body in their wake.

In the back of a cabinet in the employee's section was a hidden switch that operated a complicated lock. That lock sealed up an entire hotel-like suite behind a foot thick wall. The shop's blueprints, Vivian told him, showed it as part of the HVAC system for the building of which the shop was only a small part. In reality, despite having no windows or access to the outside world, it was rather comfortable.

The bed occupied the bulk of the space. What was left had been filled by a small table and chairs that combined areas for work and eating, and a tiny kitchen. A bathroom with what might generously be called a shower had been set into one corner behind a curtain.

Every cabinet door had been padded and the bed sat directly on the floor. Nothing in the tiny suite could have made noise.

"It's fully stocked," Vivian assured him as Apollo poked through cabinets full of Londonsberg military field rations. "It's not as nice as the KRS usually provides, but we had to make everything look like a secret Londonsberg bunker."

Apollo let out a small laugh. "Sure. Next secret mission, we should go to Dresden-Pilsen. Their bunkers come with butlers."

Vivian laughed, smothering the sound behind her hand. Away from the oppressive towers that flanked the streets, both of them were already relaxing.

"Neither of us should go out during the day," Apollo observed, continuing to peruse the cabinets.

"We're probably going to have no other choice," she countered.

Apollo paced. "You don't get it." He stopped and turned to regard her levelly. "*I* can't go out during the day. Not here."

Vivian cocked an eyebrow and made a, "continue," gesture with her hand.

"Because." He stopped. "Who is the one person in this City you would expect everyone to recognize?"

Her reply was immediate. "Duke Charlie."

"Perhaps," Apollo agreed with a shrug. "Describe him for me."

Vivian hummed. "Expensive suit. Gray hair," she hummed again. "No beard, but beady eyes and..."

"...and you just described every man over the age of sixty in this City," Apollo finished.

"Your point?" She asked crossly.

"Describe Alexander for me."

"What?"

"What does Alexander, this City's so-called 'Hero' look like?"

Over the following minute, Vivian proceeded to describe not only Alexander's face, but his build and general bearing completely. Her description was complete enough, and accurate enough, that any competent sketch artist could have drawn a perfect picture from her words alone. Not many people would have fit her description, either. Alexander possessed high cheekbones and a narrow chin. In men less accustomed to killing, his features might have seemed elfin, almost frail.

"Exactly," Apollo grunted once she was done. "You and damn near everyone else drawing breath in this concrete jungle would know him at a hundred meters. And need I remind you that Alexander's brother is one of the most wanted people in all of Londonsberg?" He paused for a heartbeat, then swept his bangs to one side in mimicry of Alexander's hairstyle. Apollo growled. "Alexander's *twin* brother?"

She narrowed her eyes in annoyance not at him, but at herself for missing such an obvious problem with her plan. The expression passed in a moment, gone before Apollo could capitalize on it. "Point made. You only go out at night."

"We both only go out at night."

She thought for a moment. Apollo watched her roll things around in her brain for a minute, judging and rejudging the situation from a hundred different angles. Finally, she nodded, agreeing. "But that means we have to move twice as fast once the alerts die down."

"That won't take long." He said. A moment passed and he simply added, "Vivian?"

Even he was not sure what was in his tone of voice, but whatever it was made her sit up and take notice. She arched an eyebrow, waiting for him to continue.

"I apologize," he said. "For earlier. I made a mistake, let my temper get the better of me."

"You apologize?"

He grit his teeth. This was harder than he expected. "Yes. I'm not sorry, which I suppose is part of the problem, but I do apologize."

Vivian nodded. A smile crept across her face. "Apology accepted."

Apollo let out a breath and, with it, a lot of his tension. "So now we sleep. And for the next three days?"

"We plan. Hell, we've got three days, we can catch up on our reading for all it matters ultimately."

He grinned. "Don't tell me one of your trashy romance novels survived the cave in."

"How did you?" Vivian demanded, then stopped. "When did you go through my bag?"

Apollo laughed. "I haven't, but I might now!"

Vivian let out a long sigh that turned into laughter. "Gods, you're a pain."

"I'm practicing on you," he said, continuing his perusal of the cabinets.

"On me?"

"Of course. If I can frustrate a highly-trained KRS agent, dealing with this City is going to be a walk in the park."

"If it had parks."

Apollo stopped. "Parks have been banned," he said with a straight face that turned into a bad movie-villain sneer. "For your protection."

Vivian laughed, a sound that sent a strange feeling down Apollo's spine. He was so unused to appreciating another person's presence that, for a moment, he had no idea what it was. It lasted for several seconds before being broken by the next thing she said.

"Apollo." A waver in her voice set off warning sirens in his mind that threatened to shatter the moment of good feelings. "You're not the only one who has something to apologize for."

The latter part of that opening confession finished the process, and a wall of crystal came down between his mind and the rest of the world. He frowned, head tilting to one side in automatic reflex.

He leaned against the cabinets and folded his arms, doing his best to project a sense of relaxation that he in no way felt. The tension that settled between his eyes and on his forehead told him that it was wasted effort, but he was going to try anyway. Apollo owed it to himself, and to Vivian, to keep things under control.

"When we met, that wasn't my first visit to the Night Market."

Apollo frowned. "I knew that. You and Sal knew each other."

"The KRS has been watching you for some time, Apollo."

His frown deepened. She was working her way around to something, but he could not yet tell what. "You already told me that."

"It was my task to watch you."

His patience thinned, but still Apollo kept a handle on things. "Bull. I never saw you."

"That was by design."

"I found you easily enough the other day."

Now it was her turn to frown. "I wanted you to, Apollo. Why do you think I brought an unusual car? It put you on alert. I came at a later hour, when the crowds were thin, and I stayed longer than anyone else. Jamie is quite excited about the carbine you built her, by the way."

Apollo narrowed his eyes, but everything else stayed carefully still. "And how long did you follow me?"

"That night, or..."

"All together."

"A year."

Jamie commissioned him to make her gun slightly less than a year ago, Apollo realized. As the months went on, her ability to pass messages and use coded language constantly improved. He thought she had been working with Sal but, while that was still a possibility, it now seemed obvious that Vivian had been training her for some time.

He found himself torn between anger and appreciation, a state that Vivian seemed to elicit more often than he wanted to admit. He knew she was good at her job, but exactly how good had remained nebulous until just then. For her to have spent a year tailing him, likely building a profile, and for her to have done so with Jamie and Sal's assistance all without Apollo noticing a thing was impressive.

It was also incredibly frustrating and left at least one question unanswered.

"Why?"

"Why you or why me?"

"Both."

She walked past him, and Apollo was acutely conscious of how close she came doing so, to take a bottle of liquor from the cabinet. From the other side of their small suite, he had not been aware of the tension in her shoulders, but from so close it was as obvious as his own. It did not put him at ease in the least, but knowing she was as uncomfortable as he was came as something of a comfort.

Vivian left a glass of deep brown liquor on the counter next to Apollo and took the other back to the table where she had been sitting. Before answering, she took a long drink from her glass, a moment which Apollo used to do the same.

Brandy, he thought as the sharp aroma hit his nostrils. Not his favorite, but it would do.

She said four words—one profession, one place, one article, and one preposition. Despite the simplicity, her statement his Apollo like a hammer.

"The Butcher of Novarus."

He froze for half a moment, then his eyes flicked upward, away from his drink, and locked on Vivian. Apollo unfolded his arms, set the glass on the counter beside him without looking away from her, and took a step forward.

The words came out one at a time. "What. Did. You. Say."

Other than setting her own glass on the table, Vivian did not move. She knew what sort of monster he was and still sat there with her eyes locked on him. Carefully, slowly, she repeated, "the Butcher of Novarus."

"Bitch!" he snapped before he could stop the epithet.

Vivian pushed her chair away from the table and took a step toward him. Apollo came closer and Vivian matched his every step with one of her own. She continued advancing through "threat range" and well into "grappling range" before Apollo himself stopped.

"This is why they sent me, Apollo," she said, still staring directly into his eyes.

"This what?" he growled.

"This!" she retorted. "I bring up something from your past which Kingsmark was, and is, very concerned about and you threaten me."

His voice came out carefully measured and level. Despite that tight control, he felt like he was watching himself have this conversation. "I've not threatened you."

"Haven't you?" Her eyes never broke from his, but a slight downward movement of her chin drew Apollo's attention. He broke eye contact with a feeling like a snapping bowstring, and looked down. Both hands remained at his side, but they had curled into tight fists without his notice.

Apollo would not back down. He could not back down. He could move literal mountains with his hands. Backing down was not something he did.

Yet Vivian, ostensibly unarmed, continued to defy him from close enough that he could have simply extended a hand and touched her. Catherine had done the same thing that night when he had too much to drink and it had the same effect now. Apollo was no longer the same broken man he had been that night and he would not be cowed by anyone.

Against his better judgment, he reached out and took both of her shoulders in his hands. He felt the muscle there, the bone. He felt the joints creak as they moved under his hands, and he knew with just a little more pressure he could turn them to pulp.

A flash of pain so minor and brief that he barely saw it flitted at the edge of her eyes, but Vivian gave no other indication of distress. Her eyes narrowed then and she repeated herself. "The Butcher of Novarus."

Apollo glared. He tried to squeeze, but his hands would not move. Instead, he ground his teeth together and asked the same question again. "Why?"

"You're unpredictable, Apollo. The KRS needed to know what would happen when we moved against Duke Charlie."

He took a long, deep breath and stepped away. As before, she mimicked his movements, taking a single step backward. He ran a hand over his head, disturbing his hair. Disgust came though in his voice. "The KRS thought I would fight to defend this City?"

"We weren't sure. Some of my superiors thought you might consider Londonsberg to be 'yours' and would defend it against us." The motion that started as a shrug ended with a wince and a roll of her shoulders. "So they sent me."

Apollo turned his back on her and made his way back to the drink she poured. With it in hand, he crossed his legs at the ankles and sank smoothly to the floor. By that point, Vivian had already resumed her seat at the table and taken her own drink in hand again.

He downed the brandy in a long swallow. "So," he said. "Why you?"

Vivian laughed, though her eyes were focused elsewhere for the first time in several minutes. "I was chosen," she said, then waved expansively. Her voice changed, becoming what Apollo assumed was a mockery of her KRS superior. "for the 'honor of investigating a potential war asset and, if possible, leveraging it against Londonsberg.'"

Apollo scoffed. "'It.'"

"Bureaucratic bullshit is a language all its own."

He made a noise that was almost a laugh, then, "I suppose some things are universal. And if I refused?"

"Termination," she replied, and Apollo surged to his feet automatically. He forced himself to stay calm, however, and leaned against the counter. His empty drink glass lay forgotten at his feet.

"They didn't realize how difficult that would be," she continued. "If, that is, they considered it all."

"I wouldn't kill you," he confessed, wondering where that sentiment came from even as he said it. It would have been simpler to express an ordinary reassurance that he, "wasn't going to," versus stating unequivocally that he would not.

"*I* know that, but that consideration never crossed my superior's desk."

"Explain."

"Oh, Apollo," she said with a derisive laugh. "They didn't send me because I was the best. They sent me to get me out of their hair. 'Send the Validian bitch to Londonsberg.'"

"You sound like they expected you to fail." Apollo wondered where the sudden flash of anger came from.

Vivian shrugged. "I'm sure they did. I can't say I'm disappointed in how it's turned out, at least."

"No, neither can I." He was silent for a minute before starting to speak again. Apollo opened his mouth once, shut it, then opened it again a few seconds later. Before he could change his mind, the unfamiliar sentiment came out again. "I'm sorry."

Vivian smiled enigmatically. "I know."

Neither of them spoke again for several minutes. When Apollo broke the silence, it was to confess hunger. With sparse conversation, they made a reasonable dinner out of the safe house's rations. Still feeling the after-effects of the ordeal in the cave, Apollo ate voraciously.

Hunger temporarily sated, Apollo dropped into the mattress that served as their bed. It proved comfortable enough to let the muscles in his back relax. He lay there, eyes closed and lost in his own meditative thoughts, while Vivian continued to work. Eventually she put her tablet down, killed the light, and slipped into bed next to him.

Some time after Vivian's breathing evened out, Apollo's mind made the transition from meditation to true sleep. Then the nightmares came.

# Chapter 12

President-Duke Charlie Maxwell regarded the man in front of him with a calculating gaze. The man, a ranking General of the Black Tie Enforcers, shifted front foot to foot. With any other person, he would have been the man behind the desk doing the intimidating. Standing there, Charlie could see precisely how uncomfortable the reversal in power made his General.

Good, he thought. Let it remind him where his uniform came from in the first place.

He regarded his General for another drawn-out moment. The Black Tie General stood tall, dark-skinned, and—despite Duke Charlie's unwavering stare—with a proud grace. Any other man would have been intimidated by being in the same room as the President-Duke, but not him.

Charlie folded his hands on his desk and smiled. The President-Duke was an unassuming man whose black hair had been shot through with silver for years. His eyes were set close together, so close in fact that they went past, "intimidating," and all the way to, "nearly cross-eyed jeweler."

He also held all the power in the world, so far as he was concerned. Between his military, the Black Ties, and his NoTech—handed down by the gods themselves, no less!—Duke Charlie knew no one stood against him. Alexander's "services" only added to his power base. Duke Charlie never pried into how his prized Captain did his job—he was satisfied that that whatever job he gave him was done at a moment's notice.

Until now, the President-Duke thought, crossly. He did not allow that frustration to show on his face, instead turning a full-face smile toward his general. Charlie's deep voice held an edge, however, that never touched any of his features. "Alexander is *where*?"

"He's in space, sir," the Black Tie repeated. Duke Charlie's glare seemed to take some off his height, but he still stood tall. "He commandeered the *Helios* this morning, sir, telling the ground crew he was on a personal mission directly from you."

Duke Charlie frowned in a momentary display of displeasure that dropped the apparent temperature of the room several degrees. He owned two space-capable vehicles: the *Helios* and the *Ra*. So far as he knew, he not only possessed two working spacecraft, but he possessed two out of only six working spacecraft within ten thousand kilometers. He used them exactly once, shortly after founding Londonsberg. The *Ra,* smaller and less extravagant, flew alongside as the *Helios* ferried him personally to the space station at Lagrange Point number 4.

Located at one of the two stable Lagrange points, the installation known colloquially as "L4" was one of two built before the Burning War. The destruction of its companion station at L5 during that war prompted the proto-government of L4 to adopt an approach of militant isolationism in regards to Earth. That policy kept it intact and it had acquired an almost mythic reputation since.

His trip to L4 had been for show, to capitalize on that reputation. He wanted the world to know that he, Duke Charlie of Londonsberg, was not afraid of space. It had worked, in its time, and since then the two ships had been on display, maintained by the Office of History and Solidarity. The Black Ties staffing the OHS had kept the ships "ready for liftoff" for a decade, but the President-Duke had never needed them.

"And where, General Carenco, did Captain Alexander take the *Helios*?"

"He told the ground crew that you had given orders for him to, and I quote, 'take care of some issues that have arisen on L4.'"

"I gave no such order."

"I apologize, sir. It was my responsibility to verify that..."

Duke Charlie waved him to silence. "No, no. You knew that my standing orders were that Alexander was to have free reign of the City so long as he did not interfere with the safety of the population. You had no reason to suspect otherwise."

"Thank you, sir. Should we prep the *Ra* to pursue him?"

Duke Charlie knew how effective Alexander was, though he had no idea why. He was strongly tempted to send a platoon of his best to bring Alexander back so that he could question him in person. Had he been anyone else, the President-Duke probably would have done just that. Alexander had always shown a competence that even the best Black Ties lacked, and Duke Charlie suspected that he had a reason for visiting L4 suddenly.

The recording devices in Alexander's quarters, usually only privy to illegal deals with corrupt Black Ties or conversations between Alexander and whomever he was bedding that night, gave him another piece of the puzzle. His prized champion was hunting someone, or a group of someones. More to the point, whoever he was after had gotten Alexander's blood boiling worse than Charlie had seen in years.

He made it a priority to have a chat with Alexander about forging orders when the man returned. On his own authority, Alexander could have seized the *Helios* and traveled to L4, and Duke Charlie wanted to know why he told the ground crew otherwise.

He shook his head, realizing that the General was waiting for his reply. "No," he said. "Alexander will return eventually. I will," he paused, "speak to him at length when he does so."

"And," General Carenco ventured, "if he does not return to Londonsberg when he lands?"

"Then the world will know my displeasure," Duke Charlie said. His voice was a low growl, not at all like the dulcet, honeyed tones he used when addressing his people. His tone abruptly shifted. "But I don't think that will be an issue. Alexander is loyal, perhaps to a fault. Perhaps it's his only fault. But he will be back, and when he is, I will get the answers I want from him."

General Carenco nodded. "Is there anything else, sir?"

When the President-Duke answered, his voice was just as neutral as it would have been to order lunch. A ghost of a smile crossed his features, one that did not extend past a slight movement of his lips. Carenco shifted uncomfortably again—he had seen that expression before, and the consequences always took lengthy cleanup.

"The 'secret' door installed by the Kingsmark Royal Service in the South-by-Southeastern octant was opened last night. Please place the City under silent alert."

"Yes, sir."

"You're dismissed, General."

"Sir," he replied, saluted, and turned for the door.

As the General left the room, Duke Charlie turned back to the issue that had occupied his attention before Carenco's arrival and subsequent addition to his day's annoyances. Perimeter Security's report simply stated that the KRS's door had been opened for a few moments. Any more information would have required enough surveillance equipment to tip their hand. The last time that happened, Kingsmark simply stopped using the door they made in the northern face of the Limits and Perimeter Security spent two years tracking down the new one.

Truthfully, General Carenco's visit had been fortuitous. Duke Charlie was minutes away from contacting him and ordering an alert anyway. Doing it in person simply encouraged the General to convey the importance of the order.

Normally, the violation of Londonsberg grounds by KRS agents was nothing of note. The news came to him, he passed it to the Black Ties, and the enemy agent would be rounded up within a short few days. With Alexander missing, however, the President-Duke found himself suffering from a distinct, if faint, feeling of dread.

Perhaps, he thought, the military itself might be placed on alert as well. That task was much easier than dealing with the Black Ties. He typed out a simple written message to alert the officers in charge of Londonsberg's regulars and shuffled that problem to the back of his mind.

That left the issue of Alexander's whereabouts. L4 maintained an independent government. Organizing his trips there had been a nightmare politically, and the right to broadcast from those stations cost more than it had to get him there in the first place. Between the station's isolationism and his inability to properly project power into space, his diplomatic options were limited.

He could not demand that L4 simply turn Alexander over as a fugitive, should he elect not to return. Neither could he launch the *Ra* and take L4 by force. Its vast arsenal of defensive weaponry dated back to before the Burning War and worked quite well. If it came to negotiations, he hoped the philosopher kings wanted something easier to produce than a hundred kilograms of rare plant seeds this time. At least he was not visiting in person and could not be "encouraged" to attend another week long symposium—could he?

Duke Charlie had no desire to see the *Ra* destroyed a hundred million kilometers short of its destination. If a similar fate befell Alexander, Charlie would be quite put out. The loss of not one but two valuable assets would be a blow to the City. No doubt Kingsmark would see it as an invitation—as would Rhineland and the DPR, assuming they could put aside their differences long enough.

The only positive aspect of the long communication lag between Earth and L4 was that it gave him plenty of time to craft his messages. One of his staff mathematicians could calculate how long Alexander would take to reach the station, then calculate the exact time lag required to get a message back to Earth. Duke Charlie would give him exactly six hours longer than that before he himself contacted L4.

He needed two messages ready. If he could announce Alexander's departure and place a positive spin on things, the morale boost it generated might just be worth the headache Alexander was causing him. On the other hand, if L4 destroyed the *Ra*, the problem would fix itself.

He smiled as he picked up his pocket comm and entered the code to contact the Office of Public Image. Yes, he thought, this might actually work out for the best.

*** 

Vivian was still asleep when Apollo woke. He sat in the perfect darkness of their hideout for some time, watching as his eyes created shapes and colors out of nothingness. Ethereal echoes from his dreams danced in front of his eyes, refusing to be banished now that he was awake. His ears rang with the sounds of imagined gunfire and screams, despite the perfect silence around him.

He held his head in trembling hands. The nightmares had been worse this time. Perhaps his proximity to Alexander was doing it somehow. Apollo wondered if the power to influence dreams was part of the Immaculata's package. Maybe that was why they were worse right after he watched Duke Charlie unveil that obscene statue of the City's "Hero."

If that was the case, then all he had to do was kill Alexander. Apollo dwelled on that for a moment before chastising himself.

"Focus," he muttered. Alexander had nothing to do with it, he added silently.

A few minutes more spent staring into the blackness of their windowless room gave him no more insights. Perhaps, he thought, the dreams continued because his psyche was damaged beyond repair or salvation. He dreamed of blood and death, fire and slaughter, exactly as he always had on nights when oblivion mercilessly eluded him.

This time, though, he had awoken before his own death. More nights than he could count, Apollo watched from within as bullets, knives, clubs, fire, or any number of worse deaths had taken him. Always, he killed dozens before death finally caught him one way or another. Sometimes his death was painless, others were full of agony—just like the deaths of his victims in his nightmares. They did not come every time he slept, but when they came, his dream self never once survived.

The problem, what disturbed him most, was that for the first time in years he felt his control slipping again. The nightmare was becoming him, or perhaps things were the other way around.

He sat still, breathing deeply. In and out, he thought, focusing on those simple instructions. He breathed, and as he did so, his heart slowed. Apollo remained like that, with the edges of his mental vision dancing with images of blood and death, for several minutes before a wash of calm and control came back to him.

"I am Apollo. I am in control," he mouthed in a single, smooth exhalation. "I am Apollo. I am in control."

Apollo checked his watch. Small, glowing dots on the hands told him it was just past Legal Night. They would have to get going as soon as humanly possible, he thought. Before he could ready any of his gear or even think about rousing Vivian, he was reminded of the first—and so far only—drawback of his new "abilities." Even the small exertion he used to smash the flimsy building facade the day before left him horrendously hungry afterward.

He searched through the shelves of their hideout, using the screen of his tablet for light. At least the KRS provided food, he thought. Apollo did not want to go back to the bland nutrition bars they brought with them.

On the shelves, he found similar bars and he sighed in the darkness. Food was food and his stomach did not want to let him take any longer to search. He hardly ate like a normal human anymore, and downed one of the high-calorie bars in seconds. Ruefully, he chewed on a second, looking for something more palatable.

Another cabinet held sealed cups of autobrew coffee. He flicked the tab on the bottom of one of the mugs and set it on the floor as the chemicals reacting inside the walls of the container brought the contents to near boiling. In moments, the earthy-yet-artificial aroma of imitation coffee filled the small room. Vivian stirred in the bed, but only pulled the covers tighter around her body. The alarm she had set was not supposed to go off for another two hours yet.

In the meantime, Apollo sat in the darkness trying to plot his next move. The only light around him came from his occasional glances at his watch to check the time. The bottom of his empty coffee cup still glowed a faint red, something that would have been completely invisible with any other light source around. In the pitch darkness of their room, it was the only light. Apollo found the deep red glow somehow comforting to stare at. It gave his eyes something to focus on, rather than creating shapes and colors out of the blackness. With his eyes distracted by the glowing cup, and his ears distracted by Vivian's faint breathing, his mind was free to think.

He crossed his legs in the middle of the floor, with the cup half a meter or so in front of him, and sat silently. No matter how he approached the problem, he could not shake the feeling that he was being played. He knew he was only a pawn of the Immaculata and their plans, but that was an arrangement he had entered into willingly. On the mundane side, Kingsmark wanted Duke Charlie gone, and to do that, they needed Alexander gone. He wanted Alexander dead, and to do that, he needed Duke Charlie gone. Their relationship, Apollo's and Kingsmark's, was mutually beneficial, but it left him feeling like an employee, not an ally.

He cursed the pounding in his chest as his frustration sped his pulse. If not them, he asked himself, wondering who else, or what else, could be the source of his unease. Duke Charlie was too stupid to even think about trying to string Apollo along. He operated an illegal weapon ring right under the President-Duke's nose for years without his knowledge, after all. Plus, he thought with relief, if Duke Charlie's "secret police" were half as effective as they were supposed to be, all of Londonsberg would have been in lockdown while they tore it apart to find whoever had murdered that Black Tie the day before.

So no, he concluded, Duke Charlie could not manage to play him, even with all of the resources at his command. Not even if he wanted to. Unless, his mind insisted on reminding him, the City was under actual lockdown, and hundreds of Black Ties patrolled the streets, just waiting on either of them to make the sort of stupid mistake that would get them caught—something like "leaving their hideout."

He mused on the remaining options, wondering who else was left. Alexander? His brother had no reason to string him along. If he knew Apollo was inside the Limits, Alexander would have been actively hunting him even if Duke Charlie was still pulling his strings.

Alexander implied at the Night Market that he could have hunted down Apollo whenever he saw fit, and had in fact watched him for some time before he finally decided to act. If Alexander's source of information followed him to the Night Market, he had to know Apollo was on his way to the City.

If the Black Ties knew he was there—again he chastised himself for his reckless attack the day before. How close had he come to sending the City into high alert?—the President-Duke would surely have ordered him found and brought in. That manhunt would not end with a random disappeared citizen.

Even if Alexander was keeping things from the Duke, the sudden shift in his behavior as he went after Apollo would surely trigger some sort of flag in the system. But even with a Black Tie ostensibly killed by a Rhineland bomb, nothing about the City had changed.

Apollo's eyes opened wide as the revelations hit. Alexander was not in the City at all!

He frowned. That was too easy. Alexander was playing some sort of long game; he had to be. Apollo needed more information, especially if he was to shake the gut feeling that his assumption was correct and Alexander was missing.

A thought struck him. If Alexander was gone, what were the two of them doing wasting time skulking around the underbelly of the City for? A flash of rage darkened his mind. All of the time it had taken to sneak into the City had been wasted. The effort and energy it had cost him to get out of that cave had been unnecessary. Vivian's company had been pleasant enough, even pleasurable at times, but that did not change the fact that he risked everything to sneak inside the Londonsberg Limits, only to find out that he probably needed to be somewhere else.

On the heels of that thought, before he could banish his anger, a vision flashed through his mind: snapping Vivian's neck, burning down their hideout, then killing and creating havoc until Alexander returned. Then they would fight, probably destroying part of the City with their Immaculata-given powers. Alexander would die, the Legion of Black Ties would probably die, and Kingsmark would roll into the City as though it were their plan all along.

And he would be left without the generous paycheck promised to him by Vivian's KRS superiors. If she died, not only would he not get paid, but Kingsmark would probably put that money into a bounty on his head. They had a military powerful enough that they could have destroyed Londonsberg easily if not for the City's NoTech. Vivian's mission—even with Apollo's "generous" fee added to it—cost less than a full-scale invasion, and he doubted that they would leave him alone if he double crossed them.

He took a deep breath, fighting his temper. Apollo ran his fingers through his hair in a gesture that quickly became him clawing at his skull.

"Control," he whispered. A deep breath, then he said, "I am in control. I am..."

The sound that emanated from his throat was more animal than man. A deep longing in his heart called for blood, for fire, and for chaos. He looked over his shoulder at the darkness where Vivian slept, unaware. One hand twitched involuntarily.

Apollo stood, the sound of his joints moving in the silence louder than his voice had been. Both hands twitched now and he clasped them together, interlacing his fingers and squeezing hard enough that the bones threatened to crack.

He took a step in the dark, measured and slow. It moved him away from the bed, away from Vivian. His hands still itched and he forced them to close into fists, then open again. His fingers made clawing motions and he put his hands on his head again, tired of fighting the urge.

No. It did not come out as a word. His mouth simply made another animal growl, but his brain screamed the word until the concept of "no" became his only overriding thought. His hands grasped at the air, closing around nothingness as though the darkness had a throat he could crush.

The darkness did not have a throat, but *she* did. Apollo turned back in the direction of the bed and, with crystal clarity, took two steps through the darkness.

Pain blossomed in his face as the force of a sledgehammer shattered his jawbone. Healing ecstasy followed as the bone knitted itself back together. He lashed out, stumbled, and crashed to his knees. Even close enough to smell the carpet cleaner, he saw nothing in the dark.

Apollo took those moments to realize that nothing attacked him. He struck himself.

On his knees, he clawed at the carpet. With his enhanced strength, he almost dug a series of gouges in the floor. Apollo raised his fist to strike, to hit something, but pulled the punch a bare centimeter before it would have cracked the floor apart.

His heart thundered in his ears as he took several deep breaths. Apollo sank back onto his heels, staring up at what should have been the sky. "I," he breathed, "am Apollo. I am in control."

He had no idea how long he sat in the dark like that. Reality softened again and thoughts started to filter back into his brain as he finally lowered his eyes to where the bed sat. He enjoyed Vivian's company. The thought of her death left him feeling unpleasant. He did not feel frightened or hollow or any nonsense warning that he was becoming dangerously attached. Rather, the idea of her dying, especially on his proverbial "watch" gave him a profound feeling of failure.

Apollo wiped the back of his hand across his face, telling himself that the wetness there was an automatic response to the pain of having his jaw broken.

Forcing another round of meditative breathing kept his nerves calm. The darkness let him think freely, but his mind was too damnably quick to dart down the darkest path possible. If he was to remain truly in control of his own desires, he would have to first master his thoughts.

Apollo's mind went back to an earlier thought. They needed more information. Going back to their bags, he took a small tablet out of its sleeve and, without turning the screen on, scrawled a simple message across it in case Vivian woke up before he returned or, more likely, in case he found out where Alexander was and pursued him. He kept the note concise, detailing as much of his logic as he could, and ending with an assurance that, if Alexander was gone and he decided to go after him, Apollo would leave a sign to let her know that he was still alive and that the KRS's plans for the City were in no danger.

He left her tablet on the table next to the bed and, atop that, his pocket watch. Satisfied that he was, if not doing the right thing, doing the best thing he could, he stood and quietly crossed the room. At the door, he felt around until he found the latch, hoping the mechanism was as silent this time as it had been before. The wheel that operated the lock turned slowly as it retracted the massive, vault-style metal cylinders out of the building's wall. The slow pace of the lock bothered him, and he flexed his fingers again.

Perhaps his enhanced strength, and the speed that came with it, was making him impatient. If that was the case, then he would have yet another thing to add to his list of annoying side effects that he had to deal with. Patience was one of the few virtues he actually possessed, and Apollo fully intended to keep it that way.

*** 

Apollo carefully made his way through the public areas of the building. Once out into the warm, stagnant air of the street—yet another thing he hated about the City—he surveyed his surroundings. A quick glance at his palm-sized tablet told him his location.

Three steps outside the shop door, the screen blanked as the NoTech took hold. He smirked, automatically brushing a hand over his pistol as though its presence reassured him. In a way it did. It, and its noise suppressor, would work inside the NoTech field, giving him the element of surprise when he encountered resistance.

He kept to the shadows close to the tall buildings as much as possible. Between the darkness, unbroken by streetlights after Legal Night, and his Mirage jacket, Apollo could remain effectively hidden even in the middle of the roads. Even so, he wanted to take as few chances as possible. The added shadow from the buildings kept even the faint starlight off of him as he moved around the City.

An hour passed.

What the hell was he expecting to find after Legal Night? Apollo demanded, directing the thought at the City as much as himself. The only ones allowed out in the open at that time of night were the Black Ties themselves, and they would not exactly be a useful source of information. Even if he could take one alive, they were in constant contact with one another and the others would converge on him long before he could get any useful information. On the other hand, a commotion like that would be the perfect thing to attract Alexander's attention.

Apollo resisted an urge to laugh, knowing the sound would be picked up. If he had to use himself as bait, so be it, but it would be on his own terms. Truthfully, he knew he was probably already being tracked, but there was a difference between knowing he was being tracked and being an idiot about it.

He walked on, scouting for areas that would make good ambush spots. The Black Ties were not used to targeting people who fought back. Apollo figured that after he killed a few of them, that they would all pull back and call for Alexander. Then Alexander would die, Kingsmark would destroy Londonsberg, and he could turn his back on the whole damned mess. Then it would be just him and the Immaculata, as it should have been from the beginning.

What Apollo would do in the meantime was beyond him. He had no idea where Alexander had gone. Logically, if he was still in the City, he would have already attacked. Alexander could be mere hours away, or he could be days or weeks distant.

He frowned, displeased. If he tipped his hand too early, the Black Ties could swarm him with enough fodder to kill him long before Alexander arrived. If the President-Duke sent them against him, they would do it knowing they would die, but they would fight him anyway.

In a way, Apollo pitied them, or he would if it came to that. Those with nothing to lose fought like mad and he had no desire to come against that sort of opposition. He sighed, resigning himself to not being able to find anything on this first trip away from their hideout.

Three sets of footsteps roused him from his reverie, and he darted into a side alley. Apollo listened for several minutes, until he could pick out slurred voices discussing some sporting event that the President-Duke authorized. Unless they were very good actors, these were not black ties.

Apollo edged closer to the street, coming even with the corner of the building in whose shadow he was hiding. Several meters away, he caught sight of the retreating backs of three men in civilian clothes.

Surprised, Apollo realized that they were ordinary citizens of the City. Not Black Ties, not covert agents of some new bureau of Duke Charlie's, but everyday citizens on their way somewhere, probably their apartments. One staggered and Apollo violently fought down a laugh as the man's two friends helped him back to his feet. They were out past Legal Night, assuming they were sober enough to understand that. If a patrolling Black Tie caught them, the lightest punishment they would receive would be a steep fine.

The reek of alcohol caught his nose, threatening to burn it off. Whatever they had been drinking was probably even more illegal than their presence on the streets after Legal Night. All was not spit-and-polish within Duke Charlie's City, he reminded himself.

Apollo's palms itched as he thought of how easy it would be to work off a little steam. They were already breaking at least two of the City's laws, he reasoned, and the Black Ties would probably disappear them if they caught them.

He clenched his fists down by his sides. "No," he grated through gritted teeth.

He was going to let them pass. They never saw him, never posed a threat to him. What good, he asked himself, would killing them actually serve?

Then he heard one of them mention Alexander's name amid a string of barely-intelligible drunken babble. His heart stopped and his blood ran cold as part of his brain registered exactly how cliché his autonomic reaction actually was. He ignored it, straining to listen for more tidbits of the drunks' conversation, but they were already too far away for their murmurs to carry anything meaningful.

He waited until they rounded a corner before coming out of his own shadowy hiding place and following them. Apollo recognized bits and pieces of his surroundings from long ago, but his mental map of the city had been degraded by time and rendered useless by construction projects.

The three drunks took side streets and alleys seemingly at random. Perhaps, he thought, it might be some ingrained path that the men developed to avoid the Black Ties and their patrols, but more likely they were simply drunk and lost.

A brief thought did cross his mind and he wondered which amused him more: the idea that the Black Ties were so corrupt that they turned a blind eye to a group of men drunk on illegal liquor; or the idea that the Black Ties were so incompetent that they somehow missed that same group as they staggered randomly along the streets.

To add to his frustration, he had not heard anything else about Alexander from the drunks since starting his chase. They ducked into yet another alley and Apollo slithered into the shadows nearby to wait for them to come out. He heard the sound of water hitting pavement, one of the drunks pissing in a dark corner, but nothing else. A minute passed, and then another, before the footsteps started again.

This time, the footsteps were headed toward him. Had he taken the time to look down the drunks' alley, he would have seen a dead end. They had no choice but to come out eventually. He entertained no doubts about whether he would be spotted unless he moved immediately. Mirage jacket momentarily forgotten, he frantically searched around for a place to hide before they passed.

He looked up. Three stories up hung a balcony, attached no doubt to some expensive apartment. It was the only projection on the entire side of the building, and Apollo wondered how much it had cost, or who the occupant had to bribe to be allowed to build such a balcony. Regardless, it would serve his needs for the moment, provided he could get to it. He saw no ladder or stairs leading up, and taking the time—and making the noise—to break into the building and go up from the inside was out of the question.

The footsteps and drunken slurring from the alley approached the street. Apollo briefly contemplated jumping and was about to dismiss it as a silly plan, when he realized that it might not be so silly after all. Whatever the Immaculata had done to him that gave him enhanced strength surely affected all of his muscles, he thought. He had used his legs to push that boulder off of his foot back in the cave, had he not? Jumping was just as strength-dependent as lifting a weight, and so he crouched and flung himself into the air.

The experience was exhilarating for the first few moments. He truly felt like he was flying, or perhaps weightless and tumbling through space. It hit him directly, unfiltered through a machine, creating a sensation more intoxicating than flying his aircar at high speed. His exhilarating jump ended up being closer to five-stories high, something he would have to practice as soon as Alexander was properly dead.

Seconds later, the realization that he had no concept of how to aim a multi-story jump shattered that feeling. Apollo was not close enough to the balconies, not moving sideways enough, and the odds of him hitting the balcony at all were far slimmer than he liked.

He stifled his momentary panic, turning the wild flailing of his limbs into a desperate grab for the balcony's rail. To its credit, and the credit of whoever built the thing, it did little more than creak as gravity did everything it could to pull them both to the ground. His shoulder was not so fortunate, though. He had only been able to touch the railing with one hand, and the force that a two-story drop suddenly coming to a stop could put on his joints was agonizing. Less so than being shot or stabbed, certainly, but the temporary immobility that came with the injury made it all the worse.

He twisted, grabbing the railing with his unhurt arm. As soon as his weight came off of the injured shoulder, his Immaculata-given healing kicked in, turning the dull ache into a white-hot needle of pain as the injury healed itself in seconds. He had to fight the urge to laugh as pleasure radiated out from the healing joint. He managed to stay quiet, though he was sure any sober person would have noticed him dangling from the balcony. Drunks had their uses. That use might simply be being too drunk to see him, but that was still a legitimate use as far as Apollo was concerned just then.

The drunks passed by below as Apollo's shoulder finished healing. The pleasure receded, allowing him to think clearly again. He needed answers, no matter the risk of blowing his cover. Three men reeking of illegal booze would not be in a hurry to turn him in. He dropped to the street.

"It's a little late to be on the streets, gentlemen," Apollo said, doing his level best to be as nonthreatening as possible.

The men turned around, wide-eyed. A tense moment passed between them before one man's frightened expression changed to a smile and he exclaimed, "Alexander!"

A great black pit opened in Apollo's stomach. He might have been looking for Alexander, but he was not ready, not then. These three drunks would have to die, probably as human shields. Perhaps Alexander might hold back just enough to allow Apollo to grab an advantage in their fight. Any other time, and he could have set up an ambush and prepared and done a thousand other things first. Then his thoughts caught up with his adrenal gland.

The man was looking at Apollo, not behind him. Did he think Apollo was his brother? It was possible, dark as it was.

"We thought," the man mumbled. He stopped, visibly trying not to vomit up whatever he had been drinking. Finally, he took a deep breath and managed, "we thought you was gone t'L4."

Apollo grinned. So that was where Alexander had gone. Apollo finally had the lead he had been looking for. Now the question foremost in his mind was whether or not the three drunks could be allowed to live, now that they knew he was here. He brought a finger to his lips in a universal gesture of secrecy.

"I un... unner... unders..." the man slurred. "I gets it. 'S a secret mission!"

Apollo nodded once. An idle voice in his mind wondered if he had been this stupid, useless, and easy to take advantage of when he spent most of his time drinking. If he was, only his own stupid luck kept him from death when he was lost to the booze. He could almost hear his own voice mocking him: "see, Apollo, here's a mirror for your life!" He narrowed his eyes into a glare, though his vision was focused inward instead of on the man in front of him.

"You ain't gonna take us..." the man slurred, apparently cognizant enough to recognize Apollo's angry glare for what it was, regardless of its intended target. "Not gonna arr... arrest us, are you?"

Apollo shook his head and made a shoo-ing gesture. The three men turned and hobbled away down the dark street, never knowing how close to death they had actually been. He had wanted to kill them; his palms itched to end their lives with knife and gun, but he fought down the urge.

He was better than that, and now he had a plan.

# Chapter 13

Apollo tried to sneak back into their hideout and failed. It might have been dark inside the locked vault, but the door still made some noise as it opened and shut. Vivian was waiting for him, sitting in the darkness like a movie cliché.

She cleared her throat and Apollo jumped, ready to kill what his brain first assumed was a Black Tie assassin. His Immaculata enhancements continued to have frustrating holes in the powers they granted—in pitch darkness he was only slightly more useful than anyone else would have been. Even Apollo could not fight what he could not see.

A click, and the overhead light came to life in a moment of blinding fury. Without streetlights, the moon outside gave just enough illumination to see by. His eyes had adjusted to that dimness, and the sudden illumination reduced everything to a white blur. Apollo involuntarily snarled, dropping into a crouch.

He fought to open his eyes against the painful light, instinct overriding the knowledge that anything that attacked would stand very little chance of killing him. Finally, he blinked away the last of the afterimages and surveyed the room. Very little had changed aside from some minor straightening, which included clearing away his trash from breakfast. Now that he could see, nothing screamed danger at him and Apollo felt his muscles slowly relax.

The last spot, a half second after the empty bed, that Apollo surveyed during his quick sweep of the room was the table. There, Vivian sat with an amused expression on her face. If the sudden light affected her at all, the effect was subtle. Three objects sat in front of her, centimeters away from her calmly folded hands. The center object was a pistol, safety off, and oriented for easy pickup. To either side sat the small tablet that controlled the room's lights and other systems, and his tablet.

Apollo growled. "What the hell?"

"To be honest, I wasn't expecting you to come back."

"I thought about it."

She quirked her eyebrow and Apollo grimaced. Vivian was getting as good as Catherine, if not better, at reading him. Not for the first time, he wondered if it frustrated other people this much when he did it to them. "And?"

He rubbed his eyes with the back of his hand. Spots from the sudden light still lingered, flashing blue and green every time he blinked. That was annoying enough, but the way they superimposed themselves over everything, moving with his eyes instead of staying in one single spot was something that always unsettled him for reasons he could not articulate.

Apollo was also surprised that his healing did not kick in to "fix" the shock from the light. True, his eyes were not actually damaged, only overloaded, but that seemed to him like the sort of thing that should have been included in his particular brand of powers.

At the very least, he thought, it should have been included right then. He blinked again and the spots hovered over the upper right corner of his vision. They could stay there until his optic nerves stopped sending false signals to his brain. If Apollo could ignore pain, he could ignore afterimages.

"And you almost shot me," he accused, stalking across the room to the kitchen and withdrawing another cup of autobrew coffee.

"I didn't."

"You didn't shoot me," he said, "or you didn't 'almost' shoot me?"

"Both. If I was going to shoot you, I would have. Probably in the head so you couldn't get up again."

"Comforting."

Vivian laughed. "Don't forget, I know how you work, Apollo. I shoot you anywhere else and it's just a distraction for a few seconds."

"You were still ready to shoot me." He turned with the rapidly-heating cup in hand and went to the table. The banter was calming his nerves, which was another strange feeling. This was the sort of conversation he carried on with someone in order to threaten them, to point out that he was in control of the situation. Instead, what it became would have been termed a "friendly exchange" if Apollo had the context for that phrase.

Vivian shrugged. "I was ready to shoot whoever came through that door. Like I said, I didn't expect you to come back."

"I almost didn't." He took the lid off the cup of coffee and set it gently on the table. The black liquid inside steamed, promising him that it was, in fact, real coffee. He knew better, but took a drink anyway. "Turns out Alexander's not in the city."

He expected Vivian to act surprised, but her expression barely changed. If anything, it became more thoughtful. "How did you figure that out?"

He related his logic, starting from the beginning with the thoughts he had before stepping outside. He carefully did not mention any of the mental turmoil that surrounded those thoughts. Apollo did tell her about the drunks and the information he gathered from them, "without torturing anyone."

Vivian nodded along until he was done, and then asked, "and you were ready to go into space after him?"

"At this point? Yes."

"Apollo," she laughed, "that's the dumbest line of reasoning I've ever heard."

He recoiled slightly, then frowned. Before he could get more than a single word out, the "what" that would have begun his demand to know what she was thinking, Vivian continued speaking.

"That doesn't mean you're wrong, though."

He took a deep breath, then another. The whole business of not simply allowing himself to act on his first impulse was growing more and more difficult. He prided himself on thinking things through, but the realization that most of his actions in life had been justified *post facto* came out of nowhere.

Apollo had been ready to leave the planet, an action available to no more than a handful of people on Earth, over a hunch and the slurred words of a group of drunks. That was not a plan made by a patient, methodical man. He stayed silent while those thoughts percolated in his brain, trying to reconcile his own mental image of himself as thoughtful and careful with the actuality that he was rash and impulsive by nature.

Vivian seemed to take his silent pondering, and the attendant frown that came with it, as encouragement to continue. "This room has no connection to the outside world," she said. "No networks of any sort. Remember when I told you the building's blueprints labeled this suite as HVAC space?"

The pair of sudden non sequiturs snapped him out of his reverie. Unable to follow Vivian's train of thought beyond what she actually said, he simply nodded and replied, "yes?"

She reached into a pocket and produced a small data drive, setting it on the table next to his tablet. "It turns out that people drop things down air conditioning vents all the time, especially people carelessly wasting an afternoon on a rooftop where Black Ties rarely patrol."

"How convenient." Apollo smirked, sweeping up the data drive in one hand and depositing it in front of his coffee cup. His next movement brought his tablet to his side of the table, and he connected the two. Deciding to skip the rest of the exposition, he asked, "what am I looking for?"

"That drive only has two files on it. The rest is, or was before I unlocked and cleaned it, junk data and encryption."

He nodded and opened the first one. Charts and tables, all cited with endless footnotes, scrolled past. The mass of numbers and seemingly random wall of text seemed at first to be another junk file, but then Apollo took a moment and actually looked at it.

Each of the footnotes in the file corresponded to an official order or unofficial communication within the Londonsberg government. Duke Charlie's comms had not been tapped, but several others high in the various branches had been compromised. Apollo wondered which were corrupt and which were simply inept, and decided it did not matter. The data showed not just Black Tie, but Perimeter Security, and even regular military information.

It took nearly fifteen minutes to peruse the entire file, during which Apollo finished his coffee and drank half of a new cup that Vivian brought him. Several things stuck out, the first and most troubling of them was the subtle shift of Black Ties into the area around their "secret" entrance into the city.

He mentioned that aloud, and Vivian frowned. "Yes," she said, "I saw that as well. I don't know if it's coincidence, related to the Tie you killed, or if the entire damn thing was leaked."

Apollo gestured with the tablet like it was a baton. "If they knew we were coming, the Black Ties would have been waiting for us when we got into the city. It's more likely that the door was bugged."

Vivian's frown deepened. "That might just be worse."

"Why's that?"

"A blown op means someone in Londonsberg got to someone in Kingsmark and money or threats changed hands. Maybe both. If they bugged the door, it means that OPS knew about it and were monitoring it. In my book, that's worse."

"Again, if they knew we," he punctuated that with a gesture at himself more than her, "were here, they would have come down on us right then. They didn't, which means even if they knew the door had been opened, they had no idea by whom."

Apollo sat back in his seat, reflecting that he could be logical when he actually made himself think things through. He picked up the tablet again and continued reading over the file. The largest movement of troops was to the spaceport where— Apollo stopped and stared at the data for a moment before reading on—it seemed that one of the ships had left the City two days ago, shortly before their arrival. A large body of regular soldiers had been sent there to reinforce the Black Ties that normally guarded the ships.

The rest of the movements were small, the sort of normal relocations that happened all the time. He skimmed those and closed the file. The second file turned out to be a video, which loaded after a moment's decompression.

The tablet's screen blanked for a second before being filled with an image of Duke Charlie's office. The camera sat just far enough away to capture the front edge of his large, empty desk. Behind that expanse of wood, the smiling face of President-Duke Charlie Maxwell gazed out for several seconds before speaking.

His smile broadened in the moment before he opened his mouth and his eyes shone with bright, reflected light. "Good morning, Londonsberg. I hope you all slept well last night under the watchful care of your Black Tie guardians.

"I'm sure by now most of you are aware, in fact some of the more industrious among you might have seen it yourself, that the *Helios* is no longer within our fair city. Already this morning, I have received many worried letters and phonecalls and I wanted to assure you all, personally, that there is no cause for alarm.

"Some of you are probably wondering why the *Helios*'s departure was not bigger news." His smile grew even wider for a moment. "That's excellent. Wonder is the key to our humanity. As these things go, I did not wish to make a formal announcement until I was sure everything would go smoothly."

Duke Charlie gave a small laugh, and Apollo almost believed his cheer was genuine.

"The reason, dear citizens, that the *Helios* left in such a rush lies with its sole passenger. Captain Alexander himself is aboard that glorious ship."

Apollo's emotions surged between anger and triumph. He was right! But now that the truth lay before him, or some version of the truth filtered through the Office of Public Image, the enormity of the task confronted him.

Before Apollo count think more, the recording continued. "Late last night, the *Helios* docked with Proxima Sol itself! That station, commonly known as 'L4,' graciously extended an invitation to my good and dear friend Alexander for a personal visit."

His smile vanished for a moment, but the twinkle in his eye never went away. When Duke Charlie spoke again, it was with the same avuncular tone. "Many of you remember my visit to Proxima Sol, so you know that such visits can sometimes take weeks, but do not worry."

Duke Charlie stared directly into the camera as he spoke his next words.

"Londonsberg again has L4's blessing. Good day."

Apollo closed the file and set the tablet down. He looked up and realized Vivian had been watching over his shoulder. "Well that's a hell of a propaganda spin."

Vivian laid a hand on his shoulder. Apollo flinched from the unexpected contact, then relaxed and leaned backwards against her. "So, you said you had a plan?"

Apollo laughed. "I do, and you're going to love the symbolism. Tomorrow, an hour after Legal Night..."

\*\*\*

Shrouded in his mirage jacket, Apollo ghosted through the streets of Londonsberg. Scenes from decades before echoed in his head, memories of similar trips out in the middle of the night. This particular trip was going to end the same way, but on a much larger scale. In those days, Apollo might have broken a few windows or doors, cornered a Black Tie or some poor bastard out after Legal Night, and then gone home to wash the blood away.

For a time, he fooled even Alexander. For the better part of a year, his brother helped the city track down the "Nightmare." Apollo pleaded his inability to help, playing on Alexander's role as the Immaculata's chosen. It worked, and Alexander's ego refused to consider that Apollo might have been the culprit.

Ironically, it had been the Black Ties who found him. Photographed in the act of slitting the throat of a Perimeter Security guard in order to leave the City for the night, Apollo instantly became a "Person of Threat." Alexander tried to kill him that day, but he displayed none of the Immaculata-granted power he gained later. Apollo disappeared into the bowels of the city for another year as the killing continued.

Finally, Apollo sneaked through the Limits aboard a passenger flier bound for Eslav. There, he became the Butcher of Novarus. He lived that life for years until he grew reckless and allowed the city-state's military to catch him. Thence, he fled to Kingsmark where his attempts at a "low profile" failed spectacularly within a year.

He returned to the city, once again becoming the Nightmare. Londonsberg had grown complacent and Alexander was missing, and the killing continued until the needless death of a child drove him from the city and to the foothills of the Visegrad mountains, where he lived until Catherine found him.

Apollo now recognized the feeling that drove him from place to place was not fear, but guilt. He was no longer the Nightmare or the Butcher of Novarus. He was Apollo, ally of Kingsmark and the Immaculata. Apollo, friend of Sal Maximilian and Vivian Jensen, had returned, and Londonsberg was going to burn.

Most of their explosives were buried in a cave outside the city, crushed under enough rock that even Apollo's enhanced strength could not free it. However, what they had left, in addition to a modest store in Vivian's safehouse, was enough to get the job done.

He dared a glance at his tablet to confirm the location one last time. The spot he chose for his "opening act" was fairly far away from any of the troop deployments that night. He was not worried for them—their time would come—but the fairly remote location meant that troops had to move away from their assigned locations to investigate.

And, thought Apollo as he pocketed the tablet and withdrew a small device with a key lock and a physical button, they were about to have plenty to investigate.

Apollo connected the device to a trail of black-coated wire. Vivian assured him, and proved it with several tests in a NoTech area, that a simple electrical circuit would still work anywhere in the city. Such things fed power to apartments and businesses and had to run through NoTech areas to do so.

Next, he withdrew a powerful battery from his pack and connected it to the device. The light atop it lit a clear, if dim, blue and Apollo grinned. He raised himself up and held the device in outstretched hands. From his rooftop vantage point, he could see the target blanketed by lightless night.

Barely resisting the urge to shout a taunt or insult, he turned the key and dropped the device. Propelled by his strength, Apollo jumped to the next rooftop before the detonator landed. He leapt to another building and then to a fourth before turning to survey his handiwork.

The explosives had done their job. None of the bombs were terribly powerful by any objective measure, but Apollo had spent two full hours placing them according to an architectural diagram Vivian provided. The building she labeled "textile factory" collapsed under its own weight as uncountable tons of fabric caught fire.

In the garish light, Apollo grinned. Sirens were already starting as searchlights on the taller buildings swept the area. Nearby, aircraft lifted off, adding their lights to the search. He sprang away again, flitting from rooftop to rooftop away from the blaze.

He got a full kilometer away from the explosion before he allowed himself the luxury of laughter. His voice rang out in the night, consumed with adrenaline. It was not the moment he had been born for, but, as far as Apollo was concerned, it was close enough for the moment.

He jumped, aiming for a taller building, and crashed into the side of it hard enough to crack the concrete. It barely slowed his trek across the City skyline as he used the sudden stop, and surge of euphoria as an accidentally shattered kneecap healed instantly, to make a sharp turn.

Before he went to the spaceport, Apollo had one more stop to make.

*** 

Salvatore Maximilian felt the explosion in his bones. Sound traveled fast through the earth, and the stone told him the story moments before the terrible sound made it to his ears. Before he could think about it, Sal drew his gun and stepped around the counter in his shop.

Rushing out through the heavy leather curtain, he nearly collided with Jamie, her Apollo-made carbine slung across her torso.

"It's burning!" she shouted.

Sal looked around the market and found a scene of pandemonium. People, most armed, ran every which way. Nothing within sight burned and he was about to ask Jamie what she meant when he completed his visual survey.

One edge of Londonsberg glowed a deep orange. The flames did not reach the top of the Limits, and the heat was lost long before he could have felt it, but the light made it to the Night Market well enough.

"What's going on?" Jamie demanded.

Sal stared at the City that took his father. He whispered, "Apollo."

"What?"

He turned on his heel. Jamie stood within arm's reach, and several others were rapidly approaching. "I said it's Apollo."

"Apollo?" someone in the crowd asked. That question was taken up by others and that name spread through the growing crowd like a fire all its own.

The din of a hundred conversations rose and rose until Sal could barely hear Jamie, next to him, asking, "is that what he meant?"

Sal nodded to her, then looked out over the crowd. "ENOUGH!"

The crowd quieted in moments. Through it continued to grow, it did so without talking. Sal looked past the crowd and at the Night Market. If the flyovers from Londonsberg ever noticed that the market had quietly tripled in size recently and was up to a great many more permanent buildings than it ever had, nothing came of it.

Sal pointed at the orange glow with a meaty hand and muscular arm. "That is what we've been waiting for, people! That is *Apollo*!"

The crowd cheered, and this time Sal let them. After a full minute, he quieted them again. To his surprise and shock, all it took was a single gesture and a wave of silence spread from his spot.

"Now is not the time for speeches," he proclaimed, "but I am going to say that I'm proud of you. Some of you may not come back, but remember why you're fighting!

"Remember what Londonsberg took from you!"

Sal raised a fist in the air. "We are not people with nothing to lose. We have *everything* to lose. Remember it, and teach my *cousin* what that means!"

He lowered his hand, but his voice continued to rise, caught up in the moment. "Two hours! Everything you're not taking with you goes into my shop. In two hours, I want to see everyone back here, armed and ready to go!"

A Marrakeshi voice cut through the cheer of the crowd. "What about the Limits?"

Sal roared with his fist in the air. "We have aircraft! *Fuck* the Limits!"

\*\*\*

With the city in uproar over the explosion at the textile factory, Londinium Square was guarded by a single sniper. Apollo's mirage jacket allowed him to cross the remaining rooftops that separated him from his destination with ease, and now that lone guard was the only thing standing between him and the message he needed to send.

As the euphoria from destroying the factory wore off, it threatened to turn into bloodlust. His thoughts coalesced around a mantra that he repeated in his head, faster and more intently now that he approached his next target.

"Keep it quick. Keep it clean. There's no need for brutality. Stay in control, Apollo. Stay. In. Control."

Apollo crept nearly on his hands and knees, silhouetting the sniper's shoulders and head against the stars above. He drew a black-bladed knife, invisible in the darkness, and clutched it tightly in one hand. The other reached out to grasp the soldier as soon as he was within range.

His lack of enhanced night vision and Londonsberg's lack of lights finally betrayed him and, with two meters to go, Apollo kicked a wooden box. It skittered across the concrete loud enough to be heard over the distant sirens.

The man whirled around, instinctively dropping his heavy rifle and reaching for his own combat knife. Apollo was faster, and had an advantage the sniper never could have suspected.

Rather than disarm him, Apollo delivered a devastating uppercut to the man's liver. That alone would kill him without medical attention—Apollo's enhanced strength was enough to rupture the organ and start the painful process of death-by-blood-poisoning. That, however, took much longer than Apollo wanted to spend on the rooftop.

To his credit, the soldier quickly recovered enough of his strength and wits to plunge his knife into Apollo's left lung. The blade slipped between his ribs like a spark of ice-cold fire. His side screamed in pain as he began to heal immediately, but each movement tore the knife's wound faster than he could heal.

The sniper pulled the knife towards him, slicing Apollo's side open like a rack of beef. Any normal assailant would have been dead on the spot while the sniper spent a few weeks in recovery. The pain burned, but nothing compared to what happened to his leg in the cave outside the City. Despite that, the wound was serious, and his vision started to blur as he lost blood faster than even he could replenish it while fighting.

The knife came out of the darkness again as his side burned itself together. By reflex alone, he shot a hand up and caught the blade. It bit into his skin, but the pain was barely noticeable against the sun-like flare in his side. Apollo twisted the knife out of his attacker's hand, rising from his knees as he did so.

The adrenaline from combat mixed with the warm euphoria his power produced while he healed. This time, he was ready for it and did not slow down. In a flash, he moved the stolen knife to his good hand. His arm uncurled like a scorpion tail and the knife struck the soldier in the right eye. Apollo buried the blade up to the hilt in the man's head before twisting it violently. He dropped to the ground, dead before he met the roof.

Likewise, Apollo collapsed as the pain from his healing wounds washed over him. In minutes, the agony was gone, replaced by receding trails of warmth and calm.

After a minute, Apollo stood and crossed the roof. He picked up the dead guard's discarded weapon, briefly considered taking it with him, and decided against it. He had another plan in mind for the weapon. Calmly, he took aim at the statue of

Alexander, exhaled, and gently caressed the trigger. The rife was well-made, he had to admit, because he barely felt the recoil of the big bullet as it exploded out of the barrel and smashed into the soft metal of Duke Charlie's statue.

To Apollo's annoyance, the statue's head did not shatter like he expected. Instead, the bullet tore through the metal not unlike a smaller bullet would have done to flesh. The hole in the front of the statue's forehead was perhaps four or five centimeters across, easily visible in the right light. He supposed the symbolism was better this way. The back of the damnable thing's head had exploded outward, showering Londinium Square with debris and satisfying his need for violence well enough.

He dropped back to the roof, panting. His wounds were not quite done healing, but would be so in another few moments. Apollo stared at the immobile stars overhead as pain and pleasure tried to turn his torso into a bonfire.

Finally, he was ready to move. He stood and looked at the broken statue of Alexander. He smiled as he imagined the panic that that one little action would cause. Burning the factory would have nothing on the long-term effects of defacing Alexander's statue. The citizens would wail and Duke Charlie would call out every Black Tie and every member of his personal army to watch inside the City for any further such "signs" or any activity by whoever had done such an unthinkable thing to his "Beloved City."

Vivian and Sal would understand the true meaning behind it. They knew who he was.

Apollo turned his attention to the spaceport. With emergency lights burning and searchbeams tracking the sky, it was an easy enough target to spot. Now, thought Apollo, it was time to leave the city again.

***

Sirens blared across the City. Smoke filled the air as a man-made star ascended to the heavens. Vivian watched as first the Black Ties and then the City's own military assembled and swept through the streets. She was exposed here, doubly so because the only people legally allowed on the streets were the military and the President-Duke's secret police. They were systematic, if rushed. The smoke came from two sources and both were being swarmed by men and women decked out in combat gear.

The first source of smoke came from Apollo's signal. More than the ease of burning a building full of fabric, she chose it for the poor road planning. Some of the most convoluted roads in all of Londonsberg wrapped around the factory district. It had to be that way to service as many trucks and freight-haulers as it did, but that same nest of twisting roadways was hell for ground response. From what she could see from her vantage point atop the building that housed their hideout, the Black Ties were concentrated more densely there than anywhere else.

Smoke also hovered over the spaceport at the opposite edge of the City, mostly residual haze from the starship that just lifted off. Its engines still twinkled in the midnight sky, but the smoke from its initial burst of thrust remained in Londonsberg's still air. Vivian suspected that some actual smoke, the sort that came from a conventional fire, was mixed in as well, but could see nothing beyond the pall of gray haze.

In her pocket, her hand brushed the pocket watch he left behind. As the City descend into chaos and fire, she realized that he had done exactly what she needed him to do.

With the Black Ties concentrated around the industrial district and the military itself vainly trying to secure an empty spaceport, no one was around to spot her. The actual populace of Londonsberg was, by and large, too cowed and fearful to even consider venturing outside. The few who would, and the fewer who would be successful, would be more interested in escaping Duke Charlie's hellhole than reporting a stray Marksman.

Still, the Black Ties and regular military were not made up exclusively of idiots. Even Duke Charlie could not weed out everyone capable of thinking for themselves, and she cursed as a trio of Black Ties marched down the street a dozen stories below her. Fortunately, none of them looked up right then and she waited until they passed before going on.

Vivian made her way down, through the building. With fires burning and sirens wailing across the City, she could move more quickly than she otherwise would have. Her main concerns now were alerting the Black Ties directly by tripping alarms. Errant noises caused by her hasty passage would not carry far.

By the time she made it to street level, the Black Ties were long gone. She had no idea where and no real desire to find out. Her job was to avoid being discovered, not to map the patrol patterns of the secret police. That would have been that night's job had Apollo not set a large chunk of the City on fire, but it was what it was. Plans changed.

No, she thought again, darting across an obnoxiously bright street and back into the safety of shadow on the other side, Apollo had done exactly what she needed him to do. He was taking care of Alexander, or had at least made sure Alexander was not in the City. In the process, he created the diversion she required.

Between skirting the light and narrowly avoiding Black Tie and regular military patrols, it took Vivian an hour to reach her destination on foot. She was rather proud of herself, as well. She made the entire trek without once having to fire a shot or even risk coming into armed combat at all. She did not—yet—want a firefight.

She crouched in the shadows of what appeared to be a high-class diner's patio. The street in front of it was just as straight as any other street in Londonsberg, but much shorter. It ran directly from the Londinium Square to what should have been the most heavily fortified structure for a thousand klicks.

She sized up the tower in front of her. It was certainly imposing. The architects had done their job well, which was a pity. It would most likely have to be razed to the ground. Duke Charlie destroyed the cities that came before him, burying thousands of years of history, and so it was poetic that his tower be likewise forgotten. It might have been her mission as a KRS agent to bring that tower down, but it was in her blood as a Validian to see it cleansed in fire.

Vivian turned her attention back to the present. With all of the commotion elsewhere, only a small token force guarded the tower. Four Black Ties flanked the entrance, but no one else was around. On any other day, the streets would not only be full of patrolling soldiers, but strategically-placed Black Ties as well. That left the platoon normally barracked on the bottom level of the tower, but Vivian watched that force march out of the tower and directly toward the spaceport an hour before.

No one else had gone in or come out since then, and the guards looked decidedly nervous at their posts. Vivian payed them no mind. She took no more pleasure from killing them than a mason would take from a solid-built wall.

Vivian, sticking as close to the building's facade as she could, unpacked from her backpack the few pieces of technology that survived the cave-in. The last one was a palm-sized device with a small screen and a variety of antennae on the top. She tapped it, and the screen came alive. A moment later, it displayed a block of text.

"System Check: Optimal
Electromagnetic Shielding: Active
NoTech: Detected
Anti-NoTech Capacitor Charge: 95% and falling
Arm: Yes/No"

The device in her hand was the single most expensive piece of technology she had ever held. It was the product of years of research into the effects of Duke Charlie's NoTech and was the best the KRS could come up with. It would disrupt the NoTech for a few moments, but it did have its drawbacks. First among them was the fact that it had to use up its own power to operate. The device, when active, had to generate a constant anti-NoTech field so that it itself could work.

Not only was its battery life extremely short, it was noisy, bright, and would absolutely destroy any stealth advantage she had. On the other hand, it was the lynch-pin to her entire mission. She set it on the ground beside her as the charge dropped to 94%, and set to work.

Her first order of business was to compose a short message to her KRS superiors. She kept it brief, more for the time it would take her to type anything longer than any concern about bandwidth or taxing the anti-NoTech device. In the message, she wrote that she was about to enter the tower, that Alexander was dealt with—and prayed to her gods that that was true—and closed with authorization to begin "Operation Medusa."

Vivian programmed the message to send automatically as soon as the NoTech field disappeared. Next in her bag was a KRS smartrifle. She was supposed to have two of the things, but one had been crushed under a boulder. She would make do with the one she had.

Vivian assembled the smartrifle and attached a lead to the NoTech disruptor. Its computer came alive, giving her a minute to sight and program it. The last instruction for its computer brain was to wait until the NoTech field vanished to execute the simple command she gave it. Unlike the guns she acquired from Apollo, the smartrifle would not operate under the effects of NoTech. The passive feed from the device was not enough power to operate the machine itself, either.

The third and final piece she withdrew from the bag was a detonator and a small pack containing a highly efficient thermobaric explosive. Once activated, a dispersal charge would spread the explosive dust around and then the second charge would detonate it.

Conscious of the falling charge on the anti-NoTech bomb, she wired the explosive quickly and then slung the backpack over her shoulders again. In five more minutes, during which she was more afraid her anti-NoTech device would run out of power than she had ever been of the Black Ties, Vivian had worked her way clear of the explosion radius and across the street.

She looked down. The device's capacitors had dropped to 40% charge, still enough. She hit the "activate" button and flung the thing into the street like a grenade.

She withdrew Apollo's pocket watch from her jacket and counted off the seconds. "Four, three, two, one."

The device went off like a flashbang. A magnesium-white flare and a whine so high pitched that it was more felt than heard followed the firecracker sound of its activation. The flash and whine disappeared quickly, or at least she thought they did. Green afterimages haunted her eyes, despite having them shut tight against the flash, and she could not be sure if the ringing she heard was her own head or something from the device.

"Three, two," she counted again, "one."

The device did not notify her in any way, but her comm should have sent the message. She dared not check it, because she could already hear the quartet of Black Ties moving around at the tower's base. Moments later, it became clear that the device did work as intended as the heads-up-display in her glasses immediately lit up in the wake of the flare. Pleased, she slipped the silver watch back into her breast pocket.

Another short countdown and the smartrifle spat its first magnetically-aimed projectile. She knew the Black Ties would have moved and so the gun had been programmed to spray its entire magazine over as wide an arc as possible. She had given special priority to the routes she assumed the Black Ties would take based on their positions, but she could not be sure and so relied instead on the ancient doctrine of "spray and pray."

She waited, counting each of the forty bullets as the gun emptied its belly on its own. The acoustics of the street were crisp and sharp, designed so that any sound would be easy to locate, and she counted a dozen return shots.

The smartrifle stopped firing and Vivian began the tensest of all of her countdowns. Five seconds after the smartrifle went silent, she heard a sound she could only describe as "poof." It was almost comical in a juvenile way, but half a second later the soft sound had been supplanted by an explosion that roared through the air like the bellows of an angry god.

Vivian waited another ten seconds. Any longer and she risked being cut off from her goal by returning troops. She rose, spun in place, and drew Apollo's pistol from her belt. Nothing alive moved on the street. The building across the way creaked and threatened to come down, but held for the moment. She suspected it would fall in minutes, which might actually help her if it blocked the road. In the chaos, she hoped that even the military would have issues requisitioning and piloting aircars around the tower.

Vivian looked over her shoulder: nothing. She took a single deep breath to calm her racing heart, and looked back to the tower. Abandoning all pretense of stealth, she ran for the base of Duke Charlie's tower.

# Chapter 14

Apollo wracked his brain all the way to L4, trying to figure out why Alexander would have abandoned the City and gone into space. L4, or more importantly the Domanantes Solis, had an unusual relationship with Earth. The station had survived countless wars on the surface of the planet by maintaining what was often referred to as "aggressively violent neutrality" backed up by efficient, long-range missiles that dated from before the Burning War.

Not only had the station lasted through devastating surface wars, it preserved and continued to advance upon the technology leftover from before those wars burned up large swaths of the Earth. The massive station was fully self-sufficient, needing nothing from the planet. That isolation and lack of immigration led to the development of a certain detachment between the people of L4 and those still on the planet.

Simply put, no one had a reason to leave L4 and travel to the station was prohibitively expensive—provided one actually owned the ship used to get there.

None of that mattered to Apollo. His only concern was finding his brother and killing him. The mystery of what Alexander was doing one hundred and fifty-six million kilometers away from the planet nagged at the back of his mind, but he refused to lose sleep over it. He told himself that Alexander's motivation was of no concern—the Immaculata said that he was to be killed for transgressing against their orders, so that was that. Apollo wanted him dead anyway; so much the better. It was only a bonus that the closest thing to a god he thought the universe possessed had granted him superhuman abilities to do the deed.

The trip to L4 took no less than four days, assuming the the Domanantes Solis allowed the landing at all. The station's missile armament was backed by a suite of long-range sensors and communications equipment. They could detect any spacefaring launch from Earth and maintain long-range weapons lock anywhere in the inner solar system. Without express permission, no one got close.

As far from the Earth as the sun, only in a slightly different navigational direction, the communications lag was significant. Including processing time, messages between his ship—not Duke Charlie's ship. The vessel was Apollo's now and he had no intention of giving it back—and L4 took nearly fifteen minutes to pass back and forth. It was worse, at least from Apollo's end, because L4 had days to decide what to do with him and was in no hurry.

Apollo barely slept the first day because he kept checking his messages, expecting to hear another reply from L4 that would always, somehow, come in after he had dozed. After resigning himself to L4's lax communication schedule, Apollo sank into routine. With nothing but the navigation system to keep him company, it came easy. He spent most of his time meditating, exercising, or reading.

Three days into the trip, the "Landing Council" at L4 decided to let him dock, which removed a weight from his shoulders. Either they bought his story about Alexander being a threat to the station—which made Apollo wonder how they let his brother on in the first place—or the Domanantes Solis planned to make him work off his admittance. Either way, it would have been an unfitting end to his journey if they atomized him with a nuclear strike twenty million miles away.

L4 was about as far as a human being could run and reasonably expect to come back to Earth in their lifetime. Mankind had other outposts and colonies, but only L4 remained in some form of contact with Earth. The other outposts—like the Hot Lab on Io, Fool's Hope on Triton, or Purgatory on Pluto—were little more than science labs or prisons according to the information in the ship's computer. There was a story about a base on the moon, but it had been out of contact with Earth for over two hundred years.

"*In vino veritas,*" went the long-cliched proverb, and an amused voice reminded him of the circumstances by which he actually came into the information. Of course the Duke's broadcast confirmed it, but that his information came from a bunch of drunks continued to amuse him.

The cornerstone of it all were Alexander's absences. That was the piece that told him Duke Charlie's announcement had not been mere propaganda. Alexander spent most of his time in recent years in the City, but when he left, someone somewhere had record of his passage. He was simply too high profile to go unnoticed. Yet, every so often, he completely disappeared from record—conveniently at the same time one of Duke Charlie's ships would be "undergoing maintenance."

Alexander had been on the planet, and in the City, until fairly recently. Either that or two superhumans with a fetish for white suits ran around. During that time, Alexander found him outside Londonsberg easily enough. Between the sensors inside the City and the always-willing human avenue of information, he should have easily found Apollo again.

Unless, Apollo reminded himself to calm the mounting anxiety brought on by the lack of communication with L4, he was not on the planet anymore.

Getting through Duke Charlie's security at the space port had been a chore. Between his bomb, the attack on the statue, the start of Vivian's attack, and what looked on the sensors like a fleet of aircars, the City's soldiers were on hair triggers. Like any paranoid tyrant, most of his weaponry was pointed inward, waiting on the day when the revolution came.

His healing power eked out the advantage in the end. Apollo simply stopped fighting and walked to the ship. He had been shot seventeen times during those few moments, but the armor-piercing rounds left neat holes in his flesh that his body immediately stitched back together. Between mounting horror as seeing him literally shrug off bullet and an unwillingness to risk hitting the ship with gunfire, the Black Ties effectiveness hit a sharp drop. Shutting the door on them ended that problem.

At that point, Apollo set the launch controls and passed out. Some time later, he awoke in orbit and devoured enough food for four days.

He fully expected that, by the time he returned in another month or more, Londonsberg would either be a smoking crater or under Marksman control. The more chaos he caused on his exit, the easier it would be for Vivian to complete her half of things.

Apollo's thoughts settled on her for a moment. Vivian had gotten him into the City and allowed him to get close to the spaceport. In return, he was taking care of Alexander, as promised. With Alexander out of the City, and Vivian handling the NoTech, Londonsberg had no way to stop the Marksman army from pouring in. Apollo had faith that Vivian opened the way wide for her people. Even if she was killed in the fighting, Londonsberg would burn.

That thought stopped him for a moment. Why did he not feel more elated about that idea? No matter what happened, Londonsberg was on the way to destruction, so why was he not happier?

It took some time, days in fact, to come to the realization that it was not Londonsberg's destruction that displeased him. In fact, that idea alone kept his spirits lifted when nothing passed the ship's tiny windows but sun-warmed blackness.

The conditional "even if Vivian is dead" was what bothered him, he finally realized. More accurately, he finally admitted it. He had realized it some days before L4 came into view, but only when the ancient space station dominated the starscape did Apollo admit that he would be somewhat distraught if she did not survive her mission. What he felt was not affection, not that he would admit, but something closer to familiarity. They had worked very closely planning their assault on Londonsberg and then even more closely afterward. If she were to be killed, Apollo realized that he might actually miss her.

Earth was a tiny dot, nearly invisible to the eye if he looked out the back windows of the ship. Its presence loomed in his mind, however, and he spared a quick thought toward the planet in general and Vivian specifically.

"Be safe," he whispered.

Looking out the window, he saw the rotating, toroidal bulk of L4 looming large. It would only be an hour or so before he docked. He would lock the ship down, making sure it would not depart without him, and then he would begin his search. Alexander could still leave on his own ship, but not easily, and certainly not without Apollo noticing.

Yes, he thought as he watched L4's slow rotational dance through his cabin window, it was about to finally be a good day to be Apollo.

*** 

Alexander never showed his face at L4's spaceport. Apollo waited for three days, sleeping in a hostel and eating food that he had to admit was actually rather good. If not for the tension in his back, knowing who and what he was here for, Apollo might have found the experience rather pleasant. By the second day, even the subtle slope of the floor passed without notice.

The first thing that stood out to him was that L4 was clean. Not just tidy and well organized, but the station was actually clean in a way the dust and grease streaked planet he came from could never be. Apollo had to admit, he expected the station to be like Londonsberg—gray, dreary, and dirty. Instead, what greeted him was a brightly-lit, clean, naturalistic environment.

It was no wonder, he thought, that the residents of L4 wanted nothing to do with the planet. Perhaps he should have stolen a starship sooner.

The laughable thing about L4, at least from Apollo's perspective, was that money was useless. It had so much space, a surprising amount of which was greenspace, and so few people that everyone's needs were met ten times over by the automated functions of the station itself. Powered by the sun, and hosting its own internal ecosystem within its hundreds of floors and thousands of kilometers, everything was next to free. The only people there to enjoy it were those few from the planet who had amassed huge stores of wealth—wealth that was now useless to them—and the population that had sustained L4 in luxury while the planet that built it poisoned itself.

After arriving, and after giving himself enough time so that even his jaded sense of impressiveness could get over the scale of the place, Apollo rented an apartment. "Rented" and "apartment" were only relative terms, used very loosely. As with everything else, the apartment was free. Using a map, he found an empty space and locked it to his fingerprint. With that done, the place was as much "his" as his house in Visegrad. The place was also only an apartment in the most literal use of the term. Like all of L4, it was huge. He could, if he wanted to spend a small fortune, move everything he owned from Earth to L4 and still have room left.

He admitted that the longer he stayed, the more the idea of remaining permanently appealed. Assuming the government of L4 allowed him to stay after killing Alexander on their streets, he might do just that.

His cynical side kept trying to find the catch. Perhaps sooner or later whoever or whatever actually ran L4 would come find him and demand that he do something to pay for his room and board. That thought never bothered him. Unless "they" wanted him to muck out the waste reclamation system or something else equally as distasteful, he would have no trouble working to pay his debt. The thought that he could simply kill them, and that he never did much like being told what to do, crossed his mind but he ignored it. There was nothing wrong with working for a living, so long as he was allowed some choice in the matter.

With Alexander gone, it would be nice not to have anyone hunting him either.

Perhaps he would be the "them" that ran L4 after Alexander was dead, he thought. That idea appealed to him as he mapped out parts of the massive station in his search. Unfortunately for him, L4 was simply too large to conduct a normal search. Even if he could go without sleep, it would take him years of walking to cover the entire station. Add to that the fact that his quarry was moving, and would quite probably be running and hiding once he got wind that Apollo was hunting him, and Apollo could search for the rest of his life without success. The only comfort was knowing that Alexander could not leave the station without Apollo's knowledge—his ship would detect Alexander's ship leaving and alert him in plenty of time to arrange his own departure.

Or he could "borrow" some of L4's weapons and do the job that way. It was an inglorious end, but it would do.

If Alexander knew Apollo was on L4, he would not leave. That left Apollo two options. The easiest would be to create a disturbance that would leave Alexander no choice but to come to him. Destroying part of the station would do, as would killing a large group of people and leaving the bodies on display.

He could think of three flaws in that plan. First, slaughtering his way across the station would take time, time that Alexander could use to hide and escape. Second, despite the planning it must have taken, his confrontation with Alexander outside the Night Market almost seemed random. The questions of "why then?" and "why there?" had never been answered. Even Catherine, who claimed to speak for the Immaculata, was no use. That meant that he had no way of knowing if death and destruction would bring Alexander out of the proverbial woodwork or not. If he really was insane, and not just a megalomaniacal asshole, then no one could predict his actions. Catherine, at least to his knowledge, certainly had not known that Alexander was going to L4.

The third flaw was that, despite everything, Apollo actually felt repelled by the thought of wantonly killing hundreds of people just to force Alexander out into the open. To be sure, the thought of all that violence sent a surge of adrenaline through his body. Picturing the blood that would result from so many dead excited him, but it also repelled him. Death had to be for a reason and mass, meaningless slaughter could never satisfy his sin-blackened conscience.

"I am Apollo, I am in control," he repeated to himself for the thousandth time since coming aboard the station. The phrase centered him and served as an anchor for his sanity. Whenever he found himself getting lost in blood-lust, which was itself an intoxication stronger than any drink or chemical, he said those words.

Slowly, hour by hour and day by day, Apollo's grip on his soul strengthened. He was in control of his mind. Lust and rage had no power over him anymore so long as he could keep that thought in his head. L4 was relaxing. The food was excellent and the people kind. Apollo found himself appreciating a beauty that Earth had long lost. He did not want to leave.

But he still needed to find his brother and kill him.

***

Apollo spent the next two weeks interrogating people. He did so with surprising gentility as well. He had killed no one since his arrival on L4, and his "information gathering" was injury free. No one on the station knew who he was beyond his identity as a new immigrant from Earth, and that felt somehow right. With none of the familiar accusations being thrown in his face, he felt none of the usual hate.

He had been rough on the first few people, kidnapping them and interrogating them harshly. It had gotten him nowhere, though. He played it off as part of "being from Earth," and explained that such behavior was common on the planet—and since he had just come from Londonsberg, that statement at least was factually true.

The next few were questioned more gently, with only threats of violence to coerce them. His, "natural reactions, being an Earther, you see," were to blame.

Ten days after his arrival, he resorted to even simpler questioning. He would stop someone, ask them if they had seen Alexander, and then send them on their way when the answer invariably came back negative. He seethed inside, fingers itching to bury themselves in someone's throat or to wrap around the handle of a gun. Each time the urge came to him, he repeated what had transcended from a mere phrase into a quasi-religious mantra.

"I am Apollo, I am in control."

The progression from rough kidnappings to conversations took two weeks, but the desire to get his hands bloody never left. As his search proved more and more fruitless each day, he wanted to strangle everyone who failed to live up to his expectations. They were of no help in his hunt for Alexander and so they had no reason to leave his presence alive. Yet, he never laid a hand of any of them. Harming them seemed wrong, like it would be bringing something to L4 that did not belong there.

Three weeks after his arrival, Apollo had almost given up his search, deciding instead to simply wait until Alexander left so that he could follow his ship. He could board and settle things personally or, as was one of his original plans, liberate some of the station's vast store of missiles and handle it from a dispassionate distance. One way or the other, it would end before either of them touched Earth again.

Apollo spent much of his time out of his apartment, trying to make himself relax in one of L4's many lush greespaces. The array of plant life was dizzying at first, and the place was far more beautiful than his meager garden ever could be, and he quickly took up the task of tending to parts of it.

To his surprise, that made him friends. That had been the most unexpected shock of all—people actually liked seeing him.

***

A week later, Alexander found him.

Alexander came at him from behind. He had no words for his estranged brother. No threats, no insane ranting, not even a taunt betrayed his presence until he was ready. Had their positions been reversed, Apollo later thought, he probably would have taunted Alexander before attacking. It was only after the fight was over that he realized how badly he would have lost, had he been in in Alexander's position and done anything but attack.

The only thing to betray Alexander's presence were his footsteps. An errant pebble on the stone pathway slid and creaked under Alexander's feet. The sound, no more than two meters distant, alerted Apollo as his would-be assassin leaped, hands searching for Apollo's throat.

Apollo would have heard the footsteps of any of L4's regular residents coming from far away. He would have recognized them as well, if not specifically then at least in the sense of knowing the person behind him was a native of L4. The steps he heard, however, were different, which could only mean one thing. That guess and his Immaculata-enhanced reflexes were the only things to save him from failure and ignoble death right then and there.

He spun around, automatically diving to one side as his hands came up to protect his face and neck. That was another reflex that saved his life, because Alexander had been moving much faster than a normal human could have managed. Alexander's own Immaculata-granted strength gave him the same boost in speed that Apollo discovered before leaving Londonsberg. His whole body moved like an arrow, angled for where Apollo's neck had been a heartbeat before.

Apollo crouched as Alexander hit the ground, turning his leap into a somersault and springing back to his feet. Alexander turned his head and opened his mouth as if to speak, but then launched himself backward and sideways, toward Apollo. Alexander twisted in midair, fist shooting toward Apollo's head like a rogue comet.

The blow hissed by his face as Apollo contorted out of the way. He grabbed his brother's wrist in the same movement and twisted further. Half a heartbeat later, Apollo grabbed the waist of Alexander's pants with his other hand and, finishing his contortion, flung Alexander onto the hard stone ground.

Apollo drew and fired his pistol in one smooth motion, sending two rounds into the exact spot where Alexander's heart had been the barest of split seconds before. Alexander, however, was on his feet again and the bullets did little more than speckle his feet with rock fragments and dust.

In a blur, Alexander's gun was in his hands. He came forward, brushing aside Apollo's own weapon and stuck the barrel under his chin.

"How many have you killed here?" Alexander demanded. His eyes were wide and jerked from side-to-side as he examined Apollo's face.

Apollo kept his mouth shut and instead used Alexander's momentary hesitation to slip backward and away from his brother's pistol as it roared in his face. The muzzle flash blinded him as the bullet carved a shallow track in his cheek where he was not quite fast enough to get away in time.

Apollo bent his knees, dropping like a stone, and lashed out with his free hand. His knuckles connected with something soft. He felt a rib next to one finger— Alexander's stomach. Apollo felt his brother's body flex under the impact and, operating on little more than guesswork, swung with the pistol in his other hand. It connected, hitting Alexander with the tip of the barrel. Apollo pulled the trigger.

Something thudded to the floor, and Apollo rapidly backpedaled as sight burned back into his healing eyes. His head was already starting to swim with endorphins and the warmth of healing as he took stock of the world around him.

The few citizens who had been in the park had scattered. Apollo was— "pleased" was not quite the right word for it—glad to see they had vacated the area. Collateral damage was for amateurs.

He looked down; Alexander lay on the ground, bleeding from a wound to the temple. It did not bleed enough to be a bullet wound, so he knew he had to move fast.

Apollo leveled his sights on Alexander's body and was about to pull the trigger when the fallen brother twitched. Apollo hesitated for a moment—he needed to know one last thing before he could end the fight.

"Why did you betray them?" he demanded.

Alexander laughed, propping himself up on his elbows. "They betrayed me!" he snapped, eyes fiery. Unlike their meeting outside the Night Market, Alexander seemed lucid and in complete control of what he was doing and saying. Gone was the maniac who had attacked Apollo in a zealous fury; replacing it was someone more like the Alexander that Apollo had once known, if only tainted by some unspeakable cruelty.

"You went rogue," Apollo accused. "Disobeyed them and broke their covenant. Why, damn you?"

"Simple," Alexander sneered. "I'm better than they are. They made me," he grinned like a snake sighting its prey and pushed up from the ground. He came to his feet and continued, "but they made me too well. And here you are, ready to jump in bed with them and you don't even know where all of your strings lead."

Apollo glared. "Don't you dare fucking mock me. I should have killed you years ago when I had the chance."

"Why didn't you, Apollo, hm?" Alexander asked with a sardonic cock of his head. "Why did you 'let me live' back then?"

"I shouldn't have."

"Everyone makes mistakes, Apollo," Alexander mocked. "Do you know why they picked me?"

"Everyone makes mistakes," he echoed.

"They thought I would be tractable!" he snapped. "That I would bow to them like gods."

"You called them gods yourself."

Alexander continued as if he had not heard. "They thought I'd do their bidding without question. Not like you, not then. No," he sneered, "you were too random, too chaotic for their purposes.

"But now you're perfect for their use. I see it all so clearly, Apollo."

"I really don't give a damn what you think their plans are, or what my plans are for that matter. They want you dead. I want you dead. They want what I want, and so you're going to fucking die, understand me?"

Alexander came to his feet, laughing. Something about his laugh kept Apollo from pulling the trigger for the moment. "Don't you see? I came here to kill them, Apollo! I'll free us both!"

"Who," Apollo retorted. "The people here? What, did you get tired of murdering for Duke Charlie's amusement?"

"Not the people, you fool. I came to kill the Immaculata. You see," Alexander spoke as if explaining simple math to a child, "when I said they made me too well, I spoke the truth. They made me strong enough to kill them! And now I..."

Apollo refused to hear any more. He had his answer. He opened fire again, emptying his magazine in an attempt to do as much damage as possible. Alexander's enhanced speed allowed him to evade most of the bullets, but several made contact. At least four fountains of red mist erupted from Alexander's back by the time the gun clicked empty. Unfortunately for Apollo, and despite the extreme pain evident on his brother's face, Alexander was still standing.

"There was a time when I wanted to help you, Apollo," Alexander growled, gritting his teeth through the pain of his rapidly-healing injuries.

"You. Help me?" Apollo laughed derisively. He roared his next words. "You wanted to fucking help *me*?"

"There was a time," Alexander repeated. Apollo watched his eyes start to glaze over the way they had been at the Night Market. He wondered if his own did that when he healed, and if Alexander's madness was the end result of that constant euphoria. He would be better than that; he owed it to himself not to lose who he was.

"You've got to be kidding me," Apollo said, half in exasperation at Alexander's comment and half at the plainly-visible degeneration of his brother's faculties.

"I wanted to bring you into the light. They had such a glorious plan for mankind..."

Apollo swore to himself, cursing whatever deity happened to be listening at that moment. Alexander looked so pathetic that Apollo almost felt pity for him—almost. "And yet they chose you," he said. "First so eager to be a sycophant and then even more eager to turn your back on them and everything they had done for you."

"I'm going to save these people from you, Apollo," Alexander's voice had thickened and he slurred his words like a drunkard. Apollo wondered exactly what drove him to such insanity. Alexander, despite his arrogance and stupidity, had once been well-spoken and dignified. Now, Apollo thought, now he was a madman.

"I'm not going to kill them." The words were out of Apollo's mouth before he even registered thinking them.

Alexander scoffed. "You're lying. You'll kill them all in time! They gave me a mission to protect mankind from people like you!"

Apollo stopped. He wondered suddenly which was the real Alexander. Maybe this was what happened to anyone who worked for the Immaculata long enough. Maybe the cogent man who cursed them was the sane one.

He shook that thought out of his head. Catherine worked for the Immaculata and she was perfectly sane, if irritating. No, Alexander was insane, and this was his insanity. After so many years, Apollo would make it right. He would, for once in his damned life, help.

He looked again. He had seen his mirror while he healed at home and his face had not looked like Alexander's. In a flash, he realized what he was seeing. The haze over Alexander's eyes was the same haze that he had seen in the mirror day after day for years as he crawled into liquor bottle after liquor bottle.

Death would be mercy.

Apollo dropped his empty gun and drew his knife as Alexander charged him. Alexander's own gun went off a dozen times, but none of the bullets hit. Apparently, without full control of his mind, Alexander's enhanced abilities were not quite so enhanced and he was not fast enough to hit Apollo as he dodged.

The sound of Alexander's ribs breaking was a wet crack as Apollo's shoulder slammed into his sternum. He drove the knife in two, three, four times into Alexander's guts and ribs before he stumbled away streaming blood.

The holes in Alexander's torso only bled for a few moments, just long enough to soak his shirt. He dropped his gun and drew his own knife, lunging for Apollo again as he did so. His eyes may have been glazed over—Apollo could only guess at what he saw—but the scowl on Alexander's face spoke volumes about his goal.

That was another face Apollo had seen many times before in the mirror. Alexander had no plans to simply injure Apollo or to cripple him; no, he would bleed him to death if it took a year.

Had he really been that far gone? Apollo asked, disgusted by the thought that he might have once been like Alexander was now. Is this what people saw when the Butcher of Novarus came for them?

In close quarters, even Alexander's diminished mental state was enough to keep pace with Apollo, who had much less experience in exploiting the Immaculata's enhancements. They both fought long and hard, trading blows and quick-healing cuts for hours. Eventually, Apollo started to wear down more than Alexander. It seemed he had found the limit to how much damage his enhanced healing could actually repair. Apollo had no idea how many hours had passed when he began to feel light headed, but he was bleeding from dozens of gashes. His body had been rent by at least six more deep wounds than Alexander's.

But finally, an opening appeared in Alexander's own tired defenses. Apollo struck, burying the knife in the side of his brother's neck. Alexander's eyes opened wide as the blade entered and his arms dropped to his sides. A moment later, Alexander fell to his knees and then to the ground.

"So," a female voice from behind Apollo said. "You finally found him."

Apollo turned, thinking Alexander was dead, to see the last person he had expected to encounter.

"Catherine?" he asked with disbelief.

She nodded. "I came here to find you, to see if you had been successful. It seems..."

Before she could finish, Alexander stirred. Using what must have been the last of his strength, he came to his feet, lunged, and buried knives in Apollo's back.

"...it seems," Catherine continued. Her face was an unreadable mask. "That you are not yet successful."

Apollo turned in time to see the wound on Alexander's neck start to heal up. Feeling his own energy ebbing, he struck out with the side of his hand at the wound, hoping to keep it open long enough for Alexander to bleed out. Something under his hand made a popping sound and he felt a sudden release of pressure.

Alexander crumpled under the blow like a paper doll meeting a hammer. His eyes rolled back in his head and he fell limply to the ground once again. He twitched, clawing at his throat as his lips turned blue. After a moment, even the twitching stopped.

Apollo, to his own disbelief, felt nothing. No sense of victory accompanied Alexander's death. He felt some small measure of vindication knowing that he had succeeded in the Immaculata's wishes and that Alexander, whose very life had plagued him for so long, was finally dead.

Rather than euphoria, a sense of overwhelming dread overcame him. He had no energy left. Everything he had had gone into fighting Alexander, leaving recovery impossible. He felt cold creeping into his extremities.

He had won, he realized, but he would die on L4.

The knives were still in his back. He reached for them, but could not get to either one. Tired, bloody, victorious but dying, he fell to the ground only a meter away from the man who tormented his psyche for years.

A pair of warm hands rolled him over onto his stomach and gently removed the knives from his back. He heard them clatter to the ground some distance away, but none of that mattered. Whoever was helping him was working in vain because he was already dead, his mind had just not caught up with his body yet.

Those same warm hands rolled him onto his back. He expected, in his last moments, to see Catherine. Her face would remind him what he had died for, that perhaps he had not died for nothing after all. And, he thought, her face would be a more pleasant last sight than dirt or his dead brother's bloody corpse.

Instead, he was greeted by a swirling blue and white effigy of light in the vague shape of a human. Two brighter points burned like stars in the inhuman visage.

"Apollo." The voice, a sound like rain and wind, came from the swirl of light. Underneath the power of that voice, he almost thought it sounded like Catherine.

"Are you..." he murmured weakly.

"Yes," burned the voice. "Apollo," it repeated. "remember..."

Remember? He tried to force his mind to work amid the blood loss. His eyes closed. He felt blood underneath his back.

"I am that which you sought."

He forced his eyes open. His voice was weak. "Catherine?"

"Yes."

"How?"

With a voice of rain and wind, she replied, "the truth has always been."

"Why?"

The burning eyes shifted somewhat, moving farther apart. The swirling face almost seemed sad. After one last beat of his tired heart, it spoke again.

"The final test," the Immaculata said, "is death."

# Epilogue

Two years after departing Londonsberg on the eve of its destruction, Apollo returned to the planet. He considered commandeering the *Helios*, but that ship stank of Alexander. He left it as a gift for the Domanantes Solis instead and personally piloted the ship formerly named *Ra* across the ocean of stars and back to Earth.

He had no name for his ship yet, but *Ra* was the name Duke Charlie gave to it and Apollo was not going to continue to call it that. For the time being, he simply called it "Ship," though it was far too nice a craft for a bland name like that.

News reports reached L4 often days after they happened on the surface and only contained events major enough to be broadcast into space in the first place. Ordinary radio broadcasts and other omnidirectional signals reached the station as well, but with degraded quality. Because of that, all Apollo knew about events on the surface was that Londonsberg had fallen and now existed as a protectorate of Kingsmark.

The multi-day trip back to the planet also gave him time to think. Ever since Alexander's death, he found himself with plenty of time to do just that. Much like his life before taking Catherine's offer, Apollo filled his free time with meditation. Only now that meditation came with the clarity of crystal and a sense of self-solidarity that no longer came from drinking until the edge fuzzed away.

Apollo fully planned to set the *Ship* down a few kilometers from his house in one of Visegrad's flatter areas. That idea went out the proverbial window when he settled into high orbit around Earth and received a message from the last place expected.

"Londonsberg astro-control to the *Ra*. Repeat, Londonsberg astro-control to the *Ra*. Please respond."

Apollo's blood chilled. He knew the City had been defeated, possibly even destroyed. The meager news reports filtering in from the surface told him that much. He could not bring himself to rage at the revelation, however, and simply pondered its meaning for five full minutes until it repeated.

He pushed across the room, floating in null-gravity. With the planet below promising real gravity, Apollo found himself wanting to preserve the ability to fly for just a little longer and had shut the a-grav off as soon as he was done with the orbital insertion.

The message repeated, or started to, and Apollo pressed the button that would accept the message as audio only.

"The designation '*Ra'* no longer applies to this vessel."

The message came back after barely noticeable lag. "Am I speaking to Ap—" Apollo heard a scuffle on the other side, a barked order, and then a rustling as what he assumed was a headset was transferred from person to person.

A moment passed and the voice that spoke was one much more familiar.

"Apollo!" Sal explained. "By the gods, man. We thought you died."

A smile crossed Apollo's face and he replied. "I did."

"You what?"

"It's a long story. Sal," he paused, "it's good to hear your voice. How's Vivian?"

"She's alive. Doing well, actually. It took Kingsmark six months to decide whether or not to pin a medal on her chest, though." Sal gave a hearty laugh that threatened to hit the volume limit on his microphone. "You know what she told them?"

"I can imagine."

"'Go fuck yourselves,' she said."

"That," Apollo laughed, "was not what I expected."

Sal's voice turned serious. "Well, see, you know how Kingsmark planned to roll in like big goddamned heroes? Well that did that, y'understand, only they did that after our asses had been tearing the place apart for sixteen straight hours."

"Sixteen," Apollo said, eyebrows raising. "It's an hour from Gothenburg to Londonsberg, maybe two if they're not mobilized."

"They were not mobilized, Apollo."

"That's," he paused, frowned. Anger came, but incoherent rage never did. "Unfortunate."

Sal chuckled. "I expected you to say you'd kill them all."

"It's tempting." Apollo shrugged. That was not entirely untrue. The bloody thoughts that followed him his entire life were still there, clawing to be heard, but now Apollo knew how to bend them to his will. He, not rage, was master now.

Silence fell for a moment before Sal asked, "how's your bandwidth? You on sound-only because of lag or what?"

"Hold on." Apollo hit the switch to activate the video feed. It lagged and distorted for a moment before coming in clear.

On the screen, Sal looked much the same except for a few extra scars. Apollo expected him to have lost an eye or be left with the sort of jagged cheek scar that stared Apollo in the face every time he looked in the mirror. Instead, if anything, Sal looked healthier—and definitely happier if a little more stressed out—than he ever had.

What Apollo did not expect was the suit. The video feed only showed him from the shoulders up, but those shoulders were covered by fabric of a grade far superior to anything the butcher ever wore before. A dark jacket that perfectly straddled the line between blue and gray gave way to a maroon shirt with a high collar. Absent was anything that could be construed as a "black tie." Instead a brilliant silver tie completed the look.

Sal raised an eyebrow. "Robes?"

Apollo looked down. In truth, after a year he had grown so accustomed to them that he no longer thought of them as any different from normal clothes. He was swathed in fabric of varying shades of gray that billowed and swirled in null-gee.

He shrugged. "It's the fashion on Proxima Sol."

"Anyway," Sal continued, "So Kingsmark rolls in after the hard parts are done. Charles is dead. Vivi and I have taken his tower. The Black Ties are scattered and we're picking the army apart with guerrilla strikes. The sun comes up, because of course they do it at sunrise, and Kingsmark swoops in and declares victory after six missiles and ten minutes of gunfire."

"I imagine you weren't happy."

Sal frowned, then laughed. "I wasn't, at least not until the DPR showed up with the *Rheinswehr* an hour behind them." He laughed again. "Then I was *really* happy for Kingsmark. I got even happier when they got everything sorted out."

Apollo raised an eyebrow. "Sorted out? You mean Dresden-Pilsen and Rhineland, or something else?"

Sal shrugged. "They backed off without a fight, even between each other. Turns out they just wanted to fire a few shot's at Charlie's City, but, see, that's what I meant when I said 'sorted out.' This ain't Charlie's City anymore."

"Oh?"

Sal grinned. "I'm still calling it 'Londonsberg' until I can think of something better, y'understand, but when General Lindholm realized who put the bullet in Charles's skull, well," he grinned again, then held his hand in front of the camera. It blurred, trying to automatically focus on something too close for its lens. Sal cursed at it, moved away, and the image resolved itself into his hand with a golden signet on the middle finger.

"Plus," Sal continued, bringing his face back into the pickup, "they're helping with the cleanup and helping dismantle the Limits. I can't fault them for sticking around."

"No," Apollo agreed, "I suppose not."

"I do have a bit of a problem, Apollo, and it's something only you can help me with."

Apollo twisted in the null-gravity, bringing himself closer to the screen. The sudden change in Sal's voice intrigued him. Something other than danger lurked there. If Apollo had to make a guess from a comm image, Sal seemed conspiratorial.

"What is it?" he asked.

"Well, you see, one of the first things I did here was to re-open trade routes. Things are flowing in, Apollo! You'd not recognize the city."

"I would hope not," he replied with a bit of a grin.

"Well, yes. But you see, that's where you come in, my friend. It seems that I've found myself in possession of a bottle of hundred-and-eighty-year-old Fras Dealanaich and, Apollo? I need some help finishing it."

Apollo laughed. Sal's face brightened and Apollo wondered if the former butcher had ever seen him do that. "I can do that, Sal."

"Good, good! Vivian's on her way. She left her—your—house as soon as we passed word to her."

"My house?"

Sal nodded. "She moved her things there after the fighting settled down here. Said to tell you two things explicitly. First, she said your garden's going well."

Apollo smiled. "Good. And the second?"

"She's gonna kill you for disappearing for two years."

"I'd expect nothing less, really."

"I'll have landing instructions sent to you in a few minutes. And, Apollo?"

"Yes?"

"It's good to see you again."

Apollo nodded. "You too. What do I call you now?"

He shrugged. "Sal's fine. Dad was a Baron and Charlie had to outdo him, so he called himself 'Duke.' I'm not sure what I'm going to do. Kingsmark called me 'Interim Director,' but that sounds so," he stopped and groped for the word.

"Boring?"

"Exactly."

Apollo chuckled. "Well, if they make you king, let me know in case I have to make you another gun."

"Funny you should mention that, Apollo. So Vivian has Charles cornered in his office, ready to shoot him and I come in. She looks at me and you know what she says?"

"I can guess."

"'This one's yours, Salvatore,' she tells me. I see the light go off in Charles's eyes. Bastard never knew who I was until right then. Probably thought I died when he had m'pa killed."

Sal's eyes turned hard for a moment. "He did not have long to ponder that piece of information. It was the gun you worked on for me, Apollo, so thanks for that."

Apollo smiled, pleased. "Glad to have helped."

Sal suddenly burst out laughing. "Helped? Buddy, you started the whole thing. You set the city on fire. You shot out that statue, which was a nice touch by the way. The Black Ties and the regulars were running in a thousand directions when we hit 'em."

"I'm glad it worked."

Sal nodded. "Hell, me too. Anyway, you land that thing and come see me in the tower and we'll have a drink or three."

"Will do."

"See you soon, my friend."

Apollo nodded and Sal ended the transmission. He twisted away from the console, floating for a minute before the computer beeped acknowledgment of his landing instructions.

"*Ship*," Apollo said, "compute landing trajectory using Londonsberg data and begin increasing gravity five percent per minute until you restore standard Earth gravity."

The computer beeped its acknowledgment and Apollo slowly sank to a sitting position on the floor as weight returned. That pull shifted sideways as the ship turned to orient itself in the direction it would soon travel, towards the city he could never leave.

The floor hummed and more weight eased into his shoulders as Apollo closed his eyes. He knew if he ever unleashed the fire in his soul, he could burn anything to ash, and so it was to stay under careful control. He took a deep breath, then let it out again and opened his eyes.

"I am Apollo. I am in control. I am Free."

# Author's Notes

"Apollo" is the product of a long, long process. It started during college at a Fantasy stage play done for my senior thesis, but something was lacking. The characters didn't *do* their thing right, so it became a sci-fi short story. That short lacked atmosphere, so it grew a little and became sci-fi-noir. At this point, everyone who read it said some variant of "I like this, but it needs more of everything." From 20 pages, it became 90, then 140, before finally settling where it is now.

Everyone who stuck by me through that process deserves congratulation, because reading *almost* the same story year after year for eight years gets old. Jason, Joseph and my wife Stephanie, my usual writing people, were there at the beginning, slogging through it with me. This time, I'd also like to thank Jay Williams who agreed to help with the final draft, and John Farmer who helped me tie up the last of the plot holes.

For me, Apollo also represents the first real step in a grand undertaking. I have this whole universe planned out. Hopefully you love it as much as I do.